DEADLY

Dr. Dale Harper was sure of one thing and one thing only. Something was wrong at Los Angeles City Hospital. Something was very wrong.

There seemed no medical explanation for the killer disease spreading among the hospital staff. There was no possible reason why it seemed to emanate from the world-famed hospital microbiology lab. There was no way that anyone would believe either Dale or his fellow doctor and lover Nina Yablonsky, if they even dared voice their growing suspicions.

Dr. Dale Harper was left with a choice.

He could abandon the investigation that was leading him ever closer to his own professional ruin and placing the woman he loved in mounting jeopardy.

Or he could pursue the trail of terror that pitted him against an enemy who used sexual prowess as a tool of power as well as an instrument of pleasure . . . and that led him ever closer to the sick secret festering in the heart of this hospital from hell. . . .

CRITICAL CONDITION

Martha Stearn

A SIGNET BOOK

SIGNET
Published by the Penguin Group
Penguin Books USA Inc., 375 Hudson Street,
New York, New York 10014, U.S.A.
Penguin Books Ltd, 27 Wrights Lane,
London W8 5TZ, England
Penguin Books Australia Ltd, Ringwood,
Victoria, Australia
Penguin Books Canada Ltd, 10 Alcorn Avenue,
Toronto, Ontario, Canada M4V 3B2
Penguin Books (N.Z.) Ltd, 182–190 Wairau Road,
Auckland 10, New Zealand

Penguin Books Ltd, Registered Offices:
Harmondsworth, Middlesex, England

First published by Signet, an imprint of New American Library,
a division of Penguin Books USA Inc.

First Printing, July, 1993
10 9 8 7 6 5 4 3 2 1

 REGISTERED TRADEMARK—MARCA REGISTRADA

Printed in the United States of America

PUBLISHER'S NOTE
This is a work of fiction. Names, characters, places, and incidents either
are the product of the author's imagination or are used fictitiously, and any
resemblance to actual persons, living or dead, events, or locales is entirely
coincidental.

To my father,
whose help and encouragement
know no bounds.

ACKNOWLEDGMENTS

Special thanks to the following people, all of whom had a hand in making this book happen:

To Dr. Robert Berlin, Dr. Chuck Everts, Dr. Jill Veber, and Dr. William Fogarty, for lending their expertise.

To my agent, Al Zuckerman, for believing in the book from the early chapters.

To Kathy Lovell, who many long years ago spotted and nurtured my budding interest in writing.

To Win and Ethan, who make it all worthwhile.

And to Dick Wheeler, special thanks.

1

"Dr. Harper, extension 103, please. Dr. Harper, 103."

The hospital page system caught Dale Harper as he bounded down the stairs, three at a time, to the cafeteria for what he had hoped would be a quiet meal. Lunch—which was also his breakfast, and could be his dinner. When you were a resident working long shifts, you were never sure.

He preferred the stairs to the elevators in his vertical travels through the thirty-floor monolith. They afforded him a little time to himself, as well as a chance to stretch his lanky legs. He sometimes speculated that the intercoms in the stairwells had been installed by some malicious administrator. No matter where you were in the maze, you could be ferreted out.

He knew only too well who was at the end of extension 103, and why he was calling. So long, lunch.

With a grimace, he grabbed a bag of corn chips from a vending machine on one of the landings, and took the elevator up to the eighth floor. He headed down the corridor of the general medicine ward. Bulky lunch carts thundered toward him like unmanned battle tanks. A cardiac arrest in the operating room was paged overhead. Not his territory, though he stepped up his pace—an automatic response to a Code Blue. A cluster of young interns and residents trailed behind a silver-haired mentor as they embarked on teaching rounds. An average day in a big city teaching hospital.

He came to a door marked "Private." He started to knock, then opened it without ceremony.

Dr. John C. Carleton, chief of medicine at Los Angeles City Hospital, looked up in absentminded surprise. He had been bent over a stack of papers heaped on his desk. His bald head gleamed with perspiration, its baldness somehow accentuated by a few wisps of dark hair. His secretary stood by, helplessly shaking her head.

"Sit down, Dr. Harper," he said, and nodding at the girl, "Take your lunch, Veronica, and don't worry about it. I'll dictate another memo this afternoon."

Dale Harper looked at Veronica appraisingly. She was attractive, with shapely legs and a cover-girl smile. And he knew she knew it.

Veronica blushed and dashed out of the room without lifting her eyes. Carleton caught the byplay, but didn't mind. When you were dealing with some form of biology all day, you weren't surprised when it cropped up under your nose. Anyway, he had been a young resident himself. Things didn't change, not like the young people thought. Some things were always the same, and romance was one of them.

And trouble was another, which brought him back to young Dr. Harper, whom he put up with, because he saw the seeds of a terrific doctor in him. Not a good doctor, but a terrific doctor, who cared about people under that crust of his, and knew intuitively how to handle patients. There weren't many like him, but still, how much could you put up with to get an extraordinary one?

Crunching one of his corn chips, Harper stepped up to Carleton's oak desk, and stuck the bag of chips under his superior's nose. "How about lunch?" he asked, knowing he was being obnoxious but not much caring. He felt an inordinate resentment toward Carleton for interrupting what little quiet time he could snatch for himself, especially after a near-sleepless night.

Carleton's first impulse was a frown. But he smiled instead. He had made up his mind he didn't want a confrontation. Not now. That wouldn't do. Not if he wanted to keep Dale Harper on his house staff. And he did, if he could keep things from getting any worse.

"Hello, Dale," he said, extending a friendly hand. "You made it here fast enough."

"Missed my lunch," said Harper, as if he hadn't already made his point.

Carleton swiveled about in his chair, looking solemn. "Doctors should get used to missing lunches."

Harper slid into a chair. "You're sure," he said, "you don't want some chips . . . low fat?"

Carleton shook his head with a frown. "Let's get down to it, Dale. I went to school with your father. But I'm not your father. And even if you were my son, I still wouldn't have time to be your father. Not around here. Yet in the few years you've been with us, you're as much on my mind as my own family. Now, why is that?"

Dale smiled, and his whole face lit up. For a moment he looked younger than his thirty-two years.

"I don't know," he said, permitting his bag of chips to slide to the floor. "It must be love."

Carleton quickly firmed up his lips as he felt some of his resolve leaving him.

"Sometimes," he said, "I think I'd love to see you disappear. But that would be too easy." He looked at his watch. "I have five minutes, and I want you to tell me why Dr. Orosco had to call me at 3:05 this morning to complain about you."

Dale shrugged. "I can't imagine why he couldn't wait until a more civilized hour." He slouched down in his chair. His surgical blues from the night before were splattered with blood, as if they were badges of merit that trivialized Orosco's complaint.

Carleton bit his lip. How different this brash young man was from his father. "Dr. Orosco says you were harassing him all night."

Dale smiled as he put a chip in his mouth. "I was merely reporting to him on a patient that he was clearly very concerned about. Besides, if he called you at 3:05, you didn't get the whole story. I reported to him at midnight and six A.M. as well."

The color came to Carleton's face. "*You* don't have the whole story. He called me *again* at 6:05." He shook his head. "I can't have any more of that."

It was time to lay it out with this young upstart, something he should have done long ago. The memory of Dale's father had always stopped him. But enough was enough. He looked the younger man in the eye. Dale Harper, the chief of medicine had decided, was an angry young rebel without sufficient cause.

"You're an excellent resident," he said. "You'll make a fine doctor. But you create problems by the way you go at things, particularly with superiors. This incident with Dr. Orosco is just a drop in your bucket of offenses."

He straightened the papers on his desk and restrained a sigh. Whatever he owed the father he no longer owed the son. His voice hardened. "Now, what do you have to say for yourself?"

Dale's brows came together. He felt his resentment fading as he saw how troubled Carleton was. He crumpled up the empty bag of chips and tossed it into a wastebasket. "I was on call last night, and Orosco ordered hematocrits every three hours on a GI bleeder. I called him after I ran each 'crit." Dale paused. His eyes widened in mock wonder. "Can you imagine? He orders a blood count that often when the patient hasn't bled in twenty-four hours?"

It was more a statement than a question, and Carleton treated it as such. He was not making a case for Orosco, so much as respect for hospital regimen. There had to be some form of order or the whole thing would come down on his head one day.

He knew all about Orosco's reputation for being arrogant and demanding, often writing orders on patients that kept the house staff running in all directions. But he made allowances. Orosco tried. What more could you ask of a doctor?

He rolled his eyes with exasperation. "Come now, Dale. You know you were looking to aggravate him. Why not admit it? You were eminently successful."

Dale had to restrain a grin. He liked Carleton. He could guess why Carleton and his father had been friends. The man had insight. But not a whole lot of backbone, he had decided.

"Okay, I was trying to prove a point. Orosco has no judgment. He orders unnecessary lab work on a stable patient. There are plenty of other ways to tell whether a patient is bleeding without stabbing his finger every three hours and waking him up." He enumerated with his fingers. "Pulse rate, blood pressure, number and color of stools. Simple bedside evaluation, most of which the nurses can do."

He tossed up his arms, his face an animated question mark. "And why should I have to get out of bed after a rough day and pester a patient just to accommodate Orosco's insecurity? If we don't get any sleep because of his incompetence, then he shouldn't either." Simple justice.

Carleton felt a certain satisfaction at hearing the confession. He relented a little, taking a gentler tone. "I understand your objections to 'slaving,' as you fellows like to put it, for the M.D.s in private practice, but that's part of training to become a good doctor. You know that. You've got to learn to put up with bull, because there's a hell of a lot of it out there in the real world. And," he said, almost as an afterthought, "you won't have me to protect you."

Dale's eyes became pinpoints as he leaned forward, his gaze riveted on Carleton. "People like Orosco shouldn't be allowed to take advantage of the system. When I'm his victim, I'm going to let him know that. That's part of the real world too."

Carleton looked away. With a half smile, he shook

his head. "Dale, Dale. What am I going to do with you?"

He moved to the window and looked out at the massive pile of granite that was City Hospital. "That is all that matters, Dale," he said. "The hospital. The patients. You and I don't count for a tinker's damn. We can be replaced overnight for any reason or no reason."

Dale was surprised at how bitter Carleton sounded. He watched Carleton's face as he returned to his desk and sat down. Carleton looked puzzled as he said, "Your intern should have been doing those hematocrits. Where was he?"

"My intern wasn't feeling well. I told him to take the night off." Dale had leaned back in his chair. He was staring at a portrait of Hippocrates, the revered Greek physician in whose name he had taken a solemn oath to serve an ailing mankind.

Carleton gave him an amused look. "Why can't you show such compassion for the rest of us?" He paused, thoughtful. "Who is your intern?"

"Ron Orloff. We've been working together for a few weeks now. He's a hard worker. When he says he's sick, he's sick."

Carleton nodded. "He's a good man, with a Ph.D. in microbiology too. One of our top medical students last year." He frowned. "What's wrong with him? He's called in sick quite a bit lately. He's not the sickly type. Rather robust, as I recall."

Dale was glad to get off Orosco. "No specific symptoms—just wiped out. Nauseated from time to time. He's been working too hard."

Carleton was about to say something, then thought better of it. Some things took care of themselves, left alone. "Well, take it easy on the boy. And on Orosco."

Dale thought he saw a twinkle in Carleton's eyes. He knew Carleton was being lenient. And he knew why. "If it will make things easier, I'll call Orosco and smooth things out." His tall frame tensed the least bit as he stood up. "But I'm making no promises, if he pulls the same nonsense the next time I'm on call."

Carleton went back to arranging stacks of papers on his desk. He sounded tired. "Do me one favor. See if you can go one week without my losing sleep over your nights on call."

Dale snapped his Reeboks together and saluted. "Aye, aye, sir."

He strode out of the office with a smile on his face. He was glad things had ended on an up note. Then he remembered Ron Orloff. Carleton was right about Ron being the robust type. He hadn't known that Ron had been sick a lot. But then Ron was the sort who kept to himself. There was something wrong. He could almost smell it, now that he thought about what Carleton had said.

He suddenly felt uneasy. He didn't know why, and that only bothered him the more. Maybe it was Carleton's mention of his father, a painful memory. Or Carleton's inexplicable bitterness. Maybe it was the talk about Ron Orloff. He frowned, making a mental note to call Ron.

2

As he left Carleton's office, Dale glanced at his watch. He had twenty minutes before staff rounds at one o'clock. Still time to grab a bite in the cafeteria. The corn chips felt like a lead block in his stomach.

The corridor was bustling with midday activity. He noticed a handsome silver-haired man in a three-piece suit heading into Carleton's office. He had the suave appearance of a drug salesman, but there was a familiar look to him that Dale couldn't quite place. He shrugged it off. People like Carleton courted all sorts of visitors all day long. And was courted by them.

He glanced across the hall to a patient's room and smiled to himself. There was the same melange of house officers he had seen earlier, swarming around the bed of a young woman who lay bare-breasted, covers down, hands clenched as she stared helplessly at the ceiling. There were six stethoscopes on her chest. Modesty and ivory tower academia didn't mix.

Before heading downstairs, he made a quick call to Ron Orloff, who had not shown up for morning rounds. Ron had slept through the alarm. He sounded embarrassed. Dale told him not to worry. Things were quiet. "Take the rest of the day off and I'll see you at dinner." He hung up and caught the elevator to the basement.

The hospital cafeteria was in the bowels of the hospital. Some staff people liked to pursue that analogy when they described the food. But Dale was usually too tired to much care what he was eating.

The laundry room sat right across from the cafeteria entrance. The constant turmoil of the giant washing machines and driers made it hard to concentrate on food, good or bad.

He grabbed a cracked, olive-green plastic tray and slid it along the steel rail, surveying the various pallid offerings of the day. The safest bet looked like a ham and cheese sandwich and a half-point carton of low-fat milk. As he stood at the cash register, he looked around for a familiar face.

He spotted Nina Yablonsky, a second-year radiology resident, and felt a quickening of his pulse. He'd had his eye on Nina for a while, but was uncharacteristically shy. He had asked around about her, chatted idly with her in the halls and cafeteria, but had never revealed his interest because of a reserve he didn't quite understand himself.

He had wondered if he lacked courage. No, he had plenty of that when it came to cardiac arrests. In fact, he felt more at ease at a dying man's bedside in his determination to bring him back than with the thought of asking Nina Yablonsky to have a drink with him. He had been like that as a teenager, that painfully awkward period when the thought of rejection could be immobilizing.

He had learned a little about her. She was from the Bronx. And despite the blue-collar background of a neighborhood school, she was a classical music buff. She dressed down meticulously, and wore makeup as though she had come out of a finishing school. But she had probably never set foot in a country club.

She was sitting alone at a small table, her nose in a book, a forkful of salad poised at her lips.

"May I?" He tapped her on the shoulder as he came up behind her.

An amused smile burnished her face as she looked up. "Why certainly, Dr. Dale Harper. You look like you've had a rough night." She waved at an empty chair. "Rest your tired bones."

She had dark brown eyes and a pleasant voice, with no trace of a Bronx accent. He craned his neck to get a better look at her book. "What are you reading?"

"Fascinating, steamy stuff. Radiation safety standards. Excuse me while I just catch the last sentence of this lurid scene." She laughed as she skimmed the page, then closed the book and tossed it on the table. "It'll keep."

Dale tore the cellophane wrapper off his sandwich. "Studying for boards?" He found himself gazing at Nina's hands as she picked at her salad. You could tell a lot about people from their hands. Hers conveyed an offbeat combination of sensuousness and efficiency, he decided. They were slim and well formed—capable-looking. He brought himself up with a start. How could you tell all this from someone's hands? Was it the hands or something in her face? Forget it, Harper. You like her. What more do you need to know?

Secretly amused by his appraisal, Nina shook off his question. "No, just boning up on radiation safety. You can't be too careful."

Dale's ears pricked up. "What do you mean by that?"

"Oh, nothing tangible. You know how it is in a big hospital. A lot of talk."

"What kind of talk?"

Nina poked at her salad. There was a brown wilted leaf of lettuce in the middle of her plate. She put down her fork. "It's pretty vague. You know, the 'Don't tell anyone I told you' sort of thing. I think it'll boil down to a few disgruntled employees."

"Who isn't disgruntled in X ray?" Dale said, downing his milk. "It's the worst-run department in the hospital."

Nina grinned, showing perfect teeth. "I've heard about your run-ins with the clerks there. You seem to specialize in run-ins."

He shook his head in exaggerated sadness. "Trying

to get an X ray out of those guys is like trying to get at snort out of a comatose pig."

"There's a story going around that you sneaked into X ray one night and threw out a bunch of films."

Dale sighed. Rumors were as common as enemas around there. "I take that as a compliment. If those turkeys had fewer X rays to look for, they could at least find the ones they've got. But I wouldn't do anything that might hurt a patient."

Nina frowned, not quite convinced.

"I mean it," he insisted, feeling misunderstood.

She sat back and smiled. "That's enough about this place. How about you? Our hard-working defender of human rights? You have quite a reputation, you know."

"I'm afraid I know all about it." He paused. "I'm on the oncology service. Nothing could be more depressing than cancer."

He took a deep breath and made an effort to lighten the conversation. He wanted her to like him. "Care to discuss my many faults over a drink some night?"

Nina laughed. "I'm sure there are some very nice things about you."

He loved her laugh. She affected him strangely. Even her laugh. He had no feeling of desire, unusual when he felt an attraction. He found himself wanting to know what went on inside her. How she thought and felt about things. What books she liked to read. And he found himself wanting her to know what he was like. This was even more unusual, since he generally kept himself pretty well insulated.

He rummaged around for a topic of conversation and found it incongruously in a field he disliked for very personal reasons. "My father was a radiologist," he said. "Maybe that's why I like you."

"Was?" Her eyebrows came up. "Has he retired?"

He shook his head. "He died. At the ripe old age of forty-eight. I was fourteen then." His voice fell.

"He was my idol. I knew he wanted me to become a doctor."

She saw the pain as he looked up. She said nothing, letting him choose his own words or end it right there. He had stopped eating and was toying with his sandwich. "I don't know why I'm boring you with all this."

She reached over and touched his arm. "I don't think you could bore me. You must have loved him very much."

He looked away for a moment. There was the hint of a tear in his eye. He tried to wink it away. He had gone deeper into himself than he'd meant to. And yet he wanted to say more. Suddenly it became very important that she understand.

"I'm still my father's son. Old Carleton and he were classmates. He wouldn't put up with me if it weren't for my father. I get a little perverse at times, and try goading him into realizing I'm my own person." He shrugged. "I suppose it's childish."

She was moved by his openness. It made her want to tell him all about herself. She had always been a little protective of her background. Her parents were Polish immigrants, and she often felt like the parent herself as she tried to help them acclimate to being American, even teaching them English. Her father, a hard-working plumber, had always wanted a son. In some ways, she thought, her tomboy childhood may have been a subconscious effort to accommodate him. It had been a struggle to find her own sense of femininity.

She looked at Dale. If anyone was a WASP, a homogeneous breed she had never felt comfortable with, it was this tall, sandy-haired resident. Somehow that didn't matter. He didn't fit any of the stereotypes she had grown up with. He made her want to reach out, pat him on the head, tell him everything was going to be okay. Instead, she veered off in a lighter vein, not yet trusting her impulses.

She smiled as her eyes ran over his strong features,

the straight, chiseled nose and the deep blue eyes. "I think you were born a century too late. There weren't so many rules then. I can see you as a doctor on horseback. On a white horse, of course." She gave him an amused look.

He finished off his sandwich. "I guess we all wonder what life would have been like in another time. But I like where I am now. Being a doctor a hundred years ago must have been frustrating."

"Why? They had a lot more respect then. Nobody even heard of malpractice."

She had struck one of his sore points: the good old days. "Who wants to spend his life holding people's hands while they die from typhoid or tonsillitis, knowing there's not a damn thing you can do about it? Mix up a few evil-smelling potions, mostly alcohol, and pray for a miracle." Dale pushed his plate away. "No thank you."

She was momentarily annoyed. She had a healthy respect for a selfless tradition—one that had attracted her to a career in medicine. "Your Carleton says there's still a lot of salesmanship required in medicine. I'm not into snake oil, which is why I opted for radiology. Nice and matter-of-fact. And no helpless hand-holding while people die, which will always happen, no matter how advanced our technology."

She chuckled as a thought struck her. "I wouldn't be too hard on the old-timers, if I were you. I'll bet you've ordered B-LAC capsules for your patients, just like the rest of us."

Dale gave her an appreciative grin. B-LAC was a joke around the hospital. It was nothing more than aspirin packaged in a fancy black capsule—a placebo promoted by some doctors as a potent painkiller for hypochondriacs and patients overly fond of narcotics.

He laughed. "It works! Some people even get a buzz."

They smiled at each other for a long wondrous moment. Yet disquieting in a way because of its emotional intensity. Dale broke the spell by leaning back in his chair and returning to the original topic, filing in his memory bank the magic they had just shared.

"The real issue is progress," he said. "Today's medicine is basically a science. A century ago, it smacked of mysticism. The primitive medicine man was a better healer than we were in those days. You know what our heritage really is? Astrology! Bloodletting, charms and amulets, human sacrifice."

As she looked at him, obviously amused, he checked his watch and stood up. "You may not think so, but 'you've come a long way, baby.' " He put his hand on her shoulder. "I'm late for a meeting. What about that drink—may I call you?" He was irritated at himself for going off on a tangent, and now he looked at her expectantly.

Nina smiled, her eyes twinkling. "Okay . . . baby."

Dale beamed. "I'll be seeing you."

She looked after him, dawdling over her cold coffee. She eyed her book with disinterest, then recalled Dale's strong reaction. Was there really something to the rumblings about safety violations? She stared at the book again, and felt an involuntary shudder.

3

The fish were a startling electric-blue. He was swimming among them, was one of them, when all at once something powerful—a crosscurrent—caught his regulator, and he was two hundred feet down without air. Suddenly he could feel the weight of the water as it wrapped around his chest like a vise. He looked up for the surface, and swam and swam but the water got darker, not lighter. And oh, my God, he was going in the wrong direction, toward death, toward more water, not less water and air. And what terror . . .

Ron Orloff awakened gasping, drenched with sweat. His pajamas and sheets were soaked. His heart was pounding like a jackhammer. He had slept fitfully, tossing and turning all night, trying to take advantage of the time Dale Harper had given him to rejuvenate himself. But his sleep was more tormenting than restful.

He'd been having drenching night sweats like this now for about a month. He lay there in what felt like a pool of body-warm water, trying to control his terror, staring at the ceiling, telling himself he was still dreaming.

But he knew he wasn't dreaming. That this nightmare was true, and that there was something dreadfully wrong.

He switched on the bedside lamp and checked the clock. Two A.M. God, four more hours before he could justify getting up and returning to the welcome distraction of working on the wards.

He sat on the edge of the bed and felt a chill run through him. He felt wrung out. He dragged himself into the bathroom and flipped on the fluorescent overhead light. The mirror was playing tricks on him. His skin looked yellow-gray. Could there be such a color? Maybe it was the light. He'd been losing weight and there were shadows where his cheeks should be. His hair was in a wet disarray, as though he had just come in from a torrential windstorm.

C'mon, Orloff, pull yourself together. Remember when you were a second-year med student? Pathology class was a riot. We were all running around feeling our necks for lymph nodes, palpating our abdomens for enlarged organs, imagining every headache to be the first insidious sign of a brain tumor. The terror was as real then as it was now. But it didn't last. And then we'd all laugh at ourselves.

A sob escaped from somewhere deep inside him. This was the real thing. There was no escaping it. He knew he had some deadly illness.

He shuffled back to his bed and started pulling the wet sheets off. Then he sat on the edge and leaned over, resting his head on his arms. He started to cry as he imagined himself dying in a hospital bed, his parents, sister, and friends filing through to pay their final respects.

Enough of this. He had to find out what was going on. But how? He refused to go to the student health service. He was certain you had to sign a statement that you hated people before you could work there. And he was afraid to let the attending staff know he was sick for fear of getting thrown out of the training program. He'd thought of drawing a blood count on himself and submitting it to the lab under a false name. Or checking himself for AIDS. He had certainly stuck himself with enough needles that had been in the veins of sick patients. Maybe he ought to check himself for tuberculosis. A simple skin test. He could sneak into the lab. Nobody would know.

Doctor, heal thyself. He snorted bitterly. It was all too much for him. He needed an objective perspective. He thought of Dale Harper. He'd only worked with him for a few weeks, but he could tell that Dale was a top-notch doc. He was thorough. And he listened. So many of them never listened. They were too busy thinking about the next patient. And didn't listen to them either.

Yes. That's what he would do. In the morning. He would talk to Dale. He got up and found some dry flannel pajamas. They felt wonderful on his clammy skin. He tossed a blanket over the bare mattress and lay down on his back, hands under his head, eyes closed. He forced himself to take a few deep breaths, and felt a tremor inside start to ease.

Dale would help him. He couldn't carry it by himself any longer. Ron felt his heartbeat slowing down. The crisis was over—for tonight. He rolled over, planted his face in the pillow, and drifted off to sleep.

4

Dale felt like a zombie as he wandered through the ward, tending to the patients he had admitted the night before. Why sleep deprivation should be part of a medical apprenticeship, he had never understood. Would you want someone who'd been working for forty-eight hours and sleeping intermittently for four hours taking care of your mother? he would ask his preceptors. The response was usually an accommodating smile and some apologetic utterance about noble tradition.

He'd had five admissions the night before, plus the usual scut work like checking blood counts on Dr. Orosco's patient. Without an intern, he'd been busier than he ever cared to be again.

At last he signed out to Andy Hamilton, the resident taking over for the night. He was finally off call. He made a beeline for the front door, feeling compelled to escape the stifling sense of being trapped by four walls and human suffering.

Besides the new admissions, you only saw the really sick ones in the middle of the night, he realized. He had spent a precious hour trying to start an IV on an semi-comatose woman whose arms had been ravaged by blood draws, IVs, and chemotherapy. Her only sign of awareness was a groan every time he stuck her. What in hell for, he wondered. Metastatic lung cancer. She'd be gone in two days. There had been times when he refused to put patients through this unnecessary torment, but he was so tired last night that he simply went with the flow. Do what they want you to do, Harper.

He needed to get out. He flung open the doors to the brisk evening air. What a relief after the dusky, dimly lit corridors of the cancer ward, where the smell of ammonia from freshly mopped floors couldn't mask the odor of human excrement, vomit, and old blood.

Dale headed across the hospital lawn to the residents' apartments. He always felt a certain thrill when he came off a forty-eight-hour stint of duty. There really was a world out there, with fresh air, people wondering whether to have chicken or fish for supper, cars speeding on the freeway, horns honking, children shouting from a nearby playground. He could imagine founding a religion to worship such wonderfully ordinary things.

The grandeur of the hospital's cathedral-like edifice loomed above him as he took in the mauve and blue streaked sky. The sun was traveling to some other part of the world, not caring that Dale Harper hadn't had a chance to see or feel it that day.

The Great Stone Mother, as she was fondly called, affected more than just the visual senses. There was a strange low-pitched humming sound, as if it were bouncing off all that stone and mortar. He'd never been able to explain it or pin it down. But it was there, night and day, enigmatically vibrating the air, setting a mood. It was as much a part of the vast medical complex as the towering walls of granite.

He stopped and stretched, sucking in the crisp air. He could feel the muscles in his shoulders and neck relax. He stole one more glance at the Stone Mother's tower, then headed into his apartment.

It was strewn with dirty clothes and dishes. He didn't spend much time there, just enough to give it a lived-in look. He went to the closet and picked out a pair of gray slacks, and a blue pin-striped shirt. He pulled off his surgical scrubs, which were limp from forty-eight hours of wear. He headed into the shower and let the hot water bring some life back into his body.

Dale met Ron Orloff in the lobby of Ron's apartment just before eight. Ron looked worried, as though he'd had a tough day. "Sorry I'm late. Life's a bitch without an intern," Dale quipped.

Ron blinked his eyes hard. "Dale, I'm really sorry to abandon you. That's what I need to talk to you about."

Dale gave him a friendly clap on the shoulder. "Hey, lighten up. We all get sick at times. Hell, if people didn't get sick, you and I would probably be working in a carwash."

Dale pointed to his beat-up white '65 Mustang parked out front. "Come on, I'm taking you to the best Italian restaurant this side of Vesuvius."

Ron gave Dale a grateful look, and got in next to him. They headed up Riverside Avenue, cut back and then cruised along Vermont. Even the neon signs were a welcome sight to Dale. Their gaudiness seemed graphically life-asserting, a visual shout for attention.

The traffic was light. The city's energy level was at an ebb. It was dusk—too late for the work-a-day bustle and too early for the all-electric night life.

The limbolike twilight meshed with Dale's mood. His thoughts turned to his father, Nina, Carleton, and the man sitting next to him. It wasn't the Ron Orloff he remembered from only two weeks ago.

He thought of their first night on call together. There had been a Code Blue. Dale and Ron had arrived together at the bedside of a man in the coronary care unit. He had complained of chest pain and then his heart stopped. When they got there, people were milling around the bed, making futile efforts to bring his heart back. Ron had taken over, barking orders, delegating authority as though he had been doing it all his life. Dale had stood back and let him. Ron saved a life that night. And now here he was, humbled and uncertain at what was happening to him. He was a different man.

They sat outside at a small table. The evening breeze gently kept the smog at bay. The table was covered with a red and white checkered cloth. The flickering flame from a candle lantern in the center of the table accentuated the gauntness of Ron's bony features. For a chilling moment, Dale had a feeling he was looking at an apparition.

Dale ordered lasagna, a glass of burgundy, and a big basket of warm garlic bread. Ron ordered antipasto.

"Not very hungry?" said Dale with a look of concern.

"Not very," said Ron, playing with his fork.

Dale ate heartily, silently, waiting.

Finally, Ron spoke. "Dale, I'm scared. I think I'm dying." His eyes seemed to double in size.

Dale saw the tremor in Ron's chin as he fought for control. The first impulse was to make light of it, to ease Ron's fears. But that wouldn't work, he knew.

Ron let it all out—the night sweats, his tiredness, his reluctance to check it out. "I don't know what it is," he said. "That's what frightens me."

Dale crisply took control. "Ron, I want you in my clinic tomorrow afternoon. Get a blood count and a chemistry profile in the morning. Then get some rest. We only have a few more weeks on this rotation." He smiled. "I'm dismissing you. We'll manage without you."

He stood up and paid the bill. They drove back in reflective silence. Ron glanced over at Dale, envying the other doctor's glow of health. He turned quickly away to gaze out the window, feeling a pang of shame as he had a fleeting wish that he could trade places with Dale.

Dale pulled up in front of Ron's place and turned off the engine. They sat for a moment, both sensing something more needed to be said. Dale stared out the window, sighed, and said, "Ron, it's going to be okay. Nothing is as bad as not knowing. We'll find out tomorrow.''

Ron's voice cracked as he reached over to shake Dale's hand. "Thanks, Dale," was all he said. He slid out of the car and walked off without looking back.

5

Willie Lee pushed the garbage cart ahead of him down the dark, empty corridor. He liked the noise that the hard wheels made on the waxed linoleum floor—like a jet about to take off.

He'd been working at the medical school now for thirteen years, and he had more seniority than anyone else. When it came to maintenance and cleaning, Willie was a star. And by God, he was proud of how spic and span that place was.

Willie's assigned areas were the two microbiology research floors of the medical school. The med school was connected by tunnels and corridors to the teaching hospital, but Willie wanted no part of that. He was afraid of all the things you could catch from sick people. He had worked over at the hospital for one year, and when there was a vacancy in the med school, Willie grabbed it, even though the pay wasn't as good.

This was his domain. He'd made friends with some of the med students, and when he came around during the day, they would hail him and ask him how his kids were doing. Willie was real proud of his kids, especially Lincoln, who was sixteen and wanted to be a doctor. Willie was all for that. He didn't want his boy to have to clean up after white people. No, Willie had great aspirations for his older son.

Willie brought the garbage cart to a halt outside the rat lab, put on his work gloves, and went in to collect the bags of waste. Sometimes, especially when he was working the night shift and no one was around, he'd sift through the bags and find some soiled syringes and other paraphernalia for his kids. They liked to play doctor and researcher.

Willie was very safety conscious. He was no dummy. He was careful to stay out of the rooms marked "Radioactive"—the ones with the big red and yellow warning signs. But even in the unmarked rooms, when he saved items, he washed them carefully before taking them home. He would never take the needles. And he only took the syringes that had been used to draw up test doses of chemicals used in experiments. Nice, clean chemicals—never any that were used to draw blood.

Willie was fifty-two years old now. He'd been raised in the streets of New York's Harlem. He wanted more for his family. He'd seen it all, the streets, crime, drugs. It wasn't worth seeing. He was going to make sure that his kids never had to find that out the hard way. Yes, Lincoln a doctor, Leroy a researcher, and Aurora—well, she was only ten—maybe a lawyer. A fighter for the cause of civil rights, helping make Martin Luther King's dream come true.

Willie rolled up his sleeves when he realized he'd been daydreaming again. He scolded himself good-naturedly, and felt his spirits rise as he spotted a plastic bag full of discarded syringes. As he carefully placed the bag in a corner of his cart, he grinned as he imagined the looks on his kids' faces when he brought them home.

6

Dr. Robert Heffron, world-renowned microbiologist, famed cancer researcher—a household word when it came to cancer and radiation—sat idly drumming his fingers on his polished mahogany desk. He was bored. Restless. He had experienced the high of being the guest of honor at last night's fund-raising dinner for the hospital. But today was another day, and whatever kick he got out of pandering to the public had already worn off. Like a drug high followed by a sudden crash.

He turned to the manuscript before him, not satisfied, but not quite certain what it needed. He felt unaccountably irritable. He looked at his Rolex watch, admiring his nicely manicured nails as he did so. Five o'clock. Mary, his receptionist, would be getting ready to go home soon. The graduate students would be finishing up.

He leaned over his intercom and buzzed his receptionist.

"Yes, Doctor?"

"Mary, please tell Tracy Hester I'd like to see her."

"Certainly, Doctor. Would you like her to wait in the reception area?"

"No, just have her come directly to my office." He felt a pleasant tingle of anticipation. "And, Mary, why don't you go on home? You've put in a difficult day."

"Are you sure, Dr. Heffron? I have a few more letters to get out . . ."

He chuckled. "Mary, you're wonderful. No, you get

on home to those precious grandchildren of yours. No job is more important than them."

He could hear her gratitude resonate over the intercom even before she spoke. "Thank you, Dr. Heffron. You're so kind."

He rang off and stood up, stretching his long arms. He walked over to the full-length mirror that hung on the closet door and took a long look at himself. He was tall, well over six feet, and slender. At fifty-four he had retained his smooth good looks. His face was angular and well tanned, elegantly set off by his razor-cut silver hair. Pockmarks from an acne that had caused him some awkward moments during adolescence now added an appealing roughness to his features. His eyes were steel-gray, giving him a hard, cruelly sensual look. He knew women found him attractive, and that fact served him well.

As though on cue, he heard a knock, and strode easily across the room. As he opened the door, Tracy Hester greeted him with a shy smile. She had long, lovely blond hair, a terrific figure with sensuously large breasts that seemed to poke through her sweater. Heffron smiled and motioned to the brown leather couch. "Miss Hester, please have a seat." He returned to his desk.

"You wanted to see me, Dr. Heffron?" She sounded nervous.

He threw his head back and laughed. "Don't tell me you find me intimidating."

She smiled again, the sort of shy smile that he found so winsome. "Well, no. I just . . . well, I just wondered if there was something wrong."

He laughed again. "Nothing, my dear girl, could be further from the truth. You're a real addition to our microbiology graduate program. I am extremely pleased with your work. So much so that I'd like your opinion of my manuscript here."

Her face lit up. "Oh, Dr. Heffron, I don't know what to say . . ."

He smiled and brought the manuscript to her, seating himself next to her on the couch. "Say what's wrong with it. It lacks a definitive punch. I need a fresh new viewpoint. Like yours." He reached out and brushed her hair away from her eyes, causing her to giggle.

He rose. "Care for some coffee, Miss Hester?"

"Oh, I'd love some," she said, her blue eyes fluttering.

He brought her the coffee, then disappeared into the lab adjacent to his office. "I'll be back momentarily."

He returned after allowing her enough time to read the article. "Well, what do you think?"

She seemed to be searching for the right thing to say. "Well, it's . . . it's good. I'm not sure I understand how you arrived at your conclusion."

"Precisely!" He sat down beside her, placing a hand on her shoulder. "You spotted the flaw. And I have picked you to write the conclusion for me. You'll be my co-author."

Tracy looked at him incredulously. He could smell the soft scent of her perfume and her femaleness. He edged closer so their thighs were touching. She didn't move away.

"But, Dr. Heffron, I'm just a first-year graduate student. It would be presumptuous of me to . . ."

He chuckled, his lips close to her ear. "You can do it, Tracy," he barely whispered. "I'll give you the raw data sheets. Take them and the manuscript with you tonight, and bring me your written conclusion by Friday. I have complete confidence in you. Now, put it down, my dear." He let his hand wander to her breast, fingering it gently until he could feel the nipple harden beneath her sweater. No bra. He liked that.

She giggled and started to pull away as she fumbled with the manuscript, but he drew her to him and planted his lips on hers. She dropped the manuscript and fell back on the couch as he slipped his other hand under her sweater and kneaded her breast. She moaned with pleasure as he moved his lips and tongue expertly up and down her neck and unbuckled his lizard-skin belt.

Heffron sent Tracy on her way with a kiss and a pat on the bottom. She had been good—very good. Eager to please. She had potential, both as his new co-author and as a pleasant sexual diversion.

After tidying up in the washroom, he returned to his office and fired up his pipe, puffing on it thoughtfully. Everyone else had left for the day, and the quietness gave him an opportunity to take stock of matters.

Christine Anselm was going to be the big problem. She wasn't going to like it if she saw an article without her name on it. Not one bit. But he thought he had timed things just right. He had found other, better uses for her. And even though she was getting a bit tiresome, she could still get him stirred up sexually.

The problem part was that she was beginning to ask too many questions, making veiled threats, showing signs of unprecedented greed. Maybe they were too much alike. Always wanting more. Never fully satisfied with a static relationship. He needed to handle her skillfully. She could be trouble. And things were going too well for him—much too well—to let anyone ruin it. Especially someone of such little consequence as Christine.

He sighed, tamping out his pipe. He wasn't going to solve anything tonight. He needed to get home. He and his wife had a dinner party.

7

As you approached the cancer ward for morning work rounds, the first thing you saw was the big blackboard behind the ward clerk's desk. That was where the names of the patients who hadn't survived the night were written. Epitaphs in white chalk, scrawled by an indifferent hand. Just part of someone's job description.

The blackboard was a necessary evil, preventing the shock of rounding on an empty bed. Or from asking a grieving relative in the hall how his loved one was doing. This morning Dale saw five names on the board. Three had been his patients. He felt relief that their agony was over. Most of them had been brought there to die. So be it.

As he perused the blackboard, Dale couldn't shake the image of Ron Orloff's anguished face from his mind. It was there when he'd awakened this morning.

He sighed. Another day on the cancer ward. Dale, oncology fellow Jon Warner, and resident Andy Hamilton, started down the hall with the patient charts piled high on a metal cart. Andy still wore the surgical blues from his night on call. They looked like he'd slept in them. He hadn't. Dale wore the standard-issue white jacket and white pants with a dark blue shirt. A stethoscope snaked out of one pocket. Jon Werner wore bland JC Penney's "civvies." They hung loosely on his small, wiry body.

The group rolled to a stop outside Room 101. Andy pulled a chart from the rack and started his presentation. He was pale and intellectual-looking with his rimless glasses and greasy straight black hair that always looked like it needed washing. Dark circles under his eyes were magnified by his thick lenses.

He sounded like a fourth-grader reciting the Declaration of Independence. "Mrs. O'Toole is a sixty-two-year-old white female who discovered a lump on the right side of her neck two months ago. She saw her local M.D. who started her on antibiotics. The lump grew, so he sent her to a surgeon for a biopsy. The biopsy showed poorly differentiated adeno Ca."

Nobody ever used the word "cancer" on this ward. Only abbreviations or euphemisms would do. Andy droned on. He looked wobbly. "She's admitted now for a workup to find the primary."

Jon Werner had been staring down the hall with apparent disinterest. As leader of the crew, he was incongruously unobtrusive-looking. He made up for his slight build with a brisk, aggressive manner. He spoke and moved quickly, as though he were always about to miss a train. He suddenly sprung to life. "Smoker?" Andy nodded. "Chest X ray clear?" Andy nodded again. "What did you find on physical exam?" Jon leafed through the chart as he hurled questions.

Dale wandered over to the water fountain. A wad of chewing gum was plugging up the drain. The water trickled out. He lost interest and returned to the cart. A group of nurses in crisp white uniforms waved at him as they hurried by.

Andy sagged against the wall. "On exam the liver is down to the umbilicus. Hard, nodular. Two-plus scleral icterus. Right lower quadrant mass."

The woman sounded sick. She had a huge liver and she was jaundiced. She had to be riddled with cancer.

Jon tapped Dale's shoulder. "What's she got, Harper?"

Dale took the woman's chart from Jon and flipped to the lab section. "Sounds like colon cancer with mets to liver and lymph nodes." He glanced at Andy. "Did you get a blood CEA?"

Andy pushed off the wall and took the chart back

from Dale. "Uhh, forgot to order one. Good baseline test." He opened to the physician order sheets. "I'll write for one now."

"Any blood in her stool?" Dale asked.

Andy slapped his forehead. "I haven't checked yet."

Jon looked impatiently at Andy. Forgetfulness was not surprising after a sleepless night, but Andy was a doctor. A doctor's training was like being in a war. You had to keep your wits about you, no matter how tough the conditions. Jon headed into the room. "Let's go see her."

Mrs. O'Toole watched the approaching doctors anxiously. She had thin, straight white hair that allowed too much of her shiny pink scalp to show. She had an orange-red complexion with chipmunk cheeks. Her bright blue eyes were couched in egg-yolk yellow. They cautiously flitted from one doctor to another. Her eyelids were puffy from crying. This was her first time in a hospital. Her breakfast tray was perched in front of her as she sat on the edge of her bed. It boasted one untouched hard-boiled egg and a black piece of dry toast. Dale felt a mild wave of nausea and smiled at her sympathetically.

Andy made the introductions and asked her to lie down so the other doctors could examine her. She did so with effort. Her threadbare hospital gown hitched up to reveal flabby thighs with unsightly blue worm-like varicose veins. She tried to tug the gown back down, but it got hung up on her fat belly.

Dale watched for a moment as Mrs. O'Toole struggled to maintain her dignity. He could hear his father's voice as he noted the pained look in her eyes: "People suffer so much when they're hospitalized. It's not their illness that dehumanizes them, it's their loss of control. Do what little bit you can to help them hang on to their humanity."

Dale felt a tightening in his throat. It was as though he could sense his father's presence in the agony of

Mrs. O'Toole. He leaned over and covered her legs with the sheet. She smiled at him gratefully and he felt a little better.

The room was a four-bed ward. Dingy yellow curtains by each bed provided trifling gestures to privacy. Dale pulled the curtain around Mrs. O'Toole's bed as Jon began examining her. The woman in the bed behind him suddenly began to wretch. Dale found a basin for her in the closet and handed it to her. He walked back over to Mrs. O'Toole's bed.

Jon glanced up with a frown as he palpated Mrs. O'Toole's abdomen. He motioned to Dale. "See what you think," he said, and stepped back. Mrs. O'Toole looked bewildered. No one seemed to know she existed above the waist. Dale smiled at her. "Do you mind if I examine you, Mrs. O'Toole? I know you've gone through a lot of poking and prodding since you've been here." He stood with his hands clasped. Jon paced around the bed, muttering to himself.

Her eyes welled up with tears as she looked at Dale and shook her head, biting her lower lip. He proceeded to methodically examine her neck, lungs, heart, and finally her abdomen. He found a fullness in the right lower abdomen and tapped his finger over it. It made a hollow sound. Her liver was huge, as Andy had said. He also felt the tip of her spleen below the left rib cage. Andy hadn't mentioned that. When he was done, he helped her cover herself back up and thanked her.

The three of them returned to the metal cart in the corridor. Andy heard his name paged and vanished. Jon tossed the file onto the cart. "Planning to go into nursing when you finish your residency, Harper?" he sneered.

Dale shrugged. Werner didn't bother him. He had him typed. Jon belonged to the prima donna school of medicine—doctors who thought of themselves as gods. Dale tolerated that attitude to a point, but had no respect for it. "Just trying to help out, Jon," he said with an indifferent smile.

Jon started pacing again. "Look, I'm trying to run an efficient service here. I don't need you running off every five minutes to wipe someone's nose for him. If you want to be a doctor, act like one."

Dale felt a flash of anger. "You mean like you?" There was no mistaking the scorn in his voice. And yet he knew that Werner was the best when it came to efficiency.

Jon opened his mouth to respond, but a nurse came up to ask him a question. He turned his back on Dale as he talked to her, which gave Dale time to regain his composure. He was fed up with a system that treated patients like practice mannequins for fledgling doctors. God save the people who came to university medical centers because they thought they would get the best care. Or the indigent, who ended up in a city teaching hospital like this one. True, they might get good care. But they might also be demeaned and humiliated.

Andy returned just as Jon finished talking with the nurse. Jon pointedly ignored Dale, and turned to Andy. "So what's your diagnosis, Dr. Hamilton?"

Andy swayed slightly. "Well, I agree with Dale. I think it's colon. I ordered a barium enema for tomorrow."

"And what will it show?"

Andy leaned against the wall. "An extensive cecal carcinoma." The cecum was the lower right portion of the colon where the mass was.

"Do you agree, Dr. Harper?" Jon was all business now.

They rolled the cart to the next room as Dale nodded and said with a thoughtful frown, "Pretty much, but I think the mass is in the ascending colon, causing obstruction and gas in the cecum. That mass is hollow-sounding to percussion, meaning air, not tumor."

Jon's eyes narrowed with grudging respect. Harper

was sharp. Even Jon hadn't noted that. But now that Dale pointed it out, he was fairly sure he was right. "We'll know tomorrow, won't we?" He turned to Andy. "Next patient?"

Rounds went on for most of the morning, with Andy presenting his admissions from the night before. They ended with Jesse Munoz, a patient of Jon's.

Jesse's chart said it all. He was a twenty-seven-year-old Mexican with cancer of the testicle. He was on massive doses of chemotherapy to blast the cancer out of him. It was also blasting his immune system, so he was in reverse isolation. This meant that everyone who entered his room had to wear gowns, gloves, and masks so they wouldn't transmit any germs to him. His fragile immunity could be devastated by things that wouldn't even make a normal person sneeze. He was as vulnerable as someone with AIDS.

The three doctors donned the sterile paraphernalia and entered Jesse's room. They looked like yellow invaders from outer space. Jesse gave them a wide grin, but it made him breathe harder even to do that. "Hey, Docs." He reached out to slap their hands. His thin, handsome face was beaded with sweat.

Jon took up the bedside clipboard to check Jesse's temperature. It was 102. He was already on three antibiotics. Jon listened to Jesse's lungs and checked his abdomen.

"Doc, I got a bad case of Montezuma's revenge, you know?" His dark brown eyes belied his ever-ready smile. However doubt manifests itself in a person's eyes, it was there in Jesse's. But Jesse would never ask if he was going to make it. He had his wife and kids and everyone else convinced that he would.

The fecal smell that inevitably accompanies diarrhea in a sick, bedridden patient permeated their masks. "It'll pass. You're doing great, Jesse." Jon's pep talk lacked its usual resonance.

For a moment the doctor and patient quietly gazed at each other. Dale guessed Werner was smiling, although the blue surgical mask hid his mouth. If Jesse saw through Werner's facade of cheerfulness, he didn't let on. "I hear ya, Doc. You can count on me, you know?"

Jon squeezed Jesse's shoulder gently. "We'll have all those IVs out of you in a few days, champ. You'll see."

The space invaders left as quickly as they had come. No intergalactic miracles today. Jesse's smile dissolved like melting snow on a hot day.

After discarding their paper garments, the three physicians headed for the doctor's lounge to discuss plans for the day.

Dale pushed aside a pair of surgical blues cast off from the night before and sprawled on the coffee-stained couch.

Jon and Andy sat at a table littered with half-empty plastic coffee cups. Andy's movements were slow. When he blinked, he looked as though he had to think about it first. "Well, you lost a lot of players last night, Dale. Guess you'll have some time on your hands today." He giggled nervously. "Want some of my patients?"

Nobody but Jon Werner liked oncology.

"No thanks." Dale shot him an understanding look. "I've got to meet with Annie Snowden's family and try to break the news about how bad off she really is." Annie was dying of metastatic breast cancer. She was only thirty-four. "Then I have my outpatient clinic." The image of a terrified Ron Orloff hounded him again.

Andy nodded. He looked miserable. He had two patients Annie Snowden's age. Oncology was either going to make or break him. Dale feared the latter. "Hey, Andy. Let's have lunch together. I should be done with Annie's family by around twelve-thirty." They needed to take care of each other.

Andy perked up a little. "Sure. Meet you in the cafeteria?"

"You got it." Dale turned to Jon. "Why not let Andy head for the library? I can tell him at lunch any comments you have for him about his patients."

Jon had been silently observing this exchange between the two residents—one a kind of quiet leader, the other slowly drowning in a sea too turbulent for him emotionally. He saw the cancer ward as a kind of test that many young doctors couldn't stand up to. Maybe it represented one of the critical crossroads where if you turned in one direction you became a cynic; the other, a compassionate human being. Jon wasn't sure which he was. The test was there each day, always ready to challenge you, catch you off guard. Dale bothered him because he thought him too involved. But Andy bothered him more. He saw the lurking cynic there, protectively hovering in the wings, waiting for the tears, the uncertainty and pain. Waiting to provide Andy with an alternative to dealing with his own suffering: You're dying? Well, tough, man—we all got to go sometime. A way to stick a finger in the dike. A way that wouldn't help anybody, including Andy.

Jon shook himself out of his musing. "Yeah, sure. Beat it, Andy. I'll pass some pearls on to Dale for you."

Andy was gone before Jon could put a period on his sentence.

Dale slumped down on the couch, as though its cushions could hide him from the day ahead. His earlier brush with Jon was forgotten. Basically, they respected each other for what they stood for. Different but equal.

"Jon," he ventured with a sigh, "you're a reasonable guy. What makes you want to spend the rest of your life telling people they only have six months to live?"

Jon tossed Jesse Munoz's chart at Dale. "Because," he almost whispered, "if this kid makes it, it will be because of me. He'll have me to thank for snatching him out of the arms of the grim reaper. That's what it's all about, man." Jon's voice had an almost evangelical fervor.

Dale laughed to himself. Touchy ground here, but he had to say it. "You mean you want to be God."

Jon was on the edge of his seat, pointing hard at Dale, who had slouched down a few more inches. Any more and he'd be on the floor. "Listen, pal," Jon rasped, "I've wanted to be a doctor since I was five years old. Sirens, flashing lights, chills up and down your spine—that's where it's at. Life and death. Every day." His head moved in quick little jerks, like an angry chicken.

"Death and death," Dale muttered as he stared absently at a teardrop-shaped smudge on the wall.

Jon ignored him. "Imagine my disappointment when I hit med school and found out that mostly you just patch people up and stick 'em back in the water—hope they don't sink.

"But if Jesse Munoz survives his chemo, he's not going to sink, my friend. He'll be a luxury liner and I'll be the one who put him back in the water." Jon punched his own chest with his forefinger.

Closest thing to walking on water, Dale thought.

It was true, though. If he survived his chemo, Jesse stood a good chance of being cured. If so, he could expect to live a normal, healthy life. A big if, judging by how things were going.

Like many other doctors in training, Dale was skeptical of chemotherapy's benefits. It seemed like a way of torturing dying people. If it served any positive purpose, it was to help people welcome death. *Adios*-mycin, they called it. But you couldn't say that in front of Jon Werner. Not if you didn't want a thirty-minute lecture about how great the stuff was.

"The odds are always against you," Dale challenged, without looking up.

Jon smiled. "Yeah, like gambling, isn't it? If the

odds were in my favor, it would get boring. Your Aunt Tillie could do it."

Dale suddenly sat up. "For chrissake, Jon, you're talking about gambling with other people's lives! They're not poker chips!"

Jon sprung to his feet. "I don't expect you to understand where I'm coming from, Dale. Not many people do. The patients do." He went over to the couch and picked up Jesse Munoz's chart. He shoved it in Dale's face. "Draw a blood count on this guy and page me with the results." He started for the door. "Get Orloff off his duff," he added without turning his head. "We've got a lot of sick patients."

You son of a bitch, Dale thought. "What about some pearls for Andy?"

"None today," Jon called as he disappeared through the door.

Dale sat there for a while, chin resting on hand, wondering what he was going to say to Annie Snowden's family.

The ward clerk, a heavyset black woman, came in with the morning lab slips and sullenly tossed them on the table next to Dale. She waddled out.

Dale leafed through them idly. Then he froze, his eyes blinking with disbelief at the blood count on Ron Orloff. The white cell count was ninety-five thousand with five percent blasts. Christ! Ron Orloff had leukemia.

8

Ron Orloff entered the large waiting room of the on-cology clinic, announced his arrival to the receptionist, and took a seat. He spotted some of his own clinic patients. Today they were waiting to see another doctor. It seemed strange to be on the receiving end. He glanced around at the walls and receptionist's desk. He was hoping to avoid catching the eye of his patients and having to explain why he was there.

The institutional green walls seemed bleak. The hot-pink vinyl and metal chair he was sitting on had a big crack in it. He was embarrassed that this was where his patients had to sit and wait for him—or for any other doctor.

Before he knew it, he found himself sitting across from Dale Harper in a cubbyhole of an office. Dale was seated at a small Formica desk that was cluttered with charts and lab slips. He looked solemn. Ron found himself focusing on small details as a way of keeping his anxiety at manageable levels. Dale had on a white coat, with one side of the collar turned under. Ron smiled to himself. Dale was not a man meant to be in uniform.

After what seemed an eternity, Dale spoke in a flat, controlled voice. "Ron, I have your lab work back from this morning." No point in beating around the bush. "I think you have CML, but we'll need to do a bone marrow aspiration to know for sure." He stopped, letting that sink in, hoping that his own affected calmness would somehow steady Ron.

Ron sat there, his ears hearing but his brain screaming at him: What did he say? Ask him what he said! Then he saw Dale's lips moving again, but all he could hear was his brain yelling at him. He looked down at his hands, spreading his fingers apart. He needed to cut his nails, he thought inanely.

He looked up again after what felt to be another eternity, and saw Dale watching him, a quizzical look on his face.

"Chronic myelogenous leukemia. Is that what you said, Dale?" That's it, his brain screamed, make him tell you again.

Dale nodded. Offer him some hope. "Listen, Ron, people with CML can do well. You know I tend to be a pessimist about chemotherapy, but this is one disease that often responds nicely to treatment."

He paused again to give Ron time to assimilate the news that would put his life into a tailspin. Dale clasped his hands on top of the desk. "The longest living patient with CML that I know of has gone eighteen years. By that time, we'll probably have a cure."

Ron felt the lump in his throat softening the slightest bit. The question he had heard many times from patients raised itself conspicuously in his own mind. He had to verbalize it. It was a way of getting rid of something he didn't like. "Why me?" He looked up at Dale, his dark eyes a kaleidoscope of fear, anger, and sadness.

Dale smiled bitterly. He had been wondering the same thing all morning. "Illness is the great equalizer, Ron. You could be a saint or a scoundrel, rich or poor. It makes no distinctions." Dale looked away, clenching his jaw. Some consolation. "I don't know," he finally said sadly.

He turned back to his desk and poised his pen to write. "I would like to ask you a few questions." He looked up at Ron, who appeared to be holding his own. "Any family history of cancer or leukemia?"

Ron shook his head. He felt drained. "Both sides

of my family have lousy hearts. Not an inkling of cancer."

"Any radiation treatment for acne or any other condition as a child?" No. "Did you grow up in any areas where nuclear testing took place or nuclear-waste dumping has been discovered?"

Ron shook his head again. "Healthy Iowa corn country. No Love Canals have been uncovered there—yet." Ron managed a smile. Humor helped fend off self-pity. He had seen it work time and again for his patients. Dale was a master at it. But not today.

Dale tossed his pen down and looked at Ron. A new thought suddenly occurred to him, seemingly from nowhere. "Ron," he asked, a feeling of nervous anticipation overtaking him, "did any of your micro research involve use of radioactive materials?"

"Never." He snorted. "I didn't want to end up with something like this."

Dale felt the momentary wave of tension pass. But he couldn't shake Nina's cryptic references to rumors about radiation safety. "Could you have been accidentally contaminated?"

The suggestion alarmed Ron. "Not that I know of . . ." The lump in his throat started knotting up again. He swallowed with effort.

Dale wasn't ready to let it go. Why Ron? He wanted to know too, and something kept tugging at his mind, making him feel restless, even irritable. It was as though a piece of a puzzle—the piece that told you what the puzzle was all about—was missing.

"Well, let me know if you think of something." Dale stood up. He came around his desk and put his hand on Ron's shoulder, leading him into the exam room. He returned to his desk and sat deep in thought, tapping his pen on the desktop while he waited for Ron to undress.

Dale's beeper interrupted his late-afternoon doze. "Call emergency," it kept sputtering, just as he was about to embrace Nina. "Damn," he muttered, waking from his dream. Just his luck. Couldn't they have held off another few seconds? He had blissfully nodded off during an oncology conference. As soon as the speaker dimmed the lights to show slides, Dale slipped into a hypnotic trance. Since the beginning of his internship, he readily fell asleep when he wasn't in motion. Situational narcolepsy, he called it. The cure would be a steady nightly dose of six to eight hours of sleep. He wouldn't have minded today's interruption if he could have finished the dream.

He looked around the room to orient himself, rubbing his eyes. At least his beeper hadn't disturbed the other snoozing house officers. When he called the ER, the gruff voice of Dr. Boyles, an emergency-room resident, accosted him. "Harper! I got a hit for you."

There was a pause as Boyles directed the receiver away from his ear. Dale could hear a man screaming hysterically in the background. Boyles came back on. "Hear that howling?"

"Is that the patient?" Dale wondered what he was in for.

"Nope. The patient is a nice sixteen-year-old black kid with what looks like acute myelogenous leukemia. Apart from the fact that you're going to get to watch him die, he should be a dream to work with. That screaming you hear is his father, who, needless to say, is having some difficulty with the news I just gave him about his son." Boyles spoke in a clipped, unemotional manner as though discussing the stock market.

God, Dale hated oncology. He suddenly felt tired. He pulled a pen out of his pocket and held it over the back of a lab slip. "What's the kid's name?"

"You're gonna love this, Harper." Boyles snorted. "Lincoln Lee. Takes you right back to the Civil War days, doesn't it?"

"Boyles, I'm not interested in your bigoted bullshit," Dale said wearily. Something kept niggling at the back of his brain. "Lincoln Lee . . . what's his father's name?"

"Robert E., no doubt," Boyles said, undaunted. Dale heard a rustling of papers as Boyles searched for the admitting sheet. "Willie. Believe me, Harper, you're gonna have a harder time calming Willie down than getting his kid into remission."

Boyles turned from the phone for a moment, then came back on. "I'm shipping them both up to you by elevator express. Good luck." Boyles slammed the phone down before Dale could rain all over him.

Willie Lee, Lincoln Lee. Jesus! Could it be the Willie Lee he knew from his med-school days? Oh, please, not that Willie. Not that Lincoln. Not when he was just trying to get through it all with his own intern. God almighty.

Lincoln was taking it okay. Boyles was right. Willie was the problem. But he was starting to settle down. As the nurses flocked around Lincoln to get an IV going and get him settled, Dale took Willie into an empty conference room to talk. It was the Willie he'd known during his med-school days. In body. Not spirit. Willie was devastated. His weathered black face sagged, accenting the sad, beaten look in his eyes. Gone was the twinkle that Dale remembered so well, especially when Willie talked about his kids. Now his eyes were a muddy brown, with the redness that tears bring. Gone too was the ever-ready broad grin that flaunted one gleaming gold-capped front tooth.

Dale had spoken in ineffective platitudes, trying to help Willie pull himself together. It was Lincoln who finally succeeded. He had called his dad over and whispered in his ear. Willie had stared at him in wonder, then stood up ramrod straight, a picture of dignity.

That was when Dale sat Willie down and explained to him all about leukemia, what the treatment would be, and what Lincoln's chances were. None of it was good. As Dale knew only too well, acute leukemia, unlike chronic leukemia, was a much more virulent disease. If a remission was achieved with chemotherapy, it most likely would not be a long one.

As Willie listened, a kind of resigned calm came over him. He was letting go of a dream and coming back to reality. He seemed to gather strength from his boy.

Willie was sipping a cup of tepid black coffee. He smiled, almost dreamily, and shook his head. "Lincoln, he's such a good boy, Doc. He was gonna be a doctor."

He looked up at Dale, his eyes revealing a glint of pride. "His teachers tol' me he was one of the smartest kids they seen in years." He put the coffee down and rested his head in his hands.

Dale sat on the coffee table in front of Willie and placed his hands on Willie's shoulders. What did you say at a time like this? He couldn't imagine that twenty more years of experience would ever make it easier to deal with terminal illness. He gave Willie's shoulders a gentle squeeze. "Willie, why don't you go on home now? I'll take good care of Lincoln. You need some rest."

But Willie was still living with the vision of a Lincoln that could never be. He sat back and propped his head on the couch pillow, staring up at the ceiling. "You should've seen Lincoln making like a doctor at home, even when he was only nine." He chuckled softly. "Yeah, I brought him some ol' white coats, ol' syringes and stuff from the med school. Stuff no one wanted no more," he added quickly, glancing at Dale. "An' he'd be runnin' aroun' the place givin' me shots and lookin' down my throat, an' tellin' me to take better care of myself."

There was that niggling feeling again. Something Willie had said bothered him. Dale frowned. "Where did you get all this old stuff for Lincoln, Willie?"

"Oh, jes' from the baskets. They was tossed out. I

never stole nothin'." If it was possible, Willie looked even more worried than before.

Dale reassured him, "Willie, that's not what I was getting at." He checked himself. "I was just wondering." He wasn't about to let Willie know why. Did Willie clean the radioactive rooms? Leukemia was probably the most common cancer due to radiation. He let the thought hang there as he walked Willie to the elevator. Willie looked up at Dale and pumped his hand vigorously. "I know you'll take good care o' my boy, Doctor. I'm sorry I caused trouble. Lincoln, he helped me. Know what he say, back there in his room?"

Dale shook his head. He'd been amazed at Willie's sudden composure after Lincoln whispered to him.

Willie smiled sadly. "He's some boy. He tol' me, 'Dad, I'm as proud of you as you are of me. Stand tall, Dad. Let the white folks know how we be.'"

Dale smiled sadly, trying to choke down a powerful feeling of anguish as he knew what was in store for Lincoln and his family. "He should be proud, Willie. He should be."

The elevator came and took Willie. Dale leaned against the wall and sighed, letting out air as though he were a punctured tire. Two cases of leukemia in one week. Strange. And it did not escape his attention that both had a connection with the microbiology research floors at the medical school. Probably just a coincidence. But he didn't like it.

9

Dale had been thinking about Nina Yablonsky more than he cared to admit. He kept visualizing her cameolike face—her high cheekbones and dark brown almond-shaped eyes. Eyes that glittered as if always amused. He craved that magic sparkle of life. It helped keep him from tottering on the edge of depression when the realities of death faced him every day.

As he lay in bed musing, he knew with a feeling of exhilaration with whom he wanted to spend his day off. He reached for the phone.

"Hello," Nina said drowsily.

"I'm calling you about that drink?" he said in the manner of an uncertain suitor. He heard a murmur of recognition. He quickly put in, reminded of his dream by the sleepy sensuality in her voice, "How about breakfast instead?"

A pause. "Sounds great."

"Our first date," he said. He felt light and alive—a sudden release from the death and despair of the cancer ward.

"Terrific! Give me a chance to shower and dress, and I'm yours for the morning."

"In that case," he rejoined with a chuckle, "don't bother dressing."

She had a lilting laugh. "Now you're the typical horny house officer, Doctor."

"God forbid," he shot back. "Pick you up in an hour?"

"It's a date."

His face lit up as an idea struck him. "How about an hour and a half? I just remembered something."

"Sounds good."

"Dress casual," he said. "Slacks." He hung up, feeling like a schoolboy stealing his first kiss. She was good for him. Full of life. An impish sense of humor. He had never met a woman quite like her.

Dale rang Nina's doorbell smiling with anticipation. Her apartment was amid a typical southern California pseudo-stucco singles complex. Already the hip weekend muscle-beach types were sprawled out by the pool, bodies oiled and tan. Male eyes hiding behind polarized sunglasses sought out the pick of the pack as the ladies wandered through the courtyard, towels and sun lotion in hand. He felt a twinge of—could it be—jealousy as he wondered whether Nina ever took part in this adolescent nonsense.

Nina opened the door, looking fit and absurdly young in her Levi's. Dressed just right for the occasion, he thought. "Hi." He grinned, a twinkle in his eye. "Our transportation awaits us." He put his arm around her and gently propelled her past a gauntlet of hungry eyes.

"Your classy Mustang?" She laughed.

"Classy mustangs," he said as they reached the street, pointing to two sorrel-red horses, saddled and hitched up to a parking meter.

She stopped short, gaping in disbelief. "Where on earth did you get them?"

"Oh, they belong to a buddy of mine," he said, enjoying her reaction. "I told him I wanted to have breakfast with a lovely lady at his restaurant. A very special occasion."

She looked up at him in mock horror. "Dale, I've never been on a horse in my life!"

"It's easy. These horses are as gentle as little lambs." At this one of the horses threw up its head and nickered.

Nina burst out laughing—a hearty, full-throated laugh. "Dale, you're mad!"

She moved closer to the horses and touched their noses. They seemed to like it. The horse with a white blaze gave her a nudge. She smiled. "Hi, big guy. What's your name?"

Dale untied the horse and gave the reins to Nina. "This is Miguel. He's a senior citizen. He's yours." He nodded toward the other horse. "That one is Pancho. He has ideas of his own. I'll take him."

She held the reins as though they were a pair of snakes. "Now what?" She patted Miguel's head as he sniffed for a sugar cube.

"Dale, isn't this illegal? Riding horseback in the streets?"

"Probably. So is stabbing people, dealing drugs, and mugging. It still happens. And we're not harming anyone." He cupped his hands near the stirrup. "Come on, let me help you up. We're only going a few blocks."

Nina's horse plodded along, flicking its ears back to tune in on its rider. Nina leaned forward to pat him on the neck. "Good boy, Miguel." She fussed with his mane, trying to push it all over to one side, which it didn't want to do.

Dale watched her, liking the way she adjusted to the unexpected. He was sharing with her one of his great loves—horses. And she hadn't disappointed him.

With each stride through the back streets of Los Angeles, Nina appeared less rigid in the saddle. Even comfortable. Dale gave her an approving smile.

"Here we are," he said as they approached a garish pink stucco building. He dismounted, tied the horses to the sign out front, and helped Nina down.

She eyed him happily as they bounded up the front steps, wonderful aromas of coffee and chiles floating out at them. She was on an adventure, ready for anything. He was getting to like her more by the minute.

Eager and fresh-faced, outgoing. Not at all worried about appearances.

The restaurant was small, with modest wooden tables and chairs. Several Mexican families were eating breakfast. They looked up as Dale and Nina entered. From behind the counter came a short, chubby Mexican with a mustache. He looked to be in his midforties. "Hey, amigo! I see you make it okay with the lady, no?" He scurried up to Dale and gave him a big embrace. "I save the best seats for you." He led them to a corner table by the window.

As Juan rushed off to bring them coffee, Nina scanned the menu. "He's certainly enamored of you," she said. "What did you do? Save his life?"

Dale gazed at her a moment. "He thinks so. When I was a third-year med student."

Juan returned with two steaming mugs of coffee. "Juan will tell you all about it. He still tells me all about it."

Juan put the mugs down and clapped Dale on the back, smiling at Nina. "He save my life, you know. I never forget someone who save my life. I make you both Juan's special, yes?"

Nina nodded enthusiastically. Juan hurried off.

"And now, Mister Lifesaver, I want to hear your own copyrighted story of how you performed your heroic feat."

"All right"—he laughed in the same vein—"you asked for it."

She steepled her fingers, thinking how handsome he was, and so unaware of it. "Please."

"Juan was sent to the medicine ward from orthopedics. They told him he had cancer that had spread to his bones. He became my patient, and even though his bone scan lit up all over, I wasn't convinced that's what he had. I was a typical compulsive third-year med student, pursuing every lead, including lots of dead-ends.

"Juan would cry and ask me how long he had to

live. I'd keep telling him he might have something treatable, trying to give him a straw to grasp at. And luckily, I'd guessed right. He did have something treatable—tuberculosis of the bone. Discovered it from a biopsy of a small mass on his rib cage. He's a cure. A great case. Grand rounds, *New England Journal*." Dale leaned back in his chair, remembering the thrill of it all—Juan's gratitude, the excitement of solving a tough case, the admiration of his peers and teachers.

She was silent for a moment, feeling close to him in her sense that this was what medicine was all about. "And now," she said lightly, masking the depth of her feeling, "he loans you his horses and feeds you whenever you want."

"For a price." He smiled mysteriously.

"You mean saving a life isn't enough?"

"It's plenty. But I also shoe his horses for him. In exchange, he lets me ride Pancho on weekends." Dale sipped his coffee. "I wouldn't have it any other way."

He was full of surprises. "You? Shoe horses? And do you also ride in rodeos?"

Dale played with his napkin, folding it into an airplane. "I worked my way through college and med school shoeing horses. It was a nice relief from the intellectual rat race. And not bad money."

Juan arrived with two platters of eggs mixed and garnished with chiles, cheese, sour cream, tomatoes. Tortillas on the side. Enough cholesterol to topple a healthy horse. But with Juan giving them an approving nod, they fell to eating like hungry animals, barely exchanging a word until their plates were empty.

Dale finished first, and tapped his fingers thoughtfully on the table as he watched Nina push her plate away.

He felt close to her, as though he had always known her. Maybe she could help him with something. She seemed so down to earth, so capable. And knowledgeable about something on his mind—radiation.

"Nina," he said, "I need your advice."

She looked up at him, instantly alert, but with an uneasy buzz in her stomach. He looked solemn, even anxious—a sudden change in mood.

He had a way of frowning when he wasn't sure of himself. He was frowning now as he lowered his voice. "I've encountered two cases of leukemia at the hospital in one week. That in itself could be considered unusual—even on the cancer ward. What bothers me is that both of them have had exposure in one way or another to the microbiology department at the med school. One is the son of a maintenance man there." He tossed the napkin on his empty plate, thinking as he talked how sketchy it all was.

Nina looked puzzled. "And?"

He moved on. "Radioisotopes. The radioactive materials they use in genetic research over there. I'm wondering if the maintenance men have to handle them."

Nina took a moment to answer as she called on her memory of regulations about nuclear medicine. "Not the regulars. There's a special team of men trained in nuclear waste disposal. That's all they do."

"That wouldn't be Willie." He seemed to be mumbling to himself.

"What are you driving at, Dale?"

He saw her frown. He didn't want to ruin a wonderful morning with his suspicions. He smiled and cupped his hand over hers. "Oh, it's nothing. Just dabbling in melodrama."

He looked around for Juan. "Listen, my car's here. I can drive you home. But I'd really like you to spend the rest of the morning with me while I shoe Juan's horses. I told him I'd do it this weekend."

"I wouldn't be in the way?" She liked being with him, listening to him, watching his face as it went through its many subtle changes. And unlike many of the men she had dated, she knew he wouldn't mind one bit if she could work crosswords better than he.

"Absolutely not! You could be a help. It's always better to have someone hold the horse."

"I'm ready!"

Dale got Juan's attention. Juan came over and chattered cheerfully. "My horses, they will want a lovely lady like you with them. Take their mind off their hoofs, that for sure."

Dale and Nina led the horses into a small corral behind the restaurant and unsaddled them. Dale transferred his equipment from the trunk of his car, and donned a tattered leather apron. Nina marveled at the transformation from doctor to farrier in a matter of minutes.

They started with Miguel, who continued his flirtation with Nina by gently nudging her with his nose. He seemed indifferent to Dale's picking up his hooves, prying off his shoes, and digging and clipping at his feet.

"Miguel has never been so well behaved," Dale said as he bent over Miguel's right forefoot. "He likes you almost as much as I do. For different reasons, no doubt."

Nina laughed. "How do you know? Maybe his father was a radiologist." She bit her lip the moment she said it. But it didn't seem to bother him. He chuckled softly and worked in silence except to occasionally explain what he was doing.

Finally Miguel's hooves were trimmed and ready for new shoes. Dale stood up stiffly, holding his hands to his back, stretching. Sweat dripped down his face. His hands were black. His rolled-up sleeves revealed strong arms with ropelike veins. "How about a Coke?"

Nina nodded. Dale tied Miguel to a fencepost and got two Cokes from a cooler behind the restaurant. Nina sat on a bench in the sun. Dale stretched out on the ground in the shade of a tree next to her.

As he downed his Coke, Nina stared at the can in her hand, her face clouding slightly. "Dale, I didn't mean to scare you off. You asked for my help, and I'll help as best I can." She looked up at him. "The stories about safety violations in radiology have made me hypersensitive. Radiologists are always blamed, even when we have nothing to do with it."

"Thanks for listening," he said. "Maybe I'm making too much of this, but it keeps coming back at me. Of the two patients I mentioned, neither one is aware of exposure to radioactive materials. Yet I can't help but wonder if they were somehow contaminated. It just seems too coincidental to be coincidental, if you know what I mean."

Nina picked a twig off the ground and sketched randomly in the sandy soil between her feet. She was not so concerned about irregularities in the microbiology department as she was about Dale. She had a feeling he was overreacting. He had next to nothing to go on. The least she could do was be candid.

"You have no idea how strictly radioactive materials are regulated," she said. "Besides, if you're thinking contamination, it would have to be a massive dose, or exposure over a long period of time—ten, twenty years. Highly unlikely." She sipped her drink, then said gently, "You're under a lot of strain. I know the cancer ward is difficult."

He felt a flicker of irritation, but he knew she was looking at it properly. On the other hand, she didn't have the whole story. He squatted in front of her, his arms resting on his knees.

She could see that he was trying to collect his thoughts, and she was more than ready to listen. She waited.

He spoke in a soft and reflective voice. "My father died of bone cancer. It was a long and painful death. In the end he was pumped full of drugs around the clock. He was pretty much out of it. But he knew who I was, right up to the hour he died. He took my hand and told me that if I became a doctor, as he wanted me to, to never fool with radiation."

He squinted up at her, gauging her reaction. What he saw made him go on. "He made me promise, with a force I didn't think he had in him. I asked him why he felt so strongly. He said it was radiation, not cancer, that was killing him, and it should never have happened."

Nina could see his pain, and she reached out to touch him. "You don't have to go on."

"I want to. I want you to know. It's important to me. No one knew what he was talking about. He didn't live to tell me anything more. Everyone insisted that he was delirious when he died. They told me not to fret about it. Not to even think about it. There was no relationship to his being a radiologist. They tried to put me off. I was only fourteen, but I knew enough to see what a reasonable man my father was. He was not an alarmist. And he was not delirious when I talked to him that day." He stared off at the horizon, his mind caught up in the emotional tumult of that time. "It's been eighteen years now, but I remember those moments like they were yesterday. And I still feel some aching need to resolve my father's death."

He took a deep breath and stood up with a sigh. "I don't even know who or what the enemy is."

"Or if," Nina said softly.

"Or if," he echoed. He strode over to the anvil and pounded out the hot horseshoes into a size for Miguel with what seemed to Nina to be Herculean force. Or was it sheer anger and frustration, judging from the set of his face?

Nina held Miguel as Dale hammered the shoes onto each hoof. They were both silent. When he finished with Miguel, Dale was drained. He would come back later to shoe Pancho. They drove to Nina's apartment and Dale trailed in after her.

They plopped down in mod chrome and leather chairs opposite each other, a glass coffee table between them, sipping from a couple of cold beers. He seemed despondent and she tried to reassure him.

"Whenever you work with radioactive materials," she said, "you have to account for every millicurie. If you don't, you lose your license to use it."

He sat up, relieved that she wasn't brushing off his concerns. "How can they keep track of it all?"

"Anyone who even enters a room designated radioactive has to log in. He has to indicate whether he worked with isotopes, and if so, how he disposed of them. Then he has to check the entire work area, even his clothing, with a Geiger counter to make sure everything's clean."

"And if it's not?"

"Then he doesn't leave the area until it is. If he wants to keep his job."

"Couldn't somebody fake it, leave an area contaminated, or carry radioisotopes into places where they don't belong?"

"Sure." Nina finished her beer and put the empty bottle on the table. "But why would anyone do something that dumb? There would be no benefit in falsifying records or taking risks. Because if they do . . ." She slashed a dramatic finger across her throat.

Dale laughed. "And who would that be?"

"The Nuclear Regulatory Commission. Our friends in Washington."

Dale didn't think much of bureaucracy. "I need to find out for myself. Call it an obsession, call it paranoia or plain curiosity. Maybe just a bungling sense of justice. I don't know."

He wandered across the room and gazed out the window at the poolside partying, his hands jingling the loose change in his pockets. "I don't want to do this alone. I can't be objective. Will you help me?"

She came up beside him and peered up at his face, a reflective look in her eyes. "You're about to get us involved in something that's not our business. You know that, don't you?"

Dale glowed. "That's a yes?"

Nina sighed. "That's a yes. Don't ask me why."

"I won't." He tilted her chin so that their eyes met. "Thank you."

He glanced at the wall clock. "I've got to go."

She walked him to the door. "All right. Now that you've hired me on, I have your first assignment for you."

"What's that, O leader of men?" He grinned, enjoying her taking command.

"I want you to check the oncology ward logbook for the past year and see if you can find any other patients who are connected with the micro department."

He understood completely. She was counting on a dead-end. "Great idea. I'll do it," he said cheerfully. He kissed her lightly on the lips and strode past the poolside scene. Most of the tanned bodies were paired off by now. For the evening, anyway.

10

Dr. Herman Moran sat in his comfortable Hollywood Hills home after a tough day at the Factory. That's what it was like, on a day like this. He perspired just thinking about it. Being a department head in that sweatshop was no small feat. Especially head of microbiology, which was a big money-maker for the medical school. Also, a big status deal. Publish or perish. Publish and perish. Something like that. People griping at him day in, day out. It got to him. More and more, it got to him.

He made himself a double martini, kicked off his shoes, and plopped down into one of the overstuffed rose-colored chairs in the television room. He loosened his tie and put his feet up on the coffee table. His middle-aged paunch stretched at his shirt as he settled back, the material gaping to reveal the soft pink flesh beneath.

He reached for the remote control and shot it at the TV. On flipped the evening news. Goddamn Arabs blowing people up again. He hoisted himself out of the chair and ambled slowly over to the wet bar in the back of the room. He felt a little woozy when he first stood up. The powder-blue deep plush carpet felt good on his stocking feet. He poured himself another martini. Just a touch of dry vermouth. No ice this time. He looked up from his bartending and regarded his image in the mirror. Too many goddamn mirrors in this house. He had told Audrey he didn't want mirrors. Everywhere he turned he saw himself.

He leaned forward, frowning at his image. He was getting a double chin. The five o'clock shadow didn't help. The slick midline part in his hair that he'd sported for so many years didn't work so well now that he was going bald. His nose was getting red and bulbous. His eyes stared at him vacantly. For a moment he felt panicky as he shrank back from what he saw. He didn't look like the dashing, aggressive genius pushing and shoving his way to the top anymore. It seemed like a long time ago now. But that's what he had been. Or how he saw himself, or how others saw him. Oh, hell. He slugged down half the martini and refilled the glass before he wove back to his cushy chair.

He started to nod off into oblivion as the TV railed at him to buy a Toyota. Then someone was shaking him, a witch. No. It was Audrey. "Herman, what are you doing home? I thought you had a meeting tonight."

Audrey had a nasal New York accent. She had been a nurse, but retired soon after marrying. She had held on to the image of wife-of-aggressive-dashing-genius quite well through the years. She was his age, fifty-five, but looked about forty. If you gave her an hour head start in the morning, that is. Makeup and face-lifts worked miracles. And she was as trim as a gymnast. No wonder. She worked out at aerobics five days a week, and played tennis three times a week with the faculty wives.

Nobody but Herm knew she was a witch, though. What? You're drunk, Herm. Your wife's not a witch. She's a lovely, gracious woman who helped shove you to the top. No, encouraged you.

He shook his head, like a wet dog. There, he felt a little clearer. "Meeting? Oh, that. No, they don't need me. The illustrious Dr. Heffron can handle it. Just piddly department policies." He smiled blearily up at his wife as she faded in and out of focus. Or was she moving to and fro?

"Besides, dear, a good leader can walk away from the office and the place still runs smooth as a baby's ass." He groped aimlessly for her breast. "Right?"

She brushed his hand away and snatched his glass. "You've had enough, Herman." She wrinkled her nose in disgust. "And your breath stinks. Why don't you go to bed?"

Good idea. You go to your bed, and I'll go to mine. They hadn't slept together in years. Their sex life, like their marriage, had been dulled and abraded by time. Herman had tried a variety of sexual substitutes outside his marriage, and had settled on feeding a previously latent desire—strapping young male medical students. Some thought that was why Herm became director of the tutorial program at the med school. More student contact. Ha, ha. But actually, Herm had been kicked upstairs. Or downstairs. Depending on your point of view. He didn't run the micro department anymore. Officially, yes. But things were happening there. Things he didn't like. Things he didn't know about.

That asshole Heffron was gradually usurping control, a big hotshot. A politician. Everybody kowtowing to him. Him and his goddamn Heffron Foundation. Such a philanthropist. So noble, pouring money into cancer research. Sponsoring graduate students from third world countries. How sweet. Where the hell did he get all that money, anyway?

Herm snorted. Philanderer was more like it. Hell, it took more than charm and money to run a department. People ought to know that. Oh, well. Herm told himself he didn't mind. He liked the student contact. Yes. A lot of medical school young men worried about their grades. But if they saw to Herm's needs, he would see to theirs. Tit for tat. It was a good arrangement. It worked.

Herm stumbled upstairs to bed. He fell asleep, fully clothed, with a smile on his face as he dreamed of a young hard body up against his.

11

Nina's suggestion backfired. When Dale went through the logbook on the cancer ward, he found two more patients who had worked in microbiology. One with leukemia and one with bone cancer. Both had died.

So here she was, much against her better judgment, standing a bit tremulously before a dozing security guard.

"Mr. Zimmer?" She gently shook the guard's shoulder. He was propped up in a chair with his arms folded, feet on the desk. His head lolled forward on his chest.

He looked up with a scowl, rubbing his eyes. When he saw Nina's white coat, he sat erect, squinting at her name tag. "Well, Doctor. What can I he'p ya with?"

The thought of what she was about to do made her hands shake. The old gaffer staring at her breasts didn't help matters any. In fact, the whole situation struck her as bizarre. Here was one of the grubbiest old codgers she'd seen in a long while, and of all things, he reeked of after-shave lotion.

"I'm Dr. Yablonsky, radiology. Did Dr. Bancroft leave me a key?"

She hadn't lied. Not really, she told herself. All she had done was ask a question that would have surprised Mike Bancroft.

Like most of the guards, he was a retiree; he had lost the edge of his younger days. He didn't seem to notice her discomfiture. He opened the top drawer of the desk that had been his footrest and sifted through an assortment of keys. Tugging at his earlobe, he glanced at the pegboard on the wall behind him. "I don't see no key here fer ya. Dr. Bancroft left before I come on duty, though." He scratched his head with ragged, dirty fingernails.

Nina registered surprise. Poor Mike. So absentminded. "Listen," she said sternly, "I've got to get into the micro lab to pick up some radioactive iodine for a procedure tomorrow." She thought she should feel bad about her little fabrication, but it was for a good cause. "Dr. Bancroft told me he'd leave it in one of the rooms, but I forgot which one."

The guard chuckled, seemingly pleased that she talked to him as though he understood the importance of her task. While he was thinking how pretty she was, and too young to be a doctor, she was noting one of his front teeth was missing. The rest looked like dried kernels of corn.

"Forgetful, these young pups," he commented. He began to squirm under her level gaze. "I could get in trouble, y'know. Ain't s'posed to hand out keys without your name's on the list, or someone on the list says so."

Nina leaned forward, planting her arms on the desk. "Mr. Zimmer." She spoke softly, mustering an air of authority as she slowly enunciated each syllable. "*I'm* saying so."

He glanced at her uncertainly with his rheumy eyes.

She elaborately looked at her watch. Midnight. "Of course, we could call Dr. Bancroft at home . . ."

Zimmer looked at his own watch. He grumbled to himself, and swiveled his chair around to the pegboard. He plucked off a key and slid it across the desk without looking at her. He tugged at his ear again. "Master key," he muttered, slouching his shoulders. "Don't tell 'em where you got it."

Nina took the key without any sense of satisfaction.

Rather, a pang of anxiety. Her heart skipped a beat. Her breathing was tight.

"Thank you, Mr. Zimmer."

It was all she could do to keep from running as she headed through the double doors toward the micro labs. As soon as she was out of the guard's sight, she slumped against the wall and let out a sigh.

As Zimmer watched her go off, he reached hesitantly for the phone. Something didn't quite ring true. He didn't want to sound any false alarms, but he didn't want to lose his job either. Tugging at his ear, he slowly dialed Robert Heffron's home number.

Dale came into the building through the rear door, which was unlocked. The corridors were dark. He moved to one of the rooms and tried the door. It wouldn't budge. The only sound was the soft whir of a refrigerator compressor. He took the elevator to the second floor, where an exit sign above the stairwell shed the only light. Its reflection made the waxed linoleum floors seem to glow from within. The greenish hue made him think of unleashed radiation, eating away at the building's foundation. He shivered, cursing himself for letting his imagination run rampant.

There was an eerie echo as he walked, even though he wore thick rubber-soled shoes. It didn't help his state of mind. At the end of the hall, he stopped and stood motionless, listening. All he could hear was his own breathing. The place was deserted. Ignoring the ominous chill at the back of his neck, he moved on. He kept telling himself it was just the adrenaline rush that came with sneaking around in the dark without permission. Nothing more.

Then he spotted Nina hunched over on the floor, her form barely visible in the dim green light. Alarmed, he quickened his pace.

She looked up as he approached. "Nina, are you okay?" He squatted beside her, taking one of her hands. Without thinking—a doctor's reflex—he felt for her pulse. Under different circumstances he might have laughed at himself.

She managed a smile. "I'm not cut out for all this cloak-and-dagger stuff." She dangled the key. "Getting this exhausted my repertoire of tricks."

Even in the poor lighting he could see lines of strain around her mouth. "You had trouble?"

"I don't like to lie. It's not me."

He squeezed her hand and took the key, wishing they were anyplace but here.

Dale played his penlight on the lock. The signs posted on the door were foreboding. A yellow poster with a purple circular symbol read RADIATION HAZARD. Below that, in purple, KEEP OUT. There was no sign of life—a fact that should have reassured him, but instead made him uneasy. He glanced at Nina as she turned the key. Together, they cautiously pushed the door open. Nina peered into the dark room and nervously laughed out loud. She'd half expected to see glass beakers glowing in the dark.

Dale flicked on the overhead light, blinking at the sudden brightness. Everything looked quite orderly. Too orderly, he thought. The room was long and narrow, lined with white counters. There was a small refrigerator near the door. Several high wooden stools sat by the counters. On one side of the room, glass hoods were propped over the counter space so technicians could handle the radioactive isotopes with little danger of contamination through inhalation.

Nina's breath caught in a little gasp. She gripped Dale's hand. "Did you hear that?"

He looked at her in surprise. Her head was cocked, a frown furrowing her brow. "Hear what?"

"I swear, I heard a noise. Like a door closing or something."

He hadn't heard a thing. "Nina, the place is deserted." He tried to make his voice light, but it seemed to hang heavily in the air.

"Then what was that noise?"

"I don't know." He suddenly found himself whispering. "I didn't hear anything."

"Okay." She wanted to believe him. She straightened, squaring her shoulders. "Let's do what we came to do," she said resolutely.

She picked up the Geiger counter near the sink and clicked it on. They combed the room together. She waved the silver-dollar-sized probe in the air, registering an occasional bleep.

"Cosmic radiation," she explained as she saw Dale watching the light on the box. "Even if Roentgen had never invented the X ray, we would still get radiation readings from the environment."

Satisfied there were no lurking evils, she handed the box to Dale. He slowly swept the probe over the sinks and countertops, as well as the white lab coats hanging behind the door. No reaction.

Nina sat on one of the tall stools by the counter while Dale prowled the premises. As she gazed around the room she was impressed with its stringent sterility. White counters, white floors, white coats, even white wastebaskets. Only one discordant note— a bulletin board cluttered with multicolored notices. Most of them appeared to summarize the rules for disposing of radioactive waste.

Dale disappeared around an L-shaped corner. Nina's eyes were caught by a red streak on the wall. She froze. It looked like blood. Her stomach did a flip-flop. She desperately wanted to pass it on to Dale, but she felt unable to move.

When he returned, he found her staring. "Nina, what is it?" He followed her gaze.

"Blood," she said, pointing.

He moved over to the wall and crouched down, examining the streak, then running his finger over it. "Rust," he said. He found it amusing—a doctor paralyzed by the thought of blood. Probably why she went into radiology.

She smiled sheepishly. "I'm sorry. I'm just a little jumpy."

"And I thought I was the one with an overactive imagination," he said, grinning.

He swept his eyes over the room one last time. It was then that he spotted several gray metal receptacles sitting on the floor in a back corner. Damn. They were probably nothing, but he had to know. He looked at her, then pointed to the canisters. "What do you suppose they're for?"

"Probably diagnostic radioisotopes." She was calmer now, eyeing the familiar-looking containers. "Most of the radioisotopes used in micro research have a short half-life—a matter of hours," she said. "You put the isotopes in these lead canisters, let them decay to a safe level, and then toss them."

She took the Geiger counter. "Here, I'll show you something." Most of the containers were padlocked, but she barely gave it a second thought. She took the top off one of the few containers that wasn't secured and held the probe over it. The Geiger counter started bleeping, its orange light blinking. The arrow on the meter moved slowly to the right.

She put the lid back on. "Not very dramatic. The isotopes have probably decayed—on their way to being harmless."

Dale nodded, intrigued. You didn't learn about things like this in a medicine residency.

They started to leave, but something stopped Dale at the door. He stood dead still, acutely aware of the silence. He held his arm out.

Nina started to give him a playful push, then felt his body go taut. "What's wrong?" she whispered, her eyes darting around the corridor.

"The light," he murmured. "It was off in that room just minutes ago." He pointed across the hall.

She gasped. "Who turned it on?"

"Maybe you heard something after all," he said, taking her arm.

He stole quietly across the hall, with Nina at his elbow. He put an ear to the door, but heard nothing. He whispered, "Someone is either in there or has just left. Stay with me, and don't make a sound."

He felt for the doorknob and quietly slipped the key into the lock, turning it ever so gently. He pushed the door open a crack and peeked in. Not a soul in sight. In the middle of the floor, however, sat a lead canister. It stood out like a traffic light in the otherwise tidy room. He pushed the door open wide enough for them both to slip into the room.

"Shall we use the Geiger counter?" Nina asked in a hushed voice.

Dale nodded and took it from her, approaching the canister. It was padlocked.

"Why would it be locked?"

"I don't know," she said.

He poked the Geiger counter probe at it, but there was little response. He shrugged and moved on. Nina followed.

There were only a few bleeps here and there as he swept the probe over sinks, cupboards, and countertops.

They turned back, and it was then that Nina spotted the closet door. She gripped Dale's arm and pointed. He understood, quickly assessing the situation. The door had no lock. He would be able to fling it open quickly. Surprise anyone who might be hiding there.

She squeezed against the wall to one side of the closet as he sneaked up and quickly turned the knob.

The door sprang open with such force that it knocked Dale off balance. Before he could recover, a ghostly figure in a khaki uniform rushed past and streaked out of the room. Nina heard a noise at the door, but her first thought was Dale. He stood dazed, with blood trickling into his eye.

She called out his name. Her cry seemed to galvanize him to action. He bolted for the door and tried to push it open. "Damn! It's locked."

He found the latch and twisted it, flinging the door open and sprinting down the hall. Nina took off after him. The uniformed figure was out of sight. They thought they had lost him completely as they searched a few more rooms. Then they heard the unmistakable growl of a truck engine. They dashed to the window at the end of the hall. A street lamp in the parking lot shed just enough light on the truck for them to make out the letters WESTERN NUCLEAR. The truck disappeared in a cloud of exhaust.

"What was that all about?" Nina asked as they stood by the window staring at the dust settling in the empty parking lot.

"You've got me," said a shaken Dale.

Nina looked at him with concern, spotting a laceration zigzagging across his eyebrow. The bleeding had stopped. She pressed her fingers against his forehead. "At least you won't need stitches."

He gingerly put his hand to his brow. "That guy sure made it clear he wasn't interested in meeting us."

Nina frowned thoughtfully. "Why would a delivery-man be in such a hurry? And so secretive?" She laughed. "Just like us."

"He was up to something," Dale said in a more serious vein.

"Maybe he was behind schedule," Nina put in, seeking a more benign explanation.

They glanced at each other dubiously. "Let's go back and take another look," Dale said.

Nina took his arm, clinging to him.

"I'll go," he said. "You wait outside."

She shook her head. "If you go, I go."

They walked back down the long corridor, hand in hand, absorbed in their own speculations. Dale turned his penlight on, bouncing the light off the walls. "I'm going to break the lock on that canister," he said.

Nina said nothing. She was puzzled by the padlock. Why put locks on canisters containing radioisotopes used only for simple research? She decided not to share her concern for a reason she couldn't quite explain herself.

As they came upon the entrance to the room with the mystery canister, she realized their troubles were just beginning. The canister had disappeared.

Dale looked at Nina. They had started this project with a thread of suspicion, and now, with sprinting deliverymen and disappearing padlocked canisters, the thread had woven itself into an intricate web of intrigue.

"Let's check a few more rooms," Dale said, picking up the Geiger counter. "My patients were never in the places we checked, anyway. Ron Orloff's research didn't involve radioisotopes, and Lincoln Lee's father doesn't clean those rooms."

They checked an unmarked room on the first floor, then took the elevator to the floor above. They entered the lounge where the employees lunched and took their breaks. The Geiger counter remained undisturbed as they entered the room, twittering mildly at a cosmic beam here and there.

As Dale moved around, it started bleeping a little faster, the needle moving rightward. A rapid if nervous calculation told Nina the reading was not significant. On the other hand, it was the only reading they had gotten since opening the lead cylinder. Dale frowned as he moved the probe around him in a circle, trying to locate the source of radioactivity. Off to his right the counter started clicking again. He tracked the probe's escalating blurpings until he found himself standing over a wastebasket by the lunch table. The basket was empty, save for a fresh plastic liner. He tore it out. Nothing.

He resumed his search, emitting a cry of triumph as it registered radioactivity in one of the sinks. Nina trailed after him, pointing out these were not levels to bring on a headache, much less leukemia.

"Let's get another Geiger counter and speed things

up," she suggested. They decided to go through the unmarked rooms on the second floor and meet back at the lounge.

An hour later they compared notes. Nina had found nothing. Dale had found one empty cupboard that barely registered a bleep.

Dale plopped down on the vinyl sofa in the lounge, setting the Geiger counter next to him. "So what does it mean?"

"Let's talk somewhere else." She didn't believe any of the levels were dangerous. Still, it was unsettling to know something like this was going on under your nose.

Dale slowly got up. He too had an uneasy feeling. "Why would there be radiation outside the places designated for radioisotopes?"

Nina shrugged. "Someone probably cleaned up a small spill and tossed the paper towels into the wastebasket without thinking."

Dale's beeper split the airwaves. It was one-thirty in the morning. A static-filled voice said, "Dr. Harper. To the ER. Stat!"

"Damn! Let's talk tomorrow," he called as he ran down the hall.

Nina returned the Geiger counters and left the key on the desk of a snoring guard who smelled of aftershave. She drove home to a few hours of restless sleep.

12

"Care to join us, Dr. Harper?"

Jon Werner's mocking smile brought Dale back to the reality of morning rounds. Werner was lecturing them on colon cancer as they finished with poor Mrs. O'Toole. Mrs. O'Toole's barium enema had confirmed Dale's hypothesis. She had a large tumor mass in the ascending colon. Jon was already extolling the virtues of chemotherapy for after her surgery.

Dale looked wearily at Jon, his eyes red from lack of sleep. He'd had a trying night on call. After he left Nina, he spent hours in the emergency room with a sixty-year-old woman who had been stable since her diagnosis of breast cancer a year earlier. That is, until last night, when a blood clot found its way to her lung. She couldn't breathe worth a damn, and her lips were deep purple when Dale arrived on the run. He knew that many cancer patients requested "no heroic measures" when they came in that sick. But in the end, the physician's judgment and compassion were usually the deciding factors.

Dale didn't know the woman. But he knew he didn't want to see her suffer. Was he treating himself or her? No time for self-analysis. He had deftly placed a tube into her trachea and hooked her up to a respirator, the machine supplying life-sustaining oxygen to her lungs. Then her blood pressure dropped, and he had to insert a special catheter through a neck vein and on into the right side of her heart for close monitoring.

She appeared relatively comfortable by the time he admitted her to Intensive Care. Once she passed through the ICU's doors, she was no longer his patient. The resident on call for intensive care took over from there. He gave Dale an appreciative nod. It wasn't unusual for the critically unstable patients in the ER, sometimes known as "train wrecks," to be dumped on the ICU residents without even an IV line in place. Passing the buck in medicine, especially late at night, was all too common.

Now, as his thoughts kept straying, Jon Werner broke in once more. "Wake up," he barked. "The war's over."

Werner squinted at him. "What the hell happened to your eyebrow?"

"Tough night," was all Dale said.

Werner let it go, still the efficient machine leading the small group of house staff and medical students around the ward behind the rolling metal chart rack.

As they came to a stop outside Lincoln Lee's room, Dale gave them an update. "Lincoln is part of the randomized double-blind chemotherapy protocol. His white count is coming down nicely, and so far he has no signs of infection." He flipped to the lab section of Lincoln's chart to find the morning's blood count.

He disliked randomized studies, where a virtual toss of the coin determined which choice of therapy a patient would receive. If you thought you had something of value to offer a patient, you ought to give it to him. Otherwise, the patient might get something less effective. A weighty paper would be published about how he might have been saved by the drugs he never got.

But when it came to cancer chemotherapy, it was anybody's guess. The outcome seemed to be about the same for all the regimens: first the patient got sick as hell, then his hair fell out, then he got an infection, then he died. Occasionally, he'd get to go home and survive a few weeks, only to repeat the cycle. Dale

knew he was overly cynical on the topic, but it was
easy to be cynical on the cancer ward.

The group approached Lincoln's bedside. He looked
surprisingly good, grinning at them. Dale was con-
stantly amazed at the good humor of terminally ill
patients. They seemed to possess a special ability to
savor every moment of life. He glanced over at Jon
Werner, thinking that maybe that was one of Jon's
subliminal reasons for picking oncology. You often got
to see people at their spiritual best.

Lincoln was sitting on the edge of his bed, devouring everything on his breakfast tray. Always a
good sign. If a patient had an appetite, especially for
hospital cuisine, you didn't worry about him so much.

"Good morning," Lincoln said cheerfully, between
bites of his rubberized "soft" boiled egg. He smiled
again as he put down his fork, surveying the crew
before him.

Dale smiled back and jostled Lincoln's shoulder
good-naturedly. "Good morning yourself." He nodded toward the remainder of Lincoln's egg. "Not too
many places where you have to slice your soft-boiled
egg."

Lincoln laughed. "Yeah, you gotta be hungry, like
me. When's dessert?" Lincoln gulped down the last
bite and pushed his tray table aside. He held his arms
out and looked down at himself quizzically. "So, when
do I get to go home? I look okay to me."

Dale pulled out his stethoscope and listened to Lincoln's chest. Janet Michaels, a fourth-year medical student, did the same. Lincoln patiently took deep
breaths as the stethoscopes lighted around his chest
like big round bugs.

As Dale finished, he pulled the temperature chart
off the footboard of the bed and analyzed it briefly.
"You're doing really well, going into remission, no
sign of infection, no bad reactions to the chemo." He
looked at Lincoln. "One more three-day course of

chemo, and if you do as well on that, you're out of here."

"And then what?" Lincoln asked.

"And then you take medicine by mouth and see me twice a week in my clinic." Dale understood that Lincoln wanted to know more than that. He believed in being up-front with patients, but why lay too much pessimism on them when you weren't sure yourself what the future held? Lincoln had already done better than anybody's wildest dreams.

"And we keep our fingers crossed," Dale added. "Hope you keep surprising us." Pessimism with an up note. The best he could offer right now.

Lincoln looked furtively at the other faces watching him, stared at his sheets, and murmured, "Forget going to medical school, though, right?"

Dale looked at him solemnly for a moment. A beautiful young life with every card in the deck stacked against him. Dale felt like putting his fist through the wall. "Lincoln, nobody knows how long you've got," he said finally. "If working toward medical school is the most important thing on earth to you, go for it. If you want to get on your motorcycle and see all that you can of the world, go for that."

Lincoln looked down at his lap and flicked a few crumbs off his hospital gown. He lifted his head, his large dark brown eyes moist. "I've made my choice," he said. "I want to be a doctor."

Dale saw Janet Michaels turn away, biting her lip. He held Lincoln's sad gaze, remembering his own exalted sense of purpose when he was Lincoln's age. Pushing through a stifling melancholy, he said, "You are quite a guy, Lincoln Lee."

Rounds continued through midmorning. Dale presented his last admission. "Alex Remy is a thirty-eight-year-old male with a two-year history of Hodgkin's disease. He came in this morning after he woke up with severe lower abdominal pain and vomiting. It looks like he's obstructed. He's down in X ray right now, then surgery will be seeing him."

They moved on past Alex's empty room. "Alex, by the way, has a younger sister with a stomach lymphoma," Dale added. "It's so unusual, I thought he would be a good patient for one of the med students to work up."

Jon glanced at Janet Michaels. "Janet?"

Janet, a dark-haired bookish type, nodded enthusiastically.

Jesse Munoz was their last stop. Jesse's temperature was coming down, and Jon seemed encouraged. "He may be ready for his last course of chemo soon."

As Andy and the two students went off, Werner and Dale sat down together in the nurse's chart room.

Werner's voice was uncharacteristically soft. "So," he said, "Orloff has CML."

Dale raised an eyebrow. Ron had wanted to keep his diagnosis under wraps. For a while anyway, until he got used to the idea of it—if he ever would.

"I found out yesterday," Werner said. "You can't keep anything quiet around here. Might as well belt it out over the page system so everybody gets the same version."

"Ron wants to go on as usual," said Dale. "He's on medication and he's feeling better. He needs to keep busy right now."

"Does he want to finish out his internship?"

Dale nodded. "Not only that, he wants to come back to oncology soon."

Werner slowly leaned back in his chair, arms crossed in front of him. "So, is Orloff's illness what's bugging you?"

Dale gave Werner a blank look. "What makes you think something's bugging me?"

"You don't usually daydream during rounds."

"No."

"No, what? No, nothing's bugging you? I don't believe you."

"No, I don't usually daydream during rounds."

Jon jumped up and threw his stethoscope down on the chair. "Harper, what the hell's going on with you?"

Dale gave a noncommittal shrug. He was not ready to talk about the micro lab, nor about his suspicions, not to Jon Werner anyway. "I'm concerned about Ron and I'm concerned about why he got leukemia in the first place."

"Well if you find out," Werner scoffed, "let me know. I'll nominate you for the Nobel prize."

"I'll take it," Dale called out as Werner left the room.

13

Robert Heffron picked up his mail from a cubbyhole behind his receptionist's desk. He began sorting through it as he moved on.

"Good morning, Doctor," she said as he walked past Mary's desk.

"Good morning, Mary. Any calls?" Something in her tone made him stop.

"Dr. Carleton and Dean Orwell. They said they'd call back."

She was a small, coolly competent woman in her mid-sixties. Heffron liked her because she minded her own business. This morning she seemed addled.

"Dr. Heffron," she said a little nervously, "there's a woman waiting in your office." As Heffron's jaw clenched, she added quickly, "She was very insistent. I told her an appointment would be necessary, but . . ." Her voice trailed off as Heffron abruptly headed to his office.

He didn't have to ask who it was. He knew. He'd seen it coming. He opened the door to see Christine Anselm sitting there, her small wiry form silhouetted against the light from the window behind his desk. She was smoking a cigarette, flicking ashes into a plastic cup on her lap.

He stood in the doorway and silently scrutinized her. What had he ever seen in this wreck of a woman? Now in her late thirties, she looked older than his wife. Her face was riddled with lines like an urban road map, and she had dark circles under darker eyes, which she now fixed on him defiantly.

"Hello, Christine," he said with controlled calmness as he closed the door behind him. He whisked past her, tossing his mail on the desk. He sat back and laced his fingers behind his head, watching her. He knew that silence made her nervous. He was silent.

She puffed hard on her cigarette, then smothered it against the side of the cup. She loudly exhaled a cloud of smoke as she pulled a thick journal from her shoulder bag and threw it onto his desk. It was the current issue of *Micronetics*. As it sailed across the desktop, an ornate porcelain cup full of pens and pencils toppled over. Heffron quietly cleaned up the mess.

"You're fucking with me again, aren't you?" Christine spoke through tight lips, as though if she loosened them, a torrent of something she couldn't control might escape.

"Christine, please stop this little melodrama and state your business. You know what our agreement was."

"And you know why I'm here, you son of a bitch." She pointed to the journal. "You have a new article in there, about radiation effects of plutonium on mammals. I'm supposed to be listed as co-author on all your articles about environmental carcinogens. *That* was our agreement. Instead you've got some little twit named Tracy Hester. Is she your latest conquest?"

She rose from the chair and walked over to his desk. She reminded him of a scarecrow with her disheveled hair, flannel shirt hanging out, sandals, and faded jeans. "My name is conspicuously absent. A little typographical error, perhaps?"

He smiled patiently. "Christine, surely you understand the intricacies of this kind of research. I told you I would help you out, get you back into the research world. Out of that menial job at Western Nuclear. But this isn't the best time to do it." He opened the journal and turned the pages as he spoke. "This is just a short little report I knocked off to meet an unexpected deadline. There wasn't time to show it to you first. I had a graduate student proofread it for me. I stuck her name on it in payment. That's all."

"It's a piece of trash anyway," she scoffed. "You must have done it all by yourself."

"Now, now," he said condescendingly.

"You might reconsider our little agreement. I imagine a lot of folks around here would be very interested in knowing who the real Robert Heffron is."

Heffron straightened, giving her an unctuous smile. "Why, Christine. Is that a threat?"

"You bet your ass it is, friend."

He said nothing, watching her emotions flit through her eyes. Finally, he saw the hurt in her doglike eyes and knew he still had the old power over her. He stood and came around the desk. He put his hands on her head and ran his fingers through her hair. "Please, Chrissie," he whispered, using the nickname he had given her years ago, "trust me. Be good to me."

With his touch, she sobbed and leaned helplessly against him. He put his arms around her and gently rubbed her back.

"How can I trust you?" she cried. "You took my research and made it over into a cheap self-serving fairy tale." She fell back into her chair, sobbing. "I can't believe I'm stupid enough to let you use me again."

He pulled up a chair beside her and held her hand. "Chrissie, I need you now more than you need me. I need plutonium for my research. It's so easy for you to get it. You know how hard it is to get a license for the amount I need." He sighed. "Maybe I've been selfish." He ran his hand up her arm. "I'm on the verge of something big here—a discovery in radiation genetics that will turn the world upside down. And you'll be part of it. You'll be co-author. You must help me." He pointed to the journal. "Don't worry about the little things. You're beyond that."

She wiped away the tears and sat back, trying to compose herself. She lit another cigarette and laughed cynically. "Why should I believe you? You never let me in on anything."

"I've told you, it's too risky. The less you know, the less involved you are. And the less likely to get in trouble."

She blew a perfect circle of smoke into his face. "You really are a bastard, aren't you?" She laughed, a hollow, barren laugh. "You made your name off my research when I was a dumb little grad student, never giving me any credit. You told me you were in love with me and you would leave your wife, and then I find out you're screwing half the grad students and telling them the same lies."

He didn't seem to hear her. His hand found the inside of her thigh. "But it was you I came back to," he murmured.

She let his hand stroke her leg, working its way upward. "I ought to have my head examined," she said without rancor.

"I ought to have mine examined, for letting you go." He leaned forward and brought his lips to hers, slipping his hand inside her jeans.

"Stop worrying," he whispered. "Everything's going to be fine." Gradually they stood and he eased her toward the door, giving her a last embrace. "Tonight?" he said. "The usual place?"

She flung her arms around him. She would be there tonight, and they would make love as they never had before. And yes, she would get him whatever he wanted. Because when she was in his arms, all her doubts left her.

Heffron went back to his desk and sat down, staring at the *Micronetics* journal. He should have known she would spot that article and make a fuss. For the present he had to go along with her. As he thought about it, it wasn't all that bad. She was skillfully provocative in bed.

He would have to cancel a previous engagement. There was nothing more important on his agenda right now. He needed Christine. But she was getting pushy. And sloppy. To the point that someone might be catching wind of it, if he was to believe that old geezer Zimmer. Some pretty doctor whose name Zimmer couldn't remember at first. Heffron was beginning to think he would need to hire someone with a few more functioning neurons, or things might start getting out of hand.

As for Christine, she was already getting out of hand. He needed to give her more perks. As busy as he was, he knew he would have to start spending more time with her. There were other solutions, but for now they didn't serve his purpose.

14

"Hi, gorgeous. When you gonna go out with me?" Lenny Perkins's pudgy face lit up as Nina breezed into his office. She smiled tolerantly. Everybody knew about Lenny, the hospital Lothario. He had never heard of catching flies with sugar. She wondered idly if he ever did catch any—girls, that is. And to think he was the chief of radiology. Fortunately, he was better at reading X rays than wooing women.

Lenny had been studying a series of X rays lined up on his viewbox. He pulled up a chair for Nina with a ceremonial bow. "Here, here, have a seat, sweetie, to what do I owe this honor?" He turned back to the viewbox and slapped up another film. "Jesus H. Christ! This poor sucker has shit for lungs." He scowled as he looked over at Nina and waved at the films. "Look at that!"

Nina saw several X rays of the chest that showed one lung almost totally whited out, the other full of patchy white densities. Something devastating was going on there. Something incompatible with life, as they used to say in medical school. She smiled fleetingly as she recalled all the people she had seen walking around with lab values and X rays that were incompatible with life.

"It doesn't look good, Lenny," she agreed. "What's the clinical history?" She was in no hurry. She wanted him in a good humor.

She knew he was a frustrated clinician who loved to discuss the patients behind the X rays. It was easy to call the shots from an ivory tower in the X-ray reading rooms, far from the blood and guts of the front lines. There were a lot like Lenny around—sideline warriors who ran at the sight of blood.

"Christ. I told these turkeys three days ago this patient was going into heart failure and they'd better start pushing the diuretics." He spread his hands in exasperation. "So what do they do? They increase his IV fluid rate to 'rehydrate' him. Rehydrate him? Hell, they're drowning the poor bastard. Goddamn family practice residents don't know their ass from a hole in the ground."

He snatched the X rays off the viewbox and dictated his interpretation with machine-gun rapidity into a hand-held recorder. Then he turned toward Nina with a grand gesture and a leer. "So, what can I do for you, my lovely? Are you gonna tell me you're free tonight?" He wiggled his eyebrows.

Nina laughed. Poor Lenny. Two divorces, short, fat, and fifty. He was a big talker. She suspected that if she were suddenly available he would as suddenly disappear.

"Lenny, you're the RSO for the department, aren't you?"

Lenny slapped his hand to his forehead and rolled his eyes. "Radiation safety officer, my ass. Don't remind me. I've only got six months to go. Then I can turn it over to some other poor slob."

His vehemence piqued Nina's curiosity. "Why? What's so bad about it?"

"What's not bad about it? How would you like to hear people whining at you day in and day out about 'so-and-so didn't shield a patient's ovaries when he shot her chest X ray' or 'so-and-so drew up the wrong dose of radiocontrast'? So what am I supposed to do about it? I run a monthly in-service where the techs are supposed to learn that the purpose of radiology is not to knock off the patient. Then I turn them loose on the public again. I mean, what the hell else can I do? Fire everybody? Shoot the goddamn X rays myself? Hell's bells!"

He looked at her suspiciously. "Don't tell me you got a complaint for the good old radiation safety officer too?"

"No complaints, Lenny. Just some questions. No offense meant."

"Hey, don't worry about that, lady. You know me. I love to complain. Eat, sleep, screw, and complain. The four essentials." He leaned toward her, elbows on knees. "Go ahead. Shoot."

"Well, believe it or not, you're not the only one who gets complaints. I've been getting a few myself, and I don't know what I should do about it." Nina sat back and crossed her trim legs. Lenny eyed them approvingly.

"So what are you hearing?" He turned back toward the viewbox and threw up a few more X rays. He always seemed to be doing at least two things at once. As if each half of his brain functioned independently of the other.

"Mostly complaints coming out of nuclear medicine. Spills that aren't cleaned up adequately. Diagnostic radioisotopes that aren't being given at the appropriate time. Dosage miscalculations." Nina thought she'd stick to the complaints brought to her by the technicians before she eased into the microbiology problem. Besides, it made her nervous. She was only too happy to put it off. "Is that the kind of thing you're hearing?"

Lenny waved his hand as if to brush it off. "Yeah, yeah, sure, sure. Big deal." He squinted at a small spot on the chest X ray before him and drew a circle around it. "What? You think we're another Three-Mile Island here? We know what we're doing." He turned his head for a moment and gave her a devilish grin. "I hope."

She wondered if he enjoyed irritating her. "Lenny, I don't like it. I don't have a handle on what's going on in radiology. And I don't think anybody else does."

He whisked the films off the viewbox, and dictated a five-second note. "Of course you don't. Nina, you and I are diagnosticians. We're not technologists. Could you fix an X-ray machine if it broke down? Of course not.

"You probably had the same Mickey Mouse physics course I had. Boring as hell. We learned about tripe like safe levels, Geiger counters, how to calibrate them, all that." He grimaced. "And if you were like me, you slept through the classes, crammed the night before the final, and aced the course. Twenty-four hours later you forgot everything. And good riddance." He tossed up a set of neck X rays on the viewbox and scrutinized them.

Nina smiled. "Lenny, you know what I like about you?"

His head pivoted toward her. "Wait, wait, let me turn the lights down low before you tell me."

She laughed. "What you see is what you get. You're as subtle as a kick in the pants."

Lenny let his shoulders sag, drooping his head in an exaggerated motion. "Shot down again." He looked up at Nina. "What the hell's my problem, anyway? Bad breath?"

Nina shook her head. "You'll find the right woman someday."

"You're trying to tell me something, right? Like, 'I'm not the one, Lenny.' " His eyes cut back to the X rays.

She reached out and patted his arm. "You're awfully lovable, though. You're . . . unique."

He took down the neck films and dictated another short note. He glanced at Nina. "All right, all right, now that I know you're not here for my body, why are you here?"

Nina stood and slowly paced the floor. "I have reports that microbiology has been sloppy with their radioisotopes. Radiation readings in the lounge area, for example."

He shrugged. "Those guys are pikers. They only have a license for a couple of harmless isotopes. I don't give a damn if they take a bath in them. Can't hurt 'em." He got up and walked across the room to pick up another pile of X rays. "Now if you told me they were eating the stuff, I'd be impressed."

It was not what she was looking for. "Lenny, how can you be so flip? How do you know what's going on if you don't check it out?"

He strode over to her and abruptly grabbed her white coat, throwing it open. "Where's your badge, Doctor?"

She blushed. "I don't usually wear it."

"You're breaking the law. Shall I report you? You know everyone in the department is supposed to wear a dosemeter. So we can protect you from overexposure."

Lenny thrust open the lapels of his own white coat. "And before you go off in a snit, notice that I don't wear mine either. Hell, it turned positive weeks ago from the sun while it sat on my dashboard." He returned to the viewbox and put up a wrist X ray.

Thoroughly frustrated, Nina said, "Lenny, you're impossible. Why have an RSO if this is how you handle it?"

"We have an RSO because the government tells us to have an RSO. If you want a license to take X rays and use radioisotopes, you play ball with the NRC." He added, with a sly intonation, "Or you let them think you're playing ball."

She sat for a moment, thinking over the night before, and decided on another tack. "Does this department ever put padlocks on its radioisotope canisters?"

"Not that I know of."

"Why would anyone use a padlock?"

"Must not want whatever's inside stolen."

She rolled her eyes with exasperation and tried

again. "What time does Western Nuclear make its deliveries, Lenny?"

"We don't use Western Nuclear."

Nina jerked forward, her heart skipping a beat. "What about the med school? Do they use Western Nuclear?"

Lenny scowled. "No, no, no, we have an exclusive contract with Bristol Nuclear. We haven't used Western for thirteen, fourteen years. Too damned expensive. Too many mess-ups."

She stood up and paced the room, clasping her hands nervously. He looked at her as though seeing her for the first time. "Having a baby?" he smirked.

"Okay, Lenny, be serious. Here's a hypothetical situation: Suppose you learned that people working in X ray and nuclear medicine were getting leukemia."

"I'd marvel at the laws of chance." He stopped to dictate a quick note about the wrist film.

She gazed at the film he had just read. "You missed something," she said.

Lenny started as though he'd been pinched. "What?"

"See the navicular fracture?" She pointed to a hairline mark on one of the wrist bones. "You read this out as normal."

"Goddammit!" He threw the film down and backed the tap recorder up to redictate. "Good call. Thanks," he muttered without looking up. "You just saved me a million-dollar law suit."

"You owe me one." Her brow furrowed into a frown. "Lenny, what if you found out that, say, sixty percent of the micro researchers were developing leukemia?"

"Ridiculous. I'd look for someone making a bomb," he said with unmistakable sarcasm. She was about to say something. But he had already put up three more films and was jabbering into his dictaphone.

15

It was the night of the Spring Fling—the annual medical center fund-raiser. A major social event, the Fling was staged in the penthouse ballroom of a dazzling downtown skyscraper. Everybody who was anybody was there. Herman and Audrey Moran made their annual appearance. Herman had to rent a tuxedo because his own was hopelessly tight around the waist, and had been for years. But he kept it as a happy memento of a past he liked to dwell on when the present got too much.

Dr. Robert Heffron was there—as usual, the cynosure of all eyes. Heffron was an impressive figure. While he was published in reputable journals worldwide, he could also write in simple language that the lay press could handle. People ate it up. They had a morbid interest in speculating about what carcinogen was going to get them next. Heffron knew how to tap into the public's fears, and his rise to fame had been meteoric.

While Heffron had been in the department a number of years, it was only within the past year or so that he had stepped out from among his genetically aberrated laboratory rats into the public limelight. He was courted by the press as an expert on cancer. Television loved him. He looked and sounded like a distinguished doctor should. Intentional or not, Heffron's public image at the medical center was doing more for its prestige and financial well-being than would a decade of Spring Flings. Especially since he started the

Heffron Foundation, infusing large amounts of cash into the medical center.

Herman eyed Heffron across the glittering high-ceilinged ballroom as people flocked around. Heffron was oh-so-charming. Herman felt like making a snide remark about the man, but he couldn't spot a soul who would snicker along with him. Not at Mr. Popular.

Heffron was surrounded by several big cheeses, including Lawrence Orwell, the dean of student affairs; John Carleton, chief of medicine; the president of the medical school; and the chairman of the board of trustees. He and Audrey had only just arrived, but already Audrey was drifting across the vast room in the general direction of Robert Heffron. Other women seemed to be meandering his way as well.

Herman swiveled his head around in search of a friendly face, and spotted the self-serve bar. His spirits lifting, he ambled toward it. He was in no hurry. He'd had a few before leaving the house. He liked to measure Audrey's getting-ready time in martinis. This one had been a biggie. Herman had killed three martinis in the TV room, waiting. And he'd drunk them slowly. Gotta be on your toes for the honchos, Herman. Play the part of honcho yourself. He glanced spitefully over at Heffron again as he searched for his favorite gin, carelessly clanging the bottles around.

Why don't they just make the bastard department chairman and take me out of my misery? What the hell would he do if he lost his position at the med center? One thing he was sure of. Audrey would leave him. That might not be all bad. He chuckled sinisterly. A bystander gave him an oblique glance.

Armed with a fresh drink, Herman felt a delicious twinge of malice. He decided to tag after Audrey and spoil her fun. Her taste was akin to his own when it came to bed partners. She liked the young men. But Heffron was a prize. That he was in his fifties would not deter Audrey. Heffron transcended statistics. No matter that he was married. Would that stop Audrey? Did it stop Cleopatra?

Herman cursed the noisy clamor of the crowd. He couldn't hear himself think. He started pushing his way through the clumps of scientists, doctors, students, and administrators, barely recognizable in their formal attire. He nodded politely to a colleague here and there. Finally he came upon Heffron, who was sitting on a couch, legs crossed, drink in hand, laughing jovially as an attractive young woman whispered in his ear. Audrey and Laurie Layton, a faculty wife, were perched on the arm of the couch chatting about the tennis match Audrey almost lost the other day. Herman smirked a five-martini smirk. Audrey hadn't gotten her foot in the door yet. He decided to stomp on it.

He marched up to Heffron, his foot knocking Heffron's shiny black patent leather shoe. He thrust out his hand and roared in a genial way, "Bob, my man, good to see you here! I can tell you're finding your way around all right, yessirree!" Herman leered at the young blonde sitting next to Heffron.

Heffron looked up, startled, then flashed a wide grin as he moved to stand up and shake Herman's hand.

"Sit down, sit down, don't get up for me," Herman bellowed.

Heffron sat back down. "How are you, Herman?" he asked with a touch of formality. He turned, smiling, toward the young woman next to him. She had moved away a few inches.

"You must know Tracy Hester," he said by way of introduction. "She's a Ph.D. student in microbiology who has honored me by applying to do her thesis under me."

Herman scanned her from head to toe, fastening on her breasts, which showed a healthy cleavage. I'll bet she'll be under you, he thought, if she hasn't been already.

"I've had the pleasure of seeing Miss Hester around the department," he said. He frowned. As department head, he must have interviewed her at one time, but try as he might, he couldn't remember her.

He gestured toward the couch, where there clearly was not room for a third person. "May I?" he asked, looking up to see Audrey staring at him from behind the couch with a mixture of scorn and dismay.

Heffron, smiling easily, said, "Why, of course." He squeezed over, but Tracy stood up, her face flushed, and walked off with a baleful eye for the department head.

Herman looked after her. "Oh, I hope I'm not interrupting anything," he said with a contrite air. He plopped down on the couch, his drink splashing dangerously close to Heffron's neatly creased trousers.

"Not at all," Heffron said amiably. "We shouldn't be talking about homework at a party anyway." He turned toward Herman and fixed him with a gaze intended to convey the message that he was the most important thing in Robert Heffron's life right now. "So, how are you, Herman?" he asked, and, looking around, added, "And where is your lovely wife? I hear she's about ready to become a Wimbledon contender."

Herman snorted and started coughing uncontrollably as part of his martini sloshed down his trachea. Heffron put his arm around him, then slapped him on the back, a concerned expression on his face. "Are you all right, Herman?"

As the paroxysm of coughing slackened, Herman looked up to see Audrey standing over him, scowling. "Why, here's my lovely spouse. The only way I can catch her attention is to feign dying. She keeps a will in her pocket that she figures I'll sign just before I take my last gasp." He tittered drunkenly.

Heffron smiled at Herman and then at Audrey, as though he realized this was domestic byplay. "What a fun couple you are," he said. Audrey, with an unintelligible sound, turned on her heel and stalked off.

As they watched Audrey's receding back, Heffron said, "Herman, let me take you out on the balcony for a little fresh air." His voice carried just the right inflection of concern, Herman noted. Not too much, not too little. Maybe the asshole should be department chief. He was smooth.

Herman nodded, and they walked out onto the balcony, high above the city. The air was cool. The traffic hummed distantly below them, as remote from their world as were the stars.

"Herman, I'm worried about you," Heffron got right down to it. "You seem distracted recently. Troubled."

He hesitated, waiting for a sign of acknowledgment from Herman, who was staring blankly over the railing. Herman grunted. Heffron took that as his cue to continue. "Is there anything I can do to help? I will if I can."

Herman sighed. A sigh colored by growing despair, bitterness, the need to talk to someone. And alcohol. Hell, maybe Heffron was okay. Maybe he could help. Herman couldn't trust his own judgment anymore, that was for sure.

"Bob, let's face it. The department's falling apart." He spoke in a monotone, his speech slightly slurred. "And it's my fault. We're not getting the big research grants. Employees are turning over so fast I haven't learned their names by the time they leave. Can't get decent applicants for the Ph.D. program."

He looked up at Heffron, his eyes damp. "Maybe you can save it. Maybe I ought to step down and give you a shot at it." He looked away, and for an awkward moment Heffron thought he was about to bawl.

Heffron put down his drink and placed both hands on Herman's shoulders, confronting him squarely. His face was almost touching Herman's. "Herman, don't be ridiculous. "I'm a very lucky man. People think

that what I'm doing is important. If their faith, their
naiveté—call it what you like—can give this department a shot in the arm, so be it. Maybe that's how I
can help. But believe me, I don't want your job."

He stepped back and looked down at the city traffic,
forty stories below. "But, Herman, for God's sake,
don't get down on yourself about this department. Do
you honestly think I would still be here if I didn't
respect this place and the men who run it?" He
paused. "I've turned down many good offers to go
elsewhere."

Herman knew that was true. Why did Heffron want
to stay here? Herman had never figured it out. Unless
he wanted to get Herman's job. That was always what
his speculation boiled down to.

He looked now at Heffron, and what he saw was
strength. "No, I don't think you would stay here if
you thought it was a cesspool." He gulped down the
rest of his drink.

Heffron laughed. "Herman, I think I understand
your problem. You're overworked and underappreci-
ated." He reached for Herman's shoulder and gave it
a firm squeeze. "But I appreciate you. And I'll help
you all I can to get the appreciation you deserve here.
There is definitely some dead wood around that needs
thinning out. I'm sure that's what's getting to you."

Still chuckling, Heffron put his arm around Moran,
the department's biggest chunk of dead wood in his
opinion, and said, "Come on, let's head back and cel-
ebrate. That's what we're here for, right?" He took
Herman's empty glass. "What are you drinking?"

Dead wood, Heffron thought with amusement, had
a purpose after all. It floated.

Ron Orloff's collar was too tight. He loosened his
tie slightly as he stood in an isolated corner of the
ballroom. He sipped at a glass of mineral water, a
lime slice floating below the ice. He wished he hadn't
come. But he was determined to keep his health prob-

lems quiet and maintain appearances. Like attending the Spring Fling. It was a dreaded but necessary part of student life. The house staff never showed up at these things, but the Ph.D. students always did.

So, here he was. Another of the many unscientific obligations he had found himself fulfilling just to get his Ph.D. Another of his many disillusionments over the past three years. He came this evening without a date, which would have been more like a burden under the circumstances. He mingled some, making sure he was seen, but mostly hung back and watched the goings-on. An astute observer could probably glean a half-dozen story lines for a soap opera simply by watching and listening to one or two of the clusters of people here.

Herman Moran had caught Ron's attention as he picked his way across the room, settling on the couch next to Robert Heffron. What a pathetic excuse for a department head. Every bit as maladroit as Heffron was suave and charming. Every bit as out of it as Heffron was into everything. Ron felt a revulsion that actually made him nauseated as he watched the two men playing up to each other. Moran the buffoon, Heffron the charmer. Together, with their rivalry, they had all but destroyed the micro department—their friction creating an environment unconducive to attracting good people.

Ron had come to the medical center as an idealistic young graduate student, ready to make breathtaking discoveries, to ride the cutting edge of science. What he found was something more akin to grade B melodrama, with serious research taking a backseat to interdepartmental politics and competitive backbiting. His decision to enter the M.D.–Ph.D. program was initially spearheaded by an effort to pull out of the micro program. Later, this negative impetus was replaced by his rewarding experiences in medicine.

As he watched Heffron guide the wobbly Moran out to the balcony, Ron wondered what was going on.

He saw Dr. John Carleton from the corner of his eye, watching the unlikely pair with what seemed to be similar wonderment. Ron's curiosity lay more with Heffron, who was an enigma. Here was a man who commanded the respect of the best in his field. Yet would not share his knowledge with his own grad students. Ron hadn't discovered this until his second year, when he began his serious thesis work on DNA and cancer-causing genetic mutations. Many of the references cited in the literature were Heffron's articles. Ron was thrilled. He'd go talk to the author himself. Get it from the horse's mouth. But Heffron didn't really appear interested in talking to him. Ron sensed a subtle hostility, even though Heffron acted genial enough. It made him not want to go back, and after a while, he didn't go back. He even found himself going out of his way to avoid the man.

Now he squinted thoughtfully at Heffron as he disappeared onto the balcony. He wondered what the man was after. And he wondered why Robert Heffron was not what he appeared to be.

16

Nina felt a hand on her elbow as she hurried down the crowded hospital corridor. Startled, she stopped short. It was Mike Bancroft, his normally placid face distorted with anger and dismay.

She smiled mechanically and resumed walking. "Hi, Mike. What's up?" she said with a turn of her head as he followed after her.

"Come on, Nina. That's what I should be asking."

She sighed, not much liking herself as she saw Mike's distress. "Mike, I didn't get you in trouble, did I? I'm very sorry."

He melted the least bit. "I sure had some explaining to do. Security asked me if I left you a key. They couldn't find it. Then Dr. Heffron called me to ask who I was handing keys out to. Pretty damned embarrassing. I had to say I didn't know, then called him back when I found out it was you." There was a whine in his voice. "I don't like being used, Nina. What the hell's going on?"

Nina stopped again. Her dark eyes softened at his helpless, boyish look. "Mike, I regret the whole thing."

She looked away, staring down the hall. The hospital corridor looked like Manhattan's Fifth Avenue during rush hour. "I guess I owe you an explanation. How about lunch?"

They pushed their way through the mob to the cafeteria. It was Nina's idea they take their trays up to the roof where it was a little more private.

They found an empty table and brushed off the black soot that had settled there. Nina considered the table with a frown, then peered upward, half expecting to see a giant black cloud. But the sky was a bright blue, accented by a few puffs of white clouds.

As they ate, she briefly went into Dale's concerns, and her wanting to help him. "Nothing turned up, and I hope that's the end of it," she said, deliberately omitting the juicy parts. "If I caused a problem, I apologize. I had to get the key. It seemed an innocuous way."

"Why didn't you just ask?" He gave her a wounded look.

"That's what I should have done, of course. But when you fancy yourself combating evil, you tend to be guarded. Everybody's suspect." She gave him an awkward apologetic smile.

Mike sat back, assuming the look of a sage, which hardly went with his round, pink face and ingenuous blue eyes. She thought he had the look of a lot of other thirty-year-old men. The fresh youthfulness of Joe College was gone, but the image lingered on.

He chose his words carefully. "Nina, I don't think you should get involved in Dale's little schemes. Don't get me wrong—he's a great guy, but he's a little off-beat, if you know what I mean."

Nina rested her chin in her hands. Recalling the horseback caper through the city streets, she suppressed a smile. "What do you mean?"

"He's always chasing after windmills or bugging people, trying to make some world-shaking statement that nobody else understands. He does things ass-backward." Mike rocked his chair forward. "I've known him a long time. I know what I'm talking about."

Spoken, she thought, like a proud sophomore. "For a scientist you're being awfully vague, Mike." She restrained a laugh. She found herself feeling immediately protective of Dale. As she watched Mike, she compared the two men in her mind. She realized what it was about Dale that made him different from Mike and other men she had known. There was something exciting and unpredictable about him—even a little dangerous. A boundlessness that both attracted and frightened her.

Mike mused for a moment. "Dale did some pretty wild things in med school. We had a physiology prof, Dr. Hunnicutt, who was gung ho on the dynamics of shock. He had a full-day lab scheduled to teach the effects of shock on the body by bleeding dogs to death. There were twenty-five dogs—four students to a dog. None of us liked the idea of watching dogs die, but we couldn't sway Hunnicutt. There was talk of boycotting the lab. Somebody circulated a petition."

Mike paused. Nina thought she saw a fleeting smile on his face. "Dale solved the problem. He broke into the animal lab the night before the class and turned the dogs loose."

Nina laughed. "What happened after that?"

"We learned about shock by watching a video of students bleeding dogs to death. Dale wasn't allowed to attend. Hunnicutt's orders." He added dryly, "Some punishment."

Nina nodded. "Is that it?"

"There were other things. He pulled a stunt in 'nutrition' class, which I have to admit was a bullshit course. On the last day of class, he ordered Big Macs, fries, and shakes for everybody, including the professor."

Nina burst out laughing. "Now, *that* is offbeat. An aspiring doctor prescribing all that grease. I agree, Dale is weird." She smiled. "And I like it. Tell me more."

Mike threw up his hands. "Okay, I know when to quit. You're hooked, aren't you?"

"I honestly don't know, Mike. I like being with him. Probably not a good sign."

Mike tossed his napkin on his tray. "I've got to get back, Nina. Think it over. Sounds like a wild-goose chase to me."

As he stacked their trays he said offhandedly. "The Geiger counters over there are a joke, anyway. Nobody ever uses them. I don't think they even get calibrated. Hell, we don't use enough isotopes in micro to warrant having special rooms for radioactive materials. Just an excuse for more rules." He gave a short laugh. "Sometimes I can see Dale's viewpoint. There's too damn many rules in the world."

She sat mulling over Mike's comments, not sure what to make of them. If the Geiger counters weren't working . . . Could they be overreading, or could they be underreading? In which case . . . no she wasn't going to tell Dale. She didn't want him going back there. He could end up with more than a simple laceration next time.

17

After rounds, Dale sat the nurse's station with a stack of charts and wrote progress reports on his patients. He chatted briefly with his medical student, Janet, then sent her off to work up his new patient, Alex Remy. He expected she would take a while. He didn't push the time element too hard, not with med students. Might as well let them enjoy their time while they had it.

He often wondered about medical schools, why they emphasized the picayune and irrelevant, while a resident had to plow through irrelevant details to get to the heart of the problem. The medical student's six-page report, that included everything from the patient's brand of cigarettes to how many pets he had, got pared down to two pages or less of bare but critical essentials. Either that, or no sleep. And certainly no tennis.

With Janet gone, and everyone else at his own chores, Dale concentrated on registering his impressions about his patients. He enjoyed this daily, ordinary task. He found it peaceful, although he knew an outsider wouldn't see it that way. For there he sat, surrounded by two shifts of nurses signing out to each other. They chattered among themselves, perched on chairs and countertops. Some of the talk was gossip, most was business. He usually had no trouble shutting it all out.

But today was different. He couldn't concentrate. His mind kept flashing back to the other night. None of it made sense. Radioactivity where there was nothing to show for it. Warning signs on doors with nothing radioactive behind them. Radioactivity registering in the lounge area, where employees ate their lunch. Padlocked canisters. A disappearing canister. A panicky deliveryman. Strange.

He propped his chin in his hand as he wrote. He was suddenly conscious of the rough stubble on his jaw. He passed his fingers over it absentmindedly. Finally, he got up and walked over to the phone, which was sitting on the counter between two nurses. He dialed Nina's extension. Gone to lunch.

He looked at his watch and frowned. Only eleven-thirty. Odd that she hadn't called. He knew she didn't really want to be involved in his project. But she could have called.

She was probably right. Nothing to get excited about. He should leave it at that. He needed to get on with his residency and patient care, and quit brooding about this radiation business. Leave Nina out of it, anyway. There was something developing between them. But if he insisted on her help, he might lose her. And he didn't want that to happen. He went back to his charts, scribbling off brief progress notes before he broke for lunch.

"Do you know what the Hippocratic Oath says?" Dale peered at Janet Michaels. You couldn't tell her anything. She knew it all.

"Not really," she replied without interest.

Dale slid a chart across to her as they sat in the doctor's lounge, going over her work. It was one o'clock. He never had gotten to lunch.

"You'll recite it when you graduate," he said. "But it doesn't hurt to know what it says now. Considering that your career is based on it."

She looked at him with a trace of a superior smile.

He paused awkwardly, suddenly sentimental. "The basic theme of the Hippocratic Oath is that you will harm no one." He saw her lips twist sardonically. "Seems absurd, doesn't it? But when you think about it, it makes sense. We're given a lot of power over people's lives—the power of life and death. We're obligated not to abuse it."

Her expression didn't change.

Dale nodded toward the chart. "Look at your orders on this patient, and tell me whether you're helping or harming her." His gaze lingered on Annie Snowden's name, written in bold black letters. In a short time that name would appear on a death certificate, and Annie Snowden would be no longer, except as a cherished memory to those who knew her.

Janet took the chart hesitantly. She scanned the orders she had written earlier, which Dale had not cosigned.

"I only ordered a CBC and electrolytes on her." She looked over at Dale with a touch of defiance. "How does that harm her?"

"What will you do if the results are abnormal?"

"If she's anemic, I'd order a blood transfusion."

"What for?"

Dale saw that he wasn't getting through. Janet looked more defiant, even belligerent.

"You can significantly improve oxygenation with transfusions for a hematocrit below thirty," she said in a tight voice. "Hers was twenty-eight on admission."

"Why do you need to improve her oxygenation? She's at bed rest. Is she short of breath?"

Janet shook her head.

Dale waited a moment, then said softly, "Janet, Annie is dying. We're trying to make her comfortable. That's all we can do. We can't rescue her this time. She's ready. She wants to die."

He saw Janet turn away, blinking back unwanted tears. "Let her go," he said gently.

Janet nodded slowly. Tight-lipped, she took the order sheet and wrote "Error" in big letters across her orders.

Dale gave her a moment alone while he went to the nurse's station for coffee. When he returned, she was sitting quietly, just as he had left her.

"Let's go on," he said. "What else do you have?" She presented her workup on Alex Remy.

She had done a good job—detailed, organized. She seemed softer to Dale. He felt better about her. She had lost some of that tough edge. She might make a good doctor yet.

They finished up in time for afternoon teaching rounds. And then out of nowhere Janet said something that made Dale sit up straight. It was like getting hit by a stray bullet.

"Did you know," she said, "that Alex's sister—the one with the lymphoma—worked at the med school before she got sick?"

Dale felt a strange tingling in his hands. "What department?"

Microbiology, he thought.

"Microbiology," she said.

"Oh," he said.

18

"My apologies for not calling sooner." Dale's voice sounded tired. It made Nina feel even more guilty about not calling him. There were too many things she didn't want to talk about—like what Mike Bancroft had just told her, and her conversation with Lenny about Western Nuclear.

"It's been a busy day," Dale went on, "sort of like yesterday—and the day before." He gave a short laugh as he realized he was feeling sorry for himself. "How about dinner tonight?"

"Did you get any sleep last night?"

"A few hours. Enough," he said. "I'm more hungry than I am tired. What do you say?"

"I'd love to. Give me an hour?"

Funny, he thought, how much he had come to depend on her. How had he ever managed before? "Great," he said. "I'll pick you up."

He rang off, stood up and stretched, slung his white coat over his shoulder and marched out of the hospital. After two days on the cancer ward, the world outside those granite walls worked its usual spell. He felt exhilarated, his lack of sleep adding a delightful heady feeling. He felt like a caged animal turned loose in its natural habitat. And the date with Nina to round out the day added to his excitement.

As he breathed deeply of the tangy air, he felt an impulse to go for a run. He tossed his coat on a bench, laced up his Reeboks, and began to lope at a leisurely pace along the path that wound around the giant medical complex. He picked up his pace as his mind raced back over the events of the past two days. His thoughts kept coming back to Nina. She was bringing something very real and precious into his life. It had to be carefully nourished, like a delicate springtime sprout just making its way through the soil.

As he ran, the sweat dripping down his back, he decided not to tell her about Alex Remy's sister. Why upset her? There was nothing she could do.

Who could say there was a connection to the other cases? Every doctor knew of the cluster phenomenon, where several cases of cancer would crop up at the same time and place. The medical journals were full of erudite head-scratching about these puzzling situations. Small towns where maybe twenty people would come down with leukemia in a five-year period. Such oddities begged for explanations. There were plenty of theories, but no proof.

When he really thought about it, what did he have? A few cases of cancer in people connected with each other only very loosely through the micro department at the med school. He was, after all, on the cancer ward, where every patient he saw had cancer. You could hardly call it suggestive when you saw two cases of leukemia in a week. It just so happened that he knew the two patients. That was all.

Somehow, he didn't find this line of reasoning satisfying. And there was still the logbook, and Alex's sister.

He sprinted hard the last five minutes of his run and came to a stop in front of the hospital, standing breathless, his chest heaving, his pulse racing. He felt better, the cobwebs cleared out of his brain, ready for a great evening.

"So why did you leave internal medicine for radiology?" Dale asked. They had just finished their coffee at a quiet, dimly lit restaurant overlooking the ocean. The conversation had been carefully pleasant. No talk of radiation, death, wrongdoing. They were getting to know each other. And basking in the feeling of warmth it brought.

Nina smiled and looked out the window. The sky still had a pink tinge to it. Two joggers were silhouetted in the sand against the ocean and setting sun. It looked like a picture postcard.

He thought for a moment she hadn't heard him. But she had been thinking. "I got tired of people throwing up on me," she said at last. "It's as simple as that."

He could see she was serious. He waited.

"It just wasn't what I'd idealized in my mind. It wasn't romantic or even dramatic. Just . . . discouraging. Saving alcoholics so they could go out and booze again. People almost dying from heart attacks, then lighting up a cigarette the minute they left intensive care. I even had an emphysema patient so eager to smoke that he lit up while he was on oxygen. He blew off part of his face. After three weeks in the burn unit, he sent his nurse out to buy him a pack."

She dabbed her napkin at some coffee that had spilled onto the saucer. "Too many people, like lemmings, seek their own destruction. I wasn't even running in place. I was running backward."

Dale understood. Any interns in a big hospital would. It all depended on what you wanted and how badly you wanted it.

When you went to sleep at night, did you feel good about saving an alcoholic from dying of hemorrhage? Or were you depressed thinking he'd probably be back in six months? When you delivered a baby, did you marvel at the magic of life, or were you bummed out when you saw the mother, a thirteen-year-old pimply-faced kid who hadn't known she was pregnant, even as she went into labor? Somehow, when it was all sorted out, the positives had to outweigh the negatives or you wouldn't stay with it. Radiology was nice and clean—if you didn't have to deal with it later. He had no criticism. They simply saw it differently, and he admired her for it.

"A city hospital isn't the best testing ground," he said at last. "It's hard-core. No place for a lady."

She smiled at his attempt at tactfulness, tarnished by a touch of chauvinism. "Actually, I was doing okay until I got to the jail ward. That's when I questioned my sanity."

He nodded. The jail ward could be trying. It was full of malingerers, dope addicts, murderers, psychotics. All trying to get out of the cell block and into the hospital, where the food was better and they could watch TV. They had a modicum of freedom, relatively speaking, even though their legs were chained to the bed. And if they could talk their doctor into it, they could even get drugs. They would do anything, even to faking a coma or seizure, to get to the jail ward. Some of them could have won an Academy Award.

"The biggest problem with the jail ward," he said, "is the way they leave it up to the interns. It's way too much responsibility for beginners. No decent backup."

"Yes," she agreed, "but knowing that doesn't make it any better. For me, it was one long, uninhibited nightmare. One night I was looking after a three-hundred-pound drunk who was gushing blood from his stomach. He was losing it as fast as we could give it to him. I had to draw a blood gas on him. But he was so combative that we needed four people to sit on him while I climbed up on the bed to draw the blood from his groin artery. He responded by throwing up a quart of blood all over me. Fortunately, he didn't have AIDS." She shivered at the thought. "One of the nurses took pictures of the whole fiasco. They're in my scrapbook with the caption 'Why I left medicine.' "

Dale smiled. He had his own memories. "Not exactly paradise."

"Not even close." She laughed, her mood suddenly lightening. Sharing it all seemed to take off the edge, and even turned up a humorous side.

"There *are* rewards," he said.

She let the waiter refill her cup. "I know that. There are times I've regretted leaving primary care. But radiology is fun and challenging. And there is doctor-patient contact."

"And nobody throws up on you."

"Nobody. It's nice to go to work knowing you'll wear the same clothes home. Not an issue for most people, but it does underline the problem. Overall, I'm glad I'm in radiology." She laughed. "Even your friend Carleton used to be in radiology. But he switched, in the wrong direction."

Dale shrugged. Another of Carleton's enigmas. "My father used to say he liked radiology because he got to look past people's thick skins every day. 'There has to be a soul there somewhere,' he'd say."

Nina wrinkled her nose. "In a barium enema?"

They laughed together as Dale hailed the waiter for the check.

They looked out at the ocean. There was a faint purplish hue above the horizon, the only sign left of the day's grace. Dale squeezed her hand. "Walk on the beach?"

She smiled and nodded.

They took off their shoes and slapped along barefoot in the wet sand through the tide, letting the cold water swirl around their ankles. The feel and sound of the surf guided them in the near darkness.

They walked along in silence until Nina's curiosity turned her mind back to the events of the past twenty-four hours. "What about the other night?" she said with a lift of her eyebrows.

"What about it?" Dale shouted over the waves.

"What do you think? Do you want to keep looking?"

Dale kept his eyes on the surf. "There were some curious things, but they don't seem to point anywhere."

She tried to read his face in the darkness. "Do you want to go back there?"

He stopped and looked at her. "Not really. I think I'm satisfied." He liked it between them just as it was. He wasn't interested in complicating matters.

He turned her around, facing the restaurant, and shouted, "Race you back!"

They ran hard—laughing, splashing, cavorting through the surf. Nina stumbled in a tangle of seaweed. Dale tripped over her, and they went sprawling in the shallow swirling water, laughing till their sides ached.

They sat like a couple of giddy kids, letting the water wash over their legs up to their waists. Nina playfully draped the tangle of seaweed over Dale. He wrapped it around his neck, and then hers, drawing them close. She stopped laughing as she looked into his eyes, so near. His wet hair was plastered to his head. Their eyes held. He pulled her toward him and kissed her. She felt an initial automatic resistance, then a delicious warmth, despite the cold sea lapping against her body.

They got up, drenched, arms around each other, and slowly headed back. They both felt the same magic and they both knew they would soon be lovers.

19

Robert Heffron stood at the door of the motel room, casually glancing down the empty hallway. He knocked. Without waiting for a response, he opened the door and slipped into the darkened room. He winced at the tawdriness of the motel, but he knew Audrey would like it. That's why he had suggested it.

Audrey Moran slithered up to him in a see-through black negligee, giving off a sickeningly sweet scent of cheap perfume. She murmured into his ear and tittered inanely as he embraced her.

Heffron knew what Audrey liked. She liked having her clothes torn off. The rougher the better. She would shriek in ecstasy if the material actually tore in the process. She "adored" being flung onto the bed. She was a caveman's delight.

He was in no mood for fantasy. Audrey annoyed him. She was too clingy, too demanding. Yet the chemistry was always there. She never failed to arouse him.

What made it even better was that as they made love, he could see old Herman Moran groveling at his feet. "Save me, save my department, Bob." And as his tongue darted in and out of Audrey's mouth, the image of Herm added a sadistic excitement to his lovemaking.

Still dressed, having time only to drop his pants in his haste, he exploded inside Audrey as they sprawled on top of the quilted bed. He mouthed the lewd words that invariably whipped her into an orgasmic frenzy.

Then came the episode that her spent ardor demanded. Mechanically almost, he nibbled at her naked breasts, her still-writhing abdomen, her moist pubic hair.

Audrey moaned softly, her eyes closed. Heffron studied her for a moment, his eyes resting on the razor-thin scar behind her ear from her facelift. As she rose to her elbows, he got up and went into the bathroom where he splashed some water in his face, and slathered his genitals generously. He studied his image in the mirror, a self-satisfied smile twisting his lips. He took a bottle of bourbon out of his duffel bag and poured two glasses, a large one for Audrey, a spot for himself.

When he returned to the bedroom, Audrey was rubbing her tattered negligee against her breasts, her eyes still closed, one hand hidden deep between her legs. She was obviously a nymphomaniac, he thought with a wrinkle of distaste. Someday, he would have his fill. The excitement would be gone, and it would be over, unless the craven features of old Herman still prodded him on.

Good old dumb Herman. Didn't have the slightest idea Heffron was pumping his wife. Not that Herman would give a damn—the miserable fag. But as long as Herman remained department head—which was where Heffron wanted him—there would likely be some fringe benefits to screwing his wife.

You never knew when you might need a friend, as the recent visit from Christine and the call from Zimmer had all too vividly reminded him. All in all, it was a good time, he decided, to renew his little friendship with Audrey. Notwithstanding the benefits of their liaison, he felt a wave of revulsion as Audrey moaned beside him.

He poured himself another drink, and kept topping off Audrey's. When she was tipsy, she would chatter, not noticing if he was listening. He turned on the television and indolently watched the news while Audrey babbled.

At length, he lifted her chin and gazed at her, smiling. He was feeling the alcohol. She looked inviting. He kissed her long and hard, plunging his tongue deep into her mouth. He put his lips to her ear, nibbled a little, then whispered. "You're a real number."

"You tell that to all the girls." She giggled, pinching his cheek.

He rubbed her thigh, his hand roaming upward. "I get around. We're alike in that way. But," he said, his voice a sensual whisper, "they all pale next to you." It never failed. Here they'd had sex less than an hour ago, and he was ready again. He had stayed longer than he'd planned. And drank more than he'd planned.

He rubbed her breasts hard. She cried out in agonized pleasure. They were both naked now. They rolled over together on the bed and this time she insisted on kissing him where she had never kissed him before. They came together once more, as explosively as the first time. He felt drained and held her panting next to him. They were both exhausted. Slowly, they got up and showered before returning home to their spouses.

Heffron slid into the bucket seat of his white Mercedes coupe and rested his arms on the steering wheel. He felt spent. His relationship with Audrey bedeviled him. He rarely thought of her when he was away from her, not until the time to see her approached. Then his face flushed in anticipation as though her lewdness were contagious. She had that hold on him.

He started the car and pulled out onto the street, watching the motel's garish neon sign from his rearview mirror.

He drove onto the freeway, his mind drifting. He thought of the women in his life. Too many to count. His wife. Devoted, unquestioning. Ready to fulfill his every need. If she knew of his escapades she never let on. She'd certainly had plenty of opportunities to find out. But she liked the same life-style he liked. Money, influence, prestige. She wouldn't risk losing those perks with a senseless confrontation about his sex life. Besides, he thought he kept her well satisfied in that area.

He was restless. Not just this moment, but in general. He found himself always craving more. More limelight, more money, more sex, more—power.

One little problem kept gnawing at him. Where you had an appetite, you had to keep it fed. You became dependent on others. If they went off suddenly, life could be difficult.

As he turned off the freeway onto Wilshire, he frowned, deep in thought. His mind flashed on Christine Anselm. She had fed more than one of his appetites. But now he was regretting it. He should have known the cunt couldn't handle the kind of responsibility he'd given her. She was asking too many questions, getting too careless. And now making threats. He should have kept her services confined to the bedroom.

He pulled into his driveway and on through the gate toward the four-car garage. He punched the remote control for the garage door and eased his Mercedes next to the Cadillac. As he shut off the engine, he decided it was time for some changes.

20

Nina studied a series of X rays on the viewbox in her small cubicle with its rows of milky white glass.

Amid the maze of cubicles and viewboxes that was the radiology department, Nina had made her spot unique. On the soundproof cloth-textured wall to the left of her chair was a tastefully framed abstract print—an arresting clash of iridescent color. Beneath the long white counter in front of her was a small compact disc player with a stack of discs, most of them classical. There was a headset plugged into the amplifier, but it sat off to one side as she puzzled over the films.

Above her dangled a showy mobile of bright-hued tropical birds and fish. Dale's head brushed against it as he quietly came up behind her and began moving his hands over her shoulders.

"You're late," she teased, reaching for his hand without looking up.

"I know. My apologies on behalf of the hopeless bureaucrats who think paperwork takes precedence over patient care."

She laughed. "Hmmm. Behind on dictating your discharge summaries again?"

"Yeah, I'm afraid they caught up with me." His eye was caught by a bulletin board overhead with a few neatly posted notes and lists. And a picture of a middle-aged couple inscribed "Love, Mom and Dad." It gave him a jolt. Her father looked like a street-tough redneck. Her mother may have been pretty at one time, but she appeared commonplace and faded as she looked up at her husband complaisantly. He marveled at how two such people could have produced someone as lovely and bright as Nina.

"How am I doing?" he said.

She looked up with a smile. She turned her neck and pointed to a sore spot. "Right there—I've got a crick in it." She closed her eyes and sighed with pleasure while he rhythmically massaged her neck. As she felt her muscles relax, the tension headache she had been developing let up.

Tension was a constant companion these days. Her life had turned upside down since the night she and Dale had kissed among the waves. She teetered between heightened excitement and an almost squeamish apprehension, not quite knowing how to accept all that was happening.

Over the past week, she had replayed that night's scene through her mind. Going back to her apartment. Inviting Dale in to dry off. His wearing her bathrobe while she put his clothes in the dryer. Her laughing riotously at the sight of him in the pink velour robe hiked above his knees. Then more kissing. Then no clothes. And then they'd made love—gently, sumptuously. Yet despite the gentleness, she had felt something more, something intriguing—an offbeat combination of trepidation and exhilaration.

Then awakening to the harsh reality of being late to work. Both of them jumping up to rush to the hospital, sheepish love-struck grins on their faces. Sharing a mug of coffee on the way to their cars, laughing as it slopped over onto their hands.

They had spent most of their free moments together since. Nina felt a closeness that she'd thought could only be achieved after months, even years, of knowing someone. At times she wondered if it was all in her head, and that Dale wasn't in fact a mirage. She didn't dwell on that thought too long. It scared her. She chided herself for holding on to the nagging fear that some fatal flaw would surface and they would come crashing to earth, their relationship shattering in the process.

"I have a dilemma here," she said, returning to the reality of the moment.

"I can see that." Dale rested his hands on her shoulders and leaned forward to peer at the dark spot on the X ray. "Even I can recognize that one. Ugly." He pointed to an area of the film, a barium enema, where the contrast material barely squeezed through. Unmistakable colon cancer. Nothing new to him these days.

She smiled grimly. "That's the patient's dilemma." She pulled down the films and put up a different set. She pointed to a tiny dark spot on one of the X rays. "This is *my* dilemma."

Dale strained to see what she was pointing at. It was another barium enema. Finally, he saw it, a dark irregularity along the wall of the colon. It was the same area of the colon as the first film she'd shown him.

"Same patient?" he asked.

"Same patient. Only this was done one year ago. That's an early cancer." She swiveled in her chair to face him. "It was read as normal."

"Uh-oh." He dropped into the chair next to her as he realized what that meant.

"Curable one year ago, a death sentence now. He's got metastatic disease," she said turning back to dictate her interpretation.

"Is whoever read it still here?"

"Not only is he still here, he's the head of nuclear medicine." She slowly took the films down and slid them back into their jacket.

"My God!" Dale was horrified. You had to wonder about a department that glorified its incompetents.

"My sentiments precisely," Nina said.

Dale immediately saw Nina's problem. Did you tell the patient that someone messed up and now he would die because of it? What would that accomplish? Yet, could you morally keep people in the dark when it came to mistakes affecting their lives?

He could see from the cloud darkening Nina's face that she was all too keenly aware of the issue.

"So now what?" he asked.

"So now I present this case at radiology rounds and watch Dr. Hendrickson's face turn purple." She gave a hollow laugh. "All he gets for his blunder is a purple face, and the patient dies. Hardly satisfactory, is it?"

"And what do you tell the patient?"

"I tell the patient's doctors, and let them struggle with it. The patient is a fifty-eight-year-old black nursing home resident. *Non compos mentis*. I did a little research on him. He has a wife and kids."

Dale mulled it over. It was, in truth, a doctor's dilemma. "So you tell the wife her husband could've been saved if Hendrickson hadn't screwed up one year ago and where does that leave her? Now she's not only grieving over her husband, but she blames herself for not having consulted someone else."

Nina tapped her pen on the countertop pensively. "Here's another hook—the patient is *non compos mentis* because the cancer has metastasized to his brain. If another radiologist had read that film, the patient might have not only a longer life, but also he'd be there for his wife and kids emotionally—not in some nursing home."

Dale saw Nina's eyes moisten. "Is a purple face really all that's going to come of this?"

She shrugged. "We all know Hendrickson is a lousy radiologist. That's one of the reasons he got kicked upstairs. Administrative duties. Keep him away from the X rays. We make sure someone overreads his films. But that didn't start until this year."

Dale grimaced. "It's a bitch," he said. "If you throw him out, he'll go somewhere else and endanger more lives. And it practically takes an act of Congress to jerk a doctor's license."

Nina sighed. "Sometimes I'm glad I'm a doctor out

of self-defense. If I ever get a barium enema, you can be sure I'll take a look at it myself."

"Take a look at mine too, will you?" Dale got out of his chair and tousled her hair affectionately. "Don't let it get you down. Don't let what other people do or don't do turn you around."

She put her hand on his. "Thank you, Dr. Harper. I needed that."

He bent down and kissed her on the cheek. "Dinner tonight?"

She nodded and smiled.

After rounds, Dale headed to the library, where he had been doing some research of his own. He was combing the medical literature on cancer clusters. He hadn't been sure where to go next. His calls to Western Nuclear had been unrewarding. The company had no official dealings with the medical center. And no one was admitting to anything unofficial. Even if he'd found a connection, he wasn't sure how it would be relevant to Ron Orloff and Lincoln Lee. He didn't have much to go on.

So he found a quiet desk in the stacks and headed up a pile of journals, leafing through them patiently. He knew he might be heading up a blind alley.

Sometimes the identification of cancer clusters led to a disclosure of environmental carcinogens, but in most cases it was inconclusive. Still, it was worth a try.

He scanned his notes to date. Thirteen cases of leukemia and nine of Hodgkin's disease in one New Jersey school district over a five-year period. No significant connection was ever found.

An outbreak of leukemia in a Massachusetts town over a fifteen-year period. Everything from well water to the local supermarkets was suspect. Extensive searching yielded nothing.

As he read on, he kept thinking he ought to find some comfort in these reports. Instead, he found himself concluding that the investigators had simply over-looked critical clues. There had to be some explanation. Chalking it off to chance was just a self-serving dis-missal of an embarrassing mystery.

He leaned back in his chair and stared out the win-dow. Statistics. That's all he was really looking at. The odds against several people in the same area getting cancer over a short period were greater than you would expect from chance alone. There had to be a reason. If you saw the tip of an iceberg, there must be a big chunk of ice beneath the surface.

He remembered his father's skepticism about statis-tics. "A poor man's crystal ball," he would say. "One in ten women will get breast cancer this year. We predict the future from the past." But it was all num-bers. No names. No explanations. Just like the cluster phenomena.

He threw down his notes in disgust. Where to go from here? He thought of his date with Nina and pushed aside the remaining journals. Another time.

He stuffed his notes into his pocket and trudged back to the cancer ward.

21

A man wearing a headset and microphone entered the studio and tapped Robert Heffron on the shoulder. "Dr. Heffron, you have a phone call."

Heffron looked at the man with fleeting disapproval. He glanced at his host Dan Worthy, who in turn glanced at his watch and scowled. "Hansen, we're about to go on the air."

Hansen eyed the wall clock and, with a perfunctory apologetic tone, said, "Five minutes, sir." He turned back to Heffron. "The lady said it was an emergency, Doctor. Otherwise I wouldn't have interrupted."

Heffron rose with a roll of his eyes. "Everyone thinks his problem is the only one on earth."

Hansen directed him to a nearby phone. Heffron closed the studio door behind him and spoke into the mouthpiece.

He was immediately accosted by an angry voice. He would have recognized it anywhere.

Heffron's voice tightened. "Why are you calling me here, Christine? I'm about to go on the air."

"Well, we wouldn't want you to be late for your precious public appearance, would we?"

He looked up, making sure no one was in range. "State your business, Christine."

"I want to know why people are snooping around the micro department in the middle of the night. I almost got caught."

"It has nothing to do with you, I assure you," he said, assuming a lofty tone.

"Nothing you say assures me. I want to know what you're doing with this stuff. It's my ass on the line."

"How many times do I have to explain to you . . ."

"All this earthshaking research, and you're protecting me by not telling me what it is. Right. I wasn't born yesterday, pal."

Her voice sounded heavy, and Heffron realized she had been drinking. As he saw Dan Worthy waving at him and pointing to his watch, Heffron changed his tone. "Chrissie, dear, let's not argue. I see it's time to let you in on it, regardless of the risks. I'll call you, all right?"

There was a pause. "It better be soon." The phone slammed sharply in his ear.

Ron Orloff removed the beeper from his belt and tossed it on the coffee table. He fell back, exhausted, into a battered recliner in the doctor's lounge. He found the remote control for the overhead TV and flipped on the late-night news.

It was his first night on call since he had learned of his leukemia. He had been feeling good, gradually returning to ward duties. He had come back, not without a battle with the top brass. They didn't want some sicko taking care of patients—he knew that had to be the issue, though they pretended their objections arose out of concern for him. Finally, with Dale's badgering on his behalf, they had given in.

He had been nervous about his return, but he knew Dale was around to back him up. In fact, Dale would let him resume call only if he promised to give the word the moment he tired.

So far, so good. It had been a quiet night. He didn't realize how beat he was until he sat down and had a moment by himself.

He stared absently at the news, his mind replaying the evening's events. A few IVs and blood draws, and one straightforward admission—a withered old woman with inoperable stomach cancer who had been vomiting all day. He gave her IV fluids and within an hour she perked up, with no more vomiting. He had just checked on her, and she was holding her own.

Though weary, he knew he wouldn't be able to sleep for a while. He was too worked up. He poured himself a cup of coffee from a tarnished metal urn. He grimaced as he tasted it. The stuff must have been sitting there all day.

As he sipped the nasty brew, he leafed through a tattered copy of the *New England Journal of Medicine*. The TV droned in the background. Suddenly, out of a corner of his eye, something caught his attention and he looked up at the television. There was Robert Heffron, big as life, dominating the screen. Ron turned up the volume and leaned forward.

Heffron wore a light blue V-neck sweater and white canvas pants. He looked southern California, his face a radiant golden hue. He appeared relaxed, his legs crossed, as he chatted with the show's host, Dan Worthy.

Worthy was the typical talk-show personality, with big eyes, a mouthful of teeth, and alternate looks of gratification, surprise, and horror. He appeared to be gratified now at the distinction of his guest. And the guest graciously accommodated this view of himself. A slightly patronizing tone crept into Heffron's voice.

"Dan, I'm afraid environmental carcinogens are ubiquitous. The more we learn about them, the more disquieting it is."

Worthy raised his dark, bushy eyebrows. "What's the old joke, Doctor? Just living is carcinogenic. And that ain't no joke."

Heffron laughed. "I wouldn't go quite that far, Dan. But we must never stop looking. And we mustn't let conventional attitudes confine our research."

"Can you give us an example of a conventional attitude?"

"Let's take radiation. Most researchers wait too

long before they look for consequences of radiation exposure. Simply because of preconceived notions."

Worthy's brows formed an ominous V in the middle of his forehead. "Radiation! There's something we have a healthy respect for. Your current research involves radiation, am I right?"

"That's right, Dan. It's a common belief in radiation research that we don't see the harmful effects until years after exposure. Consequently, many researchers don't recognize what happens to humans and animals until it's too late."

"And you feel differently?"

"Absolutely, Dan. I have always suspected earlier radiation effects. But only recently have I been able to come up with sufficient evidence."

Ron put down the journal he was reading. He was captivated. His eyes riveted on Heffron. He could see that Worthy felt he was on to something as the host glanced through his notes.

"Are you referring now to your discoveries about the radiation fallout from the Chernobyl explosion?"

Heffron nodded. "Yes, as I wrote about it."

"You have been criticized by some colleagues for going public."

Heffron smiled. "That I have, Dan, but if a scientist allows himself to be swayed by politics, then we might as well all hop into our time machines and return to the Dark Ages."

Worthy chuckled. "Spoken like a true scientist." His voice resonated with respect. "Tell us about Chernobyl."

At this point, a fascinated Ron sat up with a start as his beeper went off, instructing him to call Dr. Harper. He phoned Dale and invited him to join him in the lounge. As he turned back to the tube, Heffron was taking a sip of water and moving ahead.

"The fallout from Chernobyl first reached this country in the summer of 1986, a few months after the April explosion. Nobody disputes that." Heffron paused.

"I decided to take a look at our mortality rates for that period, and found them greater than for any previous summer on record. That also is not in dispute."

Worthy frowned. "Where, then, do you diverge from your colleagues?"

There was a sound of the lounge door opening. It was Dale. Ron pointed silently to the TV and turned his eyes back to the screen.

Heffron had smiled at Worthy's question. "I attribute the increase in mortality to Chernobyl. But most of my colleagues would say three to six months following radiation exposure is too soon to gauge its effects."

Worthy's face grew predictably grave. "What you're saying is rather frightening, Doctor. A mishap thousands of miles away can actually kill us? I, for one, hope you're wrong. But there's no sense in pulling a blanket over our heads. What are you telling us?"

Kill us thousands of miles away? Dale blinked as the thought took hold. How about five miles or six— or a hundred yards?

Heffron spoke in a normal voice, almost casually. "It's really not that complicated. It has to do with free radicals—bundles of unleashed energy with nowhere to go, if you will—that eat away at our very cell structure. The risk for cellular mutations is high, as radiation, even in small amounts, causes these free radicals to form in the body."

Dale stood in the doorway, his call forgotten.

"Are we talking cancer?" said Worthy, looking directly at his invisible audience.

"Not yet. There, I have to agree with my critics. Three months would be too early for cancer. No, these people appear to be dying from infections. It's my feeling that low-level radiation is causing sufficient damage to the immune system to lower the threshold both for acquiring an infection and for dealing with it."

Worthy grabbed at the word "immune." "Sort of like AIDS?"

Heffron pondered for a moment, stroking his jaw. "In a very narrow sense, yes. But we're not talking about a communicable disease, here. We're all susceptible, unlike the well-defined risk groups we find with AIDS."

"Making it even scarier than AIDS!" Worthy exclaimed with a look of unmitigated horror.

"In one respect, yes," Heffron responded, his calmness a contrast to the professional excitability of his host.

"In one respect?" Worthy seemed almost indignant. "You're talking about something that can affect us all, regardless of our sexual habits or life-style. Something beyond our control! Don't you find that frightening?"

"I certainly don't like it, but a scientist is trained to achieve a degree of detachment. It helps keep us from distorting data to fit the hypothesis." Heffron laughed lightly, but whatever humor he found in his comment was lost on Dan Worthy—and the two young doctors in the hospital lounge.

Worthy looked toward the camera and then back to his guest. "I'm afraid we're going to have to cut away here, Doctor. I must ask one final question. What makes you right and your colleagues wrong?"

"I don't critique my colleagues. Their reasons for opposing me may be valid. I don't have proof at this point, but the radiation connection as well as infection is strong enough to pursue. They do not see it that way."

Worthy profusely thanked Heffron. Before he cut to his sponsor, his face became grave and he repeated, "Again, I say, I hope you are wrong, Doctor."

Ron turned down the TV and looked at Dale with a blank expression. He realized that the tension he felt building up during the interview was due to the lingering question in the back of his mind: Why did this happen to me? Yet he found Heffron's ideas stimulating, even encouraging, in a climate of complacency and confusion. He made a mental note to look up Heffron's article on Chernobyl.

Dale was still standing, leaning against the door-jamb, his arms hugging his chest. "Interesting stuff," he said as he saw that Ron was waiting for his reaction. He had mixed feelings about what he had just seen. What Heffron had to say was fascinating, but something about him didn't ring true. Whatever it was, he didn't like the man. Too smooth. Anyway, he had more immediate concerns. He walked over to the couch next to Ron, flopping down on the cushions. "How's it going?" he asked.

"Not bad. Just one admission."

Dale reached for Ron's beeper.

"Hey!" Ron automatically pulled it back.

"You've had enough for one night," Dale said, pocketing the beeper. "You won't be needing this."

"Thanks," Ron said quietly, looking at his feet.

Dale pointed to the door. "Beat it!"

Ron grinned and headed for the call room. Alone, he stood over the sink, splashing warm water on his face. Looking into the mirror, he watched the water drip off his chin. He thought he was pale. He felt a twinge of anxiety that eased as he remembered the blood count taken four days ago was normal. But for how long? How long would that little white pill he took every day stand between him and the thing that would ultimately kill him?

He cursed under his breath as he saw his hand tremble. How easy it was to succumb to fear in the loneliness of the night. He wished he hadn't let Dale take his beeper. He would welcome a call of distress from a place outside himself.

He tried to divert his train of thought. He thought again of Heffron. It made him feel better to know there was someone looking for the same kinds of answers he was. Someone who wasn't bound by conventionality and medical tradition. As he drifted off to sleep, he decided he would talk to Heffron.

22

Dale fumbled in the dark to silence the alarm clock before realizing it was his phone jangling. He squinted at the luminous dial of his clock-radio. Three A.M. Jesus.

He sat up and answered with a terse "Hello."

"Dr. Harper?" It was a soft, uncertain feminine voice.

"Yes, what is it, who is this?" He switched on the bedside lamp and rubbed his eyes.

The voice appeared to falter the least bit. "Dr. Harper, this is Maggie McClellan. I'm a lab tech on the night shift at the hospital. I know it's late, but there's something you should know."

"What is it?" Dale was now fully awake, but still annoyed.

The voice again wavered. "Lincoln Lee. He's your patient?"

"Yes, what's wrong with Lincoln?" His voice was sharper now.

The lab tech finally got it out. "I had to call somebody. Lincoln's urine—it's radioactive. It may have been contaminated. I'm wondering—did he have a nuclear medicine scan or anything like that? I'm sorry I woke you. But I'm worried sick about it."

Dale was speechless. He had no idea how Lincoln's urine could have become radioactive. What on earth had made her check it?

She explained that she'd been cleaning up after using a radioisotope, checking the work area with the

Geiger counter. It had kept ticking and ticking, despite her vigorous scrubbing up. She hadn't recalled spilling anything. It just didn't make sense. Finally, she traced the reading to Lincoln's specimen where it sat on the shelf above her work space, awaiting a routine analysis.

"The Geiger counter has never read this high before," she finished rather lamely.

There was no thought in Dale's mind now of going back to sleep. It could have waited until a decent hour. But the girl sounded too distraught to be responsible. He had to find out for himself.

He hung up, tossed on his clothes, and trotted over to the hospital.

Maggie McClellan was easy to spot. She was sitting at a table watching a plastic cup tentatively, as though it might be alive. She was absurdly young-looking, with worried blue eyes and frazzled red hair.

As Dale whisked into the brightly lit laboratory, she jumped to her feet.

"Dr. Harper?" Without waiting for an answer, she waved toward the plastic cup as though it explained everything. "I wish I hadn't gotten you up. I really feel guilty."

He smiled supportively. He could see she was frightened. He motioned to the Geiger counter, which she handed to him. Switching it on, he moved around the large black lab table with its stainless-steel sinks, sticking the probe here and there for random readings. Nothing more than the occasional bleep that Nina had explained away as cosmic radiation. Then he approached the plastic cup. The Geiger counter went wild.

"Christ!" he cried. Déjà vu. Only this time, no one was reassuring him about safe levels. He blinked at the needle on the Geiger counter. It trembled in the red warning zone. He moved to the back of the lab, the Geiger counter quieting. When he returned to the cup, it tap-tapped again. The two scrubwomen cleaning up stared at him curiously.

He switched the instrument off and turned to Maggie, who had been following him around like a puppy.

"I don't know what to make of this. Lincoln hasn't had any nuclear medicine tests. Any chance this urine could belong to someone else?" He had seen frequent foul-ups in the lab.

Maggie smiled weakly. "That's always a possibility. But I don't think so. It hasn't been out of my sight."

They stood contemplating the innocuous-looking plastic cup and its contents. Finally, Maggie said, "What should we do?"

Dale glanced at his watch. Four A.M. He dialed Nina's number.

Dale marveled at how fresh and lovely Nina looked as she hurried into the lab. She must have dressed quickly, he thought, as he eyed the wall clock.

She said nothing as her eyes met Dale's, then followed his gaze to the Geiger counter. Her heart sank. She had been expecting to find him raging over a baffling X ray, not messing with Geiger counters again. If she had known—if she had only known—she would have come anyway, she thought, exasperated with herself.

"Watch this," he said gravely. He approached the plastic cup, shooting the probe out at it. The Geiger counter sang out its warning.

Nina stood with her mouth agape. "I'm impressed," she said slowly. She sat down, noticing for the first time the redheaded lab tech.

"This specimen," Dale said quietly, "came from Lincoln Lee."

"Lincoln Lee," she echoed softly. "Why is his urine radioactive?"

Dale sat on the stool next to her. "No idea. I called to see if you can help identify the isotope.

Nina shook her head. "I'm afraid I don't know much about this."

"Who might?"

She tapped her fingers on the countertop. "Probably one of the nuclear radiologists." She hesitated a moment. "I know!" Her face lit up. "Mike Bancroft!" He's up on both microbiology and biophysics."

"All right! Let's treat him to an early-bird breakfast."

Looking relieved, Maggie found a lead box to hold the specimen. Dale told her he would get back to her as soon as he knew anything. She seemed a little less anxious, now that it was out of her hands.

"You guys must be crazy!" Mike Bancroft rolled his eyes. "You think maybe somebody slipped this kid a nice little radioactive Mickey because he was running up too big a hospital bill? Jeesh!"

He downed the last of his coffee and turned to find the waitress. He caught her eye and pointed to his empty cup. As he sat across from Dale and Nina, Mike's eyes darted between them, as though he couldn't believe he was frequenting this greasy spoon at six in the morning with two crackpots.

Dale and Nina exchanged looks, suppressed smiles, and sat back to let Mike ventilate. They knew he would help. But on his terms.

Nina nudged him a little. "Listen, Mike," she said, "we weren't looking for this one. A lab tech got Dale out of bed at three this morning. There's a real problem. We need your help."

Mike melted under Nina's gaze. But he eyed Dale skeptically. "How do you know someone isn't baiting you? I can think of a few hundred people who would enjoy watching you chase your tail."

"I ordered a repeat analysis on Lincoln. The lab tech's going to check for radioactivity. That's just routine. If something's abnormal, repeat it."

"But what if it's the lab tech that's setting you up?"

"Mike?" Nina gave him a come-now look. "Now who's getting paranoid?"

"Okay. But if there's trouble about this, I never heard of you two, got it?"

Nina smiled indulgently, having got her way.

"The first thing we have to do," said Mike, his eyes brightening at the prospect of adventure, "is find out what type of emitter the isotope is. Every isotope is made up of one or more types of rays: gamma, beta, alpha. Most diagnostic isotopes are gamma. If that's what it turns out to be, we can figure it's technetium or the like—what you use for most of your nuclear medicine studies."

"But Lincoln didn't have any nuclear studies," Dale reminded him.

"Yeah, but let's be realistic. This is a city hospital. Half the employees are welfare rejects. Mistakes happen. Let's say Joe Blow in the bed next to Lincoln is supposed to get the isotope, but the tech, hung over from last night's partying, doesn't read the name band. He shoots the isotope into Lincoln instead. Bingo!"

"But what about the high reading?" Nina put in. "A diagnostic dose shouldn't do that."

Mike thought for a moment. He ran a hand through his thick curly hair. "Okay. Suppose Joe Blow weighs three hundred pounds. Lincoln is skinny, right? Maybe a hundred and twenty. He gets over twice the proper dose. That could account for the high concentration in his urine."

"Sounds farfetched," said Dale.

"So what? The whole thing is farfetched. If a palm-reader predicted you were going to get a wake-up call about radioactive urine, you'd laugh in her face, right?"

Nina saw an argument brewing. "Suppose," she said, "we go to the scene of the crime."

Dawn was poking its fingers through the windows of the medical school when the three doctors arrived at the biophysics lab.

Mike immediately took charge. "All right, now. All we need is this simple Geiger counter with an additional device called a window. That'll help narrow it down."

Dale put on the lead-lined gloves that Mike handed him, and carefully removed the specimen from the box.

Nina restlessly straddled a stool a few feet away.

Mile held up a compact device that looked fancier than the Geiger counters Dale and Nina had used. "First we'll scan the urine without the covering window, and see what kind of reading we get." He held up a flat circular probe with a metal gridwork. It was about the size of an all-day sucker. He waved it over the cup of urine. It ticked so rapidly it seemed to hum. The indicator moved to the maximum reading.

Mike's eyebrows arched with surprise. "Interesting." He looked up at Dale and Nina with an unconvincing air of scientific detachment.

He slipped a red plastic cover over the probe. "This is the window I was telling you about. It looks like it's just a cheap protective cover, but it cuts off the alpha and beta emissions. So if this isotope is pure gamma, which is my bet, putting this window on won't affect the reading." He flicked the Geiger counter back on and it ticked lamely, the arrow barely moving. As Mike peered at the meter, a frown pulled at his face.

Nina was quick to notice. "What's wrong, Mike?"

"It's apparently an alpha or beta emitter." He bit his lip. "Could be radioactive iodine. That's used for diagnostic thyroid studies."

He switched off the meter and turned to Dale. "Why don't you see if anyone else on the ward was supposed to get a nuclear scan?"

Dale shook his head. No one with cancer weighed three hundred pounds, or anywhere near it. Certainly not for very long. He couldn't go along with Mike's

theory that someone twice Lincoln's size was supposed
to get radioactive iodine. If in fact it was iodine.

"When can we find out for sure what this isotope
is?" Dale asked.

"I can probably get hold of a multichannel analyzer
this afternoon. But I think we already have our answer." Mike put the specimen back into the lead box
and closed it, tugging off his gloves as he finished. He
didn't look as confident as he sounded.

Nina thought Mike looked worried, but she didn't
say anything. Nor did she let Dale see her eyes as she
felt him watching her.

Dale poured over Lincoln Lee's chart, seeking answers he had little hope of finding. It only delayed
having to face Lincoln with the bad news. He knew
he would have to tell him someday. But not today.

He thought back on Willie Lee's confession about
taking things home from micro—little things nobody
wanted. He hadn't liked hearing about it at the time.
Now he knew why. In trying to help his son have a
future, Willie may have all but signed the boy's death
certificate. If those little gifts had been contaminated
somehow.

As he studied Lincoln's chart, Dale's eyes stopped
on an X-ray report dated two weeks earlier. It was a
liver scan, a test requiring the use of technetium, a
radioactive isotope. But technetium was a gamma
emitter, and Mike had ruled that out. He thought
back on Mike's comment about a dosing error. Maybe
Lincoln was accidentally given iodine instead of technetium. That could explain why the study was described as technically inadequate. Iodine would not be
visualized well in the liver.

He was puzzled. He didn't remember requesting a
scan on Lincoln. He turned to the front of the chart,
where he found the order. It was in Janet Michaels's
handwriting. He had co-signed it automatically along
with a number of routine orders.

He turned back to the liver scan report. With a moment of irritation he wondered why Janet had ordered it. She had no business barging off by herself. He would have to talk to her.

He read her note in the chart. She wanted the scan to follow up on some abnormal liver blood tests. Not bad reasoning, but he still didn't like it.

He too had noticed the liver abnormalities, but dismissed them as common consequences of leukemia and chemotherapy. The liver scan had been needless. He swore softly, concerned that an order of that importance had slipped past him, and that he hadn't communicated with his medical student. Wasn't she there to learn from him? It was all too easy to scrawl your signature on someone else's work if it might give you an extra wink of sleep. He would have to watch that.

He pushed aside Lincoln's chart and contemplated the pile of records needing immediate review. He felt fatigued just looking at them.

The ward clerk, cutting into his thoughts, ambled up behind him and poked his shoulder. She pointed to the phone, one of its lights flickering.

"For you," she mumbled over her shoulder as she sauntered off. He looked after her with fleeting curiosity. She had managed for three years to avoid addressing any of the doctors by name. Pure hostility. He couldn't figure it. Most of the ward clerks were black, and acted this way. But they weren't being racist. They treated the black doctors with equal rudeness.

Shaking his head in mild amusement, he scooped up the phone. "Dr. Harper."

"Dale?" Mike Bancroft. "I'm down in biophysics. I need you ASAP. Nina's already here." The tension in his voice was unmistakable.

"What is it, Mike?" Dale asked, hearing the tautness in his own voice.

"Lincoln's urine. I have the analysis done. You're not gonna believe this. It's plutonium!"

"Oh, my God!" Dale looked around the nurse's station, as though he expected everyone to react with similar dismay. "I'll be right there." As he slammed down the receiver, forbidding images raced through his mind—bombs, Hiroshima, the mysterious death of Karen Silkwood. What the hell did he know about plutonium? Just enough to send chills down his spine.

He turned to Ron Orloff, who had just come in and was watching him quizzically. "Look through these charts and sign out for me, will you? Something has come up."

Mike and Nina were frowning over a printout of computer paper that spilled onto the floor. They looked up as Dale barged through the door.

"Look at this," Mike cried. "There's no doubt about it." There was an edge to his voice, as though he expected Dale to challenge him. "Plutonium."

Mike jumped up. "Let's get the hell out of here." He hastily rolled the computer paper into a haphazard heap.

Dale nodded and offered Nina his hand. As their eyes met, he saw her fear. There was something else too—something he couldn't quite place.

They went outside and sat under a shade tree. The hospital loomed high above them, an intimidating presence of glass and stone, made more so by their discovery.

Mike quickly defined this horror. "Plutonium is not your run-of-the-mill research material," he said. "It's the essential ingredient of the deadliest radiation known to man." He licked his lips nervously. "So what the hell is it doing in some kid's urine?"

Dale's head was spinning. Now it was obvious what had caused Lincoln's leukemia. But the answer raised even more questions. Where did the plutonium come from?

Nina, stunned to silence, finally said, "Even if plutonium was frequently used here for research, how would it get into Lincoln's body?"

Mike and Dale stared at her, lost in their own speculations.

"Good question," Mike said finally.

They fell silent. Dale lay back on the cool grass and squinted his eyes at the sky. Mike sat hunched over his knees, chewing on a blade of grass. Nina sat next to Dale, clutching his hand, her own hand damp with perspiration.

"Besides making bombs, what is plutonium used for, Mike?" Dale's voice broke the silence.

"It's used in small amounts with lab animals, to study the noxious effects of radiation."

"Is anyone using it at the hospital?"

"I think Robert Heffron is the only one working with it right now. The carcinogenic effects of radiation is one of his big deals. But hell, the quantities are tiny. It would probably take a two-year supply of the amounts Heffron uses to light up Lincoln's urine like that. And even then, you'd have to figure that the kid ate or breathed it. Plutonium is an alpha emitter, meaning it doesn't penetrate the skin."

"Then why is it so dangerous?" Dale asked, sitting up.

"It's not readily excreted. It goes to the bones. Probably why it causes leukemia—eats away at the marrow. Once you're contaminated, you're contaminated for keeps. Like getting radiation therapy every day of your life." Mike spat out the blade of grass. "Plutonium's half-life is twenty-four thousand years, for chrissake."

Dale tried to digest that. He couldn't. "Heffron's in microbiology, isn't he?"

Mike whipped his head around to look at Dale. "Yes . . . yes, he is."

"Lincoln's father used to take the boy little odds and ends from the micro department wastebaskets so he could play doctor."

Mike's forehead wrinkled in a frown. "But surely he didn't take stuff out of the radioactive rooms?"

"He says not. Washed everything carefully first too." Dale paused. "I don't know if there's a connection. But there seems to be too many coincidences here." He felt Nina's grip on his hand tighten ever so slightly. He wondered if she was thinking about the same thing as he was—padlocked canisters and a mysterious deliveryman from Western Nuclear who had been in one hell of a hurry.

Mike got to his feet. "So we know the what, but not the how or why. What are you planning to do with all this, Dale?"

Dale looked at Nina. "I don't know. I've got to talk to Lincoln. Do some thinking. Maybe have a chat with Heffron."

"I don't think you should talk to Heffron," Mike said quickly. "No point in stirring things up if they don't need stirring. Talk to Lincoln. Maybe what he says will take you in a completely different direction."

"Who's the head of micro these days?" Dale asked, ignoring what he took to be Mike's attempt to put him off. He was all too familiar with Mike's penchant for keeping the peace.

Mike gave a sharp snort of disgust. "Still old Terminal Moron, I'm afraid."

Dale laughed at the nickname given Herman Moran in med school. It had stuck.

"I wouldn't waste my time with him, either," Mike said, leaning against the tree. "He's about as helpful as a case of herpes."

Dale threw up his hands. "I don't get it, Mike. Should we just forget this ever happened?"

"No. Just forget my role in it, okay? I see trouble coming, and I don't like it."

Mike reached down for the computer printout. "I'm turning this over to you." He handed it to Dale and started walking toward the hospital. "Do me a favor. Don't call me."

*   *   *

Dale watched the back of Mike's head disappear. "What spooked him? One minute he's got to talk to me stat, and the next he's out of here without so much as a good-bye."

Nina smiled. Dale could be naive at times. "Mike is an organization man. Do your job, climb the ladder, put your money in your pension plan, and don't rock the boat."

Dale laughed. "How come I like him?"

"People are inconsistent, and Mike's not as boring as he tries to be."

"You're so full of wisdom."

She looked away. He gently lifted her chin so their eyes met. "Mind filling me in on what you're thinking, O wise and wonderful one?"

"Not so wise—or wonderful. I've been sitting on information I knew you'd want. I didn't like you pursuing this radioactive business. I wanted you"—she looked him in the eye, her lips parted slightly—"pursuing me."

He embraced her, drawing her tightly to himself, and murmured, "Please stop running so I can catch you."

She melted in his arms. He could feel her tears against his cheek.

"Nina," he said softly, "what is it?"

"I feel as though I've betrayed you. I held off on telling you that Western Nuclear doesn't have a contract with the medical center. And I didn't mention that the Geiger counters in micro probably don't work." She looked up at him, her eyes still misty. "I've hindered you from doing what you want to do. And now, this. I'm ashamed of myself."

He caressed her hair, and breathed its fragrance. They held each other for a long time. Finally, Dale spoke. "Dr. Yablonsky?"

"Yes?"

"I love you."

23

"Jim Raines is a forty-two-year-old alcoholic, arrested for drunk driving," said Andy Hamilton wearily. "They had to tow his car out of a dress shop on Rodeo Drive in Beverly Hills after it crashed through the plate-glass window. The police took him to jail ward because he complained of chest pain."

As Jon Werner's morning work crew stood outside Raines's room, they could hear the man screaming that the nurses were trying to kill him. Dale caught a glimpse of the unruly patient, struggling violently against leather restraints.

"The intern on the jail ward sent the patient to us because she found a coin lesion on his chest X ray," Andy droned on. He slipped the X ray out of its yellow envelope. "His pain, by the way, miraculously disappeared as soon as the police dropped him off." He held the X ray up and pointed to a dime-sized white spot on one lung. "He's a five-pack-a-day smoker," he added with disdain.

"Five packs a day!" Werner exploded. "That's a cancer stick every ten minutes! How the hell can you smoke that much and breathe?"

Werner angrily pushed the rounds cart past Raines's room. "I can't believe they turfed this guy to us. They should have dried him out first. This is an outrage."

He snatched the chart from Andy and drew an X through the order sheet. "Send this guy back to jail. 'Don't pass go, don't collect two hundred dollars.' " He tossed it back on the cart.

Andy retrieved the chart and stared in disbelief at the order sheet, with Jon's big X staring back. He started to protest, but checked himself. If he sent the patient back, he would have wasted two hours. On the other hand, it would lighten his load. He wrote a transfer order and put the chart back, moving on to his next admission.

"Henry Tally is a sixty-year-old man with cancer of the prostate. He came to the emergency room after he saw blood in his urine."

Andy was well aware that a few drops of blood could turn gallons of water bright red, giving the illusion of massive bleeding. He tried to hide his annoyance at having to roll out of bed for something that could have waited. He ended up admitting the patient because it was less trouble than trying to reassure him. The team briefly examined Tally, then moved on to his roommate, Lincoln Lee.

Dale felt a pang at seeing Lincoln huddled in bed, his blankets pulled up to his chin. His breakfast tray was untouched. Beads of sweat dotted his forehead.

Dale scanned the vital signs chart at the foot of the bed. Damn. Lincoln's temperature had shot up to 103.

"How's it going this morning, Lincoln?" Dale asked, taking Lincoln's hand. It was cool and clammy. The pulse was faint.

"It's freezing in here," Lincoln mumbled as he pulled the blankets over his head.

Dale and Jon glanced at each other. Lincoln's immune system had more than it could handle. Somewhere there was a serious infection.

"You have a fever, Lincoln. We need to find out why."

Ron Orloff and Janet Michaels came around the bed across from Dale and helped Lincoln sit up. They examined him in painstaking detail. Lincoln moved with the dull indifference of the very sick.

Dale heard some crackles in one lung, and suspected pneumonia. He sat down on the bed as he stuffed his stethoscope into his pocket. "Lincoln, we'll need further tests on you. You won't be going home until we get this fever under control."

Lincoln closed his eyes. He asked for another blanket.

Morning rounds finished with Jesse Munoz. His dramatic improvement put a smile on Jon Werner's face. "We've licked his infection," Jon observed. "One more course of chemo and he's a cure."

Jesse's comeback was exciting. And it never would have happened without modern medicine. It gave Dale a better understanding of Werner's fascination with oncology. In a way, it was a redemption of the dead.

As they moved down the hall, Jon was the first to spot the tall young woman in the white coat. She was standing by the nurse's station, looking lost.

"Well, Dr. Yablonsky," he bellowed, still ebullient from seeing Jesse. "What are you doing in the front lines? Lose an X ray?"

Dale looked up with a start. Never before had Nina visited him on the wards.

She gave Jon a brief nod and turned to Dale. She kept her voice low. "I thought if I caught you on rounds, I could help you talk to Lincoln."

She was about to say something else when Dale took her by the elbow and propelled her to an empty corner of the nurse's station. "Lincoln's had a relapse. He's in no shape to talk."

"Oh, no! Is there anything I can do?"

"I don't know. I need to talk to Lincoln's father."

She now said what had been pressing on her mind. "Have you checked Willie's urine for plutonium?"

"What!" He turned and faced her in his astonishment. How stupid of him not to have thought of it.

"If Lincoln's contamination has anything to do with the things that Willie brought home from microbiology, then Willie may be contaminated too."

Dale was considering the possibilities when Jon Werner came over and tapped him on the shoulder. "Hey, Romeo, we need you."

Dale squeezed Nina's hand and whispered in her ear. "Let's meet this afternoon after sign-out rounds. Bring a Geiger counter."

As he rejoined the crew, Dale sidled up to Ron Orloff and said quietly, "I need to talk to you."

Was this his doctor, his boss, or his friend talking to him? He had to know, so he could figure out how to respond. Maybe it's a joke. "Hey, Orloff, ha, ha, you could be poisoned by plutonium, let's take a look at your pee!" In which case, he could say, "Take a hike, friend."

No, no, settle down, Ron. This is Dale Harper talking to you, the guy who's been straight with you from the start. And now he's telling you he wants you to pee in a cup so he can see if you're radioactive! A far-out hunch. Don't get panicky, man.

A cup, I'll find a cup. I'll be right back, Dale; wait for me, don't go away. Then a hand reaching for him, stopping him, like a gentle slap in the face. Take it easy. Nothing's certain, we're just looking. Just searching. For a cause.

A cause, yes, he could buy that. Didn't he want to find a cause? Explain why he'd been cursed with this hideous disease? Something scientific. Because even though he wasn't religious, he wanted to know, he couldn't help but wonder: Was God punishing him?

"Here it is, Dale." Ron's hand trembled as he gave the full plastic cup to his friend and doctor. "I want to come with you when you check it."

Dale studied Ron for a moment, as if deciding whether Ron could handle it. "Let's go," he said.

Ron Orloff found Robert Heffron's name heading up a number of articles in the *Index Medicus*. He moved his finger until he found the title he was look-

ing for: "Chernobyl: Early Effects of Radiation."
There were two co-authors. One was a graduate student; the other he had never heard of. He jotted down
the journal and volume number. As he went through
the stacks, his mind relentlessly went back to what
had just happened.

Dale Harper's far-out hunch had, like a summer
storm, materialized. There, in the radiology department, with Nina Yablonsky as a witness, his urine
specimen set off a frenetic burst from the Geiger
counter. The three of them had listened in amazement. And no one was more amazed than Ron Orloff.
Yet, in an odd way, he was relieved. Finally, they
were on to something, a cause for his disease. Not
that it would affect the progress of his disease. For
leukemia had an uncharted course of its own. Grimly,
he considered his own prospects—or lack of them.

And now, as he waited for Mike Bancroft to determine what the isotope was, he took some solace in
looking up Heffron's article. When he got a complete
report, he would consult Heffron, the specialist in cancer and the environment. Despite his earlier misgivings, he was sure he would find Heffron receptive and
helpful. After all, the man was a professional.

"What can I do for you, Dr. Orloff?" Heffron
smiled from behind his desk, his hands clasped neatly
in front of him.

Ron shifted in his seat, feeling alarmist and inept
now that he was here. Heffron had stayed after-hours,
just to talk to him, after Ron's panicky call.

He had to collect his thoughts. Control his voice.
And then he blurted it out, like a schoolboy. "I'm
contaminated with plutonium. I have leukemia. I
thought there might be a connection. Environmental
carcinogens being your field—I thought maybe you
could help me. I don't know what else to do. I'm
dying."

Heffron looked at Ron, his face impassive. Just

when Ron thought he would have to repeat himself, Heffron spoke. "How did you get contaminated with plutonium?"

"I don't know. But I thought maybe you could help me there. I understand you sometimes work with plutonium."

"Yes . . ." said Heffron slowly, as though trying to digest what Ron was saying.

He doesn't like me. There was that feeling again, that Ron had felt in their previous conversations. He tried to push through it. "I hoped you might give me some ideas about where to start looking." Ron smiled shyly and held up the journal containing Heffron's Chernobyl article. "I thought I might get some clues from this."

Heffron nodded, his face showing concern. "Unfortunately, it doesn't address your problem." Heffron unclasped his hands and flattened them on the desk. "I'm glad you came, Ron. I'll help you in any way I can." He looked puzzled for a moment. "How did you learn of this?"

"It was Dale, Dale Harper. He checked my urine on a hunch. Another leukemia patient of his was radioactive from plutonium."

Heffron listened intently. "Who's the patient?"

"Lincoln Lee. His father works in maintenance here."

Heffron got up from his chair, lifted a book from its shelf, and handed it to Ron. "I'd like you to read this. Try to think of everywhere you've been in the past fifteen years as you read. Then we'll meet again in a few days, after I've done some investigating. I'll need a detailed personal history from you."

Ron stood up. He decided Heffron's coolness was simply the scientist talking. He found the thought reassuring. "Thank you. I'll get to it right away," he said, tucking the book under his arm.

Heffron extended his hand as they parted. He watched Ron hurry off. He stood in the doorway a

long moment, frowning thoughtfully before he finally
returned to his desk. It was time to have his little
rendezvous with Christine. But first he had to make
a few phone calls.

24

Dale Harper pounded a nail into the horse's hoof with a ferocious swing of his hammer. The horse jerked its head in protest. Dale freed the hoof and patted the horse's muzzle. "Sorry, Tonto."

Shoeing horses usually helped him relax. But today, Tonto's skittishness reflected his own mood. He slid around the horse, inspecting his handiwork. Satisfied, he slipped Tonto's halter off and turned him loose with a slap on the rump. He watched the stallion prance toward the far end of the corral, his tail streaming like a banner.

Dale tossed his tools into the car and waved at the horse as he drove off. As he negotiated the winding canyon road, his thoughts drifted from the earthy diversion of horses to the sharp reality of Ron Orloff. He wondered if he had made matters worse for Ron, throwing him into the quicksand without any hope of getting him out. But without Ron there was no pattern. Not much to go on. A second case of plutonium contaminations was hardly coincidental. In act, it was bizarre.

Yes, he had been right to tell Ron. Even a clumsy treatment of the truth was better than manipulating it. He had learned that early on, when the husband of one of his first patients had insisted that his wife not be told she had cancer. It would devastate her, he had insisted sternly.

Dale had fumed with anger. "It's her body," he stated. "She has a right to know." And he told her.

The man gave him a hard look. Dale held his gaze, and then witnessed the man's tears as he turned away. It was he, the husband, who was devastated. And it was his wife who helped him through it, until her death two weeks later—of cancer. Knowing the truth had given her the strength they both needed.

The memory of that brave woman brought a mist to his eyes as his thoughts turned back to Ron, who had taken the news about his poisoned urine quietly. But Dale had seen the fear behind the pale mask as Ron spun around and stalked off, ending any discussion.

Dale turned off the canyon road toward Nina's apartment. She had insisted on going with him today. They were returning to microbiology with a calibrated Geiger counter to check for radiation—this time, plutonium.

Dale pulled up in front of Nina's apartment and jumped out of the car before its old engine coughed to a standstill. His dark mood lightened at the thought of seeing her, and he bounded up the stairs.

"Hi!" He grinned as she opened the door. As usual she was ravishing. She wore Levi's and a pin-striped blouse with a tailored burgundy blazer. "No trench-coat, Holmes?" He leaned over and pecked her cheek.

Her eyes danced as she returned his kiss. "It's at the cleaner's, along with my houndstooth cap. I've got my pipe though." She proudly produced a corncob pipe.

Dale sniffed at the pipe. "Which of your boyfriends left this?"

"Chauvinist! Can't a woman smoke a pipe?" She jammed it in her mouth with a smile.

His jaw dropped. "You're kidding!"

"It helps me think. I've always loved the aroma of pipe tobacco. It doesn't taste as good as it smells, but it's great on a lonely night when a woman has a lot to think about."

He shook his head in mock horror. "You know something, Dr. Yablonsky? You're a little crazy."

He drew her to him and held her close. The only sound was the thud of the pipe hitting the floor.

"Like you," she murmured.

Nina gasped softly as they drove into the medical school parking lot. Dale followed her gaze to a dusty delivery truck pulled up at a loading dock. He looked at her questioningly.

"Don't you remember?" she said. "That's the same truck. It's from Western Nuclear."

The truck's insignia was obscured by the dust. But it did look familiar. "Let's sit here a minute and watch," he said as he switched off the ignition.

They saw a person in a khaki uniform roll a bulky canister on a dolly up the truck ramp. He disappeared back into the building with the empty dolly.

"He's making a pickup," Dale said, thinking it strange. "You'd think he would exchange empty canisters for new ones."

They waited in silence for the deliveryman to return, which he did after five minutes, with four more canisters strapped to the dolly. After vanishing into the back of the truck, he emerged empty-handed and closed up.

Dale jumped out of the car and started toward the truck as the deliveryman climbed into the cab. He tried to wave the driver down, but the truck pulled away with a screech of its tires, forcing Dale to jump aside. He was close enough to make out the lettering on the back of the truck. Western Nuclear.

There was a lone maintenance man mopping up as Dale and Nina approached the micro lounge area with Mike Bancroft's key. The man looked up indifferently and went back to his work. No one else was around on this Sunday morning except Mr. Zimmer, the useless old guard whom Nina had encountered before.

He nodded at them and flashed his yellow-toothed grin.

They slipped into the lounge and closed the door behind them. Nina pulled the Geiger counter out of her oversize purse and turned it on.

"It's been calibrated. Should be right on," she said, handing it to Dale.

"Good work." He looked around the room, spotting a Geiger counter on the back shelf. "Let's use that one too."

Nina crossed the room and picked up the counter. She blew the dust off it and flicked it on. "It's dead."

Dale frowned. "Let's get one of the instruments we used last time." He handed her a key, another gift from Mike Bancroft.

Dale swept the probe around the lounge area. He checked the wastebasket that had been radioactive before, and watched the needle go far to the right and sit there, ticking so fast it hummed.

He was standing mesmerized over the basket when Nina returned. They looked at each other, the hum capturing their attention like the opening notes of a dark symphony. Nina broke the spell by turning on her counter and holding the probe over the basket. The needle edged up, but not dramatically.

"One of these instruments is batty," he said, annoyed.

"It's mine. Remember, I calibrated yours." She turned hers off and sat in the middle of the floor, burying her face in her hands.

"Hey, what's wrong?" He pulled up a chair and wrapped his arm around her.

She was shaking her head. "I should have told you when I first found out that the Geiger counters here were off."

He gently turned her face toward his. "You act as though you're to blame. That's nonsense. Nobody else would have taken the risks you have."

She sniffed and sat back, regaining her composure. "I'm sorry."

He stood up and held out his hand. "Come, Holmes, while the scent is still fresh."

She laughed, as he'd hoped she would, and let him pull her up. "Okay, my dear Watson."

They went on to the research rooms, picking up an occasional bleep. As they were leaving one of the rooms, something caught Nina's eye. She pointed to the floor. Dale could plainly see the rings of dirt and rust.

"Looks like a canister was here just recently." He squatted down and saw droplets of a thick, nondescript fluid. He flicked on the Geiger counter and held the probe to the floor. It went wild. He looked up at Nina. "We've got something. Let's find a lead container."

She nodded. "I can get one from radiology. And don't touch that slime while I'm gone."

He turned off the Geiger counter. "I'm not that crazy."

On Nina's return, they carefully collected the fluid into the protective lead container.

After a call to Mike Bancroft, they prepared to leave when Nina said, "I just realized something!"

"What's that?"

"All the padlocked canisters that were here last time are gone."

"Yeah, and I'll bet our friend from Western Nuclear had something to do with it," Dale said, his eyes narrowing.

"Do you think someone tipped him off?"

"It's beginning to look that way."

"Well, you guys are wrong on this one, thank God." Mike Bancroft looked tired, his curly hair matted to his forehead. "This is radioactive iodine. Just what you'd expect to find in a micro lab."

"On the floor?" Nina lifted a skeptical eyebrow.

Mike sighed and slouched back in his chair. "So,

somebody was a little careless. A container leaked. Big deal."

"Big deal? Mike, are you nuts? If people around here are that sloppy, it could turn up anywhere. Maybe next time it won't be iodine, it'll be plutonium. And it won't be the floor, it'll be the table you're eating from."

"Oh, come off it, Nina. You're worse than Dale."

Dale followed the exchange with mild amusement. Maybe Mike was right. Though he couldn't help but admire Nina, so full of fire as she lit into Mike.

"Pull your head out of the sand, Mike," she said. "You can't ignore this."

Mike jumped up. "I don't have my head in the sand, goddammit! Who the hell has been working on all this for you? I'd rather be slugging rats at the dump, for chrissake. I can't believe I'm spending a Sunday afternoon sitting in a goddamn laboratory churning out data for a couple of ingrates. I ought to have my head examined! Yeah, you said it—I must be nuts!" The vein on Mike's forehead popped up.

Dale stepped in. "Hey, let's cool off. We're all a little edgy. You've been a big help, Mike." Dale rested a hand on Mike's shoulder. "What do you say? Buy you a drink?"

Mike started to say something, then looked at Nina. He smiled sheepishly and nodded. "Sure."

Nina reached for Mike's hand. "I'm sorry, Mike. I'm just uptight."

"I'm sorry too. Hell, I'm just trying to survive in this crazy world." He shrugged. "I'll take that drink."

25

Christine Anselm quietly took in the elegant surroundings. She was impressed. Waiters in tuxedos. White linen tablecloths. Half a dozen roses on the table. A violinist playing classical music. The resonant clinking of crystal. It represented a world she had scorned but secretly yearned for.

Her trysts with Heffron had always been in a cheap motel or an isolated office. Never in this world.

She hadn't minded shedding her jeans and sandals for the occasion. She wore light makeup and a simple cotton dress. She had even gone to the trouble of styling her unruly hair.

Heffron smiled at her from across the table as the waiter handed him the wine list. He thought she looked like a caricature of herself. The makeup seemed to accentuate the deep lines of dissipation in her face. "How about some vintage Cabernet?" he said.

She nodded, too preoccupied with her suspicions to relax. She didn't trust him. Why should she? It would be just like him to have something up his sleeve.

The dinner passed uneventfully, though she remained on edge, despite plenty of vintage Cabernet. She ordered beef Wellington, and Heffron had the shrimp scampi. She could smell the savory garlic sauce across the table, and for a moment she wished she had ordered the scampi instead. She ordinarily would have helped herself off his plate, but she wanted to avoid any implications of intimacy. He was not going to get around her this time with his old tricks. Yet even at the bare thought of this she felt a quiver of desire.

He had a way with women, of every age and description. She hated him for it, except when she was in bed with him, and then she was like all the rest. She guessed he had never known a woman he couldn't twist around his little finger. But not tonight, no matter what or how much she drank. She had decided that.

They ate in silence, not touching. There were no pleasantries. The strain finally got to her.

"Why did you bring me here?" she said. "It's hardly like you to treat a person like me so lavishly."

He smiled and reached for her hand, not appearing to notice when she pulled away. He had finished with his scampi and was sipping a cappuccino.

"You know," he said in a gentle way, "I got to thinking about what you said the other day. And, as usual, you were right. I've been a complete cad, not giving you the credit or benefits you've earned. I meant to protect you, to keep you from incurring any risks, but then, I'm afraid, I sort of lost track of things."

He gave an apologetic wave of his arm. "What can I say? I want to make it up to you." He smiled. "You do remember how much we shared together. It's not over. It never is when you've had what we have."

She sniffed into her glass. She had already downed a liter of wine, but she was ready for his little games. "I imagine you'll propose marriage next. Pardon me, but I'm not that stupid, Herr Professor."

He saw she was going to be more difficult than he had anticipated. He looked around the restaurant as the waiter brought back his credit card and two giant strawberries dipped in chocolate. He reached across the table and touched one of the strawberries to her lips.

"Forget it," she said as she stuck a cigarette in her

mouth and lit it. "You don't get around me that easy."

"We can't talk here," he said, nodding at the nearby tables. "I want to settle our little difficulty," He smiled. "You'll have no complaint after we're through."

He looked up, as though struck by a sudden thought. "There's a special place—very private— where we can talk. You'll need to follow me in your car. You'll see what I mean when we get there."

She shrugged. "No games, now."

He put his hand on hers. She let it rest there for a moment.

"You know better," he said.

She arched her eyebrows and blew a smoke ring in his face.

"Pretty fancy," Christine said, her bright, careful eyes glowing despite herself.

Heffron smiled as he stood at the door of the rustic yet comfortable and well-appointed cabin. Log walls. Plush carpet on the floor. A giant bed in the middle of the room. A stone fireplace across the way with a large painting of a stormy seascape over the mantel.

"The place belongs to a friend of mine," he said. "I use it on rare occasions."

She was still baffled by his behavior, though tantalized by the thought he still found her attractive. Her mind had been clear as she followed him down the dark, winding canyon road to this hideout in the Santa Monica Mountains. Only the rich, she thought, could afford this kind of privacy in a city the size of Los Angeles.

He rubbed his hands together. "It's chilly. How about a fire?"

She tossed her purse onto the bed and strolled around, fondling the furniture and knickknacks, enjoying the thought of him getting his hands sooty. "I'd love it," she said.

At last to be treated like an equal. They were all the same, these dirty old men, falling all over themselves when you lashed back at them. It struck her for the first time how much older he was. Nearly twenty years. He should be grateful for what she gave him. Not always carping at her.

He had squatted down next to the fireplace and turned a switch. There was a brief hissing sound, and then a soft proof as propane-driven flames lapped around a fake log.

She emitted a harsh laugh as she watched the instant fire ignite. She should have known. He wasn't the type to do dirty work. That's what he had her for.

He stood and walked to a cabinet in one corner of the room. "How about an after-dinner drink?" He held up a bottle of bourbon.

"Sure," she said, dropping into an easy chair in front of the fire.

"So how's it going?" he said, handing her a whiskey glass brimming with bourbon and ice. He sat down in a leather chair next to her and put his feet up on a matching ottoman.

Here it comes, she thought. She eyed her drink, as though debating whether to hold on to her last thread of sobriety. She felt him watching her. She put the drink to her mouth, and took a generous swallow. The warmth hit her brain almost instantaneously. "How's what going?" She had the vague notion that she sounded too mellow. She was loosening up.

"The deliveries. Any problems?"

She looked at his profile, highlighted by the light of the fire, which he seemed to be studying. He didn't appear worried. In fact, casual. All too casual, considering the topic at hand.

"What do you care?" She took another gulp of her drink.

He leaned over and laid his hand in hers. "Christine, I want to make amends. I've asked too much of you. You deserve a proper reward. Let me know what you want. And it will be yours. Just name it."

She drained her glass. He was used to her drinking, and knew that she carried it well to a point. She had not yet reached that point. He got up to refill her glass. He didn't remember how much she had consumed, but it was plenty. She had handled the car well on the mountain road, but the alcohol would soon be catching up with her.

"So what do I want?" she mimicked, crossing her legs and allowing his hand to stray to her knee.

"If I keep delivering, and that's a big if, you're going to have to cough up some real dough, sweetheart. Someone's onto your little game." She looked around the cabin, suddenly dizzy as she turned her head. It passed quickly. She waved her hand. "Big bucks like your friend here has." She thought of Heffron's leather-upholstered Mercedes and tailored suits and stuck out her chin. "Like you have."

"Why would anyone be onto my little game as you so elegantly put it? Have you slipped up?"

She laughed knowingly. "So that's it. You think you're gonna wine and dine me into taking the rap for you. Well, you got that one wrong, buster."

He looked at her with amusement. "The rap? For what?"

"I did a little investigating on my own after those two idiots caught me with your precious stuff. They're all excited about plutonium lighting up people's urine. Is that your big project now?"

She wanted to intimidate and hurt him, as he had done so many times to her. "I can see it now—the runaway bestseller: *How to Kill People Without the Inconvenience and Expense of Bombing Them.* I'm dying to see my name on the dust jacket."

He shook his head and smiled. "My dear, I think you've had too much to drink."

"Yeah? Well I want another." The words burst out of her defiantly.

"You came to the right place," he said, filling her glass from the bottle he had brought over from the bar. "By the way, did you get all the canisters out?"

"Sure. Nothing to it. They're in my basement."

"Good. They were leaking. How did that happen?"

"Just a minute, pard. You're not gonna pin that on me."

"I'm afraid you used the wrong canisters, Christine. Plutonium is extremely corrosive. You should have known that." He took a sip of his own drink. "But don't worry. It will be our secret."

Suddenly she felt confused. Her eyes wouldn't focus for a moment. Heffron had told her there was a slight problem with the inspectors. Now he was telling her the canisters were leaking. But not to worry. Sure, it wasn't his hide.

"Wait just a minute," she drawled, her speech thick. "Time out. I'm the one who's got that crap glowing under my living room. What're you using it for?"

She threw her legs over the side of her chair until her skirt hiked up her thighs. "Of course, if you don't want to tell me, I knew a coupla people who'd just love to hear from yours truly."

He laughed aloud. "You wouldn't be thinking of blackmailing me now, would you, my dear?"

She was too far gone to care about anything but the immediacy of his presence. A flood of muddled memories of their sexual past swept over her. She looked up at him dreamily as he sat on the arm of her chair and stroked her face.

"I have an offer for you, Christine—one you can't refuse," he said as he rubbed her neck. "But first, why don't we enjoy ourselves?" He took her hand and put his lips around one of her fingers, sucking it gently. She looked at him with the old hunger, unable to help herself. The alcohol had removed what few inhibitions she had.

As he felt her resistance dissolve, he led her to the bed, where they made love for the last time.

* * *

She looked almost tranquil as she lay sprawled on the bed. He hadn't removed her clothes. Everything should look as natural as possible. She was under, way under. He hadn't needed the phenobarbital. The simpler the better. A sky-high alcohol level would explain it all.

She was in such a stuporous sleep that her breathing was becoming irregular. She was snoring, and saliva trickled out of the side of her mouth. As he sat on the bed watching her, he was overcome with a sense of revulsion. He had just made love to that . . . creature.

Well, no one would ever know. He got up and quickly changed into a black sweat suit and a pair of cheap tennis shoes he had picked up at a discount store. He stuffed his dress clothes into a duffel bag, along with his polished black leather shoes. He ran through her purse, finding her wallet, and threw it all into his bag. He pulled on a pair of latex exam gloves and looked around the cabin for any telltale signs. He washed and dried the glasses and put them away.

He went out to his car and tossed his belongings into the trunk, locking it. He opened the passenger door of Christine's car, a small green Japanese job that he had instructed her to park next to the garage on the asphalt. Asphalt held secrets far better than dirt and gravel.

Back in the cabin she was still spread out on the bed. Had she moved? For an uneasy moment he wondered if she was faking it. It would be just like her, the bitch. He eased up to her and pinched her neck—hard. She groaned, but her head fell back and he knew she was out.

He picked her up, cradling her in both arms. She was surprisingly light. He carried her out the front door, looked up and down the dark desolate canyon road, and hauled her over to the Japanese piece of junk. He placed her in the passenger seat. She fell over against the door after he slammed it shut.

He slipped into the driver's seat and drove about a mile up the road to the pullout he had spotted earlier in the week. He parked, ran around the car, gathered up her limp body, and carried her to the driver's side. He dumped her into the driver's seat, letting her slump forward onto the steering wheel. He considered fastening the seat belt, then decided against it. What drunk used a seat belt?

Just then he heard a car up ahead, and could see its lights penetrating the darkness that hung over the canyon. He shoved Christine down in the seat and moved to the far side of the car where he hunkered down, out of sight. The oncoming car screeched around the curve without a sign that the driver noticed or gave a damn about the abandoned vehicle parked on the side of the road. Another drunk, no doubt.

After the car passed, he stood and strained to hear any other noises in the distance. Nothing but a few crickets and frogs, their innocuous chirps bouncing off the canyon walls.

He turned the ignition of Christine's car and fired up the engine by reaching a hand in and pushing the gas pedal. She had an automatic shift, which helped. He repositioned her against the steering wheel, not that it would matter when they found her charred remains at the bottom of the ravine. He cranked the steering wheel, slipped the gearshift into drive, and got behind the car to give it a shove over the enbankment.

He watched with satisfaction as the Japanese toy tumbled over and over, deep into the ravine. And as he had anticipated, there was an explosion and a burst of flames on final impact.

Good-bye, Christine. You were a little too greedy, my dear. He stood watching the flames engulf the car. After a couple of minutes he tugged off the latex gloves and jogged back to the cabin, enjoying the fresh night air.

26

Herman Moran stared at the bottom drawer of his desk, where he kept his vodka. He preferred gin, but a man of his position couldn't afford to smell like a juniper berry. He was thinking of this position as he considered the busybody sitting across from him.

"Correct me if I'm wrong, Dr. Harper. You think there's some hanky-panky going on with radioisotopes in the microbiology department?" His eyes slid past Dale's and fixed on the clock overhead.

"If you want to put it that way."

Watching Moran fidget brought back memories of medical school, and Moran's spreading stories of a Harper attitude problem. It had baffled him, until he recalled a hospital party where he had rebuffed Moran's drunken advances. It was apparent that Moran had never forgiven him.

"And why, may I ask, do you give a damn?" Moran was saying.

"I'm a doctor. That's why." He found Terminal Moron's glibness annoying. "Radiation kills people. Those big 'Hazardous Materials' signs you see around aren't just some first-grader's poster project."

Moran seemed not to notice the barb. "I have two questions about this little, er, investigation of yours."

"Yes?"

"Number one, why the hell are you nosing around in my department, and number two, what do you expect me to do about these little revelations of yours?"

Dale had been under no illusions about this visit.

He knew if he did not go through channels and talk to Moran first, there would be trouble later.

"It says 'Department Head' there." He nodded toward the door behind him. "Doesn't that mean you're in charge?"

Moran's eyes flared. "You're not telling me anything, buster. I know all about radiation violations in this department. It's nit-picky stuff. The state inspectors have to justify their existence, so they slap us with a few citations. Most of it's just paperwork. We fix the paperwork, they look good, we look good. When they want a raise, they find something else to complain about. More paperwork. Ad nauseam."

He permitted himself a malicious smile. "Paperwork infractions haven't been listed as a cause of leukemia yet, to the best of my knowledge. Of course, I haven't seen this week's *New England Journal.*"

Dale plowed on. "What about plutonium in the urine of one of your Ph.D. students? What about radioactivity in the lounge where your people eat their lunch?"

"I don't know anything about that. We don't use plutonium in this department." Except for Bob Heffron. He suppressed a smile as the thought struck him. Heffron and Harper. A chance to put two thorns in his side together. Hopefully, they would destroy each other. He chuckled to himself. How appropriate.

"Wait a second," he drawled. "How could I forget Dr. Heffron? He uses plutonium. You'll want to talk to him."

Dale could see this was the end of the discussion. It was Heffron he wanted anyway. "Is he around today?" he asked with studied casualness.

"You bet he is!" Moran leapt from his chair. "You two will find lots to talk about. Cancer is Bob's research baby, you know."

Moran led Dale down the hall and ushered him into Heffron's office without knocking. Heffron looked up from his desk, holding back a frown. He half rose from his chair.

"Bob, my boy, meet Dale Harper, an old student of mine who's very interested in your work."

"Yes?" Heffron glanced first at Moran, then at Dale. A stiff smile worked at his lips. So this was Harper. Christine Anselm's snoop.

"Dr. Harper here has a strong interest in your plutonium research. Thinks maybe you're poisoning his patients—just joking, just joking." Moran snickered and pushed a chair behind Dale, motioning him to sit down. "Seriously, you two really should, er, visit. Nothing like the present." He turned to leave. "Let me know if you need me."

As the door closed, Heffron and Dale faced each other. "I'm sorry to intrude like this," Dale said. "I can come another time."

Heffron sat back in his chair. "No, please stay." He laughed easily. "You certainly have my attention. Dr. Moran has a way about him, doesn't he?"

Dale felt a bond with Heffron as they silently acknowledged their contempt for the bumbling department head. "Dr. Moran," Dale said, "has trouble dealing with anything more controversial than Mother's Day."

Heffron chuckled and relit the pipe that had been burning down in his ashtray. He puffed casually and leaned back. "What is this about plutonium poisoning?"

"Two of my patients have been victims of radiation exposure. It may have happened somewhere in this department." He saw nothing but understandable astonishment in Heffron's face. "As soon as I mentioned plutonium to Dr. Moran, he brought me to you."

Heffron tamped down his pipe. Moran was a damned fool. "And you think I may have the solution because I use plutonium?"

"I don't know what to think."

"I'm afraid my use of the material is too minuscule to affect anything bigger than a rat. That doesn't mean

I'm not interested in helping you. But you really ought to be looking over in biophysics."

"One of the patients is a microbiology research student," Dale said, prompted by what he took to be Heffron's put off, "and the other is the son of a maintenance man in micro. Micro is the only common denominator so far."

Heffron frowned. "What are their names?"

Dale shook his head. "Patient confidentiality." He felt protective toward Ron and Lincoln, though he knew Heffron could scout around and come up with the information.

"Yes, of course." Heffron puffed a cloud of smoke. "So what can I do for you?"

"Tell me about your use of plutonium."

Heffron felt a growing distaste for this intrusive young nobody, which he glossed over with an air of candor. "I use literally microcuries—tiny amounts. It's stored in a small lead container behind my office here." He gestured toward an unmarked door in the far corner of the room. "It never goes beyond here because the lab I use for plutonium research is also behind my office." Heffron put down his pipe. "Would you like to see the setup?"

Dale nodded, mildly surprised at Heffron's readiness to cooperate.

Walking a little ahead, Heffron led him down a long hall into a laboratory full of the stench of experimental rats. It was about what he would have expected. Heffron opened a cupboard door and pointed to a small lead cylinder. It was labeled "Plutonium." "That's the extent of it, I'm afraid."

Dale looked around the room. There was only one entrance, from Heffron's office. He examined the door, which was devoid of warnings. "I see this room isn't designated for radioactive materials."

Heffron laughed easily. "You got me on that one. I don't think anyone cares, and the arrangement is quite convenient for me. What I'm doing here could not harm your patients. Or anyone else for that matter." Heffron led Dale back to his office, locking the door behind him. "We're extremely careful."

"Mind if I check this over with a Geiger counter sometime?"

"Be my guest." Heffron returned to his desk. "Any other questions? I have a meeting in a few minutes."

"Just one. Where do you get your plutonium?"

"Bristol Nuclear services all the nuclear medicine needs of the hospital and medical center." He stood up. "Now if you'll excuse me, Dr. Harper . . ."

"What about Western Nuclear?"

Heffron cleared his throat. He was disliking Harper more by the minute. "As I just told you, we use Bristol Nuclear."

"Right." Dale held Heffron's steel-gray eyes for a long moment. He thought he saw a chink in the smooth facade. And he wanted Heffron to know he saw it. He grinned with an exaggerated cheerfulness. "Thank you for your time, Dr. Heffron. I expect we'll run into each other again."

"Come anytime," Heffron said with a smile. "I'll eagerly await news of your investigation."

He leaned against the doorjamb, watching Dale move down the corridor with a self-confident swagger. He pulled out a lighter to reignite his pipe. The tobacco tasted dank and tarry. He shoved the pipe into a rack and grabbed the phone, punching out the number of Audrey Moran.

"This is so-o-o naughty," she said, giggling as he tore off her housedress.

"Isn't it." Heffron crushed his lips to hers, stifling her childish blabbering.

"My husband's bed," she murmured as they pressed their bodies together. She was breathing heavily.

He was bored. Somehow the erotic magic wasn't there. He just wanted to get it done with.

She giggled again, her laugh suddenly becoming

deep and sensual. He thought for a moment she would choke. "Oh, I'd *love* to see Herman's face right now."

So would he. At the thought, he felt a sudden surge of desire and roughly forced her before she was ready. She gasped as he quickly reached a violent peak of satisfaction. Spent, limp from his effort, he turned over and flopped down beside her, oblivious to her need.

She ran her fingers through his hair. "Hey, what about me, big boy?" She raised up on an elbow and gave him a lascivious grin, her mouth loose with desire. He reached over and stimulated her with his hand until she arched her back and moaned in a frenzy of climactic ecstasy. He watched her idly as she kept twisting and turning, his mind elsewhere.

"Let me freshen your drink," he said as she lay back, exhausted.

"God," she said, "you're wonderful!" She took a deep breath. "Can you imagine what it's like to be married to a faggot?"

He shrugged. "That's your problem. Mine's getting a drink." He stepped into his pants and headed downstairs to the bar. On his return, she was sitting up, watching him with a mixture of worship and puzzlement. He poured two martinis out of a decanter and clinked her glass with his. "How about a toast?"

"To fucking in my husband's bed," she said, shrilly laughing.

"No," he said solemnly. "To us."

They propped themselves up with pillows and stared at the foot of the bed. Finally, Audrey turned to him. "You're different, somehow. Is there something wrong?"

Without looking at her he said slowly. "I'm sorry you noticed." He took a sip of his drink and looked down. "I didn't want to spoil our time together."

She reached out, her face clouded with concern, and gently touched his brow. "Oh, you silly. Tell me about it. Please."

He put his drink down and took her hand, kissing

the back of it. Her hands, veined and bony, gave away her age, he thought with a twinge of distaste. He sighed to himself, thinking of what he had to put up with to get what he wanted. All these silly women.

His eyes held hers. "I'm in the midst of very important research. Every scientist works toward the pinnacle of his career. A research accomplishment of such magnitude that the world is changed forever by it."

She wiggled closer to him. "Why, this sounds like something to rejoice about, not for pouting!" She touched his lips. "Now, let's see those turn into a smile, right now." She laughed, but then quieted when she saw her attempt at levity had no impact.

He studied her a moment, frowning. "It would be as you say, dear lady, were it not for your husband, who can't stand to see me succeed."

She cried out with amazement. "Herman?! How could an incompetent ass like him be anything more than a pebble under your foot?"

"He has help," Heffron said sadly. "And they're trying to sabotage my efforts."

"My God," Audrey gasped. "Who would think Herman could be that clever?"

"It's not cleverness. But a hatred so overwhelming the mind looks for ways to destroy its enemy. In this case, he found two residents, young and naive enough to be awed by a department head. One's an inveterate troublemaker. The other his girlfriend."

Audrey was resting on her elbow, watching him. "Herman is such a useless parasite," she said with a scowl. "The thought of a man like you having to answer to him makes my blood boil."

He allowed himself a sardonic laugh. "He only thinks I answer to him. He's too inept to know differently." Which, he didn't add, suited him just fine. He liked to work amid chaos. It allowed him the freedom to do as he pleased. The setup had been working just fine. Till now.

Audrey glowed at Heffron's closeness, wanting him

now more than ever. The thought of seeing him again and again gave her a thrill of desire. Herman had suddenly become a very useful commodity. "Herman is my husband," she said with a sly smile. "I know it's silly, but I feel partially responsible for him. I want to help you."

He shook his head. "It would mean getting those residents—especially the troublemaker—out of my hair. I couldn't ask you to do that. I wouldn't even know what to ask."

She sat forward, her face intent. "I'm a nurse, you know. Nurses can make doctors look like shit warmed over. Especially when it's a poor, inexperienced, beaten-on resident."

He leaned over and planted a kiss on her forehead. "You're so good to me. But you can't afford the risk . . ."

"Nonsense. What's this troublemaker's name?"

There was a long pause. Finally he said it, as though it had been wrenched from his lips. "Dale Harper."

27

It looked like more of the same. Dale groaned to himself. He was getting tired of this particular scene, and he knew Carleton was too.

He leaned back in his chair, his eyes taking in Carleton's office, as though he had never seen it before. Green velveteen drapes, plush gray carpet, a massive mahogany desk, and bookcases adorned with expensive little trinkets of ivory and jade. The somber elegance stood in sharp contrast to the garish fluorescent-bright hospital corridors he had just traveled. He wondered what emotional sustenance, if any, Carleton gleaned from this oasis of rich finery.

"Why do you keep picking on Dr. Orosco? We would all like to know," Carleton said in a world-weary voice.

"I'm not picking on him. We don't see eye-to-eye, that's all." Tired from a night on call, he wanted to be done with this. The chores were piling up.

"Orosco called this morning. He says you told one of his patients that Orosco didn't know what he was doing, and the patient subsequently left the hospital." Carleton removed his glasses and slowly rubbed his eyes. "Well?"

Dale sighed. That would be how Orosco saw it. He ought to feel sorry for the man, but he didn't. "Last night one of Orosco's patients slipped and fell. The charge nurse asked me to check him over. He started telling me why he was in the hospital and how much he wanted to go home. He asked my opinion, so I told him."

"You told him to go home?"

"I told him it seemed reasonable." Seeing the frown form on Carleton's face, Dale went on to explain. "The patient was admitted a week ago for pneumonia. His chart showed he hadn't had a fever for five days. He was on oral antibiotics, no IVs. He was eating well and feeling good."

Carleton's frown deepened. "You don't find it inappropriate, advising a patient to go against a doctor's orders?"

"Not when the doctor is Orosco."

Carleton had a pained look. "And if the patient suffers because he went home too early, who is liable?"

It was more a statement than a question, and Dale took it as such. Twin patches of red appeared on his cheeks. As he leaned forward his stethoscope fell to the floor. "What about the hospital's liability for letting a man like Orosco on the staff? Everybody knows he overadmits patients. He herds them in like cattle so he can pay for his yacht and his Malibu beachhouse. At best, he's a mediocrity."

From the look on Carleton's face, Dale saw that he had gone too far, but he was too fired up to care. He picked up his stethoscope and angrily slung it over his neck.

"That's not for you to judge," Carleton snapped.

"Then who does? Some bureaucratic review board, made up of people like Orosco? They thrive on rules and red tape. It makes them important. They exist because doctors don't take care of their own problems." Dale threw up his hands. "So a bunch of bureaucrats does it for us. Great. And what about the patient?" He shook his head with frustration. "It's all wrong."

"Your arrogance is insufferable." Carleton rose from his chair and moved to the window. He tugged at his collar, twisting his neck uncomfortably, as he stared at the hospital's cold granite walls.

Dale felt compelled to go on, despite Carleton's obvious disapproval. "Maybe you're right," he said in a voice that admitted no such thing. "But that doesn't change the fact that Orosco is incompetent."

Carleton shook his head. "You think that unless you, Mr. Hero in Scrub Clothes, are right there, the world is going to hell in a handbasket. Well, Dr. Kildare, you have another think coming."

Dale said nothing.

Carleton took his silence as acquiescence. It softened him a bit. "I agree that Dr. Orosco is not among the best, a rank held by only a few. Most doctors are average, or mediocre, as you choose to put it. And a few are substandard. As in any profession. Part of maturing as a professional is recognizing that and turning it to one's advantage."

Dale put in a word for old Hippocrates, whom he considered the lost and forsworn idol of all true men of medicine. "Mediocrity may be okay for car salesmen or ward clerks. Not for doctors. Not when human life is at stake."

Carleton moved slowly back to his chair. "Mediocrity, as you call it, is as much a part of life as illness, or death. I prefer to use the term 'average.' Without it, there would not be enough healers in the world. The challenge to those of us who teach is to turn average into effective."

To Dale, Carleton's attitude was offensive. It smacked of the Peter Principle—performance at the lowest common denominator. The gulf between them was too great to bridge. "I guess we'll just have to agree to disagree." He started to rise from his chair.

"Please, sit down." Carleton waved his hand. "Orosco is not why I asked you here. I need a moment more of your time."

Dale sat back.

"Tell me about Ron Orloff."

So that was it. Dale actually felt a certain relief. Ron's illness was becoming harder to handle. He could use Carleton's help. Carleton was stodgy and conventional, but he had a blend of experience and—yes—wisdom. He'd give him that. He had misgivings, nevertheless, about how much he should tell Carleton.

"He has leukemia." He paused, knowing that Carleton already knew. "I think I know how he got it." As soon as he said it, he wished he hadn't.

Carleton looked puzzled and concerned. "What are you talking about?"

"Ron has somehow been contaminated with plutonium. We found it in his urine."

"And why did I have to prod you for news of this importance?" Carleton was plainly annoyed.

"Ron didn't want anyone to know he was sick. And I felt we had things under control. You know how it is when you're a resident." He smiled briefly. And he wondered why Carleton wasn't blown away by the news.

"Yes," said Carleton with a wrinkled brow, "it's easy to get overprotective about these matters." He chuckled softly. "You know, I'm not here just to badger you. I'm also here to help."

Dale nodded. "I do feel protective of Ron. And that throws my perspective out of whack."

"*You?*" Carleton made a gesture of mock surprise, and they both laughed. Then Carleton's expression became grave. "It's a tragic mishap. We need to be sure the proper authorities look into this."

Dale was irked. Turn it over to some chief of some department somewhere. Carleton seemed to think that organizations had more intelligence than people.

"Notify them if you want."

"And you will confine yourself to your duties as a resident. I'll take care of this. I know the chain of command around here. That's my job, and I'm good at it. You're good at your job. There's no need for overlap here."

Dale, about to object, thought better of it. He could continue on his own. He was pretty good at it. Hadn't he just caught Robert Heffron in an outright lie? All he would get from Carleton was disapproval and an order to cease and desist. Carleton, no matter how much he might care about Ron Orloff, had the school's reputation to protect. And that would include the life-sustaining Heffron Foundation. That's what he was paid for. If Ron's well-being and the school's well-being came into conflict, he knew who would come out ahead.

"Yes," Dale said, "you are good at your job."

As he started to rise, his beeper went off. "Code Blue, Coronary Care Unit! Code Blue, CCU!"

They both knew what that meant as Dale bolted out the door, their conversation cut short by a need to respond to a cry for help—the reason they were all there, within those granite walls.

"I said a straight blade, goddammit!" Ron Orloff hurled the curved laryngoscope across the room, where it clanged against the wall, leaving a streak of saliva and blood. His hands trembled as he snatched the straight-bladed laryngoscope from the nurse. He pried open the dying patient's mouth and sought the vocal cords, then shoved an endotracheal tube down her throat. He looked up, breathing hard, to see the CCU nurse had stopped pumping on the patient's chest.

"What are you standing there for?!" he barked. "Continue CPR! You know what that means, don't you? Pump!"

"Doctor, she has a blood pressure," the nurse said quietly, pointing to the monitor.

Suddenly embarrassed, Ron took refuge in listening to the patient's heartbeat, which was now strong. He saw she was breathing on her own too.

She was going to live. He took a deep breath and

closed his eyes. When he opened them, he saw the patient looking at him, her eyes terror-stricken.

"You're going to be all right, now. Your heart acted up for a minute, but it's fine now."

As Ron walked around the bed to retrieve the laryngoscope he had thrown, Dale came racing into the room. "Is everything under control?"

Ron pointed to the patient. "She had a couple runs of ventricular tachycardia. We brought her out of it."

They left the patient and moved over to the monitor. Dale scanned the rhythm strips and the list of medications administered during the arrest. "Good work, Ron."

"I almost lost it in there." Ron wiped the sweat from his brow.

Dale gave him a hard look. "Let's talk."

Ron stared at the floor. "Just let me check this for a minute." He went back into the patient's room. Dale could see him talking to the nurses, then speaking to the patient, his hand on her shoulder. When he returned, they went to the doctor's lounge.

As Ron flopped down on the couch, Dale handed him a cup of coffee and sat on the table in front of him. "What's wrong, Ron?"

"Everything. I acted like a total asshole during that arrest. It could have cost that woman her life." He set his coffee down, and buried his face in his hands.

This was, Dale knew, the intern's eternal lament. He reached out and touched Ron's arm. "We all get uptight during a cardiac arrest. The fact remains, you saved that woman's life."

Ron grunted halfheartedly. "I was not in control, Dale. I've never screamed at a nurse in my life. This was the second time in a week. I don't know, maybe I should get away from all this sickness. I have enough trouble handling my own."

"My offer stands. Don't come to work. You'll get credit for your rotation. I'll take your call. I have to be here anyway."

Ron studied his hands, then looked up. "Maybe you're right. I could use the time to do some research. Dr. Heffron gave me a long list of articles to read."

"Heffron!" Dale couldn't believe his ears. "He keeps popping up like bad news."

A look of reserve came into Ron's eyes. "I've gotten to know him, Dale. Remember that talk show? It got me to thinking. So I went to see him. He wants to help me. He's given me hope. I know I've had my doubts, but I think he's an okay guy."

Dale stared at him. Ron was his intern and his friend. Whatever he thought, he knew it would be unwise to question Heffron's help. It was something to grab on to. Something Ron needed that he, Dale, had been unable to give him. One thing was perfectly clear. Right now Ron Orloff believed in Heffron.

"That's good enough for me, Ron," Dale said, wishing deep down he believed it himself.

28

The nurse moved like a shadow through the dimly lit cancer ward. She was sure no one saw her, but she acted completely naturally, as though she belonged. She had picked the all-night graveyard shift because it was always quiet. It was so quiet she could hear her starched uniform rustling against her white nylons, and her white rubber-soled shoes softly kissing the floor as she walked. If anyone were to notice her, she would fit in with the almost funereal atmosphere of drowsing patients, dark corridors, and the unmistakable odor of sickness.

The nurse knew about the blackboard behind the ward clerk's desk, where the names of the newly demised were etched in chalk. The slate was clean tonight. So far.

She looked at her wristwatch. There was only one nurse on duty this time of night, a pitiful reflection of the nursing shortage. One nurse for twenty or so patients. A male nurse at that. She had seen him starting his nightly vital signs checks. He would be moving methodically from room to room, bed to bed. She was counting on the fact that he would be totally occupied. She did not expect him near the medication room or the nurse's station for at least twenty minutes.

As she approached the nurse's station, she glanced down the empty hall. Reassured, she moved toward the chart rack and removed one of the blue vinyl looseleaf files. She looked through the order sheets, then put the chart back. She scanned through two more until she found what she wanted. She smiled and tucked the chart under her arm as she headed for the medication room, which was set off in a corner apart from the patient rooms. She was pleased to see the light was already on. Probably to discourage the drug thieves among the employees from sneaking around in the dark for a fix.

Well, she was no drug thief. That was for sure. She was a drug giver. A giver of long-sought peace, of freedom. She smiled again and lifted her chin as she thought of herself in that light. She took one last look down the hall before slipping into the med room and locking the door behind her.

She parked herself on a stool and opened the chart, running her finger along the most recent chemotherapy order, which had been written several hours earlier. It was a single-dose order for one of the most toxic chemotherapeutic drugs.

"I'm ready," she whispered to herself as she wiped her moist palms on her thighs.

She looked through the glass doors of the medication cupboard and found the drug she needed. She sorted through the keys Heffron had slipped her. She tried each until she found the one that opened the cupboard. She held her breath as she heard footsteps outside the door, then slipped off the stool and knelt on the floor, as if looking for something. The footsteps faded. She stood up and began quickly extracting what she needed from the cupboards and drawers.

When she was finished, she held a syringe full of brilliant scarlet medicine up to the light, double-checking the dose. She glanced at the order sheet again, and thought the small change she had made looked authentic. She cleaned the counter meticulously, leaving everything as she had found it. Only then did she tuck the chart under her arm, flick out the light, and put the syringe and empty vial in the pocket of her uniform before emerging from the med room. She returned to the nurse's station and put the chart back in its slot before glancing at her watch. She thought she could hear the floor nurse finishing his duties at the other end of the ward. Perfect timing. He wouldn't be going into the patient rooms again for a while.

She could feel her heart throbbing. She felt a-tingle, a little heady. She sat down and lowered her head to normalize the circulation. No time to be having one of those silly hot flashes! She tossed her head, as if to shake off her nervousness, stood up with alacrity, and moved on to her destination.

Ah, how peaceful and serene he looked, lying there. As if he knew, even in his sleep, what was about to happen. She felt an impulse as she stood over him to wake him, show him the syringe, let him know that it was she who was about to save him from his agony. It was she who would let him carry the serenity she now saw on this young—oh, too young—dark, handsome face into eternity.

She could not resist the urge to lean over and gently touch his forehead, perhaps to convince herself that the sweat she saw was real—a sign that he was not as serene as one might think. He was suffering, even in his sleep. She knew that. She knew he would have been grateful for her visit, could he have known why she was there.

She felt her heart jump as she heard the patient in the next bed groan. She stood stark still as she watched him turn over to face her. She peered hard at him. Even in the poorly lit room, she could see that his eyes were closed. But what if he opened them? He might not understand, might call out. She moved around the bed and drew the curtain.

Returning to the young patient, she turned on her headlamp so she could find the injection port on his IV tubing without having to grope for it. Spotting it, she pulled an alcohol swab out of her pocket, and began cleaning it. She suppressed a nervous giggle as she suddenly realized the incongruity of this ingrained habit. Protecting someone from an infection he would not live long enough to acquire.

She threw down the swab and quickly pulled out the syringe with its ruby-red liquid, only to catch herself in yet another old habit. This time she was holding the syringe up to the light and squeezing the bubbles out. Her hands trembled momentarily. She had all her life been trained to save lives—to remember the tiniest slip could cost a life, including shooting a few bubbles into a patient's bloodstream. And now . . .

"Know that you are not a messenger of death, but an angel of mercy," he had told her. Her hands stopped trembling as she reminded herself of that.

She cocked her head and stopped moving. Yes, footsteps, nearing the room. She turned off her headlamp and backed into the corner toward the head of the bed, crouching and holding her breath. The floor nurse came in, his headlamp on. He walked over to the curtain she had drawn closed and threw it open. The light from his headlamp gave his face an eerie quality. She could see he was frowning. He looked terribly young.

He left after perusing the room briefly without so much as a glance toward her. Thank God. She had almost blown it with something as simple as drawing a curtain. She could not allow herself to stop and wonder what had brought the floor nurse back.

She moved quickly now, plunging the needle into the rubber-covered IV port. She deftly pushed the red liquid into the plastic tubing, and on into the sleeping man's vein. Red, like blood.

After the syringe was empty, she flushed the red medicine through the tubing with the clear IV fluid that hung on the pole next to his bed. She thought she saw him stir, and guessed he might be feeling the sting of the strong drug in his vein. She hurriedly put the plastic cap back on the needle of the syringe and shoved it into her pocket.

She walked briskly to the door and looked toward

the nurse's station. She saw the floor nurse sitting at a desk, his head down as he wrote his reports. She slipped to the stairwell around the corner. She hurried down the stairs, every nerve of her body quivering with the excitement of what she had done.

29

Dale Harper stepped off the elevator, a doughnut and coffee in one hand, and a folder of X rays in the other. He heard the overhead page system reel off one command after another as the morning grind gathered momentum.

The paging sounded louder than usual, and somehow irritating, as he headed toward the nurse's station.

"Dr. Reynolds to surgery!" "Dr. Switzer, call extension 213!" "Dr. Orosco, to the ER stat!" And on and on.

As he walked, he wondered what the page operators looked like. It struck him as strange that the voices bossing people around all day actually belonged to human beings. People who had kids, bought groceries after work, watched television, and suffered colds, like everyone else.

As he approached the ward, his eyes automatically scanned the blackboard behind the clerk—the Black Death board—as some smart-ass had named it. After four weeks on the cancer service, the blackboard held no surprises for him. Except this morning.

Jesse Munoz.

He squinted in disbelief and moved closer to the board, a lump forming in his throat. He set his things down on the ward clerk's desk.

Jesse Munoz—dead. Maybe, when he overcame the shock, he would feel the grief. Shock, because they all believed that Jesse had beat the odds. He had finished his chemotherapy the day before. He had survived the infections, conquered the cancer. He was to go home today.

Jesse Munoz, dead at twenty-seven.

Dale felt a shiver run through him as he stood there, staring blankly at Jesse's name. He resisted an impulse to grab the eraser and wipe it out.

As he grappled with the immediacy of Jesse's death, he thought of Jon Werner. It was going to be hard on him. Jon probably already knew about it since he was usually on the ward before the others. Pulling himself together, Dale turned and headed for the doctor's lounge to find him.

"Hey, man, you wanna get your junk off my desk?" The ward clerk called after him.

She might as well have yelled at a wooden Indian.

As he pushed through the door of the lounge, Dale felt the lump in his throat tighten. He saw Jon slumped over the table in the middle of the room, his back to Dale. Ron Orloff sat next to him, looking worried and helpless.

Dale nodded silently at Ron as he walked up behind Jon. He gently rested his hand on Werner's shoulder. "Jon, I'm sorry." He didn't trust his voice to say anything more.

The rest was a blur. The screeching, grating sound of Jon's chair as he pushed back and leapt to his feet. A reeling sensation as something hit him and pitched him backward. Then Jon pressing him against the wall, his face so close their noses almost touched.

"You killed him, you son of a bitch! You goddamn son of a bitch! Murderer!" Jon screamed, his eyes rolling wildly.

Dale, stunned, finally reacted. He pushed Jon off him with such force that he threw him to the floor. "What in the hell is wrong with you?" He planted his feet over Jon, fists clenched, his eyes blazing with anger.

Jon bobbed back up, like a wiry prizefighter. Orloff rushed forward to restrain him as he came back at Dale.

Dale warded Ron off with his arm and shoved Jon onto the couch. He dropped down next to him, gripped him by the shoulders, and shook him. "Have you gone mad?" he shouted. "I ought to beat the hell out of you, you arrogant bastard! You can't accept death without finding someone to blame. And you call yourself a doctor!"

They glared at each other, breathing heavily. Finally, Dale relaxed his grip and got up, snorting with disgust. He paced the floor as Jon watched him in silence, still gasping for air. He stood over the table and leaned his arms on it, then crashed down on it with his fists.

Taking a deep breath, he straightened up. "I'm going to see my patients now." He struggled to control his voice. He could still feel his heart pounding. He pointed a trembling finger at Jon. "Don't you come near me."

He stalked out. As he passed the ward clerk, she whined, "Hey, you gonna get your stuff off my desk?"

He spun toward her. She stopped filing her nails and drew back, averting her eyes from the fury in his face, as, with one sweep of his hand, he sent the coffee and doughnut flying into her lap.

Dr. Carleton looked grim, his lips tight and unforgiving. What a thankless job the man had, Dale thought, as he sat across from the chief of medicine for the second time that week. Carleton's formality was not lost on Dale. He sat rigidly, waiting to hear why he was summoned, though certain it concerned his confrontation with Werner. He wondered too, whether Heffron had registered any complaints. Somehow he didn't think that was Heffron's style.

Carleton cleared his throat. "These are serious charges against you, Dr. Harper. This is not just an

Orosco complaining about an insolent resident." He bent over the paper on his desk. "This is an assault on a colleague, scalding the ward clerk, and, finally, the death of a patient, which appears to be the direct consequence of an order you wrote." He looked up and peered at Dale over his glasses.

Dale felt himself tense up as he again heard, without the anger, the absurd accusation that he had caused Jesse Munoz's death. He had tried to put the incident out of his mind, attributing Jon's outburst to emotional instability.

But now, here was Carleton, making the same charges, in a grave tone. And being coldly specific about it.

Dale looked the older man squarely in the eye. "I don't know why Jesse died," he said. "I had nothing to do with it."

Carleton arched his eyebrows in surprise. He held up a sheaf of papers bound together with rubber bands. "You don't think ordering fifty milligrams of andromycin is sufficient reason?"

Dale looked at his chief incredulously. Fifty milligrams was an outrageous dose. He couldn't recall what the amount was that he had written for, but he knew it wasn't anywhere near that much. "I don't know what you're talking about. I wrote for a standard amount, most likely five milligrams." He reached out his hand. "Is that Jesse's chart? I'd like to see it."

Carleton pulled the rubber bands off the papers that recorded Jesse's last days, and found the sheet with Dale's order on it. He pushed it across the desk. "Did you write that order for andromycin, dated the eighteenth?"

Dale began to nod, then drew back, startled, as he saw that it did in fact say fifty milligrams. "No, not for fifty milligrams! I wrote it for five milligrams."

He looked up at Carleton, visibly shaken. Could he have accidentally stuck a zero on there? And if he had, wouldn't the nurses have picked it up? They would have known fifty milligrams was an error—a lethal dose.

He stared at the order again, oblivious of everything but the figure "50," looming up at him like a newspaper headline. His mind buzzed with possibilities as he tried to pull his thoughts together. He had been tired that morning—not unusual after a night on call. Mistakes happened. They had happened to him. They happened to every doctor. But this? It just wasn't possible.

He looked up at Carleton, his face taut. "I don't know what to say. The order is in my writing, but I'm sure I wrote for five milligrams. I had to figure the dosage by hand because I couldn't find my calculator."

Carleton said in a gentler voice, "You perhaps meant five, but inadvertently wrote fifty. You may have been overtired."

Dale put the paper down and cradled his head in his hands. He ran his fingers through his hair. No matter how you looked at it, there it was. How could he deny it? "Maybe Jon was right. Maybe I did kill Jesse Munoz," he muttered, shaking his head.

He looked up. "I don't see how I could have made a mistake like that. Nor why it wasn't caught. It doesn't make sense."

Carleton stood up, and walked over to the window behind his desk. He removed his glasses and gave Dale a thoughtful look. "Dale," he began in a tired voice, "medicine is an unforgiving mistress. We all make mistakes. We're only human. But because someone may die from our mistakes, we must go that one extra step that other professions needn't take: We must be infallible."

He looked almost kindly at Dale, who sat with his head buried in his hands. "Of course, no one actually is infallible. But we have to keep seeking it, like an impossible dream. If we let ourselves believe, even for a moment, that it's permissible to make a deadly mistake, we're finished as professionals. We become the mediocrities that you so despise."

Carleton sighed heavily as he moved back to his desk. "Let's look at the facts. You made a mistake. It may have, and probably did, cost a young man his life. But before you go off feeling sorry for yourself, you need to realize one thing." He hesitated as he saw Dale slowly lift his head.

Carleton sat down, clasping his hands. "Any doctor who tells you he has never killed a patient is lying, to you and to himself."

Dale searched his mentor's face. Carleton had touched on a delicate subject, one that doctors rarely discussed. Death was no stranger. He had toiled with the guilt of the "what-ifs" alone. Cases where he might have saved a life if he had just done something a little differently. What if he had thought of getting this lab test or that X ray? What if he had put the patient in the hospital sooner? What if he had given the patient a different drug, or no drug at all? Alone in his speculations of his own flaws, he had no idea what other doctors suffered through.

The person he least expected as a kindred spirit was Carleton. Carleton, whose job it was to call him down, was offering some understanding at this most painful moment. He felt a flush of gratitude.

"Knowing that others may have made a similar mistake doesn't make mine any easier to accept," he said.

"Nor should it," Carleton put his glasses back on and began reading from another report. "In your case, you've been distracted by matters other than medicine."

As if to demonstrate, Carleton moved his finger along the sheet of paper, reading. "I have here a report regarding your snooping around in the microbiology department after hours." He looked up. "You have gone against my advice, and have continued prying into a matter that is none of your business."

Carleton held up the pages of Jesse's chart, giving Dale a hard look. "It's taking its toll, and it has to stop. Otherwise"—he hesitated a moment—"you will be dismissed from the program. No matter what I might do to stop it, if only for your father's sake." There was a note of warning—a finality—in his voice.

Dale listened to Carleton with a certain distraction, his mind consumed with the image of Jesse Munoz, that last day he saw him alive. A bright smile on his face—the look of a man who had conquered the impossible and was justly proud of it.

Then, an image of his father on his deathbed. The father he had worshipped and tried to live up to.

"My father wouldn't want you protecting me," he said, "not for his sake. He would want me treated as anyone else." He stared down at his hands. "And that's what I want too."

Carleton swiveled slowly in his chair until his back was to Dale. "All right," he said to the window behind his desk. "Any more trouble, and I will propose an indefinite leave of absence."

An indefinite leave of absence. Propose. How good we become at couching our words in this profession, Dale thought bitterly. "How long will I have to take this drug, Doctor?" "Indefinitely." Because "forever" was too hard to explain. And "until you die" was too cruel.

"I am sorry," was all Dale could say to Carleton, whose silhouette seemed to cut a hard, unforgiving edge. "I am sorry for Jesse Munoz and his family. And for all the Jesse Munozes in the world. I will never forget him."

He slowly rose from his chair and walked toward the door, feeling a heaviness of spirit he had never imagined possible. Carleton's shadow remained unmoving behind him, like a dark, flat painting, smudged against the Los Angeles sky.

30

"To death! How's it go? 'Death be not proud, though some have called thee mighty and dreadful,' blah, blah . . . Oh, yeah—'Die not, poor death, nor yet canst thou kill me!' " Dale brandished his drink, clinking Nina's glass in a clumsy toast. The contents splattered and dribbled down his hand.

Nina smiled uneasily. She had never seen him like this. Abrupt and withdrawn. He had whisked her off to dinner without a word, responding to her efforts at conversation with unintelligible grunts as he gunned the car down the freeway. When they had arrived at Gift of the Sea, Dale promptly ordered them each a Manhattan and guzzled his down while Nina was still stirring hers. After his second drink, she noticed his speech slurring. He had never taken more than one drink before, not with her.

"I thought you despised Manhattans."

"I do," he replied as he hefted his glass once more. "To death, without which our economy would crumble. Think of all the unemployed undertakers, coffin makers, grave diggers, lawn mowers, weapons makers, evangelists, and, above all, doctors—were it not for death!"

Nina noticed people glancing toward their table. She reached for his glass.

"Enough speeches—an orator you're not." She clasped her hand over his and looked for a telltale sign of what was troubling him. As his wandering eyes came to rest on hers, she caught a glint of pain, but then it was gone.

"Dale, what's wrong?" She gripped his hand firmly.

He looked at her for a long moment. His heart ached at what he saw. She looked so beautiful, but . . . frightened. And a little blurry at the edges. He took a deep breath. It was time to own his pain. He could see that. It was the one valuable lesson he had taken away from psychiatry in medical school. Learn to own your feelings—face them head on. Then, and only then, could you master your ship.

What was he accomplishing by guzzling down these sickening drinks? He felt like kicking himself as he marked the cloud darkening Nina's brow.

He slipped out of his side of the booth and sat next to her. He drew her to him and gently ran his hand over her soft dark brown hair.

She sensed there was something terribly wrong, but by the tenderness of his touch, she knew he was no longer fighting it. He would tell her in due time. She guessed it had something to do with a patient and she knew what it must be.

As a radiologist she no longer had to deal with the agony of standing by to watch a patient die. She could almost feel his anguish as she tried to imagine the burden he was carrying.

Dale broke the silence. "Are you hungry?"

Without looking up, she shook her head.

He lifted her chin with a gentle finger. "I'm sorry. I'm not myself."

She sat up, dabbing at her moist eyes with a tissue. She knew she was overreacting.

"Let's do something fun," he said. "How about the Marx brothers? They're playing at the Nuart."

Nina smiled. The two of them had a special niche in their hearts for the Marx brothers. Uncannily, their all-time favorite was the same, *Duck Soup*. That surely meant some kind of kinship, though it was hard to attribute any depth to the Marx brothers.

"I'd love to," she said, gratified to see his eyes light up.

He paid for the drinks and they drove in silence to the theater. It was a favorite retreat, though almost everything they saw there could be rented for two dollars at a video store. This, Nina thought, was another thing that showed how much alike they were— even amid a hodgepodge of dissimilarities. A movie was a movie, meant to be viewed on the silver screen, in a darkened theater, popcorn on your lap, sticky spilled Cokes under your feet, couples laughing, crying, whispering, fondling each other, all around you.

They settled back in their seats with a giant carton of popcorn. The feature, incredibly, was *Duck Soup*. They guffawed together as Groucho and company marched out hailing Fredonia in a style reminiscent of Gilbert and Sullivan. They snickered and held hands as Groucho and Chico mimicked each other in the famous mirror scene. And afterward, they left the theater, arms around each other, seemingly holding each other up as they lockstepped their way toward the street.

They drove home a circuitous route, up the Pacific Coast Highway and through Malibu Canyon. High in the Santa Monica Mountains, they pulled off the road and got out of the car to watch the sun sink into the sea. And it was there, moved by the transcending beauty of Nature, that Dale turned to her. In the dim light she could see how pale he had become.

"Nina, two days ago, a patient died because of me." He looked at her forlornly. "I don't know how to handle it. I can't live with the fact that my carelessness cost a life. Right now, I can't tolerate the idea of being a doctor."

Nina leaned against the hood of the car, still warm from the labors of the old engine beneath it. What he was struggling with was nothing new to her. Medical school. First they told you what great healing powers you would learn, bolstering your ego. But they never told you what to do with your feelings when your first patient died.

She stood and waited, letting him tell her in his own time. And this he proceeded to do, in the halting, yet driven voice of the confessional.

"I accidentally wrote an order for ten times the intended dose of chemotherapy for Jesse Munoz, the man with testicular cancer, and it killed him. One stupid decimal point. One stupid doctor." He paused, glancing at Nina as she quietly listened.

He pushed on. "I thought old Carleton was wrong at first, then I saw the order myself. Fifty milligrams, instead of five. I didn't want to believe it, but there it was. He shoved it right in my face."

Nina bled for him silently. "You must be going through hell," she said finally. "You don't have to go on."

"There's not much more to tell. The nurse who administered the medication insists she gave five milligrams, but nobody believes her."

Nina frowned. "Why not?"

"They say she's just trying to cover herself. A nurse is supposed to catch gross errors like that. God knows how many times a nurse protects the patient when the doctor fouls up."

Nina's eyes brightened as she saw the hole he had dug for himself. "You obviously don't believe her either."

"What do you mean?" He gave her a puzzled look.

"Well, if she says she gave five milligrams, and you think you killed the patient, then you're as much as accusing the nurse of lying." It seemed plain enough to Nina. In her excitement she grasped his shoulders and shook him. "Don't you see what this means? If she's not guilty, then you're not guilty. Dale, you didn't do it!"

"I hadn't thought of it that way."

Nina turned to face the ocean with her arms clasped to her chest, shoulders hunched against the cold breeze coming off the ocean. "What about that poor nurse? Have you talked to her?"

"No. I never thought about how she might be feeling." He chuckled quietly. "I've been bogged down feeling sorry for myself, without giving a thought to Jesse, his family, or that nurse."

He saw Nina shivering and he threw his jacket around her shoulders. "You're cold. I'll take you home."

She shook her head. "You need to talk to that nurse, and I'm going with you."

Something glowed inside of him.

Lou Ann Hayes was a curly-haired blonde on the frail side, but attractive in a shy sort of way. She kept playing with her opal ring, shifting it from one hand to the other. She eyed Dale and Nina nervously. The three of them sat around a small table in the oncology lounge, where only a few days before Dale and Jon Werner had been at each other's throats. It was Lou Ann's last night on duty. She had been fired.

"I gave Jesse Munoz five milligrams of andromycin, Dr. Harper. I know I did." She spoke slowly but not, Dale thought, with much conviction.

"I'd like to believe you, Lou Ann. But how can you be sure?"

"I can see it in my mind's eye." She closed her eyes as if to establish her point. "Andromycin comes in thirty-milligram vials. If I'd given fifty, I would have had to open a second vial. I would have remembered that."

She slipped her ring back onto her right hand and looked up at Nina, as if expecting more assurance from another woman. "And besides, I know fifty milligrams of andromycin would kill a person. I wouldn't have given it if you had held a gun to my head."

Nina nodded. "What would you have done, Lou Ann?"

"I would have called the charge nurse. But I didn't

have to. The order said five milligrams. And that's what I gave."

"Why were you fired?"

The nurse shrugged unhappily. "Nobody believes me. I hear they found a lethal level of andromycin in his blood."

Dale had not heard the autopsy results, and the news startled him. His doubt returned, taking an even firmer grip than before. "How do you explain that?"

"I can't, unless someone else came and gave it. Maybe someone was trying to kill Jesse. But then, why wouldn't they just give him the drug? Why fool with the order sheet and draw attention to themselves?" Lou Ann's eyes moistened. "I just don't know."

Dale and Nina looked at each other. "Why would someone want to kill Jesse, Lou Ann?" Nina asked.

"I don't know, I just don't know. I guess everyone has enemies. All I know is I'm out of a job, and I'll probably never find work in nursing again." Her face was glum. She removed her ring again, rolling it between her palms, as if to make a wish.

Dale stood up abruptly, rubbing his hands together as a new possibility dawned. "Someone came along after you gave the drug," he whispered, as though to himself, "and changed the order. Slipped a zero in there after the five. Then gave him the fatal dose."

Lou Ann shrugged her slim shoulders. "I suppose it could have happened like that."

Dale's excitement grew as he thought about it. Someone had made it look as though he had been responsible. For what reason? That too was becoming all too clear—if he was guilty, he was discredited, maybe out of the residency program, out of everyone's hair. Maybe Jesse Munoz had enemies, but certainly Dale Harper had them.

"Lou Ann, aren't there carbon copies of the order sheets?"

"Yes. The carbon goes to the hospital pharmacy."

"And when is it removed from the chart?"

"As soon as the order is taken off by the nurse, she pulls the carbon and takes it to the pharmacy to get the medication."

"So if someone changed my order by adding a zero, they would need to find the carbon?"

"If they were on their toes," Nina chimed in.

Lou Ann seemed flustered by Dale's questions. "I guess. I don't really know. I do know the carbon said five milligrams, because that's my final checkpoint before I draw up the drug. If someone changed it, it was after I did my job."

"That's it!" Nina exclaimed, jumping to her feet. "Lou Ann, can you show us where the carbons are kept?"

Lou Ann glanced around the room, as if seeking help from an invisible source. "I suppose so." She wiped her clammy palms on her skirt. "What do you expect to find?"

"Just how clever our tamperer is," Dale said.

Lou Ann's key let them into the pharmacy, the room where the drug that killed Jesse had been drawn up only days earlier. Below the medication cupboards were file cabinets, marked alphabetically. The room was small, and the files were in plain view. "This must be where they keep the carbons," Lou Ann said, pointing.

Nina stopped at the file marked "M" and tugged at the drawer. It was locked.

"Try this." Lou Ann handed her a key, one of many on her belt.

Dale perused the shelves of medications until he found a bottle of andromycin. Through the glass, he could see that Lou Ann was right. Andromycin was in a thirty-milligram vial. That was a good omen. It lent credibility to her story.

"Got it!" Nina exclaimed, as the drawer slid open. She and Dale riffled through the files until they came to Munoz, Jesse. They pulled out a stack of flimsy yellow sheets and spread them over the counter. There were duplicate medication order sheets for every day of Jesse's long hospitalization—except for the day of his death.

"Holy Jesus!" Dale turned to a startled Lou Ann, who in turn looked at Nina.

A smile came to Nina's face as she understood. "The person who changed the order found the carbon and destroyed it!"

Lou Ann looked puzzled as she watched the two of them rejoicing over a missing piece of paper. "I don't get it," she said.

Nina explained as Dale put the file back in order. "If someone added a zero to the original, to make it appear authentic they would have had to find the carbon, put it under the original, make the change, then put the carbon back where it belonged. They probably didn't have time to do all that."

"Or they didn't think of it at the time," Dale said, closing the file drawer. "So they covered their tracks later by destroying the carbon, which still said five milligrams." He beamed at Lou Ann as though she were his savior. "I could kiss you!" He paused and laughed the hearty laugh of a man who has just broken the shackles of his bondage.

Nina happily threw herself into his outstretched arms. As he held her, he suspected this moment of vindication would be short-lived. He could almost feel a black cloud positioning itself over his head. The picture was becoming clearer. Someone was out for his hide. But seeing the joy in Nina's face, for one blissful moment he didn't give a damn.

31

Hector Cantrell felt like he was drowning. His eyes moved frantically around the dimly lit room, as if seeking a source of air. He hadn't felt so great the day before, but this was different. In the morning, just before the nurse checked his blood pressure and temperature, he felt dizzy, and he told her so. When he tried to sit up he thought he would keel over. She nodded perfunctorily and went on about her business, which apparently didn't include him.

Then a team of doctors came through, smiling, asking questions, chatting among themselves. But none of them asked him if he was dizzy. They didn't give a damn, and he was getting dizzier by the minute, his brain wobbling chaotically. Even worse, he wasn't sure which one of those guys in the white monkey suits was his doctor. He had been in the hospital four days and he swore he had a different doctor every day, not one of them looking as old as Danny, his oldest son.

He slept fitfully through the day, and when his doctors came by on afternoon rounds, he missed his chance to speak up because he was dozing.

He wished to God those doctors were here now. The breathing problem had started about an hour before. For a while previously, he was actually feeling better, the dizziness relenting after a nurse finally listened to him and paged the on-call doctor around ten P.M. Yet another doctor he had never seen before! But this one helped him, at least for a while. Told him he was going to give him more fluids. Whatever, at least he was able to get some sleep.

Now his breathing was becoming unmanageable. He could feel his body straining with the effort of moving his chest. He propped himself up, getting a little relief, but then went into a coughing fit. He was alarmed by the white froth he brought up. Panting, he groped for the call button and pressed it with tremulous fingers. He squinted at the clock and saw it was six A.M. He heard the guy in the next bed snoring. He wished he could move air that effortlessly.

His team of doctors would be in shortly, but he was panicking. He couldn't wait. He hoped they wouldn't think he was a hopeless hypochondriac.

Damn! Where was that nurse? He'd get better care lying in the street! His head swam as he started to get out of bed and find a goddamn doctor in this goddamn miserable excuse for a hospital. Came in with a stomachache, for chrissake, and now he was smothering to death. Thanks to his goddamn wife. She made him come to the emergency room in the dead of the night. He should have known better.

He had one leg over the siderail, making good progress, he thought, when his vision went gray and he struggled for consciousness. He was vaguely aware of white shoes dancing jaggedly before his eyes, like bad TV reception, and his last thought as he hit the floor was, What do ya have to do to get a goddamn nurse around here? Die?

Nina left Lenny Perkins's office in a quandary. He had railed at her royally for her part in Dale Harper's escapades. He brandished a pile of incident reports under her nose, making ugly threats. She stood up to him, but the confrontation took its toll, and she shakily hurried back to her cubicle to page Dale. When her phone rang she snatched it up. "Dale?"

An impersonal female voice responded. "This is the

oncology nurse. Dr. Harper is in the middle of a procedure. Can I take a message?"

Nina tried to contain her disappointment. "You're a professional," she whispered to herself. Those three words had seen her through some difficult times, helping her remain cool. Like when she had to do her first rectal exam on a male patient. Or when a patient was rude and she felt like responding in kind.

"I beg your pardon?" the nurse asked, sounding impatient.

"This is Dr. Yablonsky, in radiology. It's important that I talk to Dr. Harper as soon as possible. When will he be done?"

The nurse retreated slightly. "Well, he's inserting a central line, but he's just started, so I'd say about twenty minutes."

"Thank you, I'll call back." She paced the office with her hands clasped behind her. It seemed as though her worst fears were coming true. Dale attracted trouble like a magnet. It couldn't go on like this. It had to stop somewhere. They had to talk, and right away.

"Where is Dr. Harper?" Nina asked the ward clerk.

The clerk, a corpulent Hispanic woman somewhere between thirty and fifty, stared past her. "He's gone, miss," she said after turning her head slightly as if looking for him.

"You're a professional," Nina told herself as she checked an impulse to grab the clerk by the collar and shake her. Instead she spoke in an even tone. "He's here. Find me the charge nurse right now, please."

The ward clerk looked hesitant, as though considering whether this was part of her job, when one of the nurses approached and pointed down the hall. "Dr. Harper is in room 602."

"Thank you." Nina strode briskly to the room and looked in. She saw a tall figure in a blue paper gown, mask, and head cover. He was leaning over a patient who was mostly hidden by blue paper drape cloths. A nurse stood across from him. While she was sure the figure was Dale—she thought she would know him in a clown suit—Nina felt suddenly shy, as though intruding. She tiptoed into the room.

The gowned figure looked up. She could see the pleasure in his eyes. He waved a gloved hand. "Nina, come in. I could use your help."

He stepped back from the bed, his hands raised to avoid contamination. "I'll need a larger bore needle," he said to the nurse. "Let's go with a fourteen-gauge."

He moved toward Nina as the nurse left the room. "I'm putting in a central line. This woman has no veins left; that's all the good chemotherapy has done her." He shook his head. "I don't know why we're giving chemotherapy to a comatose patient who has maybe two or three days to live."

Nina looked over at the patient, a black woman. She was beautiful, despite the dry, chafed lips, the gaping mouth, the beads of sweat, and the scant patches of hair. Nina felt a pang as she realized the woman was probably younger than herself. "Who is she?" she whispered.

"Annie Snowden. Breast."

Nina nodded. He had told her about Annie. She felt as though she knew her.

"I canceled her chemo last week, but Werner reordered it. He thinks the stuff will raise the dead." He sighed. "It doesn't matter now. He can have his way. It can't hurt her anymore."

Nina looked at him. "But you're hurting."

He turned away from her as he saw the nurse returning, and reached for the needle she handed him. "You don't need to stay, Joan. Dr. Yablonsky can help me." The hospital was so short on nurses that he was glad to let her catch up on other duties. And he wanted to be with Nina.

Nina moved next to Dale and watched as he deftly slipped the needle under Annie's right collarbone.

Annie didn't even flinch. Proper placement of the needle in the large subclavian vein was established as dark
red blood gushed out. He quickly took the guidewire
that Nina handed him and threaded it into the needle,
arresting the blood flow. He then slipped the needle
out, leaving the guidewire in place. Nina handed him
a plastic catheter that he threaded over the guidewire.
Then he pulled out the guidewire and hooked the
catheter to plastic tubing connected like a lifeline to
a bottle full of liquid nutrients.

"Why give her IVs at all if she's dying?" Nina
asked. "Aren't you just drawing it out?"

Dale was suturing the catheter to the skin to prevent its dislodgement. "One thing I can't do is let a
patient die of starvation or dehydration. I've seen it
happen."

"But look at her. She's not feeling anything." Nina
couldn't take her eyes off that face, that beautiful,
youthful face.

He peeled off his gloves and mask and tore away
the drape sheets. "Maybe I'm just indulging myself.
But I can't let her starve. Besides," he added as he
stared solemnly at his patient, "who are we to say that
someone in her state is feeling nothing? Maybe she
has dreams, and if she's hungry or thirsty, she could
be having nightmares about being stranded on a des-
ert, or in a concentration camp. Who knows what
she's really going through?"

Nina shuddered. You didn't have to face this horror
when you were a radiologist. She turned away, trying
to lose herself in the banality of cleaning up the mess
Dale had made. Invasive procedures, such as inserting
a central IV line, led to bloodied bedclothes. What
would the family think, if they saw her like this?

She helped Dale untie his gown. She stood behind
him and let a hand rest on his shoulder. He turned
around, his eyes soft. "Thank you," he said, "for
understanding."

*   *   *

They sat in the doctor's lounge, both drained. Dale offered Nina coffee that she took black. He poured himself a cup and flopped into an old lounge chair.

"What's on your mind? I know you didn't turn up just to help with a CVP line." He smiled, but she could see it was an effort. The cancer ward was sapping his spirit each day. Somehow he found the resilience to spring back, but she wondered if he lost a little ground each time he lost a patient. She wished she could wave a wand and take him away from all this.

Even Lenny's tirade might be a welcome distraction. "I just had a rousing conversation with Lenny Perkins. He says you're in big trouble."

Dale chuckled. "So what else is new?"

"We need to take this seriously, Dale. Lenny says there's going to be a high-level meeting about you soon. And it could be bad news." She sipped her coffee. "I'm in trouble too, it appears."

He leaned forward, immediately concerned. "What do they want with you?"

"They want me to mind my own business."

"And not hang around with me."

She nodded. "I'm sure that's part of it."

Dale got up and put his arm around her. "Nina, I don't know how serious all this is, but maybe we'd better stop seeing each other for a while."

She shook her head vigorously. "We're together. And we'll go through it together."

He touched his fingers to her chin and turned her face toward him. "I love you for standing by me, but it isn't worth your career."

"And what about yours?"

He pursed his lips thoughtfully. "I don't think they would dare throw me out. They know I wouldn't go quietly. Bad publicity is worse than having a nosy resident around."

"Maybe they'd take a chance on the publicity."

Dale gave a short hollow laugh. "All right. So I'm

taking a chance. But I don't want you taking the same chance."

She was touched more than she showed and kissed him softly on the forehead. "Dale, can't you see what's happening? Someone is setting you up. That someone wants to get rid of you. Have you forgotten Jesse Munoz?"

"That may be true, Nina. But I'm not about to run for cover. I have to go on doing what I think is right, and getting through this blasted residency of mine. But"—his tone softened—"you're not part of it. I'm sorry I ever brought you into it."

She leaned back and sighed. "I want to ask you a question, and I want you to think it through. You don't need to answer now. You can sleep on it."

He looked at her, waiting.

"What would change if you stopped all this investigating now? Isn't it presumptuous to assume you're going to make that much of a difference? We became doctors because we want to make a difference. But don't you make a difference when you help an Annie Snowden meet death with peace and dignity? And isn't that enough?"

He sighed. He did believe he could make a difference. He had believed that all his life. He wanted her to understand. "Maybe it is presumptuous, Nina, but if there's a difference to be made, I can make it. And if there are people who are threatened enough to try to stop me, then they must believe as I do. That I make that kind of difference."

Nina laughed, shaking her head with exaggerated hopelessness. "I am really dumb. All I've done is fire you up even more. You thrive on conflict."

He shrugged, feeling a measure of rejection. His beeper went off, directing him to call Dr. Rodale. He and Nina looked at each other, both somehow relieved that chance had ended a conversation that wasn't going well. He picked up the phone and dialed

Rodale's extension. When he hung up, Nina saw his jaw tighten.

"I have to get down to the ICU," he said in a flat voice. "Another patient has turned bad."

32

Dale pushed through a pair of swinging white doors into the Intensive Care Unit. It was like entering a different world. The place seemed to vibrate with an energy all its own—like an invisible force that refused to let the dying die.

There was the constant sighing of the ventilators as they breathed life into the near-dead. Well over half the patients were hooked up to these mechanical white knights.

Then there was the inharmonious bleeping of cardiac monitors as pictures of green spikes and peaks flitted across banks of televisionlike screens. Nurses, doctors, and technicians bustled in and out of patient rooms. Only the patients were still.

Dale moved toward the nurse's station that was the hub of the ICU. From there the nurses could see into any one of the sixteen rooms, a layout that helped them keep a close eye on their charges. He spotted Steve Rodale coming toward him and waved. He didn't like the grim look on Steve's face.

Steve was a good resident. He had tall dark good looks and liquid brown eyes that made the nurses swoon. He was gay.

Steve and Dale had worked together many times during their training, and Dale had watched Steve become one of the most highly respected residents on the staff. Even some of the tough guys, known to beat up fellows like Steve in the dark corner of a bar, stood in line to be his patient. Sexual preferences became irrelevant.

Steve smiled at him, but Dale could see the tension in the classic features of his face as he motioned to the doctor's dictating room. As they walked through the ICU, Dale thought he saw Hector Cantrell in one of the rooms, nurses and respiratory therapists swarming all around him. He felt a cold hand grab his heart.

"What happened to Hector?" he asked as they entered a small room full of dictaphones and shelves of reference books.

Steve pulled out a chair for Dale and back-straddled another, facing him. "That's what I need to talk to you about. Before you hear it from Carleton."

Dale waited. Hector was in big trouble, and it looked like he was too.

"You saw Hector last night?"

Dale nodded. He could see the chart tucked under Steve's arm, and sensed that Steve was uncomfortable with the role of inquisitor. He was having trouble framing his questions, finally adding, rather inanely, "And what did you think was wrong with him?"

Dale began to answer, then suddenly stopped, angry. "Steve, why don't you just get to the point? Did I do something wrong?"

Steve hesitated a moment. "Well, yes. You gave him so much IV fluid he went into congestive heart failure. He had to be intubated. I . . ."

"Just a minute," Dale interrupted. "I gave him a fluid challenge because he was dehydrated. He had an orthostatic drop in his blood pressure of thirty millimeters, he was hypotensive, and he was dizzy, which he said he'd been trying to tell his doctors about for two days!" He could hear his voice rising. But hell, Hector had been ignored and neglected by his own doctors, and here he was—in the hot seat for trying to help. It seemed unjust.

Steve held up his hand. "Whoa! Don't get mad at

me, old boy. I never saw this man until they rolled him in this morning.''

Dale grinned sheepishly. Of course Steve hadn't been one of the culprits. They both knew that. When a patient went to the Intensive Care Unit, he shed one set of doctors and acquired a whole new team who specialized in critical care medicine. While this arrangement interrupted continuity of care, it made more sense for seriously ill patients to have the full attention of a specialty team.

"I'm sorry, Steve. I didn't mean to jump on you.'' He reached for the chart. "May I see that?'' He wondered what had gone wrong. Hector had looked so much better when Dale checked him the second time. He couldn't help but wonder if this was going to be another Jesse Munoz.

He turned to the morning's progress note. "Patient in florid pulmonary edema secondary to fluid overload. Severely hypoxemic. Transfer to ICU. May need intubation.'' The signature was, like most doctors', illegible.

Baffled, he turned to the physician order sheets. He saw his order for the fluid challenge, then flipped the page. An eerie feeling stirred in his stomach as he searched through the orders. He was aware of Steve's voice, but he was fully absorbed in the chart, for something critical was missing. He turned back to the progress notes and found that the page where he had written his impressions was also missing.

"Dammit! Someone is trying to ruin me!'' His eyes shot up to see Steve staring at him incredulously.

He rose, waving the chart. "Can't you see what's happening? I saw this patient twice last night.'' He poked two fingers into the air. "I gave him fluids and returned in two hours to see how he was doing. His dizziness had completely resolved, his blood pressure had improved, so I put his IV rate back to fifty cc's per hour. But someone tore out my order sheet and made it look like I ordered two hundred cc's per hour for the rest of the night. Of course he went into failure, at that rate."

Dale opened the chart to the progress notes and stuck it in front of Steve. "And look at this—I wrote two progress notes, and neither one is there. Someone took them."

He sat back down, trying to get a grip. He felt like the victim of an unseen malevolent force.

Steve sighed, shaking his head skeptically. "I don't know, Dale. It's not like you to be careless. But this conspiracy theory of yours . . . well, frankly, it's getting around the hospital that you're . . . not yourself." A doleful expression clouded his dark eyes, which he turned back toward the chart.

Dale leaned forward, slamming his fist on his knee. "I hate to have to prove myself, but I will, by God." He started to rise. "Hector can tell you I saw him twice last night."

"Dale, Hector is in a coma. He arrested right after he got here. Ventricular tachycardia."

Dale fell back in his chair. He felt torn between concern for the patient whose life might be slipping away, and for saving his reputation, which was definitely slipping away. "Let's go see him, Steve. Maybe I can at least help him out of this mess."

Steve nodded, closing the chart. He was clearly thankful to do something other than reproach a friend and colleague.

Dale nodded at the masked house officer who was gloved up and gowned, working over Hector Cantrell. He looked up at the monitor as he pulled out his stethoscope. Hector's heart was racing, and his pressure was low. He was barely recognizable with the endotracheal tube down his mouth, tape all over his face, and another tube down his nose. His eyes were closed, the eyelids swollen and twitching.

After he listened to Hector's heart and lungs, and checked his eyes for a light reflex, which was barely present as a sign of brain life, Dale addressed the house officer, whom he recognized as one of the medicine interns, even through the garb. The intern seemed to be struggling, trying to wend a catheter through a needle inserted into Hector's neck vein.

"Need some help?"

The intern looked at Steve, who stood behind Dale. Steve nodded. The intern stepped back with obvious relief. Dale guessed it was his first try at putting in a Swan-Ganz catheter, and as usual with inexperience, he was struggling through it at the patient's expense.

Dale pulled on a pair of sterile gloves, the thin latex snapping against his wrists. He took hold of the catheter from the intern's bloodied hands, and felt an involuntary shudder. He was tired of the "see one, do one, teach one" philosophy that permeated most residencies. You were supposed to sail through procedures like this one the first time you did them, and then teach the next poor sap who came along. It never worked that way, and it was the patient who suffered, along with a few house staff egos. The intern had probably been working for an hour already, and without adequate supervision was having trouble getting the catheter to go where he wanted, which was the pulmonary artery. Once there, it would give valuable information about pressures on the left side of Hector's heart, and help them decide which medications would be best for getting him out of trouble.

"Is the balloon up?" Dale asked, looking at the intern, who had pulled off his mask. Seeing the intern's blank expression, he turned to the nurse standing on the other side of the bed. She was squeezed awkwardly between Hector and the big machine that was breathing for him.

"No, it's not," she said. He thought he could detect a note of exasperation in her voice. The ICU nurses were good. This one had probably been standing by, controlling her desire to snap orders to the bungling intern, but carefully keeping her own counsel.

Dale pulled the catheter back toward him a few inches, and eyed the pressure wave on the monitor until he saw the tall peaks and valleys that he was looking for. "Okay, it's in the right ventricle. Now inflate the balloon." He gestured toward the nurse. Once the balloon was up, it would allow the catheter to float with the blood flow on into the pulmonary artery. As he advanced the catheter, he looked up at the monitor. Soon the pressure wave changed, confirming proper position.

Dale called out some pressure readings for the nurse to record, then stepped back and turned to the intern. "Go ahead and suture the catheter to the skin. And don't forget to inflate that balloon next time or the catheter will just flail around in the ventricle."

He peeled off his gloves and stepped over to where Steve stood watching. "His wedge pressure's way up, which is no surprise, but his vascular resistance is up too, so I think I'd give him some nitroprusside along with dopamine."

Steve nodded. "Good idea. We'll get it started after we measure some cardiac outputs."

Dale stepped over to the bedside again to look at the bag attached to yet another catheter that was draining Hector's bladder. "Looks like he's starting to make urine," he said, looking at the clear fluid forming in the transparent tubing. He knew Hector's kidneys had to kick in soon if he was going to survive. "How much Lasix has he gotten?"

"Forty milligrams," the nurse replied.

"I'd give another eighty," he said. He watched her hurry off to get it without bothering to check with Steve or the intern for confirmation. She'd probably been standing there for an hour biting her tongue to keep from recommending more Lasix, a potent diuretic that might get Hector's kidneys going again.

"He barely rolled in the door before you came . . ." Steve explained.

"I know."

His beeper sounded as he and Steve stood quietly at Hector's bedside. "Dr. Harper, call extension 103 please, extension 103."

He and Steve exchanged looks. They both knew who that was.

33

Herman Moran belched, then scowled as a burning, sour taste washed into his mouth. He put his glass to his lips and scowled again when he found it empty. He turned his head toward the bar, as though looking at it would produce a fresh drink and save him the effort of getting out of his easy chair. He shifted his gaze to his watch and gave an I-could-have-told-you-so snort, directed at no one in particular, since no one else was in the TV room with him. Eight o'clock, and they were supposed to be at the party by seven-thirty. What the hell was Audrey doing up there? Giving herself a face-lift?

He stared at his empty glass, rested the stem on his paunch, and closed his eyes. If he could summon the energy to get up and make himself another martini, he might just break a record tonight: a four-martini wait. He couldn't figure why Audrey was taking so long. She had even protested going. A bunch of boring professors droning about boring subjects. But he was department head, and he had to go. She had damned well better go with him.

"I'm ready, Herman." He thought for a moment he had been shot in the back, but it was just Audrey, standing at the door behind him, stabbing at the neurons of his alcohol-sotted brain with her harsh nasal voice. She even had the audacity to sound impatient.

"Well, let's hurry along, by all means, dear," he said, leaning forward before daring to stand. He had learned that moving slowly helped ease the wooziness that was coming with fewer and fewer drinks these days. He saw Audrey's image in the mirror in front of him, distorted by the liquor glasses. The play of light gave her a soft, benign appearance. He let a loud guffaw erupt at the incongruity, not caring what she thought.

"I'll drive," she announced tersely as she spun on her heel and left him to struggle to his feet.

"I'll drive," he mimicked in a slurred falsetto, wrinkling his nose Audrey style. "I'll drive," he said again, a pitch higher, drawing out the words. He plunked his glass down and shuffled toward the car.

When he arrived in the garage, Audrey was gunning the motor of the Wagoneer. The garage door was closed, and the exhaust billowed around him. She's trying to kill me, he thought. Herman, go put your mouth on the exhaust pipe. He coughed as he lurched toward the passenger side. The door was locked. He pounded on the window and noisily worked the door handle.

She flicked the automatic locks and he flung the door open. "What the hell are you trying to do, kill me?" He coughed and sputtered as he climbed in.

"Don't be absurd, Herman." She backed out of the garage so fast he had to brace his arms against the dashboard.

He looked over at her. She had her hair pulled back, which was becoming, but lent an edge of severity to her features. She was wearing a black sequined dress cut low across the bosom, with a fur shawl slung around her shoulders.

"You know, there aren't going to be any great lays there tonight. Or are you just going to drop me off and meet a friend?" He said "friend" with extra punch and winked wickedly at her.

"You're sick, Herman," she snapped, keeping her eyes straight ahead. "You need help."

"Nothing wrong that a little loving couldn't cure,"

he croaked. He reached for her hand but she batted him away.

"Herman, you need to see someone about your drinking. You're an embarrassment. I can't imagine why you haven't been fired."

He frowned. "You'd leave me if I got fired," he muttered. "That's it!" His eyes lit up with drunken mischief. "That's why you took so long to get ready tonight! Trying to get me smashed, make me look bad in front of my *compadres*. I get canned and old Bobby Heffron takes over. Of course! Don't think I don't know you've got the hots for old Bobby-boy, sweetheart."

He snickered with pleasure at his stupefying insight. "But he doesn't know you exist. I'm afraid you're stuck with me," he bellowed triumphantly, as though he had just cracked the genetic code.

Audrey made an exasperated tsking sound and put her foot to the floor.

Herman greeted their hostess, Rhonda Guest, with an exaggerated bow. Audrey smiled tightly and extended her hand. "How are you, Rhonda? I haven't seen you on the court in a while."

Rhonda, an attractive silver-haired woman in her late fifties, smiled graciously as she took Audrey's shawl. "I've been busy typing up Royal's final draft. Publish or perish, you know. Right, Herman?" She shifted her glance to Herman, who swayed next to Audrey. He thought Rhonda's lipstick, shocking pink, was a bit too shocking and a bit too pink.

"Publish, then perish," he sputtered. "That's how I do it, right, dear?" He placed a heavy hand on Audrey's shoulder. "Kill two birds with one tome!" He snorted at his pun. He saw Audrey roll her eyes with disgust.

Rhonda drew Audrey aside, soliciting advice about where to buy a new tennis racket. Herman drifted toward the bar. His host, Royal Guest, came up behind him and gave him a friendly clap on the shoulder.

"What can I get for you, Herman? You're a martini man, aren't you?"

"Right you are, Royal, but I make my own. Only a martini drinker knows how to make a good martini. No offense." Royal Guest. Jesus. Royal's parents must have hated him.

Royal was one of the less prominent members of the micro department. The students found him boring and his publications were usually rehashes of someone else's work. To Herman, he even looked boring, with his puttylike skin, bland features, rimless glasses, and his quiet, colorless eyes. Herman wasn't sure why, but he liked having Royal around the department.

"So, Herman," Royal said as he freshened his own drink. "Are you taking a cut in salary to help out the department?"

"Oh, sure, Royal. You think I want to take out a third mortgage on my house?" He frowned as the oddity of Royal's question struck him. "What are you talking about, Royal?"

"Just kidding, Herman, just kidding. I heard Audrey has gone back to nursing, that's all. I'm sure she's just doing it to get out of the house and off the tennis court, but I couldn't help giving a little dig about money. We academics are all so rich, you know." He tasted his drink, then added a little more club soda.

Herman found a stuffed olive to plunk into his martini, stirring the drink with his finger. "Royal, have you had one too many?" he asked, sucking the vermouth off his finger. "Audrey working? She wouldn't be caught dead in a nurse's uniform."

Royal arched his eyebrows, signs of life creeping into his bland face. "You mean you don't know Audrey's working? Goodness, I hope I'm not letting out any secrets. But why wouldn't she want you to know?"

"Ahh, you're crazy, Royal." Herman started to move away from the table. Royal was a worse gossip than any woman he knew. What was more, he was wrong half the time. If you were going to spread rumors, they ought to at least be plausible. Audrey, working! Jesus. She was too busy spending his money, philandering, and playing tennis.

Royal wasn't going to leave him alone. He tagged along behind him. "Look, there's Sue Alderman over there. She's the one who told me. Ask her."

Royal shot ahead of Herman and called out to Sue, a graduate student who worked odd jobs and odd hours at the hospital. She smiled and approached the two men as she saw Royal waving at her. "Hi, Dr. Moran." She nodded at Royal. She had an innocent, fresh quality about her, and hid a natural attractiveness with a hideous hairstyle that left her with bangs almost hiding her eyes. Even though she didn't wear glasses, she looked as though she wished she could, Herman thought. She wore a dowdy pastel-blue pants suit, the kind often favored by senior citizens. Trying her damnedest to look like a studious bookworm.

Royal put his arm around her, as though drawing her into a conspiratorial huddle. "Sue, didn't you tell me you saw Audrey Moran at the hospital the other day?"

"Why, yes, I'm pretty sure it was her." She looked at Herman as though she expected him to confirm her statement.

"Well, tell Dr. Moran, Sue. He thinks I'm pulling his leg."

Herman waited skeptically. Royal was acting as though he were leading the hunt for the Red October. This ought to be a good one, he thought.

"Well, I was working in the business office late one night," Sue said, "when I saw we were about to run out of outpatient requisitions. You would think there would be someone in charge of making sure you never run out of something that basic. Anyway, I went downstairs to central supply to get another box. That's when I saw Mrs. Moran—I recognized her from the Spring Fling—and she was in a nurse's uniform."

Herman swiveled his head around until he spotted Audrey, still chatting with Rhonda Guest. He pointed to his wife. "Is that who you saw?"

Sue's gaze followed Herman's finger. She saw Audrey Moran, this time in black, instead of starched white. "That's her, Dr. Moran." She turned back to him with a nervous smile, as if aware of a storm brewing, perhaps caused by her. She brushed at her bangs absently.

"Did she see you, Sue?" He suddenly felt stone-cold sober. He may not have Audrey under his thumb, but he sure as hell didn't like the idea of her running around the hospital in a nurse's uniform without telling him. It made no sense at all.

"I'm pretty sure she didn't. She looked like she was in a hurry. I saw her as I stepped off the elevator."

"Well, well, what a pleasant surprise," he said, trying to make light of it as he noticed both Sue and Royal staring at him. "My birthday's coming up. She's probably trying to earn a little money on the side to get me that Mercedes I've always wanted." He laughed robustly, but nobody laughed with him. What the hell was wrong with these people? This was a party, for chrissake.

"Aha! Look who's here!" Royal cried. He patted Herman's arm in a parting gesture as he headed for the new arrivals. Herman looked toward the front door. There was old Bobby Heffron with his adoring wife hanging dutifully on his arm. Was he imagining it, or was the whole roomful of people drifting toward Heffron? What an egocentric jerk. He turned back to find Sue, but she was gone. Had he imagined it all? He looked at his martini, as though he could chalk it all off to the effects of alcohol. His wife disguised as a nurse? Surely she wouldn't be working as a nurse. She hadn't touched a patient in what, twenty years? Nobody in his right mind would hire her. He'd always suspected that she hadn't voluntarily retired. She must have been fired. Nurses were supposed to be caring, compassionate. Audrey didn't even know the meaning of the words.

Watching Heffron attract the guests like moths to a lighted window, Herman felt like puking. He threaded his way through the throng, making his amenities.

"As usual, you made a drunken fool of yourself tonight," Audrey seethed, her arms braced against the steering wheel as she drove them home.

Herman slouched in the passenger seat. He felt dizzy and sick to his stomach. Sometime during the evening he'd had to slow down on the booze because he couldn't stand up. Now he was starting to sober up, and he didn't like the feeling. He let Audrey's tirade wash over him. But he kept remembering that graduate student and Royal trying to cram something down his throat, something about Audrey. He'd forgotten about it as his hatred for Robert Heffron consumed him for the rest of the party. Now this other was pushing its way through the alcohol, demanding attention.

"Audrey, why are you running around the hospital in a nurse's uniform?" He stared out the window. Raindrops were forming on the windshield.

Audrey whipped her face toward him, causing the car to swerve. "What are you talking about, Herman?"

Herman sat up, surprised by her vehemence. "Better watch the road, Audrey. The idea of dying in a car with you on top of me isn't very appealing."

"I said, what are you talking about, Herman?" This time she kept her eyes on the road, but he noticed her foot was getting a little heavy on the pedal.

He hadn't elicited this much interest from Audrey in years. He was beginning to enjoy himself. "Oh, I'm sure it was just a case of mistaken identity, but one of the graduate students thought she saw you in a nurse's uniform at the hospital one night."

"Of course," Audrey said.

"Of course what?" Herman looked at her. Her face was a mask.

"Of course it was a case of mistaken identity. What on earth would I be doing in a nurse's uniform?"

"My thoughts, exactly, Audrey. It wasn't even Halloween."

"Haven't you got anything better to do than gossip at a department party, Herman?"

"You mean I should do something more noble, like you? Look for young studs to roll in the hay with?"

"I'm afraid the young studs are your department, Herman."

"Oh, low blow, Audrey. Aren't we being cute?" He looked at the rain on the windshield, wondering why the hell she didn't turn on the wipers. "Besides, I was just minding my own business when Royal Guest assaulted me. You know what a gossip he is."

He could see Audrey turning toward him again, out of the corner of his eye. "Royal told you this? I thought you said it was some graduate student."

"It was, but she told him, you see. Now everybody knows, dear." He thought she squirmed ever so slightly. "Audrey, you just went through a red light."

"Well, that's disgusting. As head of the department, you shouldn't be letting gossip spread around like some . . . disease. You must call Royal tomorrow and put a stop to this."

"I rather enjoy it myself. Why are you so hepped up about it, anyway? Who gives a damn if you're working or not? I laughed it off and told them you wanted to buy me a Mercedes for my birthday."

He heard Audrey snort at the absurdity of his white lie. He felt a flash of irritation. It was okay for him to make sarcastic cracks about the joke that was their marriage, but she didn't have to be so overt about agreeing with him. He felt a compulsion to keep needling her, looking for a response, though he had no idea what response he would find satisfying. "What's the matter, Audrey, aren't I worth a Mercedes?"

He saw her eyebrows arch with surprise, though she kept her eyes on the road. She turned on the wipers, finally, as the rain poured over the windshield like transparent melting candle wax. "Herman, you know you're not worth a beat-up pickup truck to me."

He knew she meant it, even before she said it. Nevertheless, it rankled. "But Bobby Heffron would be worth a Rolls-Royce, wouldn't he?" He chuckled. "Too bad he won't give you the time of day."

Audrey careened the car into the driveway and punched the garage door opener. Herman swayed with the motion of the car, then jerked forward as she slammed on the brakes. He smiled smugly at the impact of his barb.

Audrey turned to him, her face a caricature of anger, every line of it screaming at him. "You fool. You stupid, blundering fool. Robert Heffron and I are lovers." He saw saliva spray from her mouth, fire leap from her eyes. He saw her grab her purse and gloves, jerk the keys from the ignition, and slide out of the car, slamming the door. Even though he knew she was moving with rapid-fire speed, the whole scene played out before him in slow motion.

Herman rubbed his eyes and blinked as he sat in the quiet empty car. He could hear the rainwater trickling off the roof. He played back in his mind what Audrey had just said. She and Heffron. Lovers. He could take anything she could dish out. He could watch her having an orgy with a lineup of young studs, even in his own bed. But screwing Heffron. His wife? That was beyond the pale. More than he could accept. More than he could imagine.

He shook his head, as if to clear it of an hallucination. But he knew that what had happened had happened. And he knew Audrey was telling the truth. If it had been a lie, she would have taunted him with it much sooner, and not begrudgingly, with a touch of pity, as she just had.

He suddenly felt very old. And very lonely. A momentary sense of doom passed over him as he broke out in a sweat, and felt his heart pumping in his throat, like it was reaching up to strangle him. Then he felt an anger, more like rage, well up in him. He thought for a moment that he could kill Audrey. He wanted to hurt her, really hurt her, for doing this to him. Sleeping with a despicable enemy. Throwing it in his face. He straightened up in his seat, opened the car door. He would get her for this. Sweet revenge.

34

Dale left Carleton's office feeling defeated. He walked slowly, aimlessly, through the medicine ward toward the elevator. He'd never felt this way, as though he'd had the starch knocked out of him and couldn't come back. Maybe he had been called down one too many times. More likely, it was fearing Nina might be in trouble too. Worse than he had even anticipated. She was likely to have a "voluntary leave of absence" pressed on her as well if she stuck by him.

He came to a stop and leaned against the wall, looking around the ward from the painful perspective that his days here were numbered. He felt a pang of love for the place. Crazy. How could four walls become such an integral part of your life? Even shape your life, as he felt these walls had? From medical student to seasoned house officer.

He stood, his hands at his sides, his feet frozen to the floor beneath him. He watched an orderly push a patient in a wheelchair toward the elevator. They both looked dejected. He concluded they must be going to the X-ray department, where they could count on spending the afternoon waiting around like lost luggage.

He noticed a priest hurrying down the hall toward a cluster of crying people, at least three generations of them, their arms around each other. He watched with a numb interest the priest's calming influence. It probably included promises of an afterlife far better than poor mortals could imagine. How often he had seen religion step over a threshold that medicine could not cross. Not religious himself, he refrained from judgment. He had learned to view the clergy as his colleagues, often there to lend a hand at the most troubling of times.

The page system, like canned music, droned non-stop. He was conditioned only to hear his own name, or a Code Blue. How many times had he run to its beck and call, like an eager, obedient servant?

He smiled at his own nostalgia, then let the sadness he had been fighting off finally wash over him. The ignominy of being suspended from his training finally struck him full force, despite his efforts to feel ennobled by it. No, he wasn't being asked to leave because he was a white knight banging at the doors of the black force of evil. But for negligence. He, Dale Harper, negligent. It offended everything he had ever stood for, with his passion for serving the sick. And he had taken the woman he loved into this quagmire with him.

Now, as he thought again of Nina, a feeling of purpose freed him to put one foot in front of the other, and he moved to find the nearest phone.

"Dr. Yablonsky."

He marveled at the sureness in her voice. He envisioned her in her crisp white coat. Her ID card hanging from her left front pocket with a picture that didn't do her justice. A radiation badge pinned to her other front pocket. No doubt she was cricking her neck to hold the receiver while she jotted down her impressions of the X rays she was studying.

"Hello? This is Dr. Yablonsky." Now impatience pushing at the sureness.

"Nina . . ."

"Dale! Is that you? I can barely hear you. Are you all right?" Now he heard concern.

"Nina, I need to talk to you. About my meeting with Carleton."

"Are you . . . have you been suspended?" Now a whisper.

"Not yet. But I'm on probation." He didn't bother adding that he might just as well have been suspended, because he knew this was merely a formality. Like giving someone two weeks notice that he'd been fired. Or telling a family member on the phone that he'd better get to the hospital quick without disclosing that his loved one had already died.

"Where are you? I'll come meet you."

The urgency in Nina's voice alarmed him. Watching Carleton's office down the hall, he said, "We'd better talk outside. How about a little stroll?"

"Okay. I'll just pick up a beeper in case they need me. Meet you out front in five minutes?"

"I'll be there." Dale slowly put the receiver down, strode past the elevators and down the stairs.

"Dr. Yablonsky! Nina!" Nina turned to see Ron Orloff wending his way toward her through the crowded hospital lobby. His pale face stood out like a flattened marshmallow. She had an impulse to turn around and keep walking, which annoyed her. Actually, it was Ron who annoyed her. But why? She barely knew him. Maybe that was the problem. She knew him mainly as one cause of Dale's current predicament. She found it hard to muster any compassion for him. And her, a doctor, for God's sake. Sometimes she hated herself.

"What is it, Ron?" She stopped abruptly, causing him to bump into her.

"Oh, God, I'm sorry, Nina. I wasn't expecting you to stop like that. Listen, I've got to talk to Dale, do you know where he is?" He was gasping for breath, just from that short excursion through the lobby. She winced.

"I'm going to meet him right now," she said. She allowed a pause, hoping Ron would sense that she didn't want him along.

"I'll come with you."

"Ron, Dale is in serious trouble, and he and I need to be alone together right now."

"Oh, well . . ."

She couldn't bear the crestfallen look on his face.

"All right." She started walking again, and he trailed behind her, even aware by this time that he wasn't welcome.

Dale was waiting on the front steps of the hospital. He sat, looking into the sun. Nina watched him a moment, putting a finger to her lips as Ron started to speak. Dale appeared so peaceful, looking out at what—the pink-brown polluted air? She didn't have the heart to interrupt him.

Finally, aware of Ron's restlessness, she brought herself to approach Dale and tap him on the shoulder. He turned, his face beaming upon seeing her. Then he saw Ron. He rose. "Ron, what's up?"

"I think I know how I got contaminated," he said bluntly. Excitement began to burn in his dark eyes, making his face appear even paler by contrast.

Dale and Nina looked at each other. Whatever they had to say to each other could wait. "Tell us!"

Ron motioned with his arm toward the lawn in front of the hospital, and the three of them headed down the steps. It was late afternoon, but the sun still hung high, like a bright disk refusing to be engulfed by the contaminated atmosphere beneath it. Nina thought how pleasant its rays were on her face. It gave her a feeling of well-being and confidence.

Dale slipped down on the grass and drew Nina down with him, cradling her head with his hands. "Let's hear it."

Ron remained standing, pacing in small steps back and forth. "I think it's the micro department, all right. Everything points that way. You told me you picked up radiation in the lounge." He suddenly spoke with shocking ferocity. "And I used to eat there all the time!" He seemed to loom over them, his lips trembling.

Dale frowned. Nina stared at Ron's pale, pinched

face. He seemed almost crazed, grasping frantically at straws.

"How did you arrive at this, Ron?" Dale asked with concern as he watched a fine sweat coat Ron's face like a patina of fear.

Ron squatted in front of them, his hands moving excitably, telling a dramatic story that he seemed unable to verbalize. "Plutonium. It's the only place in the medical center where it's kept. Robert Heffron thinks Moran was storing it, against regulations. Probably for illicit purposes, though he didn't exactly say that."

"Moran!?" Nina sat up incredulously.

Dale turned to Ron. "You've been talking to Heffron?"

Ron nodded. "He's been a big help to me," he said defensively. "He's arranged for me to check into Sloan-Kettering in New York. He has a friend there who's one of the leading experts on leukemia."

"And he thinks Moran did this to you?"

"Not intentionally. Moran is such a poor administrator that nothing gets done right, including the storage of radioactive materials. Heffron says the department is on its umpteenth warning with the state radiation safety board."

Ron's fervor notwithstanding, Nina couldn't find it in her to take Moran seriously. "Moran hasn't got the gumption for anything like that. He's a sheep in sheep's clothing."

She screwed up her eyes in a speculative look. "Maybe Heffron is trying to shift suspicion from himself. Now *there's* a wolf."

There's a wolf, all right, thought Dale, remembering Heffron's lie about Western Nuclear and his oily, patronizing smile. For reasons he was unsure of, he hadn't even told Nina about his ever-growing doubts regarding Heffron.

Ron glanced at Nina. She thought he was glaring for a moment, but then it was gone. "That thought," he said slowly, "occurred to me, Nina. I've never trusted him myself. But I've had reason to change my mind. Besides, everybody knows what a jerk Moran is."

"He's incapable of anything," Dale said, smiling.

"What do you propose to do, Ron?" Nina asked.

"I'l like to see the son of a bitch fired," Ron said with cold fury.

After an awkward silence, Dale said, "Everyone would like that, Ron. But I'd hate to see you waste your time, especially without proof." He didn't say what he was thinking, that Ron might not have that much time left. He hadn't seen a blood count on him for a while, but the symptoms were there. Ron had stopped consulting him, which Dale understood. If he had a terminal illness, he wouldn't want someone as inexperienced as a resident, however good he was.

What had bothered him, though, was that Ron had never discussed it. He just stopped showing up, and when Dale asked him why, he mumbled something about seeing a specialist. God, he hoped Heffron wasn't the "specialist." And now, this unleashed hatred. So uncharacteristic. Was Heffron somehow using Ron, poisoning his mind?

He noted Ron's countenance. Pale and sickly. Feverish. As though not only his body, but his mind too, was consumed with something sinister.

"I intend to get proof," Ron said. "And I don't need your help. I just wanted you to know the score."

Dale could see the sweat form beads on Ron's forehead, even though the breeze was cool. He shrugged, not exactly sure what Ron wanted from him. "Okay, Ron. Good luck. Let me know what I can do."

Ron nodded curtly and walked back to the hospital. Nina turned to Dale with indignation. "Doesn't he realize how you've stuck your neck out to help him?"

"I think he knows. And I think he's having trouble handling the guilt. I guess the whole purpose of that little visit, whether he knows it or not, was to tell me he's taking over. A kind of dismissal. Maybe for my own good."

Nina laughed hollowly. "Well, at least someone is looking after your welfare. Your list of friends gets shorter by the day."

He scooted up close to her and wrapped his arms around her waist. "As long as you're still there. That's what counts. I need you."

She looked up and kissed him. "Always," she murmured.

He realized they hadn't talked about his meeting with Carleton. But it didn't matter. Just being with her was enough.

35

"So, Dr. Harper, you're in a little hot water. Uncomfortable, is it?" Herman Moran snickered, enjoying himself as he watched Dale Harper sitting stiffly across from him. Did he see a flicker of fear? Maybe so. He hoped so, though that was not his purpose in summoning the resident to his office.

"It isn't pleasant," Dale said. He wondered why Moran wanted to see him, especially on a Saturday morning.

"Is that all you have to say for yourself, Doctor?" Moran drew out the word "doctor," as though accusing him of engaging in something smutty.

Dale felt a surge of anger. Moran was an embarrassment to the profession—a buffoon. He studied the department head's slack red face, bulbous nose, and baggy eyes, and his anger was softened by pity. What a pathetic creature.

"Maybe there's some mistake, Dr. Moran. Your secretary told me you wanted to see me."

"Yes, well, let's put aside social pleasantries and get down to business." Moran's fingers did a drumroll on the desktop.

Dale waited. Moran cleared his throat. When he spoke, he took on a surprisingly serious tone. "Don't think I don't know what you're going through, Harper. I admire your—pigheadedness. You've believed in something, and you've put your ass on the line. And," Moran leaned forward and said, in a conspiratorial whisper, "I am going to help you."

Dale kept his expression wooden, unrevealing, at the same time feeling a turbulence rise in the pit of his stomach. If Moran expected applause, he sure as hell wasn't getting any from his corner.

Moran shifted in his chair, thrown off by Dale's unresponsiveness. He laid his cards on the table. "I think you have been on the right track, looking in this department for the source of the trouble."

He squinted at Dale, then frowned. He might as well be conversing with the draperies. "The plutonium? Your patients, the ones you came to me about earlier?"

"Yes?" Dale sensed a trap.

"Are you no longer interested in your little investigation, Dr. Harper? Has the threat of suspension killed your curiosity? Don't think I don't know all about what they're trying to do to you."

Moran mustered an expression of indignation, which on his dissolute face appeared laughable. "It's inexcusable," he said. "Penalizing those who seek the truth."

"My 'little investigation,' as you put it, was not provoked by simple curiosity, Dr. Moran."

Moran chuckled. "You're a tough cookie, aren't you?" He paused, then went on when Dale didn't take up with his attempt at lightness. "As I said, I can help you. I've stumbled across some rather . . . embarrassing information. I would really prefer not to have it exposed by anyone, but I see now that it's relevant to your investigation, and therefore helpful to others."

"What information?" Dale asked with a clinical detachment. He wasn't budging.

"Information that I fear verges on the sensational. How should I put it?" Moran cleared his throat again. "I'm afraid our colleague, Dr. Heffron, has been a bit lax with his plutonium. As you know, he uses it in his research. The state radiation board has cited the department several times for violations, as you probably also know. When you and I last spoke, I made the mistake of trying to protect Heffron. Departmental loyalty. Fear of scandal. But in doing so, I realize others may have been harmed. As head of this department, I have responsibilities to more than one man."

Moran waved a hand in the air—as though signaling this absurdity must stop. Dale noticed the redness of Moran's palm, not uncommon with heavy drinkers. He wondered if Moran already had his drink or two this morning.

"Why are you telling me this now?"

Moran laughed, spreading his hands with a shrug, as though illustrating the obvious. "Even I have a conscience, Dr. Harper."

Dale looked at him askance. Whatever the reason, it would be to Moran's advantage. He knew, behind those alcohol-glazed eyes, there was a hidden agenda. He looked at his watch, then back at Moran. He had time. He tapped his fingers on his thigh, and permitted himself a skeptical grin.

Moran studied his own fingers, splayed out before him on the desk. "You don't believe me, do you?"

"No."

"You're right not to."

Dale's fingers became still. He leveled his eyes on Moran's, his eyebrows arched.

Moran averted his gaze. He hauled himself out of his chair and came around to sit on the edge of his desk. One leg dangled, his trousers hitched up to show white, hairless flesh. Dale noticed the ankles were swollen, and found himself again speculating about Moran's health.

Moran closed his eyes for a moment, then abruptly opened them and blurted out, "My wife is having an affair with that son of a bitch." He leaned close enough that Dale could smell the sourness of his breath. His eyes gleamed with hatred. "I want you to get the bastard."

Dale started to push himself up out his chair. "I'm sorry, but I'm not interested in being anyone's pawn. Find yourself a marriage counselor."

"Sit down, Dr. Harper!" Moran shouted, jumping down off the desk.

Dale sat down, despite himself. He felt a sudden concern for Moran as he saw the man's face turn an ugly purple hue. He watched Moran shuffle back to his seat, realizing by the disappointment he now felt that he was hoping Moran wasn't talking through his hat. There would have been a feeling of satisfaction in bringing down that smug phony, Robert Heffron.

But Moran was still trying to pin the tail on the donkey. "Let me tell you about our friend Robert Heffron, Dr. Harper. Then judge for yourself. Forget my motives. My wife screws everyone, but I draw the line at that slimy bastard, and I want you to know why."

Moran's color was changing from a bluish-black to its normal ruddiness. Dale breathed more easily.

"Go ahead," Dale said, torn between walking out on this pitiful lout or staying for his sordid tale. He sat on the edge of his seat, more as a statement of his ambivalence than a show of interest.

Moran was so caught up with himself that the didn't notice. "Robert Heffron is a parasite. He's a smooth operator who talks big and knows little. People see what he wants them to see, and what they want to see." Moran laughed mirthlessly. "That's why he's so well received. He appeals to the phoniness in us all."

He reached into a drawer and pulled out a half-empty bottle of vodka. He poured himself a drink, then held the bottle up, gesturing to Dale with a nod of his head.

Dale politely declined.

Moran tilted his head back and tossed down half his drink. As he set the glass down, he smiled, and Dale marveled at how much better he looked, his eyes taking on a hard brightness.

Moran's eyes moved over Dale, dwelling a little too long, making Dale feel uncomfortably self-conscious. The alcohol was bringing out some qualities in Moran that Dale recalled from his medical school years when he had to tactfully but firmly fend off Moran's drunken groping at a party.

"I'll level with you, Harper," Moran went on, the alcohol loosening his tongue. "It would serve my purposes well to have Bobby Heffron out of my life. But there's no doubt—he's your man. The one you've been trying to track down, that is. He has to be. He's the only one in the department using plutonium." He smiled a predatory smile. "You rub my back, I'll rub yours. Together, we can do everyone a big favor and put the scoundrel where he belongs: out on his ass."

Dale's disappointment grew. So far there was no substance to any of Moran's accusations. Just hateful peregrinations. "Where's your evidence? I already know Heffron's the only one who uses plutonium. So what? I can't accuse him of poisoning people just for that." He paused. "Or because he sleeps with your wife."

Moran grinned, a knowing glint in his eyes that made him appear to be leering. "Let me ask you this: Are you satisfied that he's innocent? Do you have evidence to *that* effect?"

Dale stared at him. This man wasn't as out of touch as he seemed. He was playing on Dale's own dislike for Heffron—a dislike that he had not professed, but which Moran clearly saw. Finally, he answered, "No, I'm not satisfied."

"I knew it!" Moran sat back triumphantly.

"Dr. Moran, if you have nothing more, I really need to be going." Dale felt a strange disinclination to leave, but he saw no point in staying.

Moran lowered his voice, assuming a confidential tone. "I don't have any answers for you, but I've got some questions that may pique your curiosity—oh, excuse me, I didn't mean to use such a simple word." Moran snickered as he shuffled papers around on his desk. "Let me see, now, where the hell is that list I made? Oh, yes, here we go."

He looked up, then back at a sheet of paper, which Dale noticed was shaking in his grasp. "Number one: Why does Heffron use Western Nuclear to deliver his radioisotopes when the rest of the medical school and the hospital use Bristol Labs?

"Number two: Why does Heffron show up here sometimes at midnight?" Moran looked at Dale and chuckled. "There aren't any good places to fuck around here, believe me. I've tried."

He returned to his list. "Number three: How come someone by the name of Christine Anselm co-authors most of Heffron's research when she isn't even affiliated with this program?

"And, number four: Is it more than coincidence that this co-author of his, Ms. Anselm, also works at Western Nuclear?"

Moran put his list down and sat back, looking every bit like the cat who ate the canary. "Well?"

Dale felt his head spinning. Western Nuclear. Heffron's lie. And now, Christine Anselm. No, it couldn't be coincidence. He looked at Moran, wondering how he could have come up with these questions that in themselves were provocative of answers. "You have something—something worth looking at," he said at last. "I have to admit it."

Moran grinned, or rather was still grinning. His expression hadn't changed since he had first noted Dale's reaction. No more conversing with the draperies. "Gotcha hooked, eh?"

"How do you know about this Christine Anselm?"

Moran wagged a pudgy finger at him. "Ah, ah, ah. No answers until I'm sure you're with me. For all I know, you might take all these goodies and go running to old Bobby-boy with them."

Dale erupted. "Maybe we've reached an impasse. How do I know you're not just trying to get me into deeper trouble? Or, as you clearly indicated earlier, you just want to use me to stab Heffron in the back to get at your wife?"

Moran's grin widened. "Even if those were my motives, I still have information that can be useful to
you. Besides, you're quite capable of cutting your own
throat. You don't need my help, that's obvious
enough."

Dale was beginning to appreciate a level of cunning
that hid a gram of wisdom. Moran was right on one
point. He was already in hot water. If someone like
Moran wanted him out of the program, all he had to
do was lie back and do nothing. Not offer information
that could backfire on the informant.

He put his arms behind his head and sat back.
"Okay, you have my interest. What do you want from
me?"

Moran came around his desk to give Dale a clap on
the back, his hand lingering a moment longer than
necessary. "Now you're talking! Come with me, my
dear boy."

36

Nina sprawled on the plush sheepskin rug in her living room, the smooth, haunting sounds of the Moody Blues playing softly in the background. Dale was equally engrossed in massaging her shoulders—imparting pleasure while enjoying the intimate contact himself. He wondered if this was what marriage would be like. Marriage? And he a struggling resident about to be bounced out on his ear.

They had finished a marvelous dinner, Mediterranean pasta. It was Nina'a own concoction, with Greek olives, fresh tomatoes, feta cheese, garlic—you could never have too much garlic—artichokes, and a magical mixture of spices. They were both mellow from the chardonnay and overeating. The candles still flickered on the dining table, creating a dreamy light show on the ceiling.

"Mmmm, a little more on the upper arms, please." The oversize, colorful woven pillows supporting Nina's head seemed to be exuding muffled gurgles of ecstasy.

He stroked her upper arms, working his thumbs in a circular motion, as he knew she liked it.

She raised her head slightly. "Any regrets? About medicine, I mean."

"Never," he said without a moment's hesitation.

"Not even in the past few months?"

He laughed. "These few months have convinced me I was lucky I didn't go into politics."

"You considered politics?"

"No, thank God. But that's what I've had to deal with."

He started working on her spine, egged on by the pleasurable sounds she was making.

She turned onto her side, and he could see her staring across the room, lost in thought. "Sometimes I have misgivings," she said. "Radiology is not where I saw myself when I dreamed of being a doctor. Sitting in front of a viewbox looking at people's innards isn't very glamorous."

"And what is?" He let a finger wander over the contours of her firm breast beneath her silk robe.

"Oh, I don't know." She rolled onto her back and looked up at him lazily. "Maybe acting. I used to fantasize myself being an actress until I realized it was the roles they played that I found exciting. Women playing doctors, judges, lawyers, journalists. Then I thought, why choose a profession where you only pretend? Why not just *be* one of those people?"

"And so here you are."

"Here I am. Minus the opening credits and name on the marquee." She looked over at the stereo, which was now quiet. "Let's have some Cleo Laine." She reached out to put on another disc. Dale kissed her under the arm.

She sighed. "I love it. You have great hands."

As Cleo started crooning "Send in the Clowns," Nina reclaimed her spot on the sheepskin. Her lean, long legs looked as though they had been sculpted of marble. Dale leaned down and kissed her lightly on the neck. "I always thought of glamorous as superficial, phony. But you're glamorous. And you're authentic. Real. With so many facets, you're still a mystery to me."

He sat up and reached for the giant teddy bear propped near Nina's head. "For example, how can a woman as sophisticated as you possess this unsophisticated worn-out old teddy bear?" He laughed as he held it up.

She smiled, raising up to sip her wine. "That's Snuffy. He's been the most important bear in my life, bar none, since I was five years old. So be nice to him."

He grinned and winked at her as he gave Snuffy a hug and put him down.

As she lay back she slowly unbuttoned his gray canvas shirt. "You know, I don't feel very mysterious. You see what you want to see."

He took her hand and squeezed it. "I see a strong, beautiful woman who doesn't let anyone push her around. Not even me, which isn't fair."

"Oh, be quiet, and get back to work," she teased, rolling over so he could finish doing her back.

After a few rapturous moans, then silence, Nina mumbled through the pillows. "What's going to happen to you? To us?" He could feel a subtle tension building in the muscles of her lower back.

He chose to take her lightly. "I'm going to massage you until you beg me to stop, then I'm going to seduce you."

"No, seriously."

He stopped to sip his wine, then kissed her ear, whispering, "I think we need more ominous, dramatic music for this part. How about 'Carmina Burana'?"

"Oh, you're terrible," she said.

"No, just hungry."

"Hungry? How could you be hungry? You ate nearly a pound of pasta, not to mention the sauce and half a loaf of bread!"

Dale shrugged, rubbing his stomach. "It's all your fault."

She got up and started for the kitchen. He groaned. "Not right now, Nina. I was just discovering your glamorous parts."

"Come along, you bottomless pit," she said, grabbing his arm.

She led him to the refrigerator where she pulled out

a quart of Häagen-Dazs. She pointed to the cupboard. "Get me the can of fudge sauce in there, please."

"Yes, ma'am." He handed it to her and she emptied it into a saucepan.

"I also need the sliced almonds."

She built him a mountainous hot fudge sundae and started the coffee brewing.

As he watched her, he decided to answer her question. "I don't know what's going to happen. I'm on probation with the likelihood of joining the ranks of the unemployed if I so much as sneeze too loud or say the word 'plutonium,' even in my sleep. You'll be on probation if you're so much as seen with me, other than looking at an X ray. I haven't uncovered any more cases of plutonium poisoning. Robert Heffron says it's all Moran's fault, and Moran says it's all Heffron's fault. And I'm being used by each to help annihilate the other. Ron Orloff is acting weird, and has dropped out of sight. Lincoln Lee is critical. And to round it out, someone is mucking with patients' lives and making it look like I'm responsible."

As she watched him dabble with his sundae, she wished she had said nothing. The wonderment of the evening had been spoiled. When would it end? And how?

She got up to pour them each a mug of black coffee, then frowning as she sat back down, she shook her head. "There must be some reason Moran thinks this Christine person is involved."

Dale stared into his coffee. "I think it's self-evident. He showed me a pile of Heffron's journal articles over the past two years. She's co-author on almost all of them. But nobody's ever heard of her at the medical center. Moran says she was a graduate student of Heffron's about ten years ago, back East. They started collaborating then."

Nina sipped her coffee thoughtfully. "You know what keeps bothering me?"

"What?"

"Lincoln Lee. Why did he get leukemia while Willie didn't? If the stuff that Willie brought home is what contaminated Lincoln, surely Willie had even greater exposure."

Dale smiled. "Great minds think alike. I've wondered the same thing. But I came up with some answers that make sense to me. One, Willie wore gloves. Two, Lincoln was a young kid when he first started playing with those syringes. Kids are always getting stuff in their mouths. Remember what Mike told us? It has to get inside him somehow. And three, kids are more susceptible to leukemia than adults."

Nina nodded. "You're a genius."

He reached for her hand. "You know the smartest thing I ever did?"

She squeezed his hand. "What would that be?"

"I hooked up with you."

"Western Nuclear. How may I direct your call?"

"Christine Anselm, please."

"Ms. Anselm no longer works here, sir. Can someone else help you?"

Dale thought a moment. "Personnel, please."

"Just a moment, sir, I'll connect you." The woman's voice was impersonal, with a distinct Southern drawl.

A few clicks and hums later, "Personnel, Shelly speaking."

"This is Dr. Harper at City Hospital. I need to locate Christine Anselm."

He thought there was a moment's hesitation, longer than necessary. "I'm sorry, Doctor, but Miss Anselm has left our employ."

"I understand that. Do you know why she left?"

"I can't tell you that. Perhaps someone in Miss Anselm's department can help you."

"Yes, thank you. May I speak to Miss Anselm's replacement?"

"Just a moment, please."

He heard Muzak's sickeningly sweet rendition of

"Aquarius" ooze over the line while he waited. How to ruin a wonderful song. He would have much preferred silence. Finally, a brusque male voice came on. "Deliveries."

Deliveries! His mind flashed to the day he chased after the Western Nuclear deliveryman. Could it have been Christine? He remembered thinking the figure was rather slight for a man.

"Dr. Harper from City Hospital," he said with what he hoped was impressive formality. "Christine Anselm, please."

"She ain't here no more. Whatcha need?"

Dale took a shot in the dark. "I'm from the microbiology department. You're late on our plutonium delivery."

"Plutonium?! This some kinda joke?"

"What's the joke?" Dale felt a stir of excitement.

"We don't handle plutonium for City Hospital."

Dale sensed anger in the man's voice. "Christine Anselm. I'm sure she was the one making our deliveries." He paused long enough to be checking something. "Why, yes. I've got her signature right in front of me," he lied.

There was a long silence. He tried again. "Sorry to bother you. I'm sure Miss Anselm could straighten it out."

That broke the silence. "Well, she upped and disappeared last week. And good riddance. Always messin' up her orders. Runnin' around in the company truck like she owned it. That's what happens when you hire a woman to do a man's job."

Abruptly, as though afraid he had revealed too much, the man said, "Listen, gotta go. Sorry." He didn't sound at all sorry.

Dale hung up slowly. One more strange twist in the puzzle. He cradled his chin with his hand and drummed his fingers on the table, wondering where to turn next. Finally, he reached for the phone book and turned to the A's.

37

Dale went through five directories and finally found a Christine Anselm in the Glendale book. It was a piece of luck. He dialed her number expectantly, only to be put off by a recording. Service had been disconnected.

On a hunch, he jumped in his car and drove to Glendale. It didn't take him long, considering the Sunday afternoon beach traffic.

He spotted the street number in a dingy run-down neighborhood. The house was a ruin. He parked and sat in his car, looking the place over, pulling his thoughts together. The squalid neighborhood hardly befitted the life-style of someone in league with Robert Heffron.

Some of the houses surrounding the small one-story hovel appeared abandoned, the windows boarded up. Graffiti was splashed over walls and sidewalks. What lawns there were had taken on the brownish discoloration of dead grass. But the weeds continued to grow to great heights. Most of the yards were littered with cast-off machine parts and broken toys. A small mongrel dog sat forlornly in the front yard, staring at him.

Did he have the wrong Christine Anselm? Maybe he should have gone through a few more phone books. He hesitantly slid out of the Mustang and crossed a patch of weeds rather than pick his way through the cluttered sidewalk. He rechecked the address in his notebook one more time before knocking on the paint-chipped door. The doorbell didn't work.

He knocked again, putting his ear to the door. The

mongrel apathetically turned its head to watch him. Dale noticed a few suspicious eyes on him—mostly black and Hispanic. It made him feel squeamish. He was glad Nina hadn't come. Finally, he tried the door, and it creaked open.

He stood scanning the room before him, or what was left of it. Lamps, tables, and chairs were knocked over. Papers were strewn all over the floor. Two plants had been emptied from their pots, soil and leaves scattered. Shards of broken glass glittered in the sunlight filtering through a broken window.

A primitive sense of self-preservation told him to turn and leave, but curiosity drew him on. He was intrigued by the enigmatic Christine Anselm whose name kept popping up.

His shoes crunched on the litter strewn on the floor as he stepped into the room. He moved on through the house to the bedroom, encountering the same disarray. He explored the rest of the house, including a small bathroom and kitchen. He was aware of a rotten stench as he entered the kitchen. The odor almost knocked him over. Dirty dishes were heaped in the sink. A two- or three-day-old pizza sitting on the table was black with flies. The refrigerator door was ajar.

The smell was so pervasive he considered the possibility of decomposing flesh. He looked everywhere—under the bed, in the shower, in the closets. Nothing.

The mystery drew him on. He scanned the scattered piles of papers lying around. As he squatted on the floor and started to ransack the papers, he thought of his fingerprints. He was already in enough trouble.

He returned to his car, where he kept his black doctor's bag stowed in the trunk. Finally, that relic would come in handy. A freebie from the drug companies his second year in medical school, he had eagerly stocked it with everything a doctor might need in an emergency. He had toted it around proudly for a while, then cast it aside as he realized its uselessness. It was a status symbol that had lost its substance in an age where house calls were as rare as smallpox. Ah, well. There were still the rubber exam gloves, almost designed for the task at hand.

He pulled on a pair of the gloves, and went through the papers on the floor. They were mostly bills, addressed to Christine Anselm. She apparently was behind in her payments on many things. He saw the phone bill, with the disconnect notice. He started to discard it, then examined it more closely. He saw two calls that were made to the medical center exchange, nothing particularly striking. Unless they were on Heffron's exchange. He stuffed the bill in his pocket.

Bills, invoices, receipts. He saw a stack of periodicals next to the tipped-over coffee table and went over to take a look. Most of them were technical journals, including *Micronetics,* a well-known microbiology journal. He looked through the table of contents, and, with an extra beat of his pulse, found an article by Christine Anselm and Robert Heffron. He turned to the page and saw it had been torn out.

His excitement building, he started leafing through the other four journals lying there, but found no more Heffron or Anselm authored pieces. He sat back against the couch, wondering why the article had been removed. It seemed that every time he was onto something, it disappeared on him. One thing was sure—he was on the trail of the right Christine Anselm. Maybe old Terminal Moron knew what he was talking about after all.

The remainder of his search brought no further surprises. He removed his gloves and left the place looking much as it had when he arrived. He had the phone bill in his pocket and the *Micronetics* journal under his arm. As he threaded his way through the weeds and junk toward his car, he was again uncomfortably aware of watchful eyes. He stopped a moment to look around. He noticed a Mexican man working on an auto engine in the adjacent yard. He was wearing a greasy, sleeveless T-shirt and equally greasy baggy blue jeans. Dale knew the man had been watching him, but as soon as he cast his glance in the man's direction, he appeared fully absorbed in his work.

"Excuse me," he called, waving toward the Mexican.

The man looked at him with a blank expression.

"Hable inglés?"

The Mexican stood up. Dale noticed his fists were clenched. "A little," he said, his accent thick. *"Porqué?"*

Dale gestured toward Christine's house. "I'm looking for the woman who lives there. It looks like someone broke into her place. And she's gone. Do you know her?"

"No, sorry." The Mexican squatted down and resumed tinkering with the engine.

"Do you live here?" Dale pointed to the run-down stucco house adjoining the yard.

"Sí. But I know nothing."

Dale wasn't about to let him off so easily. He crossed over to the Mexican's yard, uninvited. "I am a doctor. My name is Dale Harper." He pulled his ID card out of his shirt pocket and held it out. "At City Hospital."

He had discovered it was handy to carry his ID, even off duty. One day at the beach he had witnessed an elderly man collapse on the sand. Dale rushed to his aid, starting CPR when he found no pulse. He was just beginning to see signs of life when the victim's son came bounding over and pulled him off. "What do you think you're doing? Wait for the EMTs," he had shouted.

"I'm a doctor! He's coming to!" Dale shouted back, struggling to free himself from the son's grip.

"The hell you are!" The son, a fat, hairy-chested man in his fifties, probably thought Dale was just some starry-eyed kid. He had been an intern, looking much younger than his twenty-nine years. While the two of them struggled on the beach, surrounded by dumbstruck onlookers, the old man died. When the

EMTs arrived, they took the poor fellow to the morgue. He wished it had been the son.

The Mexican seemed to relax ever so slightly when he saw Dale's laminated name and picture before him.

"I work days," the Mexican said. "I hardly ever see the lady lives there."

"Do you know whether a robbery was reported? It's a mess in there," Dale said, pointing to Christine's house. He wanted to be sure someone knew it had been like that before he arrived.

The Mexican shrugged. "Doctor, there's robberies 'round here all the time. The gangs."

The Mexican eyed him askance. "What you want with her?"

"She may have some important information that could help a patient of mine." Dale put his ID card back in his pocket.

The man nodded. "I seen her a couple times. Long straight hair. Kinda small. Wears jeans all the time, don't dress like a woman." He smiled for the first time. "She looks mean. I keep outta her way."

"When's the last time you saw her?"

The Mexican frowned. "A while. Can't say for sure." He turned back to the engine.

Dale sensed he was being dismissed. He didn't think the Mexican knew any more. If he did, he wasn't about to share it. He reached out his hand. "Thanks. What's your name?"

The Mexican wiped his hands on his thighs and shook Dale's hand. "Roberto."

"*Muchas gracias,* Roberto. If you think of anything more, please give me a call." He turned to leave. The mongrel dog was still sitting in the same spot, his eyes apathetically following Dale. It was that kind of neighborhood. Apathetic.

38

Dale weaved in and out of the thickening afternoon traffic. On the track of the elusive Christine Anselm. But all he had found was a ransacked house in Glendale. And a deepening mystery. He eased his car toward the exit ramp, skillfully gliding between a sleek red Mercedes convertible with a couple of yuppie lovebirds and a battered old Dodge van packed with kids.

He stopped at a gas station and dialed Nina's number. No answer. Frustrated, he looked up Moran's number. Moran wasn't much, but he was a connecting link.

"Hello?" A woman's voice, abrupt, flattened his ear.

"Is Dr. Moran there, please?" A jackhammer was stuttering nearby, and he had to put a finger to his ear to block it out.

"Who's calling?"

"A student."

"One moment."

He waited, interminably, it seemed. He watched the cars lining up for gas—people topping their tanks, always a sure sign of tension in the Middle East.

Finally, Moran came on the line. "Hello, hello." His voice sounded muddy.

"Dr. Moran. It's Dale Harper. I have something about Christine Anselm. Can we talk somewhere?"

"Yes, yes, of course." There was a long pause, and

he wondered if Moran was still there. "Why don't you come to my house tomorrow night?"

He couldn't imagine a worse place. "What about your wife?"

Moran laughed. "No problem. I don't want to meet at the medical center for obvious reasons."

Dale hesitated. "All right. I'd like to bring Nina Yablonsky."

"By all means!" Moran cried. "We'll make an occasion of it. Break out some vintage Cabernet."

When Dale entered the radiology department, the place was bustling—unusual for a Sunday. This much activity usually signified an emergency—a multivehicle accident, a gang shooting, or a building collapse.

He threaded his way through the corridor traffic to Nina's cubicle, only to find it empty. He retraced his steps and called to one of the X-ray technicians wheeling a man with a gaping head wound down the hall. "Is Dr. Yablonsky around?"

"Haven't seen her," the tech said, hurrying on.

He went back to her cubicle. Her white coat was gone, so he guessed she was about. He had her paged, and within minutes her phone rang. He scooped up the receiver. "Nina?"

"Dale! I've been trying to reach you. About Ron Orloff. Let me finish this CT scan." She was breathless. "This place is a madhouse—a head-on between a tour bus and a truck. Fractured skulls everywhere. I'll be a few minutes. Don't move!"

Nina came hurrying in, a worried look on her face. Dale had been flipping through a radiology journal. He jumped up to greet her with an embrace. "Am I glad to see you," they said in unison, then laughed with the joy of lovers.

He watched as she put a series of X rays on her viewbox—fine slices through a not-so-fine brain. Muttering something about brain surgery as her sharp eyes surveyed the films. She made a brief dictation of her findings into a recorder, sighed, and then, her shoulders sagging, turned to him. She flung her white coat on a chair.

"I don't know where to begin," she said. "I'm worried sick about Ron. He's become a raving fanatic."

Dale nodded grimly. "Like a person who knows he's dying. Where did you come across him?"

"In micro this morning. Mike Bancroft asked me to stop by, so I visited with him between scans. I saw Ron in the hall as I came out. He looks like death warmed over."

Dale frowned. "He hasn't shown up for rounds. He doesn't return my calls."

"Denial. You'd think a doctor would know better. He's pushing us all away." She smiled sadly. "I feel sorry for the poor guy."

"I do too. What did he have to say?"

"He said he was going after Moran. He wouldn't say why. I asked how he explained Lincoln Lee and the others. He got upset and clammed up." She shook her head. "He's so pale. And he's lost so much weight, he's almost a skeleton."

"There's nothing we can do . . . Did he say what he was doing there? He's too sick to be working."

"No, but here's the bizarre part. Heffron came gliding by, smiling graciously, put his arm around Ron, and whisked him off." She lowered her voice. "I followed them—into Heffron's office."

Dale gave her an amused look. "And?"

"I put my ear to the door. I heard snatches of the conversation. They were talking about Ron's illness. Moran's name came up, of course." She paused. "So did yours. But I couldn't hear what they said."

Dale snorted. "It's hard to take these clowns seriously. Moran is trying to get me to finger Heffron. And Heffron's trying to get Ron to finger Moran. Meanwhile, the ship is sinking, and our mystery remains unsolved.

"I keep coming back to Christine Anselm. She seems to have disappeared. Moran may be the key. He's invited us to his house for drinks tomorrow night. Will you come with me?"

She reached out and kissed him. "Try to keep me away."

Robert Heffron sat with his feet on the desk, a cold meerschaum pipe parked in the corner of his mouth. He toyed absently with the jade paperweight. After a while he reached for his lighter and fired up his pipe, then leaned back and studied the ceiling.

It was time, he knew, to take a different tack. Dale Harper was not the type to be stopped by threats. If anything, he appeared to be inspired to even greater activity by the clouds gathering around him.

Heffron, who prided himself on knowing what made people tick, had gravely misjudged on this one, and it irked him. What irked him even more was the fervor with which Harper's girlfriend joined in the hunt.

He puffed on his pipe thoughtfully. Getting Harper in trouble had not been much of a challenge. Audrey had done her job admirably, as he knew she would. With her nursing background she was suited perfectly for the job. It hadn't taken much to deal with what little conscience she had by invoking the you'll-be-taking-them-out-of-their-misery bit. The right to die with dignity and all that nonsense. She was conventional enough to balk at the thought of cold-blooded murder. But call it a mercy killing, and she couldn't wait to get her needle into some poor slob's vein.

Nonetheless, she'd messed up royally on Cantrell. Now, if Cantrell identified her, Heffron knew it wouldn't take her long to implicate him. Of this Heffron was sure. Women were like that. No loyalty. And certainly no strength. No, it was the Harpers of the world—and the Heffrons—who had that. It all boiled down to the primal issue of turf, like a stallion fighting for supremacy over the herd. And, like the stallion, he would not be at peace until his rival was eliminated, one way or the other.

They approached Moran's house—a white stucco affair in the Hollywood hills—with a certain excitement. It was a sprawling two-story villa, with a nicely landscaped approach of shade trees and bright splashes of colorful bougainvillea.

They had dressed casually. Dale wore jeans and a red flannel shirt with a brown corduroy jacket, and Nina, a navy-blue blazer with brass buttons over a teal shirtwaist dress. He looked at her with approval.

"Looks like Herman does all right for himself," she said as they climbed the brick steps.

Dale nodded, ringing the doorbell. Within moments Moran flung the door open. "Come in, come in!" he roared. "So glad you could bring your lovely colleague." He raised Nina's hand to his lips, bowing melodramatically. Dale could smell the alcohol on his breath.

Moran looked all set for an evening of leisure. He wore a black velveteen robe with red trim, a pair of gray slacks, and Moroccan leather slippers. Nina and Dale looked at each other with amusement.

"Be prepared for a bizarre experience," Dale muttered as they dutifully followed their host.

Nina rolled her eyes.

Dale grinned. "Worry not. I'm the one he'll flash."

Moran seemed totally oblivious, humming to himself as he led them down a long corridor. He turned and waved them into the living room. They followed obediently and sat down together in a rose-colored love seat. Dale's eyes traveled over the room. He was struck by the number of liquor bottles lined up on the shelves. The mirrored backing didn't help any.

"What can I get you?" Moran asked, heading for the wet bar.

"I'll have a gin and tonic," Nina said. "It's been a rough day."

"Me too," said Dale.

Figuring that Moran already had a few drinks under his belt, Dale decided to get to the point quickly. "I've told Nina about Christine Anselm. I found where she lived, but her place has been broken into. And she's gone."

Moran snorted. "Old Bobby probably trying to wipe out the evidence. Find anything?"

"A phone bill. She made some calls to Heffron last month, at his home number—a few to his work number." As Moran turned, Dale searched his face. Moran's lips were twisted in a nasty grin. "It seems you were right, at least about their connection."

Moran shuffled over with the drinks. "Of course I was right." He went back for his own drink, then fell into his easy chair, placing his drink on the glass table between them.

As if on cue, a woman entered the room, circling around behind Moran. She put her hands on his shoulders. "Who are your friends, dear?" she asked sweetly, squeezing Moran's shoulders, her long red fingernails digging in like painted daggers.

"My dear Audrey, imagine you home at this **hour**. Did your tennis cancel?" He tilted his head for a better look at her. She wore a dark green housedress, and looked sleek in it.

"Herman, you know I don't play tennis on Mondays." She stepped toward the love seat and extended her hand. "I'm Audrey Moran." A stiff smile crossed her face. Dale noticed she was heavily made-up. She was attractive, but there was a brittle coldness about her, and he found himself hesitant to take her hand. Her eyes locked on his.

"I'm Dale Harper, and this is Nina Yablonsky," he said, putting his arm around Nina.

"Are you students of Herman's?"

"I'm a medicine resident, and Nina's a radiology resident."

Audrey smiled. "How nice. Herman, I would like

a Dubonnet on the rocks," she said, keeping her eyes fixed on Dale.

"Certainly, my sweet." Moran hauled himself out of his chair and moved toward the bar.

Audrey perched on the edge of the coffee table. "You should let me know when we're having guests, dear, so I can be at my best."

"I didn't want to bother you with business, love. But you're certainly welcome to join us." He pecked her on the cheek. "And you're always at your best."

"Well," she said, sipping her drink and moving her eyes around the room, "don't let me keep you from your business. Please, go on."

Moran looked perfectly at ease. "What we're discussing, Audrey dear, is the concern these two doctors have about radiation contamination at the medical center. I've offered to help them."

"Goodness!" Audrey exclaimed. "This sounds super-serious."

"And so it is." Moran took a gulp of his drink and seemed to sink deeper into his chair. "Dr. Harper here, and his lovely colleague Dr. Yablonsky, have come across evidence that seems to implicate our esteemed colleague Dr. Heffron."

Audrey smiled. "Oh?"

"Tell Audrey what you've come up with, Dr. Harper."

Dale didn't like the way things were shaping up. "Please go ahead, Dr. Moran. You're the one with the information."

Moran cleared his throat, for the first time appearing unsure of himself. He shifted his weight around in his chair, then went to the wet bar for a refill. He wobbled ever so slightly. "As you were saying, Dr. Harper, this woman, Christine Anselm, has apparently been having an affair with Bobby Heffron." He smiled at Audrey, who chose that moment to spill her drink. "You know about Bobby's reputation with the young ladies, dear. At any rate, this Christine person appears to have been writing his articles for him. Can't say it comes as a shock."

For a moment the only sound was the gurgling of the gin into Moran's glass. Then the fizzing of the tonic water. He moved leisurely back to his chair and sat down with an air of nonchalance.

"I did a little digging—belatedly alas—on Bobbyboy. Seems he was faking his research back East. They threw him out. Got him to 'resign' by promising they would keep it quiet. Helped him get a good position here. He learned his lesson well. Instead of faking research, he got one of his grad students to do it for him, and took all the credit. You might say he knows how to . . . use his resources, eh?" Moran's eyes flitted toward his wife, who was sitting rock still, her face expressionless. There was an uneasy silence.

"What's the connection between Christine and Western Nuclear?" Nina asked with an air of innocence.

Moran gave her a triumphant look. It was the question he was waiting for. "To provide him with plutonium, of course!"

Nina frowned. "Am I missing something? We know that Heffron uses plutonium. What's so special about Christine delivering it?"

Moran's eyes widened. "Surely you don't think it's a coincidence?"

"So what?" Nina was clearly puzzled. "What's the big deal? Is he getting it free? He uses it for research, right?"

Moran's mouth widened into a gloating grin. "That's why we're all here! To find out what dastardly deed he's up to this time." His arm swept toward his wife. "Except for Audrey, of course. She thinks he's hot stuff, don't you, sweetie?"

Audrey stood up, her lips curling in contempt. "I've had enough of this nonsense, Herman. You'll have to entertain your little guests by yourself."

He flashed her a mocking smile. "Oh, don't run off, darling. We were about to talk about the virtues—and sins—of nursing." He turned to Nina. "Audrey is a registered nurse, but she's only recently returned to the working ranks, right dearest?" He winked wickedly.

Audrey spun to leave, but apparently thought better of it, and took a stance in the middle of the room. "You'll have to take what my husband says with a grain of salt, I'm afraid," she said with measured exactness. "He's an alcoholic." She leveled her eyes at Moran. "I'm sorry to have to bring this up in front of your guests, Herman."

There was an awkward silence as Audrey turned her gaze back toward Dale, continuing to ignore Nina. She sighed and said quietly, "My husband needs help."

Moran's eyelids were drooping. He grinned good-naturedly and went on like a bulldozer, as though nothing had happened. "Tell us, Audrey, why you went back to nursing. Doctors always find these matters fascinating." He tossed the rest of his drink down.

Audrey rolled her eyes and smiled tightly. She glanced around the room, her eyes lighting on Dale, this time with a strange—almost vulnerable—look. Dale gave her a noncommittal shrug. Moran might be an alcoholic—that was certainly no news—but he had said enough in his drunken ramblings to stop his wife in her tracks.

Dale gave Nina's hand an I-know-what-I'm-doing squeeze and said, "I would be interested in hearing why you went back to nursing, Mrs. Moran."

As Audrey's eyes flared, Moran rambled on. "Audrey has trouble remembering, so I'll help her along. It seems she chose the graveyard shift to make her reappearance. You always were the night owl, dear. I would never have known if a colleague of mine hadn't spotted her at the hospital."

"It was a case of mistaken identity. I told you that," Audrey broke in.

"Oh, come now, dearest. You are one of a kind. Nobody looks like you. You spend thousands of dollars a year to make sure of that, in fact. And so," Moran went on, ambling to the bar again for a refresher, "we're left with Audrey Moran, mystery nurse. Has a nice ring to it, don't you think? The stuff for a racy novel.

"Let's see, what night was it, Audrey? I have trouble remembering—a problem we alcoholics have. So I link something unmemorable with something memorable, and bingo! A way to remember them both! In this case, it was the same night, Dr. Harper, that your patient Jesse Munoz died. I remember that very well, because I'm on the frigging review board. Got yourself in a little hot water with that one, eh?" He slopped down his drink and screwed up his face. "Ugh. Forgot the damn ice."

"I'm warning you, Herman." Audrey's voice had dropped ominously. "If you keep this up, you'll be talking to my lawyer."

"Hah! That sleaze-ball you belly up to at the club?"

Audrey's face turned a shade of red. "I've had quite enough, Herman, and I'm sure your guests have as well." She made a waving motion with her arm. "I'm afraid I'll have to ask you to leave now. My husband clearly needs his rest."

Dale saw that Moran was already appearing to nod off. Nina gave him an unmistakable let's-get-out-of-here look. He nodded and stood up.

He was furious. Moran had been playing with all of them. Dale wanted to give the man a piece of his mind, but he knew it would be hours before Moran would be conscious enough to hear him.

He and Nina walked wordlessly toward the front door as they accepted Audrey Moran's cold invitation.

39

Herman Moran rolled over in bed, burying his throbbing head under his pillow as the phone jangled insistently. He let a hand grope for the body next to him, resting it comfortably on a firm hairy thigh. He felt a savory stirring, then a fleeting moment of uneasiness as he tried to remember who he was with. God, he must have had one too many. He couldn't recall how he ended up here, in his own bed, naked. His last memory was of Dale Harper and his girlfriend leaving, rather abruptly.

He peeked out from beneath the pillow, but it was too dark. The anonymity—the sheer wickedness—of the circumstances aroused him, and his fingers kneaded his partner's thigh as they crept upward to find a hard, tumescent organ. He moaned with anticipation.

But the goddamn phone kept ringing. Hell, maybe Audrey would answer it. That is, if she had returned, after peeling out of the garage in a cloud of exhaust. *That* he remembered, with considerable amusement. Ten rings, twelve rings. Shut up!

"You ought to answer it. Maybe it's an emergency," the voice next to him whispered as a hand lifted up the pillow.

"Yeah," he muttered. "Maybe my dear wife drove off a cliff." He reluctantly took his hand away and reached for the receiver. "Hello."

"This is Dale Harper. I think you owe me an explanation."

It took a moment for Moran to realize what the hell

Harper was talking about. He sounded angry, and his voice seemed to bounce around in Moran's head like a racketball, aggravating his headache.

"I owe you nothing, and you've got one hell of a nerve calling me like this." He sat up and turned on the bedside light, casting his eyes surreptitiously toward the figure beside him. It was one of his medical students, who had been flunking microbiology. Herman was helping him out. Special private tutelage. Goddamn Harper! He smiled at his student—what the hell was his name? Rolling his eyes with exasperation, he pointed at the receiver with a grimace.

"I'm tired of your sick games. It's time for some straight talk." Dale's voice assailed him with its fierce intensity.

"You couldn't have picked a more convenient hour," Moran whined sourly. "Call my secretary in the morning and make an appointment, like a normal person." He observed his fat paunch hanging out, glanced at what's-his-name, and flipped off the light. "Good-bye." He heard Dale's voice crescendoing in anger as he gently placed the receiver in its cradle.

He rolled back toward the student with eager exploring hands. "Now, where were we?"

Dale entered the lecture hall from the upper door. A few heads turned with mild interest. He was wearing his white coat, so he didn't look out of place. The lights had been dimmed and Herman Moran was below in the lecture pit, talking and showing slides. Even in the dim light, Dale noted Moran's characteristic slouch.

Dale stood there a moment, feeling an unexpected nostalgia in this amphitheater, where he had spent eight hours a day as a medical student, listening to one lecture after another for two years. How he had yearned for patient contact, and to escape this sterile prison of cushioned red seats, row after row. No windows. No fresh air. Parades of professors, most of whom wouldn't demean themselves to touch a patient, but who were willing to step out of their ivory towers for an hour in the name of education.

Despite the starkness of the lecture format, his mind had eagerly soaked up what tidbits of useful information were thrown at him. Unfortunately, most of the lectures had been deadly, with Moran's microbiology course taking the prize. Terminal Moron. Some things never changed.

His eyes swept the hall, where some one hundred second-year students sat in varying stages of wakefulness. One, more fortunate than the others, was actually snoring, his chin resting on his hand. Two other students were whispering intently over a diagram. The woman seated by the aisle where he stood was doodling. They all looked so young.

He drew in a deep breath, determined to get on with his mission. He moved on down the steps and took a seat in front. He pulled out a bag of potato chips and opened it noisily. Moran, still talking, looked in his direction but didn't appear to recognize him in the near-dark auditorium.

"And so, right here you can see these two bacteria undergoing phagocytosis, while this one, resistant to the antibiotic, appears to have an invisible mechanism to fend off the body's white cell defenses." Moran touched a pointer to the images of the bacteria on the hugely magnified electron micrograph that lit the screen. An amoebalike organism, the white cell appeared to be engulfing two perfect spheres. He turned off the slide projector. "Lights, please."

Dale jumped up and went over to the side wall switch, flicking on the auditorium lights. "Is that good, sir?"

Moran, immersed in his notes, said, "Yes, yes, fine." He sounded slightly annoyed.

"I'm sorry. I didn't hear you, Dr. Moran." Dale stood by the switch, munching loudly on his potato chips. A few of the students began snickering.

"What?" Moran looked up and froze. He put his pointer down and shuffled through the papers on the podium, collecting himself.

Finally, managing a weak smile, he said, "Why, Dr. Harper, what a pleasant surprise." He was astute enough not to ask why Harper was visiting his class. He looked up at his students. "Any questions?" he kept his eyes high, avoiding Harper's gaze.

Moving back to his seat, Dale's hand shot up. "Yessir. I have a question."

Moran's eyes scanned the audience, ignoring Dale. Finally, he saw another hand up, way in the back. "Mr. Rosen?"

The student stood up. "Could you explain again, what you meant by . . ."

Dale interrupted. "Wait, I had my hand up first." He pumped his hand up and down, like a first-grader who desperately needs to go to the bathroom. He crumpled up the empty bag of chips and dropped it on the floor.

"Yes, Dr. Harper?" Moran nodded tentatively and motioned for Rosen to sit down. By now the class was fully awake.

"Well, actually, sir, I have several questions. But"—he shrugged nonchalantly—"we'll just have to take them one at a time."

Moran fidgeted, eyeing the clock.

"The problem with the basic sciences," Dale said, "has always been how to apply them to real life. Now, this diagram you just showed us. One organism devouring another. I think a concrete example would be helpful."

The students began to murmur together in hushed tones. Moran sat down unnerved. "Dr. Harper, please make your point. You're wasting our time."

"I'd be glad to, Dr. Moran. Just for the sake of example, suppose that a medical resident is one of those bacteria, and you're that bloblike white cell, trying to devour him. And that resistant bacteria off to the side is, oh, let's say, one of your colleagues. Now, let's suppose . . ."

The class was now fully enjoying itself, with the students edging toward the front of the auditorium in their excitement.

Moran sputtered, "Get out of my class, Harper, before I call security."

"No, you won't call security." Dale looked around the lecture hall, then stretched his legs and yawned. "Shall I go on?"

Moran stood up. "Class dismissed," he snapped. "Go on, all of you, get out of here." He waved his arms, trying to move people along. Dragging their feet, they filed out, wistfully looking back over their shoulders. Dale sat quietly, his arms across his chest.

As the auditorium emptied, Moran went back to the podium and stood there rigidly, gripping its sides as if to keep from falling. He looked at Dale with an inscrutable expression. Neither of them spoke.

Finally, Moran walked over to the exit, closed the door, and took a seat near Dale. He faced Dale, as if to speak, and then turned away, burying his head in his hands. His body began to heave with huge, fitful sobs. After a while, he raised his head, sniffling, his eyes red.

Moran's collapse was unexpected but not totally surprising. He has been skating emotionally on a razor's edge all too long. Dale felt no sympathy, only a kind of cold clinical pity. He didn't like the way he felt, but he knew for once he was seeing the real Herman Moran. He waited, letting Moran speak when he was ready.

Moran pulled a handkerchief from his pocket and blew his nose. He leaned back and took a deep breath. Like so many alcoholics, he seemed to swing from one self-destructive mood to another.

"I hate myself," he said in a dull voice. "I'm a failure. A total failure. My marriage is lousy—my wife hates my guts. My students think I'm a bore. My colleagues laugh at me behind my back. And don't think I'm unaware of my nickname. Terminal Moron." He laughed quietly, bitterly. "I'm a drunk, and I have no one to blame but myself."

He looked at Dale ruefully, then forged on, as though purging himself in the catharsis of self-flagellation. "It's true. I hate Robert Heffron. He has everything— looks, cleverness, charm, money. I'll never forgive my wife for throwing her affair with him in my face. For that I despise her."

"Enough to lie about her?"

"What I told you yesterday about Audrey was not a lie. One thing I'm *not* is a liar." He seemed to be grasping onto this virtue as if it were the last thread of his unraveling self-respect.

Dale was like a hungry dog with a bone. "You implied your wife poisoned Jesse Munoz. Didn't you?"

"I thought it all came together. Her association with Heffron, her secrecy, the timing."

"Circumstantial evidence," Dale said. "The kind that gets thrown out in court." He felt disappointed. Moran was finally leveling with him, and he didn't seem to have much. So typical.

Moran suddenly sat up straight. "Wait a minute. You got into trouble one other night, didn't you?"

Dale looked at him with surprise, as though seeing him for the first time. "Yes. The Hector Cantrell case. How did you know . . . ?"

"I told you. I'm on the review board. Not because I'm any great judge of weighty matters. Simply because I'm a department head." He spoke with irony and self-contempt. Or perhaps, Dale thought, his contempt was for a system that would make someone like him a department head.

Dale felt a surge of excitement. "The incident with Cantrell was on the twenty-third of last month. A Tuesday. Where was your wife that night?"

A crafty smile slowly formed on Moran's face. Dale knew in that moment that the window to Moran's soul, as smudged and small as it was, had just slammed shut.

"I don't know," Moran said, his eyes gleaming. "But I'll find out."

40

Dale's weeks on the cancer ward seemed an eternity. His relations with Jon Werner were increasingly strained. Ron Orloff's conspicuous absence left Dale with double duty. Even his medical student, Janet Michaels, looked at him askance. Only two people seemed to believe in his innocence: Nina, and the rattle-brained Herman Moran.

To make matters worse, while on probation all his orders needed to be countersigned. The nurses had to call Werner or Andy Hamilton for verification. At least, Dale thought, they went through this formality begrudgingly.

These were hard times, but he tried to focus on the good things. All he had to do was think of Nina, and it was as though a weight fell off his shoulders. And he would smile. Sometimes, he would be drawing blood, or starting an IV line, and he would think of her. At such times, his smile earned him an odd glance, which made him smile all the more.

Tonight, as he sat at the nurse's station, writing his chart notes prior to signing out, he felt unaccountably irritable. Maybe it was because Nina wasn't feeling well. Home with the flu, she had said. He had wanted to come by, but she insisted he stay away. "That's all you need. To catch this miserable bug of mine."

The prospect of his upcoming evening stretched out before him like a vast, yawning, empty chasm. He was barely aware of Andy Hamilton self-consciously sticking a chart in front of him.

"Uh, Dale, did you really mean to order a stop to Annie Snowden's potassium? It was low last week." Andy giggled, that damn self-conscious giggle that drove Dale crazy.

Biting his lip, he said, not looking up, "Yes, Andy, I meant to. Isn't that what the order says?"

Andy was apologetic but determined. "Well, I'm not sure I can okay it, Dale. I mean, like I said, her potassium was low, and, well . . ."

Dale threw down his pen and glared at him. "I wouldn't want you to compromise your principles, Andy. Don't countersign it if you think you'll lose sleep over it."

Andy quailed as though the pen had hit him between the eyes. "Oh, come on, Dale. I don't like this any more than you do. Stop making it hard for me."

Dale turned in his seat to squarely face Andy. "Andy, I'm just trying to take care of my patients. Do you think I'm doing a bad job?"

"No, but . . ."

"Then countersign the goddamn order and leave me alone." He went back to writing his notes.

Andy was abashed for a moment, then held his ground. "Well, could you at least tell me why you stopped it?"

Dale suddenly felt hot, and saw his fists clench, as though they weren't part of him. He knew Andy was thinking of his own skin. He took in a deep breath, then grabbed Annie's chart, flipping to the lab section. "Her creatinine is 3.6, Andy. She's slipping into kidney failure. Potassium will kill her. Is that good enough?"

Andy giggled. "Oh, I didn't see that. Good point. Right. Thanks, Dale." Andy strode off with a look of relief, scribbling his signature next to Dale's.

Dale decided he should have let it go. Annie was still hanging on, still in coma. The potassium probably would have ended her misery mercifully.

He tossed aside the chart he had been working on,

and took up Lincoln Lee's record. Lincoln. He had almost died, thanks to the chemotherapy, but he had pulled through. A tough kid. Dale had written a discharge order the day before, but Jon wouldn't countersign it. He wanted to put Lincoln through the latest "surefire" course of chemo. Dale had been livid, but he didn't argue. He knew it would be useless. The more you went up against a guy like Werner, the more you pushed him in the wrong direction. He might order a double dose of chemo, just to show how right he was. So Dale Harper, the hospital pariah, had a better idea, and he was going to carry it out now, before he left tonight. The hell with them all.

He leafed through Lincoln's chart one more time, checking the day's lab values, just to be sure there were no surprises. Everything looked in fine order. He slipped the chart under his arm and headed for Lincoln's room. He found Lincoln sitting on the edge of his bed, munching away. On his plate was a pile of mashed potatoes and green beans, with slices of a gamey-looking meat. Mystery meat, they called it. It looked worse than it tasted, thank God.

"Lincoln, you're looking good."

Lincoln waved. "Hey, Doc. I feel great. I about cried though when Dr. Werner told me I'd have to be here at least another week. Thought I was gonna be set free." Lincoln scooped a mound of potatoes into his mouth. His cheek bulged as he chewed.

"That's what I want to talk to you about." Dale sat down next to him. "I think you should go, Lincoln. Tonight. Against medical advice. There's a form you can sign."

Lincoln laughed. "Hey, man, how can it be against medical advice if you're telling me to do it?"

Dale smiled. "Dr. Werner and I disagree about your care. I don't think it would be wise to put you through another round of chemotherapy right now. Especially when you almost died from the last round. But he has the final say."

Lincoln stopped chewing, and regarded Dale with his big brown eyes. "You saved my life, Dr. Harper," he said softly.

Dale shrugged. Who knew what forces were at work when someone pulled through against all odds? "You have a strong will to live," he said. "That helped."

"Yeah. But I couldn't have made it without you." Lincoln stopped eating and scowled. "What about Dr. Werner? Wouldn't he be mad at me, if I left?"

"No. He'd be mad at me."

Lincoln poked thoughtfully at his mystery meat. "I don't want to get you in trouble." He looked up, the soft brown pools he had for eyes started to gleam. "But I sure would like to get out of here."

"You've got to remember, Lincoln. A hospital is not a prison. You can leave anytime you want."

"Then what would I do? Do I have to take any medications? Do I get to see you again?"

"I have a clinic every week. I'd like to see you next week. We'll check some bloodwork. I have a prescription here for you, if you choose to leave."

Lincoln started to shovel another load of mashed potatoes into his mouth, stopped, put his fork down, and pushed his tray away. "Where's that form?"

Dale tossed his mail on the table and flung himself down on the couch. He lay stretched out, his hands behind his head, thinking about Lincoln Lee. He felt a thrill of pleasure as he remembered the sight of Lincoln, light-footed as a dancer, leaving the hospital. Then he felt a deep sadness, an impenetrable sense of melancholy, knowing that no matter how happy Lincoln was now, his days were numbered, short of a miracle. Life seemed so unfair. Nothing made that more real to him than the cancer ward.

He stared at his phone, expecting it to scream at him any moment, as soon as Jon Werner found out what he had done. Sorry, Jon. You'll have to find some other sucker to experiment on.

He trudged into the kitchen and threw open the refrigerator door, looking for something to eat, even though he didn't have much of an appetite. Nothing looked appealing, but there wasn't much selection. He ate most of his meals out. Even the hospital cafeteria beat eating at home, but the thought of staying in the hospital one minute longer had been unbearable.

Finally, he put two slices of ham between two slices of whole wheat bread and popped open a can of Coke. He wandered back into the living room and turned on his answering machine.

"Dale, this is Dan Church. I need my horses shod in the next week or so. Please give me a call at 786-9821. Thanks."

He flipped on the television, keeping the volume low as the messages reeled off, looking for the sports scores.

"Dr. Harper. This here's Willie Lee. I'm wonderin' if you could call me about when Lincoln's coming home. The number's 491-8734." He smiled. Willie would get his answer in person tonight.

Damn, the Dodgers lost again to the Cardinals. It looked like it was going to be a pennant year for the Cardinals, the bums.

"Dr. Harper, my name is Chris Anselm. I, uh, heard you wanted to talk to me." Dale plunked down his Coke and stood over the machine, pen and paper poised. "Well, I, uh, want to talk to you. I'm on the move, so I'll have to call you back." Damn! He threw down the pen and paper, frustrated. The ever-elusive Chris Anselm. At least she was alive. It turned out to be a good night to stay home—glued to the phone.

He turned off the machine and flopped back down on the couch, stretching his legs out on the coffee table. The phone rang just as he was getting comfortable. Probably Werner.

He reached for the receiver without having to move off the couch. "Hello," he said brusquely, unconsciously bracing himself for Werner's onslaught.

"Dr. Harper?"

He sat bolt upright. "Yes?"

"This is Chris Anselm. I'm in a big fix. A friend of mine told me you might be able to help me."

"I hope I can. I've been trying to find you. I think we can help each other."

"I'm staying at a motel in Pasadena. I'm afraid to go back home."

"I'll meet you. How about tonight?"

"No. We mustn't meet," she said emphatically. "I'm too scared to come out. Can we just talk on the phone?"

He couldn't believe his luck—finally.

"Sure. Right now?" He lodged the receiver in the crook of his neck while he grabbed pen and paper.

Her voice was soft and musical. "It's hard to know where to start. I was a graduate student of Robert Heffron's, years ago. he taught me everything I know. I've continued to publish articles with him, thanks to his generosity and encouragement." He could hear her take a long drag of a cigarette. "I've had a tough road—being a woman in a man's field. But he stuck by me, all the way."

Dale was baffled, and fascinated. It was a little too easy. "What happened at Western Nuclear, and why did you leave?"

She laughed. "You should have been a detective. Dr. Heffron helped me get a job there. There were no openings for me at the medical center. I followed him out here from back East. I had a crush on him, and I guess he felt a responsibility for me. Unfortunately for him."

There was a long pause and Dale thought he might have been cut off. But it was only uncertainty. "I might as well get it all out," she sighed. "It so happened we slept together a few times. Dr. Moran found out and threatened to go public. Unless I would supply him with plutonium from Western Nuclear. He would never tell me what it was for, but he made me promise not to keep any records, and to make the deliveries secretly."

Dale frowned. It was all a little too pat. He wished he could record the conversation.

Another long drag on her cigarette, and then she swept on, almost as though she were reading from a book. "The amounts kept growing. I started getting scared. I told him I couldn't do it anymore." Dale could hear her tamping out her cigarette and lighting another. "That's when he threatened me. He said he would see to it that Robert Heffron was ruined, and it would all be my fault. I decided to disappear.

"I went back to my place to get my things and get the hell out, and it had been ransacked. As I was packing my stuff, I got a phone call—a death threat.

"That's when I knew it was time to get help. A friend told me you might be interested, so I called."

"Who was the friend?"

"I can't tell you that."

Dale sat transfixed, tapping his fingers on the arm of the couch. "Why didn't you call the police?"

"I didn't want to get Dr. Heffron in trouble."

"You have no idea why Moran wanted this plutonium?"

"No. But I do know the amounts were large—more than he would need for research."

"Why don't you just go to Heffron and tell him what you've told me?"

He heard a break in her voice. "I feel like I've betrayed him."

Dale shook his head, confused. He didn't like any of it. Why was someone going to all this trouble? He knew enough to guess she had been put up to it. But why?

He stood up, shifting the receiver to his other ear. "Listen, I don't know how I can help you. Where can I reach you?"

She sounded hurried. "I'll call you again. Be careful. Moran's a madman."

"I'll do what I can, Christine."

He heard a sigh. "Thank you, Dr. Harper. I'm glad I called."

"So am I."

The dial tone buzzed in his ear.

As she hung up the phone, she looked at Robert Heffron with a tentative smile, like a child seeking approval. "How'd I do?"

"You were great, Tracy." He sat down on the couch and pulled her down next to him. "If you weren't such an excellent graduate student, I'd advise you to take up acting." He put his arm around her and tilted her chin up as he smiled at her reassuringly. He was pleased. Harper would be confused for a while. Enough to be put off the scent until Heffron could proceed with a more definitive solution.

She giggled. "Oh, I'd love to be an actress." Her lovely brow furrowed. "Who is this Christine Anselm, anyway?"

He threw his head back and laughed. "She's a thorn in my side, no more important than a Herman Moran or a Dale Harper. The world is full of incompetents, seeking to destroy their betters. Your little act tonight will throw up a few roadblocks. Confuse and conquer." He smiled. "Napoleon. Have you heard of him, my dear?"

Tracy was not to be put off. She pouted coquettishly. "But an actress should understand her character . . ." Tracy's voice trailed off as Heffron cupped her breast in one hand and slipped his other hand under her skirt. His tongue fluttered in and out of her ear.

"Oooh, Dr. Heffron . . ."

41

Dale stared at the phone, perplexed. He looked at his watch—nine o'clock already. His stomach rumbled, and he couldn't remember if he had eaten. As if in answer, a twinge of heartburn crept up his chest, accompanied by the sour taste of half-digested ham. He swallowed the rest of his Coke to chase it down.

He stood up and paced his small living room, thinking. Then he dialed Moran's home.

"Hello?" It was Audrey's distinctively abrasive voice.

"Dr. Moran, please," he mumbled, hoping she wouldn't recognize his voice.

"Who is this?" she demanded.

"A student."

"Name?"

He wondered if she had been an army nurse. "Ron Orloff," he said. A loud noise assailed his ears as she dropped the phone and called for Moran.

After a good wait, Moran came on, his slurred voice a distinct contrast to his wife's. "H'lo, Ron."

"This is Dale Harper. I just had a very strange phone call from someone who claims to be Christine Anselm."

"Harper?! Jesus, why can't you leave me alone? If I'd known it was you . . . goddammit, we're about to go out."

"Did you hear me?"

"Harper, you have no sense of proportion or priorities. You get obsessed with something, and nothing else exists. You need to get hold of yourself, boy." Moran spoke in measured sentences, like a man who knows when he's had too much to drink.

"Your priorities are *real* clear. First your booze, then your scheming," he retorted.

In the ensuing silence, Dale surmised something he had said was filtering through the alcohol to Moran's soggy brain.

"What the hell are you talking about?" Moran finally exploded.

"Christine Anselm says you're trying to ruin Robert Heffron, and that *you're* the one using plutonium."

"Christine Anselm? Where the hell did you find her?"

"She found me. Five minutes ago."

He heard Moran turning away from the phone, telling Audrey to go on ahead. He would catch up. His tone now was a little plaintive. "Listen, Harper. Why don't you come over and we'll talk? Audrey's going on without me."

Remembering all too well the earlier meeting, Dale rejoined, "Let's meet at my place."

Surprisingly, Moran agreed. After giving him directions, Dale peeled off his sweaty hospital whites, showered, and changed into jeans and T-shirt.

While he waited for Moran, he called Nina. He was relieved at the lightness in her voice. "I'm worlds better," she said. "I slept almost all afternoon."

He told her about his conversation with the alleged Christine and Moran's upcoming visit.

"I want to be there," she said.

"Are you sure you're up to it?"

"I wouldn't miss this one if I had the plague."

When Nina arrived there was still no sign of Moran. Dale was so glad to see her that Moran's tardiness went unnoticed. He was happy to have time with her alone. He deluged her with questions about her health.

She rolled her eyes. "Will you stop being the doctor? You're off duty, you know."

As her hand moved, he spotted a bruise on her wrist. He held her arm to the light, pulling back the sleeve of her sweater. "How'd you get this?"

She shrugged. "Gosh, I don't know. I'm always bumping into things."

He lifted her other arm, again rolling up the sleeve. "Any others?"

"Not that I know of," she said with an edge to her voice.

He drew her closer to the light and rolled down her lower eyelids. "You don't look anemic."

She jerked away from him. "Dale, I don't have leukemia! Now will you stop it? I'm not another Ron Orloff."

He embraced her, stroking her hair. "I'm sorry, Nina. I worry about you."

"I'm fine. I can't wait until you get off that miserable cancer ward. It's making you morbid." She took his wrist and looked at his watch. "It's late. Where's Moran?"

"Probably stopped at a bar to fuel up. I'd better call."

There was no answer at Moran's. Dale began to feel uneasy. Nina suggested they leave a note on the door, and go check Moran's house. They piled into the Mustang for the short jaunt.

They knocked and rang the doorbell, with no response. They looked at each other. "Let's try the garage, see if his car's here," suggested Dale. Both garage doors were locked. He tried to lift them, but they wouldn't budge.

They returned to the front door and found it unlocked. They slipped in and Dale was about to call out, but thought better of it. Putting his finger to his lips, he led Nina down the hall to the living room, which they could see was lighted.

There, slouched in his easy chair, his head back, a drink spilled in his lap, was Moran. He was a ghastly sight. His mouth hung open and saliva was dripping down his chin. Was he comatose or just in a drunken, stuporous sleep? Or dead? Dale was relieved to see his chest move.

He crouched down next to Moran and felt for his pulse. It was strong and regular. "The son of a bitch must have decided to have one for the road and it zonked him. Let's wake him up."

Nina looked for the kitchen. "I'll make some coffee."

"Good. I'll slap him around a little." He shook Moran's shoulders and tapped him on the face, eliciting a few grunts. "Herman, wake up!"

He walked over to the wet bar and found some ice. He put a few cubes down Moran's back and took another and slid it over his face. "Rise and shine, Herman."

"Aaaaggh." Moran began coughing and thrashing, his eyelids twitching.

"Come on, Herman. Time to face the music." Dale unbuttoned the top of Moran's shirt and dropped an ice cube down the front.

Moran came to abruptly, his eyes popping open with a mixture of horror and annoyance. "What the hell . . ." he sputtered, his lips foaming.

Nina came in with a mug of coffee and gently put it to his lips. "Ow, hot, goddammit!" He tried to push it away, but she forced it on him.

"Herman, you know where you are?" Dale tapped him again lightly on the face.

"Yeah, yeah, yeah. Disneyland. Spare me the Mickey Mouse questions." He rubbed his head uncertainly. "What the hell happened?"

"That's what we want to know."

Moran sat up, alertness sneaking into his eyes. "I know. Audrey slipped me a Mickey. She'd kill me if she thought she could get away with it."

Nina and Dale smiled at each other. Moran caught the exchange. "I'm not kidding. She's a shark." He looked around. "God, I need a drink." He started to get up, but Dale gently though firmly pushed him back.

"You need to sober up." He felt like he was humoring a child. He put the mug of coffee in Moran's unsteady hand. "Chug-a-lug."

Moran gasped and wiped his mouth with his sleeve. He motioned for Dale and Nina to sit down, took a sip of the coffee, and wrinkled his nose.

"I'm a cad," he said, very matter-of-factly. "I should have gotten back to you. Turns out Audrey wasn't home the night of the Hector Cantrell fiasco. She was, quote, playing bridge, unquote, with Marge Anderson. I checked. Marge was out of town that night."

"Did you ask her about it?" Nina said.

"Ask Audrey for the truth? Let's be realistic."

"What about Christine Anselm?" Dale put in.

Moran screwed up his face. "She says she was delivering plutonium to me? Outrageous. Old Bobby-boy put her up to it. Believe me, Harper, I'm not your villain. Let's face it, I'm not clever enough."

"So you say," said Dale, but he silently agreed.

"Dr. Moran, if your wife was going around in a nurse's uniform to make Dale look like a criminal, there might be some clues lying around," Nina said.

"Like what?"

"Like a uniform, or an identification badge."

Moran waved an airy hand. "Take a look around. The shark is out looking for little fishes." He guffawed. "Her room's at the head of the stairs. Hell, look around for plutonium. Look anywhere you like. I could care less."

"This doesn't feel right," Nina said, puffing at the top of the stairs.

Dale eyed her with concern. She looked tired. "What doesn't?"

"Invading a woman's privacy. It's an assault."

"Somehow I can't get worked up about it," he said dryly.

He took in Audrey Moran's bedroom as he stood at the threshold. There was a basic austerity, despite obvious efforts to make it decorative. There were two paintings over her super-sized bed that, while colorful and grand in scale, looked as though someone had gone through his paint cupboard and randomly splashed it over the two canvases. The bed was neatly made, accented by a deep violet comforter and lavender pillow shams. Dale realized, finally, what it was that bothered him. Although there were windows, the natural light was shut out by heavy violet draperies, giving the room a funereal feeling.

Nina wandered around, touching objects as she came upon them, trying to get a handle on the woman who was Audrey Moran. "I'm just a little spooked, like the night we prowled around the micro labs."

"Audrey Moran is a spooky person," Dale said, knowing exactly how she felt. "Why don't you check her closet, and I'll search around here?"

"I'm looking for a nursing uniform, right?" Nina found a walk-in closet and pulled on the light cord.

"That, or anything else that might arouse your suspicion. Sometimes you don't know what you're looking for until you fall over it."

She chuckled. "Spoken like a true scientist."

He crossed to the bedside table. On it were a reading lamp, a clock, and a stack of paperback books. Most were novels by Danielle Steele and the like, which didn't fit his image of Audrey. There were a few mysteries by authors he didn't recognize, and an old copy of *U.S. News and World Report*. A Los Angeles phone book. Nothing exciting. As he was opening the drawer, he heard Nina call out.

"Good grief, this woman has more shoes than Imelda

Marcos! And a wardrobe to match. Hmmmm, I wish she were my size."

"Something white, look for something white," he reminded her, rifling through the papers in the drawer. A few bills. Two parking tickets. A tennis club membership card. And a vibrator.

"Wait. Two uniforms." Nina brought them out and hung them on the closet door. They didn't look new. Nor did they look twenty years old. She ran through the pockets as a matter of course. Her hand came upon something round and cool. She pulled it out, and stared at it, a small empty vial. She read the label. Speechlessly, she passed the vial to Dale, her eyes riveted to his face.

He took it from her, and read the label aloud, the syllables sticking in his throat. "Andromycin. Thirty milligrams. Expires 3/94. Littleton Laboratories."

"You two indulging in hanky-panky up there?" Moran's voice wheezed at them from below. The gasps between words suggested he was coming up the stairs.

Nina and Dale stood handling—fondling almost— the andromycin vial. They did not speak. It seemed clear this small glass bottle was Dale's ticket to absolution. Far more convincing evidence than the missing carbon of his andromycin order. They could, as they tipped the vial upside down, even see a residual of the potent red liquid trickle along the sides.

Nina ruefully observed that they had ruined whatever chance they had to identify Audrey's fingerprints.

Dale shrugged. "She won't know that."

Nina considered the implications of their find. How could they prove that Audrey Moran had poisoned Jesse Munoz, especially if her fingerprints were no longer detectable? Then, as Moran's muddled voice filtered up the stairs, she had another, more horrifying thought. What if Moran had only been using them all along to get back at his wife?

"Dale," she said with studied calm, "suppose Moran planted that vial in his wife's uniform? Or planted the uniform, for that matter?"

Dale could hear Moran's heavy breathing moving closer. "We're almost finished up here," he called. "We'll be right down." He needed to decide, quickly, whether to let Moran know.

"Listen"—his voice dropping to a whisper as he drew Nina behind the door—"I've got to trust Moran. If he can't help me, I'm gone. I haven't caught him in a lie yet, which is more than I can say for our friend Heffron."

She could see the tension in his clenched jaw, the grim, tight lips. "You have to go with what you feel, Dale." She tried to smile, but her lips wouldn't do her bidding.

"I've got to play along with him, Nina. If he's using me, that will become clear soon enough. I can't imagine things getting much worse."

Just thinking of Moran made her nauseated. But she would go along with him. She restrained a sigh.

Dale pocketed the vial while Nina returned the uniforms to the closet. "We've got something," he cried.

She was not so sure.

Moran's eyes gleamed as he sat back, panting, in his easy chair. He held the vial to the light as if scrutinizing a rare diamond for flaws. "Well, well, Audrey, we have been busy, haven't we?"

"You can't tell Audrey about this," said Dale quickly. "She'll cover her tracks like a snowbird."

Moran handed the vial back, a malicious grin signaling his intentions. He threw his head back, muttering to himself. "Let's see, Audrey, my sweet, you'll get ten to twenty years for this, if you're good." Reaching for his drink, he added, "And since Bobby-boy is the mastermind, he'll get a good deal more. Too bad jails aren't co-ed yet." He gave a raucous laugh.

"Dr. Moran," Dale said as a thought struck him, "do you have a recent picture of Audrey?"

Moran looked at him as though he had just noticed he had company. "Hmmm?" He shook his head. "I'm not a photographer. And if I were, I wouldn't waste my Kodachrome on Audrey. But her picture was in the *Herald*'s sports section about a month ago. She was a runner-up in one of the local tennis tournaments." He snickered. "That's Audrey. Always a runner-up."

Nina leaned forward. "Would you have a copy of the paper?"

"You've got to be kidding." He frowned. "What do you want it for?"

Dale shrugged and slipped the vial into his pocket. "We can find a paper at the library, I imagine. We'd better get back."

42

Nina stopped at her mailbox as she hurried into the radiology department. She was late and her day was jam-packed. She spotted a large box along with the usual interhospital correspondence and departmental memos. Putting down her briefcase, she pulled the box out eagerly. It had her name scrawled on it and she guessed it was from a grateful patient. Even radiologists could touch people's lives. Usually the gifts were chocolates or homemade goods.

The box was in a plain brown wrapper and fairly heavy. She guessed something homemade. She grabbed her briefcase and the box and entered her cubicle where she set everything down. She tore open the wrapper and lifted the lid off the enclosed shoebox. Inside was a jar of what looked like raspberry jam. She smiled. One of her favorites. A small white envelope with her name typed on it was taped to the jar. She slit it open and pulled out a card.

As she read the message, she stood still in shock for a moment. Then she kept turning the card over with trembling fingers as though questioning the reality of what lay so innocuously in her hand. She picked up the jar again and it slipped out of her uncertain grasp to the floor. The glass shattered and the red contents oozed out around her feet. The color of blood.

She looked at the card and read it again. Typed in capital letters, with no signature, it said, "THIS TIME PRESERVES. NEXT TIME PLUTONIUM."

* * *

Dale shot down the stairs. Nina hadn't told him what it was about, but he knew from her voice over the phone that something terrible had happened. He left an incensed Jon Werner in the middle of morning rounds. No matter. There was no love lost.

As he came upon Nina sitting next to a pool of reddened glass, his first thought was that she had been injured. He rushed to her and gathered her in his arms. She buried her face in his chest, and without speaking pointed to the typed card on the counter. He picked it up and read it aloud.

He shoved the card in his pocket and held her tight. Neither uttered a word, each caught up by the heaviness of the moment.

Finally, he said, "I'm getting you out of here."

She stepped back and looked at him. His agitation had the effect of calming her. She had overreacted. And now he was overreacting. For all they knew it could be a hoax, a thoughtless prank. She was coming to her senses. "I'm sorry, Dale. I can't just drop everything because of some idiotic note."

He seemed not to hear her, as though drawing further into himself. His eyes were a kaleidoscope of shades and tints, each reflecting a thought or mood. Suddenly he gripped her arm and led her into the hallway. She had to break into a jog to keep up with his long stride. He came to a stop in front of the women's rest room.

"Nina, go in there and bring back a sample of your urine."

She gave him a blank look. "What?"

"Nina, just do it. Now. I have to know."

"Know?"

Suddenly she understood. It was as though her mind had been keeping her from taking in more than she could handle. She shrugged off a moment of fear. Plutonium in her urine? Absurd. She had to bring all this nonsense to a halt. Before they both went mad. She squared her shoulders and entered the ladies' room.

She returned with a cup in a few seconds. So ordinary-looking, she thought inanely. Even as she held it, Dale was on it with the Geiger counter. There was no sound, no movement of the needle. Under different circumstances she might have felt relieved. But now she was acutely aware of the absurdity of standing in the hospital corridor hovering over a specimen as though their lives depended on it. She noticed people looking their way.

Suddenly, she laughed. One roll of laughter after another. He looked at her vacantly for a moment. And then he laughed with her, picking her up and swinging her around, as though she were light as a feather. Miraculously, not a drop of urine spilled.

With a greater sense of urgency than ever, Dale hunted down Steve Rodale in the ICU, where the house officers were just finishing morning rounds. A smile crossed Steve's pleasant face.

"Dale! Good to see you. I thought you'd have been by sooner. Hector Cantrell's doing great—we're transferring him to the medical ward today."

Dale nodded. "I've been keeping in touch through the grapevine. I never know what to expect when I come in here. People love scapegoats. Even doctors."

Steve grimaced. "I don't care what those yahoos on the review board say. Haven't they gotten off your back yet?"

"There's a meeting on Friday. They'll decide then whether I stay or go." Dale extracted a newspaper clipping from his pocket. "I'm supposed to meet with Carleton before that." He handed the clipping to Steve.

"Here's a picture of the woman who may have increased Hector's IV fluids to make it look like I fouled up. Maybe he can recognize her, if you think he's up to it."

Steve studied the picture, which showed two women smiling into the camera. One held up a trophy, the other had her arm around her. The caption had been cut off. He frowned. "Which one—and who is she?"

"I'd rather not say. If I'm wrong, it will only cause more trouble." He took the clipping back. "You're better off the less you know. Let's leave it to Hector."

"I think Hector's up to it. I'll see that you have some time alone with him."

Dale extended his hand. "Thanks, buddy."

"Mr. Cantrell, remember me?" Dale asked gently, standing at the man's bedside. He still had an IV running into his arm, and plastic prongs in his nostrils, feeding him oxygen. Doing great, Steve had said. Everything was relative. At least he was alive.

Cantrell's dark eyes peered up at him listlessly. Dale thought he saw a glint of recognition. Cantrell smiled weakly. "Hi, Doc. I remember your face, but not your name. *Lo siento.*"

"No need to apologize. I'm Dr. Harper. Remember the night I saw you?"

"A little. It's mostly a blank. They tell me I was on a breathing machine. But I don't remember nothing about it."

"Do you remember how many times I saw you?"

"No, sorry." He tried to push himself up in bed but fell back.

Dale felt a twinge of disappointment. "Let me help," Dale bent down. "You push with your feet, and I'll lift." He put his arms under Cantrell and pulled him up, then sat on the bed.

"Mind if I ask you a few more questions? We're still trying to figure out what happened that night."

"Anything, Doc. Ask me anything. I wanna get well and go home. I don't want no more surprises."

"Do you remember seeing any of the nurses adjusting your IV?" He pointed to the tubing that ran between a bottle of fluid and Cantrell's arm.

Cantrell squinted, furrowing his brow. "I remember one nurse come in, didn't say nothing, just puttered around with the hose in my arm. I asked what she was doing, and she didn't answer." He reached a bony hand up and scratched his thatch of black hair. "I didn't think nothing of it. Nurses treating you like dirt."

Dale pulled out the clipping. "Mr. Cantrell, I know it seems a long time ago, but did that nurse look like either one of these women?"

Cantrell squinted again as he studied the clipping. After a minute or so, which seemed like an eternity, he pointed a shaky finger. "That one, she looks something like her. But like I say . . ." His voice trailed off as he handed back the clipping.

Cantrell had pointed to the wrong woman. And she didn't look a bit like Audrey Moran.

Dale decided to look up the student who had reported seeing Audrey Moran in the hospital the night of Jesse Munoz's death. He called Moran and got the name. Sue Alderman. He looked at his watch. He had enough time to run over to micro before Grand Rounds. On the chance that Nina might be able to break away, he gave her a call.

"Dr. Yablonsky."

"Hi, sweetheart. I have a little errand to run over in micro. Think you could join me?"

Nina looked at the stack of unread X rays and cringed. "I'd love to," she said.

"I'll swing by."

He picked her up and they marched down the dimly lit tunnel connecting the hospital with the medical school. After an elevator ride and another long walk, they came upon a spacious lab area, where they looked without success for someone fitting the description Mike Bancroft had given them.

A nearby student filled them in. They followed a pointing finger and came upon a young woman with horn-rimmed glasses seated at the counter next to a microscope. She was jotting down notes and looked preoccupied.

"Excuse me," Dale said as Nina stayed in the background. "Are you Sue Alderman?"

She stared back at him. "Yes. Who are you?"

"I'm Dale Harper, a medical resident, and this is Nina Yablonsky, a radiology resident." He swept a hand toward Nina as she came forward and smiled at Sue.

"Umm, can I help you?"

"We hope so." He saw there were already a few heads turned their way. "Is there someplace private we can talk? It shouldn't take long."

Sue looked around hesitantly. "There's a small lounge area around the corner. I guess . . ." She suddenly caught herself. "What is this about?"

"Let's talk in the lounge."

She turned off her microscope light, closed her notebook, and led them to the lounge, a hodgepodge of a room with a few plastic chairs, a vinyl table, and a shelf of reference books. Not so different from the shoddy accommodations for doctors at the hospital.

They sat down and Dale began on a casual note. "Dr. Moran told me that you saw his wife at the hospital late one night a few weeks ago, dressed in a nurse's uniform."

Sue batted her forehead with her hand and laughed. "Oh, that. Me and my big mouth. A case of mistaken identity, that's all."

Nina couldn't contain her surprise. "You're saying you did *not* see Audrey Moran that night?"

Alderman nodded without looking at them. Dale and Nina exchanged glances, both wondering the same thing. Who had gotten to her.

"Who did you see, then, Sue?" Dale asked softly while thinking he would like to hang her upside down and shake the truth out of her.

She shrugged with a self-conscious air. "Just some

nurse. You know how it is, late at night when you've been working hard. Your mind plays tricks on you."

Dale knew she was lying. His voice turned harsh as he looked right through her. "Who," he demanded, "told you to lie?"

She kept her eyes downcast. He could see her lips begin to tremble. "Oh, please. Leave me alone."

"I know you're lying. People have died. More people could die and"—he paused—"you could be one of them. What you saw is obviously important enough for someone to try to keep you quiet."

She shook her head. "I can't help you."

Nina leaned forward and let her hand rest on Sue's shoulder. "Sue, we know what you're going through. Don't try to go it alone."

Sue looked up uncertainly. Nina gave her a sympathetic smile. She sensed that Sue desperately needed to unload the truth. She just needed the right circumstance.

As though reading Nina's mind, Sue burst into tears. "It's been a nightmare."

"Tell us about it," Nina said.

Sue looked up with reddened eyes and moist cheeks. She blew her nose and stared at the crumpled tissue in her hand. "Audrey Moran phoned me and told me to stop spreading malicious lies about her. She called me a vicious gossip, when all I did was mention it once in casual conversation. Then she told me I could be thrown out of the graduate program." Her breath caught for a moment. "She was just awful to me."

"Is their anything else, Sue?" Nina handed her another tissue.

"One of my professors called me and said the same thing."

"Was it Dr. Heffron?" Dale asked.

"No, it was Dr. Guest."

"And you're sure? You're sure it was Audrey Moran?"

She shook her head. "What's so terrible is that even though I was sure at the time, after all this I'm no longer certain."

Dale brought out the clipping and showed it to her. "Was it one of these women you saw?"

With the wadded-up tissue to her nose, eyes puffy and red, Sue Alderman nodded and put her finger on the newspaper likeness of Audrey Moran, tennis trophy runner-up—and angel of death.

"Whew," Nina said, back in the radiology department. "That poor girl."

Dale slammed his fist on the countertop. "What in the hell is that witch Audrey Moran up to?"

"She's out to get you. But why?"

"Heffron. It has to be," Dale muttered. "He knows we're catching up to him. First he tries to discredit me and now he's trying to get to me through you."

Nina didn't know what to say. She had no fix on Heffron's connection to plutonium and the poisonings. He couldn't be using human guinea pigs, as Moran had implied. No journal on earth would publish the results.

Dale stared at Nina. "You're staying with me," he said. "Till this thing's over."

She smiled. "But my things . . ."

"I've got room for your things."

She knew, by the determined look in his eyes, that he wouldn't give up. Besides, she liked the idea. "All right. Tomorrow night."

"Tonight."

"But I've got so much to do. And I have to go home and pack some clothes."

"Then do it. I'll go with you."

She laughed. He could be unbearably stubborn. "No, I can do it myself."

"Okay," he said solemnly. "But I want you at my place no later than ten."

"Yessir." She saluted him with an amused smile.

* * *

With all the distractions of the day, Nina didn't finish up until dark. And that without a break for supper. She was famished. Checking her watch, she knew it would be impossible to get to her apartment, clean up, eat, and get to Dale's by ten o'clock. She tried to reach him to let him know she would be late, but he wasn't around or answering his page. She would try him again when she got home.

Stepping outside the little world of her cubicle, she was surprised to find no one else around. The radiologist on call was most likely in the emergency room. She realized she had never been completely alone in the department before, and there was a stark coldness about the place. All those lines of viewboxes, usually brightly lit, looked like a bank of vacant windows. She was reminded of the one-way mirrors in the psych department, and had the momentary chilling sense that maybe someone was watching her through the milky rows of glass.

She shrugged it off as a case of nerves, hung her white coat on a hook, and grabbed her briefcase. She experienced another disquieting moment as her feet stuck to the floor. The custodian had done a poor job mopping up. Grimacing, she slung her purse over her shoulder and hurried out.

She walked briskly through the parking lot toward her car, the click-clack of her heels making a loud echo. Usually there was a security guard in the lot at night. There had been several muggings and one rape so far this year. And the female staff had been encouraged to request an escort to their cars after hours because of the soaring crime rate. She hadn't thought much about it, having grown up in a much tougher neighborhood and knowing something about taking care of herself. But tonight, as she moved amid the shadows, she had second thoughts about those uniformed old boys offering her an arm. The card had bothered her more than she let on.

Fortunately, the lot was well lighted, and she had already spotted her car, an electric-blue Honda Civic. She quickened her pace. She heard a rustling somewhere behind her, and shot a look over her shoulder. She was relieved to see a guard patrolling the area on foot. But when she recognized the snoring Mr. Zimmer, she ducked her head in embarrassment. With her back to him, she tossed her things in the car and slid into the driver's seat. She locked all the doors and made sure the windows were rolled up, then felt annoyed at herself. She had never been this jittery before.

At the familiar purr of the engine she began to relax. She flipped on her favorite classical music station and looked forward to the drive home. By the time she pulled into her parking spot beneath her apartment complex—which Dale dubbed Singlesville—she had been able to put the day behind her.

As she climbed the steps, she saw a couple sitting in the Jacuzzi, and she found their presence reassuring. She waved, even though she didn't recognize them.

As she entered her apartment, she switched on the light, put her things down on the coffee table, kicked off her shoes, and flopped into a chair, putting her feet up. She looked at her watch. Nearly ten. She felt too tired to move. She dialed Dale's number to tell him she was fine and she'd be okay here tonight. After five rings, she frowned, let it ring a few more times, then hung up. Where was he?

She decided to have a frozen dinner and a beer to help her relax, and padded toward the kitchen. As she puttered around, she began to feel an inexplicable uneasiness. She didn't know why until she headed into the bathroom. There was a faint perfumy odor that she knew wasn't there when she left this morning. While there was a familiarity to it, she was sure it wasn't hers.

She stepped into the hallway, turning on every light

she could find as she moved down the hall. She sniffed
the air. There it was again. The scent was stronger
as she approached her bedroom. Suddenly, she was
terrified. She knew, beyond a doubt, that someone
else had been there, or was still there. She stood stark
still, her ears straining. There was only the monoto-
nous hum of the microwave. She stared toward the
bedroom at the end of the carpeted hallway. The door
was half-closed.

She felt something drawing her onward, down the
hall, toward the bedroom, as though she were sleep-
walking in a nightmare. She had a compelling need to
know. Nothing was worse than what your own head
could conjure up. She tiptoed stealthily along the corridor, which suddenly seemed endless. She realized,
as she started to feel light-headed, that she was holding her breath. She took two big gulps of air. She
sneaked back to the kitchen, returning with a healthy-
sized butcher knife.

She was almost to the door when the phone rang.
It made her jump. She waited, counting the rings. Ten
times. Her watch said ten-thirty. It had to be Dale,
wondering where she was. Oh, God, should she answer it? Finally it stopped.

She waited a moment longer, listening for signs of
life. Then, with all the strength she could muster, she
leapt across the threshold, threw the door open,
switched on the light, and brandished her knife like a
savage, all in one profoundly fluid motion. Her eyes
quickly scanned the room. Nothing was out of place.
Or was it? Something was missing, but she wasn't sure
what.

The bed. There was something wrong with the bed.

Then she knew. Her cherished teddy bear, the one
remnant from her childhood that had followed her
into adulthood, was gone. Where was Snuffy?

She cautiously slinked around the perimeter of the
room, her head pounding. The odd perfumey scent
hung in the air. Then she spotted Snuffy. Behind the

door. What was left of him. He had been sliced to shreds. And taped to one of the precious brown plastic eyes that had watched her grow up was a typed note. "THIS TIME YOURS. NEXT TIME YOU."

"Answer, dammit!" She must have dialed Dale's number twenty times as she sat on the edge of the bed, her hands shaking, tears streaming down her face. She kept the knife on her lap. She didn't dare leave the room.

She slammed the phone down and realized the thudding she had thought was her heart was coming from the other room. They were back!

She grasped the knife, turned out the light, and hunkered down behind the door. There was thumping, yelling, then the crashing sound of glass.

As she crouched quivering in her hiding place, her life flashed before her. Just as it might with a drowning man. Years of timeless images consolidated into seconds. That, followed by a strange sense of cold calmness as she heard footsteps in the other room, crunching the broken glass.

She was ready for it—whoever, whatever, it was. The terror was gone, and in its stead a simple acceptance. There was no turning back, no running away.

She heard him coming closer, and poised the knife above her head. She heard his footsteps, heard his breathing, smelled his sweat, saw his face through the crack . . .

His face! It was Dale! A metal pipe in his hand.

What was she doing on the floor, looking up at him? He was holding her, talking to her, but he seemed so far away. He disappeared and then he was back with a glass of water. He sat her up, his hand supporting her. She drank down the cool liquid. She shook the cobwebs out of her head and he suddenly came into focus. Then she could hear him again.

"Nina, are you all right?"

She put her hand to her head. Her hair was damp with sweat. "What happened?"

"You passed out for a few seconds. Shock. At first I thought someone had knocked you unconscious."

"Now I remember," she said. "I heard you out there, and I thought it was someone here to . . . kill me. I had my knife ready. My God! Dale, I might have stabbed you!" She could feel the tears start up again. She pointed to the remains of Snuffy and the note.

She watched him read it. She saw his face turn to stone. They were beyond the point of reason. And she saw no way out.

43

Dr. John Carleton's face was solemn. His lips formed a thin line with no hint of leniency. He clearly meant business. Despite his own predicament, Dale found himself feeling sorry for Carleton. He looked as though he carried the weight of the world on his shoulders.

Dale sat and waited, his arms crossed in front of him. His eyes came to rest, as they had many times before, on the portrait of Hippocrates above Carleton's head.

Carleton cleared his throat. He looked down at his hands. He leaned back. Finally, he spoke with rigid formality. "We have considerable ground to cover before your meeting with the review board Friday." He paused. "I want you to know that I am on your side. However, on Friday, I must, like a juror, cast aside my inclinations and review your case objectively. It is expected of me."

His eyes glided past Dale's, then returned to the papers on his desk. "You face very serious charges indeed. I want you to know what they are."

Dale had a sinking feeling. "I would appreciate that," he said, endeavoring to keep his voice firm.

Carleton donned his reading glasses and peered at the documents on his desk. "There are several issues, the principal one being the death of Jesse Munoz." He looked over his glasses at Dale. "I understand you have, against my advice, continued your own investigation. Perhaps you have accumulated evidence to help establish your innocence. I hope so." His voice remained rigidly correct, the formality disconcerting.

"I know I'm innocent," said Dale, "but I'm not ready to say who *is* guilty. Not until I'm sure."

Carleton studied him for a moment, then went back to his papers. "Of course not. Then there is the Hector Cantrell case. What's your position on that?"

"Someone tore my orders and progress notes out of the chart, making it look like I put him into congestive heart failure. Whoever it was flooded him with IV fluids. Cantrell remembers a strange nurse fiddling with his IV that night."

"That's what nurses do. They fiddle with IVs. Is that all you've got?"

Dale shrugged. "I'm working on something. I'm close. That's all I can say right now."

Carleton sighed, shaking his head. "I have an incident report here from the oncology fellow, Jon Werner. He charges you endangered the life of a patient by telling him to leave the hospital, against Werner's advice." He flashed a yellow sheet of paper. Even from where he sat, Dale recognized Werner's oversize scrawl. To match his ego, he thought bitterly.

"That's a matter of opinion," he responded. "No one should be faulted for discouraging a patient from an experimental drug protocol. Especially when the patient's doing well and wants to get on with what life he has left."

He thought he saw Carleton's expression soften momentarily. "Of course the committee will make allowances for matters of opinion," said Carleton.

Carleton removed his glasses and rubbed his eyes. "Be prepared to discuss your conflicts with Werner." He repositioned his spectacles on his nose.

Dale nodded. "Thank you for the warning. Will Werner be there?"

Carleton made a notation. "We'll see what we can arrange."

"What about Dr. Heffron?"

Carleton started to look up, but went back to scrutinizing the papers on his desk. "There are some miscellaneous matters here, which I do not consider serious, such as the complaints your friend Dr. Orosco has lodged against you. Or the ward clerk who claims you assaulted her with a cup of scalding coffee. But these irregularities do add up."

But what about Heffron, Dale wondered. Why was there no answer? Before he could say anything further, Carleton frowned and squinted at a paper on top of his stack. "There is one last allegation here, which warrants attention," said Carleton, his tone severe.

Dale braced himself. It had to be Heffron.

"It's from Ron Orloff," said Carleton, peering over his glasses and holding Dale's gaze.

"Ron Orloff! What on earth is that about?" He could feel the uneasiness rising from his stomach, and lodging like a lump of putty in his throat. Ron Orloff was his friend. Not an Orosco or some incompetent ward clerk, or a two-faced phony.

Carleton held up the report. "He says that you and Dr. Moran poisoned him with plutonium."

Dale gripped the arms of his chair. He felt as though he was being sucked into a bottomless vacuum. He was only vaguely aware of Carleton rising, then looming over him. He felt Carleton take his arm, as if to draw him back to reality. He felt the rim of a glass touch his lips.

"Drink this water. You look faint," Carleton said, coming clearly into focus, two images melding into one.

Dale sipped the water and rattled his head back and forth. "Thanks. I'll be okay." He took a deep breath. Carleton handed him a handkerchief, and he wiped his forehead.

Carleton moved back to his desk and sat down. "You knew nothing of this?"

Dale took another sip of water, using the time to regain his composure. Finally, he looked up at Carleton.

"When did you get that report?" he asked quietly.

"Two days ago. I've not spoken with Orloff. It came through the mail."

"I can't imagine where he got that. We're friends."

"Unfortunately, he's not here to explain. He's in New York."

"New York . . ." Dale muttered.

"He checked into Sloan-Kettering. They have a new drug protocol."

Surely Heffron was part of this. "Why New York?"

Carleton shrugged. "Maybe he has family there. The point is, he's not here to elaborate."

Dale took a moment to collect his thoughts. "You mentioned Moran. Does he know about this?"

"Yes. Dr. Moran knows."

"He must have thrown a fit."

Carleton permitted himself a thin smile. "That may be understating it." There was an edge to his voice. "Dr. Moran carries very little credibility at this point. I advise you to stay clear of him. Any connection with him can only hurt you."

Dale leaned back in his chair. "You know, when I dreamed of being a doctor, even in medical school, I never imagined I'd get in a mess like this. I just wanted to take care of patients, make their lives easier, longer, healthier. I naively thought doctors were above politics and back-stabbing."

Carleton straightened the papers on his desk into a neat pile, his head down. Finally, he looked at Dale. "I wish I could tell you more about the Orloff business. But that's all I have."

"May I see the report?"

Carleton shook his head. "You have the essence of it. Enough to give you pause." He slipped his glasses off. "Mark my words, Dale. Herman Moran is no friend of yours."

"Is there anything else, Dr. Carleton?"

Carleton laughed. It had a hollow sound. "Isn't that enough?"

* * *

Dale somehow ambulated himself out of Carleton's office. His head was throbbing. He made a detour to the men's room and caught a glimpse of himself in the mirror. His face was like chalk. He dug around in his pockets for some aspirin. Naturally, he didn't have any. Nothing was going right.

He came upon Nina as she headed into an X-ray room. She looked at him in alarm. A fine sweat coated his face.

She looked around. The corridor was bustling with activity, and no one gave them a second glance. She was late for a fluoroscopy, but it would keep. "You look like Custer's last stand."

"I just saw Carleton. Ron Orloff has filed an incident report against me and Moran."

Her eyes widened incredulously. "Why?"

"For poisoning him with plutonium."

She stared at him. "You can't be serious?"

"What's even worse, Ron's in New York City and I can't get to him."

She checked her watch. "Give me a minute to run a fluoroscopy. Then we can go for coffee."

As usual, the unexpected occurred. In a matter of minutes, she had her hands full with an obese woman who reeked of what was wryly known around the wards as Lily of the Valley. She watched the barium flow down the woman's esophagus as she lay on the table, and identified a ragged area in the duodenum that looked like an ulcer. She took a flat object like an oversize Ping-Pong paddle and compressed the woman's abdomen. More Lily of the Valley.

"Let's get some spot films of the duodenum," she called to the technician, "including an oblique."

She looked at her watch and sighed as she waited for the films to develop.

They sat in the near-empty cafeteria during the lull between the breakfast and luncheon crowd. They sipped at the stale black coffee and tried to make sense of Ron Orloff.

"You know," Nina said, "people do crazy things when they learn they're dying. Unless you've been there, it's impossible to understand how their minds work. I had a friend, an only child, whose father adored her. The week before he died he disinherited her. He left his fortune to charity. She was a struggling college student at the time."

She was babbling to no end. But it was true. She had seen it time and again. Dying people did crazy things. Sometimes inexplicably mean things, as the father of her friend had done.

Dale smiled wanly, appreciating the effort. "Ron isn't the vengeful type."

"What I'm saying is it doesn't take a type. It takes a circumstance. We all have our breaking points."

"That's true enough." He stroked his chin thoughtfully. "But I keep coming back to Heffron. You saw them together. And Ron told me earlier that Heffron was helping him. He talked of Heffron with stars in his eyes."

"You think Heffron arranged for Ron's trip to New York?"

"Yes. And had him file his charges first."

"Interesting," Nina mused, taking another sip of coffee. "Why would he do that?"

Dale looked at her with a shade of surprise. "To discredit me. People are his pawns. Audrey Moran, Christine Anselm. Why not Ron Orloff?"

"Dale, you're obsessed with that man. It's telling on you."

He frowned. "If someone keeps getting hit between the eyes with the same rock, would you call him obsessed when he ducks the next time he sees it?"

"You have a point. But even so, you have no proof."

"Exactly. And the missing link is Christine Anselm.

Once we find her, we'll have what we need to nail Heffron."

"And how do you propose to find her?"

"I have a better idea of what to look for. Plus, I've enlisted the help of the police."

Her eyebrows shot up. "The police!"

"I went down to the station house yesterday and filed a missing persons report."

"Oh, my God," she said, putting her hands to her head.

He took her hand. There was a hard, cold edge to his voice that she had never heard before. "I'm going back to Christine's place, tonight after work. Wait for me at my apartment. Don't answer the phone, and don't let anyone in."

She straightened in her chair. "I'm going with you," she said quietly.

He hesitated. "Okay," he said finally. "At least that way I can keep an eye on you."

44

They pulled up in front of Christine's house and Dale turned off the engine. "This is it." The neighborhood looked even seedier than he remembered, and he felt like turning around.

"Let's go," Nina said, her hand on the door handle. Suddenly she froze as her eyes wandered past him. He followed her gaze.

"Well, look who's here," he said, hunkering down in the seat with her. "A ray of sunshine all the way from Belair."

Robert Heffron was striding down the walk, away from the house, a grim expression on his face. The mongrel Dale had observed a few days earlier sat watching Heffron with the same disinterest.

Nina whispered, "We'd better stay out of sight."

Dale watched Heffron turn the corner. "You stay put. I'm going to have a little chat with our friend. We may have caught him with his hand in the cookie jar."

Nina clutched his arm. "Please don't."

Dale looked at her in surprise. "I'll be right back," he said as he jumped out of the car.

Nina moved over and started the car, trying to find a spot to squeeze into the heavy traffic. She cranked the wheel, watching the two disappear in the rearview mirror. In her haste she backed into the car parked behind her. And then burst into tears.

Dale had turned the corner, loping past crowds of

street people. He saw Heffron getting into his Cadillac some distance down the block and picked up his pace.

Heffron, apparently preoccupied, was tinkering with the glove compartment. Dale arrived just as Heffron put the key in the ignition. He flung open the passenger door and jumped into the car. He snatched the key, then sat back out of breath.

Heffron turned in surprise, momentarily caught off guard. He was as smooth as ever. "Dr. Harper, I presume. Do you live around here?" He smiled as he reached for the keys.

Dale, still breathing hard, dangled the keys over his head. "Not so fast, Doc."

Heffron threw his head back and laughed. "I rather admire your style, Harper. You remind me of myself when I was a small boy." He beckoned toward the keys. "Now if you'll hand me those . . ."

"Get out of the car," Dale said, staring Heffron down.

"What was that?" Heffron's face tightened.

"Out. Now." Dale leaned over and opened the door, giving Heffron a shove.

"Just a minute. This is no longer amusing." Heffron's face puffed and he turned a fiery crimson as he gripped the steering wheel.

But Dale was younger, stronger, and ignited by a deep-seated dislike of the unscrupulous manipulator. All the feeling, which had simmered in the back of his mind, exploded now in a burst of force.

"You're right, Heffron. It's not amusing," he said as he yanked Heffron from behind the wheel and pushed him out of the car.

He followed Heffron out the driver's side, slammed the door, and leaned against it. Heffron stood facing him, still holding on to himself.

"I want to know what you're doing in this neighborhood," Dale said, twirling the car keys.

Heffron's eyes flared. "I don't see how that's your concern."

"I'll be the judge of that."

"Give me those keys now. Or you'll find yourself blacklisted by every medical center in this country."

Dale folded his arms across his chest. "I'm waiting, Heffron. You're not going to bulldoze me, like you do everybody else—like Christine Anselm."

He thought he saw a flicker in the other man's eyes. Suddenly Heffron appeared to melt as if the game was not worth all the trouble.

"All right," he said. "If you must know. I came here to see Christine. She's a colleague of mine. I hadn't heard from her in a while, and decided to stop by her house. Now I find it's been burglarized and I'm concerned about her." He gave Dale a sardonic smile and held out his hand. "Give me the keys, like a good boy."

As Dale shook his head, Heffron's smile broadened. "I'm afraid that's all. No devious plots, no dastardly deeds." His voice was almost apologetic.

Dale was not to be put off. "How is she your colleague?"

Heffron rolled his eyes with just the right degree of forbearance. "She edits my manuscripts."

"And you make her co-author for that?"

"There's more to it. We're good friends—if you know what I mean." He lit up a pipe he had removed from a pocket with an amused air.

Dale resisted an impulse to wipe the smile from Heffron's face. "Did you do away with her?"

Heffron laughed. "You're being absurd, Harper. My keys, please." He moved toward Dale, his pipe dangling from the corner of his mouth.

Dale slipped the keys into his pocket. "Now, tell me why you're trying to scare us off."

Heffron sighed, as though in relief, still Mister Smooth. "That's what's troubling you? Quite frankly, I'm glad for an opportunity to set the record straight. I am doing nothing of the kind."

As they took stock of each other, there was a

screech of brakes. Nina brought the Mustang to a rocking halt alongside Heffron's Cadillac. She jumped out and ran to Dale, brushing by Heffron.

"Why, Nina, how wonderful to see you," Heffron sailed on with a pleasant nod of his head.

She looked through him as if he didn't exist. She turned to Dale. "Dale, let's go. Please."

He squeezed her hand, his eyes riveted on Heffron. "In a minute."

Heffron's pipe chose that moment to go out. He reached into his pocket for his lighter. As he pulled it out, a white envelope floated to the ground at his feet. He edged one foot toward it.

Dale's eye was drawn by the sudden movement. Heffron bent to pick it up, but Dale beat him to it. He turned it over in his hand, taking note of Heffron's malignant look. The envelope was unsealed, and several papers had been jammed into it.

Dale handed it back without examining the contents. "What's the matter, Heffron? Something incriminating in here?" He smiled. "Don't worry. I already have enough to nail you."

"Thank you," snapped Heffron as he snatched the envelope and buried it in his pocket.

"Thank *you*, Dr. Heffron. Tell me, are Ron Orloff and Lincoln Lee the victims of your latest research?" He was so intent he was barely aware of Nina tugging at his arm.

Heffron laughed easily and turned to Nina. "Your boyfriend has a vivid imagination. And so sure of himself. A dangerous combination. Very dangerous, indeed."

Dale reached into his pocket and tossed the keys at Heffron. "Don't threaten me, Heffron. And leave Nina alone, or I'll make you wish you had. Now take your keys and get out of here."

Heffron had a last smirk. "I'll remember you, Harper."

"You won't have to, Heffron. You'll be seeing me again, I'm sure."

Dale and Nina drove around the block to Christine's house. Nina had a worried look. "I've never seen Heffron quite so rattled. He's a powerful man, Dale. If he didn't hate you before, he does now."

"I can handle it." He put his arm around her shoulders.

"I wonder what was in that envelope."

"Something he didn't want us to see, that's for sure."

She smiled. "You really knew how to play him. I swear, you would make a terrific poker player."

He chuckled.

They approached Christine's house in silence. They looked up and down the street. No one in sight. They turned the knob and walked in.

Nina looked around in dismay. She had never seen such a disarray. The smell that had bothered Dale before was now almost intolerable. Obviously, the break-in had gone unreported. It was understandable. This was a neighborhood where the police spelled trouble.

"What we need," Dale said, scooping up a pile of papers on the floor, "is an address, a name. Anything that might lead us to someone who knows Christine. Friend or relative."

"Here's a handwritten envelope with a return address in Santa Cruz," Nina said, waving it over her head. "Nothing inside, and no name."

"Hang on to it. But a name would be better. Someone we could call." He pushed the couch to one side and came on a new pile of papers.

"What about her co-workers at Western Nuclear?"

"They know as little as we do. Whatever she was doing for Heffron was on the sly."

"Here's something!" Nina plumped down on the couch, waving an envelope with a gasp of excitement. It was white and square, the kind for greeting cards. "Rita DeVici. And it's a San Bernardino return address."

Dale paused to examine it. "Let's check it out."

Heffron brought the Cadillac to a stop in front of the garage and jumped out. He stalked into his study, brushing past his wife. The beginning of a smile faded as she gave him one look and moved out of his way. She returned to her soap opera.

He slammed the study door, sat down at his desk, and punched out a phone number.

"Zimmer here," came a sleepy voice on the other end.

"Wake up, you fool. It's time."

Zimmer sat up and took his feet off the desk. "Yeah?" He looked around to make sure no one was within earshot.

"Take care of the girl." He knew how to get to Harper.

Zimmer smiled, running his tongue over his yellow teeth. "I been lookin' forward to this. She shore looks juicy."

"Shut up and listen. You need to get her in the morning. When you're done, call me."

Zimmer's tiny eyes gleamed. "I'll set out first thing."

"You remember the plan?"

"You betcha."

"You had better tell it back to me, one more time. No mistakes."

The guard chortled, tugging at his ear. He repeated the plan in his own crude fashion.

"Good," said Heffron. "And remember, you're to call me when you've got her." He started to hang up.

"Hey, Doc."

"What is it?"

"Mind if I have a little fun with her?"

Heffron rolled his eyes. Zimmer was a stupid animal. But he was greedy, which meant he could be depended upon. "Have all the fun you want, my friend. You have my official sanction."

Zimmer burst into a raucous laugh. "You're my man, Doc."

Heffron hung up. He paced the room. Up to now he had just been toying with Harper. The time had come to demonstrate he was not a man for games. Rather, a teacher, about to impart an important message. Especially now with Harper on the scent of Christine Anselm. It was time to give the cocky resident a lesson he would never forget.

45

Four insistent rings. A child answered, maybe five or six years old.

"May I speak to your mother, please?" Dale asked softly.

"Mom! Phone!"

There was the raucous sound of a television in the background. Finally, "Ricky! Turn that thing down!" And then a rasping "Hello."

"Mrs. DeVici? My name if Dr. Harper." Time to invoke whatever status a doctor might have these days. "I'm looking for Christine Anselm."

A pause. Then, with a brittle edge to her voice, "And you think I know where she is? That's a laugh. And I could care less." Another pause, a rise of concern. "Are you her doctor?"

"No. But she may be in trouble." He decided to play out a hunch. It was that moment of concern prickling through the hostility. "Are you related?"

"I'm afraid so." There was a sigh. "Sister."

Dale, on firmer ground now, pressed on. "When did you last talk to her?"

"About a month ago. Ricky! I told you to turn that damn thing down! Sorry. The kid's a game-show addict."

"A month ago?" He tried the psychologist's trick of feeding back a patient's words. And he had help—a deep, underlying resentment ready to explode without too much prodding.

"Yeah, that's about right. Whenever she needs

something. Money, a shoulder to cry on. You name it. A real deadbeat."

She sounded so bitter he was afraid she might angrily hang up on him. "Mrs. DeVici, I'm in Los Angeles. I'd really like to talk to you in person." Silence. "It's important—for your sister's sake. Please believe me. If you care for her at all?"

She sniffed. "Sure you're not a lawyer?"

He laughed. "Positive."

Her voice hung for a moment. "Well, I'm here. Ricky! I'm not going to tell you again!"

Dale knocked. There was no doorbell. Nina stood at his side. They both wore their hospital identification tags, to allay the suspicions of a hostile Mrs. DeVici.

A woman in her late thirties opened the door. She had teased platinum hair down to her shoulders, with black roots emerging an inch from her scalp. Her narrow face was drawn, and without makeup. She was thin, and wore tight-fitting jeans and a T-shirt that said "Shit Happens." The TV was blaring. Apparently Ricky was still at it.

"Mrs. DeVici? I'm Dr. Harper, and this is Dr. Yablonsky." He pointed to their badges.

She laughed mirthlessly. "You cops or something?"

Dale smiled. "No, we just wanted you to know we're what we say we are."

The tension in her face let up a trace. "Come in," she said without enthusiasm. She led them to a small living room. Crayon marks littered the walls. A drooling baby sat gibbering in a playpen. A freckled, towheaded kid had his bright eyes glued to the TV. His mother walked over and turned it off. She whispered something and he left, snatching a curious look at the visitors.

She sat down, lit a cigarette, and crossed her legs. "So what's Chris up to now?" She blew the smoke out through her nose. "Have a seat," she said, almost as an afterthought.

Nina sat in a beat-up easy chair, covered with food stains. Dale straddled a worn ottoman that had seen better days.

His face was solemn. "As I said, we think she may be in trouble. Her house has been turned upside down, and she's disappeared. Out of sight."

Rita kept her face expressionless and took another drag on her cigarette. "Well, she's got nothing worth stealing. God knows what she spends her money on." She stubbed out her cigarette. "You try her at work?"

"She apparently left Western Nuclear."

A hint of alarm flickered in Rita's eyes, but she quickly looked off. "Nothing new. She can't stay put anywhere."

Nina and Dale exchanged looks. "Mrs. DeVici," Nina said, "do you know anything about your sister's social life? Any friends she might have looked up? Maybe a boyfriend?"

She had touched the right button. The woman's lips twisted into a scowl. "Chris has tagged along after some guy for years. She's obsessed." She lit another cigarette. "She's not the little sister I grew up with. She gave up a good career in medical research because of this guy. She's the one person in the family who could have made something of her life." She waved a hand around the ramshackle room as if to summarize her own status.

Dale leaned forward. "And this man's name?" He knew what it would be. It could be nobody else.

She rifled through some papers and came up with one of the articles Christine had a hand in. She tossed it to Dale. "There's his name. Heffron. Robert Heffron."

Dale and Nina gave each other knowing looks. "Have you ever met him?"

She snorted. "He's married. You don't sleep around with a married guy and show him off to your family."

"No, I guess not. Do you have a picture of your sister?"

"What do you want with a picture?" Her dark eyes narrowed. "I thought you knew her."

"I never said I met her. What I said was I thought she was in trouble. There's no trace of her. A picture might help us find her."

"If you never met her, why do you care about her?"

"Because of Heffron. We think he's messed her up."

Rita DeVici exhaled slowly, her eyes moving from Dale to Nina and back again. "She's always in trouble. She thrives on it."

She muttered to herself for a moment, then rose and left the room. She returned with a color Polaroid. "This was taken a few years ago."

Dale took it and showed it to Nina. There was a drawn face that held a hint of faded beauty. The lines of discontent around the mouth spoke of someone who had never quite gotten what she wanted out of life.

"She looks sad but tough," Nina said.

"Yeah, she's tough all right. She's a sucker, though. This heel she follows around plays her like a drum."

Nina's forehead wrinkled into a frown. "You really hate this man. Yet you've never met him?"

She spat out a shred of tobacco and snuffed out another cigarette. "Ever meet Hitler?"

After a moment of awkward silence, Dale stood up. "We've taken enough of your time, Mrs. DeVici. If we learn anything, we'll let you know."

"Thanks a lot," she said. "I won't hold my breath."

"May we keep the picture?"

"Sure. Pin it on your wall." She let out a harsh laugh and rose to show them out, closing the door on them without so much as a good-bye.

Dale and Nina stood transfixed on the outside doormat that said "Welcome." They both knew where their next stop would be.

Western Nuclear's public relations director was a short chunky man in his late thirties with a soft chubby face the color of putty. He wore a three-piece suit, which seemed absurdly out of place in the barren atmosphere of his run-down office.

He sat at a cheap-looking yellow metal desk—the kind whose drawers jam. The window behind him had no curtains or blinds, just soot. The floor was a dingy gray linoleum. A couple of landscape prints in cheap frames from the local discount store hung crookedly on the walls.

Dale and Nina had been funneled through the plant until they ended up with Albert Chase. They weren't impressed with what they saw. Neither the office nor the director.

Chase stared at them uneasily, as if he would like nothing better than for them to disappear. "How may I help you?" he asked in a solicitous voice.

Dale took the direct approach. "Are you aware," he said as he flashed his identification badge, "that one of your employees has been delivering large amounts of plutonium to our medical center?"

Albert Chase's head came back. "I beg your pardon?"

"Her name is Christine Anselm," Dale said, noting Chase's sudden attentiveness.

"I thought you wanted a tour . . ."

Nina smiled, flashing her badge as well. "We asked to speak to the head of Western Nuclear, and we got you, Mr. Chase."

"Well, that's nice of you," he said apropos of nothing.

"Christine Anselm. Do you know her?" Dale pressed on. "We thought we'd do a little groundwork ourselves, rather than bring in the State Radiation Safety Board."

Chase suddenly seemed to get the point. He turned to his computer and summoned up a roll of employees. "Hmmm. We did have a Christine Anselm employed here, but she was terminated. Last week, it says here." He pointed to the monitor.

"Why?" Nina put in.

Chase drew himself up, straightening his tie. He seemed distressed now that he may have gotten himself into something. "May I ask how this is pertinent? All I was told was that you wanted a tour."

"Yes, we would like a tour," Nina again chimed in. "We would like to see where you keep your plutonium."

"We don't keep plutonium here," Chase said as though it were a personal affront to even suggest such a thing. "It's not a material that stores well."

"Meaning?"

"Meaning, it's highly corrosive if not sealed properly. The canisters required to store it are expensive. It's much easier to simply pick it up at the Hadley Plant when we get an order—which is infrequent. Plutonium is a government commodity primarily. Our clients are from the private sector."

"The Hadley Plant. You mean the nuclear energy plant?"

"That's right. Twenty miles up the coast."

Nina leaned forward. "Which of your clients orders plutonium?"

Chase studied them a moment, as though debating what would be worse—talking to this meddlesome pair or the state inspectors. He sighed unhappily, turning back to his computer. He slowly pecked at the keys.

After a few bleeps and chirps, he swiveled the monitor around. "See for yourself," he said with a noise that sounded like satisfaction.

They stood up to scrutinize the screen. On it was a short list of private research labs. City Hospital was not one of them. No Robert Heffron. No Herman Moran.

Dale nodded politely. "Thank you, Mr. Chase."

"You're welcome," Chase said with a note of relief in his voice.

At the door, Nina turned. "Mr. Chase, one last question."

"Yes?"

"Who makes the runs to the Hadley Plant when you do have an order?"

His fingers flew over the computer keyboard. As he searched the screen, a look of surprise illuminated his otherwise dull face. He cleared his throat uncertainly. "Christine Anselm. But she's no longer . . ."

"Thank you, Mr. Chase."

"So, what do you think?" Nina asked as they drove back to the hospital.

"Two things. Christine had access to plutonium. And her visits to the medical center were a deep dark secret."

"Which means there was some hanky-panky, to borrow one of Moran's favorite terms."

"It sure looks that way."

"But we have no proof that Heffron was her client."

"No, but plenty of evidence pointing that way."

"On the other hand, if Heffron *was* storing plutonium in micro, then the canisters could have been leaking."

"But we never did find any plutonium," Dale countered.

"Here's the sixty-four-thousand-dollar question," Nina said. "Why would Heffron poison people with plutonium?"

"I've thought about that. It may be unintentional. If he's handling large amounts of plutonium, for whatever reason, there's a great risk of accidental contamination. We know what a mess it is in the micro department. Isotopes leaking all over the place and nobody giving it a second thought. On the other hand, he's unscrupulous enough to turn humans into unknowing victims."

Nina frowned. "Suppose he is hiding plutonium in the micro department? Unlikely places, like the cupboards in the lounge. Some of it spills or leaks. Someone stores his sandwich in there, and . . ."

Dale looked at her. "And plutonium with mayo on

whole wheat." He paused, appalled by the thought. "Or, if there's enough of it, whoever takes a break in the lounge inhales it. Or he gets it on his hands, then contaminates whatever he eats or drinks."

She nodded. "However it happens, he gets it internally. And it has to be either by ingestion or inhalation since it doesn't penetrate the skin."

"So, we postulate that there's plutonium, large amounts, sitting around micro. A fairly safe bet at this point."

"And," Nina added, "let's figure Christine Anselm is the supplier. She has—had—access, through her job. She knew Heffron, maybe one or both of the Morans."

Dale tapped his fingers on his leg. "So let's assume it's Heffron and Anselm. What are they doing with this stuff? Possibly research," he said. Unethical as hell. Unfortunately, not terribly uncommon in medical science.

"The only other use I can think of for plutonium is making bombs," Nina mused, staring at the car ahead of them. She remembered her outrage at Lenny Perkins when he shot off a wisecrack to that effect.

Dale mulled it over, then shook his head. "Heffron making bombs, along with all his other projects? Seems unlikely."

"I agree," she conceded. "Maybe he's selling it. The black market. He does live in ritzy Belair."

He nodded. "It's an intriguing thought, I have to admit. But such a massive operation?"

She waved a hand. "Not massive at all. A dogfood can's worth would be a start on a bomb big enough to blow up a small country."

"Hmmm. There must be big money in selling plutonium. Think of all the countries that want the bomb."

She nodded with an air of certitude. This was her field of expertise. "And it really doesn't take a lot of technology, once you have the plutonium."

"But we keep coming back to the fact that we've

never found any plutonium in micro," said Dale, swerving into the right lane toward the exit ramp.

"How about this? Heffron learns we're snooping around. He gets rid of the plutonium. But because of the leakage, we still pick up radioactivity."

"Very possible. Where would he take the stuff? Supposedly he stored it at the medical center because there was no other place. He wouldn't dare take it home."

"If he was selling it, maybe he just had his buyer come get it."

Dale squinted thoughtfully, his eyes on the traffic. "Damn," he said. "What a slippery guy."

"How about following him?"

He gave Nina a quick glance before turning onto Vermont Avenue. "A stakeout."

"Yes," she said, the thought of it animating her face. "We'll park ourselves in front of his house and watch him like a hawk."

It had possibilities.

46

"Christine Anselm is dead."

Dale held up the police report for a moment. He felt cold inside.

Nina took the report from him and stared at it. She placed it on the coffee table, speechless over the death of a person they had never known.

"They say it was an accident. Her car went off the road in Malibu Canyon. Blood alcohol level sky-high."

Nina felt numb. She knew Dale didn't think it was an accident. She didn't think so either, though she wished she could. A net seemed to be closing in on them.

"When did they find her?"

Dale fell into a chair opposite her, dropping his keys with a clang on his battered coffee table. "Late this afternoon. A hiker spotted a wreck down a ravine and called the police. They had a hard time making an identification. Her face was charred. The gas tank exploded."

"How could they get a blood alcohol level?"

"She was thrown from the car. Only her face was devastated. She died from internal injuries." His voice was a dull monotone. "She had no identification on her. They used dental records." He pointed to the report. "It's all there. I just came from the police station."

She didn't care to read it. "I could use a drink." She got up. "How about you?"

He nodded, watching her disappear into the kitchen. He liked the way she had made herself at home.

She returned with two Heinekens. He glanced at his watch. Almost eleven. "Let's turn on the news."

She flipped on the television before sitting down. "Will they have the story already?"

"They should. The police have notified next of kin."

"Rita. Have you talked to her?"

"Yeah. No surprise. She acts as though Christine had it coming. Hardly the grieving sister." He took a gulp of his beer. It tasted good. Even though it was ice-cold, he could feel it warming his insides.

They turned to the television as anchorman Jerry Landau launched the local news. "The body of a Glendale woman was found in a Malibu Canyon ravine this afternoon after a passerby spotted a wreck from the roadside. Christine Anselm, a thirty-eight-year-old employee of Western Nuclear, was thrown from her car, which then burst into flames. She had apparently been dead for several days. Forensic specialists report that she had a high alcohol level, and believe she may have fallen asleep at the wheel. She died of a broken neck and multiple internal injuries. Miss Anselm had been reported missing two days earlier."

Landau shuffled papers and went on to the next item, Christine's death another traffic fatality, as common as sushi in Los Angeles.

"Other news in the Southland tonight, the Malibu fund-raiser for the homeless is expected to draw a large crowd, says April Anderson, the project's organizer. The event will take place tomorrow night at the . . ."

Dale shut the television off with the remote control. Nina turned to him. "What now?"

He took another swallow of beer and slouched deep into the chair. "I don't know. I told the police she may have been murdered. They laughed politely. Just another drunk in their book."

Murdered. Nina felt a shiver down her spine. He had put a name on their fear, and now there was no avoiding it. "You think it was Heffron?"

"He keeps cropping up, doesn't he? He's written articles with her, faked research with her, gets plutonium from her, presumably made love with her. Then we see him hurrying down the walk of her ransacked house."

"*If* she was murdered," Nina reminded him. "It could be an accident, as they claim."

He gave her a morose look and grunted skeptically.

She sat on the arm of his chair. She brushed his hair back from his forehead. "You look exhausted. There's nothing more we can do tonight, Dale. Why don't we get some sleep and we'll talk after morning rounds?"

He took her hand. "I'm sorry I'm in such a rotten mood. I keep thinking I could have prevented it. I was two steps behind her all the way."

She smiled. "That's the doctor in you. You run through that guilt trip every time a patient dies."

"I suppose so."

"It'll pass. It always does."

He hauled himself out of the chair and lumbered toward the bedroom. "Boy, am I beat." He turned and gave her a perfunctory peck on the cheek.

"Hey, you can do better than that," she scolded lightly, trying to shake off the mood that the news had left them in.

"Yes, especially with encouragement." He laughed, and they engaged in a long, luxurious kiss, the best thing that had happened all day.

After morning rounds, which had turned into a session of escalating hostility between Dale and Werner, Dale swung by Moran's office. Moran had left a message at the nurse's station. Moran's secretary let him through with no questions.

"You wanted to see me?" he said to the harried-looking Moran.

Moran waved. "Come in, come in."

"You heard about Christine?" Dale said, taking a seat.

"No, I haven't heard a thing about Christine," Moran said with little interest. "Listen, I think we can nail Audrey."

"Oh, God," Dale muttered under his breath.

"An ex-friend of Audrey's—and she has lots of those, by the way. Women, you know, get peeved when their friends sleep with their hubbies." He chuckled. "Anyway, one of her ex-friends whose hubby porked old Audrey told me the name of Audrey's favorite hangout. She plucked it out of her husband, threatening a scandal if he didn't cough it up."

Dale tapped his fingers impatiently. "So?"

"So, I wandered over there, had a little talk with the proprietor." He screwed up his face. "It's a dumpy motel. Fits Audrey to a tee. This bozo saw her there with old Bobby boy. Recognized him from a talk show. How about that?" Moran thumped a fist on the desktop.

Dale frowned. "So what? You already knew Audrey was sleeping with Heffron. She told you herself."

"For a star resident, you're not too bright. Let me spell it out. They go there about once a week." He winked. "Dollars talk. For a few bucks I was able to arrange something. The proprietor is going to bug their room. We'll catch their conversation."

Dale let a scornful laugh escape. "Conversation? You mean like discussing which position to use? Whether to do it on the bed or the ceiling?"

Moran scowled defensively. "It's worth a try. We

can also use the tape for a little leverage, if you get my drift."

Dale got his drift all right. Disgusted, he stood up. "Is that all?"

Moran poured himself a drink. "Why don't you come down off your high horse?" He paused with the drink at his lips. "Because if you don't, someone's going to knock you off. Things aren't looking real good for you right now, bucko. The board is going to take a hard line tomorrow."

"What do you care?" He thought about Carleton's warning. And here he was. He wanted to run. Instead, he moved slowly toward the door so as not to provoke a malicious outburst.

"We're in this together, remember?" Moran threw at him. "I rub your back, you rub mine. You're not a hell of a lot of help to me if you're out on your ear."

"At least I've got Carleton in my corner."

Moran's jaw dropped. "Carleton? You really are in left field, aren't you?" He waved toward the chair. "I think you'd better have a seat."

"I'll stand, thanks. I've got to be going."

Moran gulped down half his drink. "Carleton is your biggest hurdle. He's been pushing your suspension."

Dale sat down. "What are you talking about? I just saw him yesterday. He said . . ."

Moran leaned across the desk, his eyes blazing with an intensity that even vodka couldn't dampen. "I don't give a damn what he said. He's lying. I told you. I'm on the board. I have to listen to the pompous ass. He wants you out. O-U-T. Get my drift?"

"I don't believe you." Dale felt a surging anger. His whole world was tilting in the balance. Carleton? His father's friend. *In locus parentis.* Impossible.

Moran brandished the vodka bottle like a trophy. "Maybe now you have an idea why I like my liquid friend here. It doesn't lie, cheat, disappoint, or take advantage of you. It just leaves you with a nice warm glow, a little escape from all the bullshit." He emptied his glass with a flourish, then coughed, his face turning beet-red.

Dale looked at him with a mixture of revulsion and pity. And, amazingly, caring. At least Moran suffered for what he was, and didn't pretend. He balanced this against Carleton, who he thought had been kind and straightforward with him. And tolerant almost to a fault.

He didn't want to believe what a gut feeling told him was true. "How do I know you're telling the truth?"

"Why the hell would I lie? Wait until tomorrow if you don't believe me. Carleton is no friend of yours. He's a politician, like the rest of us. Only he's too hoity-toity to admit it."

There was some grain of truth in this, Dale knew. Carleton was an indecisive man, trying to rise above the petty politics built into his position. Maybe he had failed down the road somewhere. He sighed. So why stop at friendship?

He got up to leave. "Good luck with Audrey," he said, feeling totally detached. "I'll see you at the meeting tomorrow."

"Wait a minute," Moran said with a frown. "What's this about Christine? It slipped by me."

"She died in a car crash. Presumably an accident."

"An accident! Bullshit! Heffron killed her. She was going to spill the beans."

"You don't sound surprised."

Moran gave him a sideways glance. "Why should I be?" He paused, fingering his empty glass. "You don't trust me, do you?"

The absurdity of it all suddenly struck Dale, and he threw his head back and laughed. He was caught between two hard rocks, hopelessly trapped.

He was still laughing when Moran jumped to his feet, pounding his fist on the desk. "Shut up, goddammit! Have you lost your mind?"

Dale shook his head, his face damp with tears. "I'm sorry," he said. "Is there anything else?"

Moran shuffled papers around randomly, not looking up. "No, I'll see you tomorrow," he said, mustering what dignity he could with two double shots of vodka on board.

47

Nina was with a patient in the fluoroscopy room when the secretary hurried in. "You have a phone call, Dr. Yablonsky."

In the midst of performing a barium enema, she frowned, watching the screen. She thought she saw a suspicious-looking lesion in the lower portion of the colon. "Please take a message," she said. "I'll need some spot views of this," she called out to the X-ray tech.

"He said it was urgent," the secretary whispered. By now, the patient on the X-ray table was squirming uncomfortably.

"Who is it?" Nina asked, feeling a mixture of irritation and foreboding.

"He wouldn't say."

She hesitated, watching the anxious patient. But ultimately her curiosity—and fear—won out. "All right," she said. "Please have Dr. Stratton come in and finish up."

She removed her lead apron and picked up the phone just outside the X-ray room. "This is Dr. Yablonsky."

"Doc? This here's Zimmer, the security guard over in microbiology?"

She felt her body go taut. The man gave her the creeps. He was like something from under a rock. "What is it?"

"I have a message from Dr. Harper."

"Yes?"

"Cain't tell ya on the phone. What he wants, he wants me to bring ya to him. Says he come across somethin' real important."

"Just tell me where he is," she demanded, her tension mounting.

Zimmer chuckled. "He warned me ya might be kinda superstitiouslike. But he says I gotta bring ya."

"All right," she said. "Where shall I meet you?"

"I'll pick you up right out front the hospital. I got a beat-up ol' Chevy, light brown."

"I'll be there." She grabbed a beeper, slipped it in the pocket of her white coat, and headed for the elevators.

As Zimmer wound in and out of traffic, Nina wondered where on earth he was taking her. He was sticking to the city streets, heading into the warehouse district. He hunched over the wheel humming to himself or chatting idly, evading her questions.

Finally she sat quietly, her hands folded in her lap, as she looked out the window. His car stank of old cigarettes and stale sweat. There was another sickening odor that she couldn't quite place.

"You're too pretty to be a doc, Doc," he said, cackling. He took his eyes off the road and the car meandered across the center line as he leered at her.

"You'd better keep your eyes on the traffic," she said as he swerved back into his lane. "How much longer till we get there?" She was beginning to realize she had made a big mistake. She should have tried to reach Dale first, but she had been too frantic to think straight. This secretiveness wasn't like him. And the more she thought about it, she was sure Dale wouldn't entrust a message to anyone, much less this seedy character.

Just then, Zimmer pulled up to the curb in front of what appeared to be an abandoned warehouse. As he reached across her to get something out of the glovebox, she got a good whiff of him, and a bolt of fear shot through her. He reeked of after-shave. And she recognized it as the same odor that had permeated her apartment that terrifying night. Now she was sure there was no message.

Her mind raced as Zimmer sat back up, humming to himself, a stupid grin pasted on his homely face. She could tell he sensed nothing awry. He was just proceeding with whatever insane plan he had in mind. No doubt someone else's plan, for that matter.

What to do? She would just play along, having the single advantage that he didn't yet know she was on to him. She looked around the bleak neighborhood. Gutted-out slums, abandoned cars, trash strewn on the streets. It looked like a war zone. Even if she made a run for it, she didn't know where she could go.

Then she remembered the beeper. It was a two-way. She could only talk to the switchboard operator at the hospital, but she could try to get a message through to Dale. It was her best hope. She looked at Zimmer, who was fooling with the trunk of the car. She looked at the warehouse and spotted a number over the warped wooden door. But what was the street?

She decided to take a chance. When Zimmer came over to her side of the car, she rolled down the window. "I've never been in this part of town," she said innocently. "What street is this?"

He scratched his head. "This here's Franklin. Not hardly a place you rich kids'd go on a date, is it?" He chuckled. "Well, let's get goin'."

She nodded. "Okay."

He started to open her door, but she drew it closed. "If you don't mind, I'd like to put some fresh lipstick on." She smiled at him.

He gave her a knowing wink, as though he liked the idea, as though she were doing it for him. He stood staring at her.

"Could I have some privacy?"

"You bet." He ambled toward a nearby tree. As soon as his back was turned, she grabbed her beeper and slouched down in the seat. She hoped she wasn't out of range. She pressed the button to bring the operator in, but all she got was static. Please come in, oh, please come in! Then she heard the faint voice of the hospital operator.

"Operator, this is Dr. Yablonsky! Can you hear me?" All she got back was multisyllabic static. She could only hope she was relaying better than she was receiving.

She saw Zimmer cast a glance back toward the car, and she slouched down farther. "Operator. This is a matter of life and death. Page Dr. Harper. Tell him I'm at 1045 Franklin Street. Tell him . . ."

Zimmer was coming back. She slipped the beeper back in her pocket and moistened her lips.

He opened the passenger door. "C'mon now. Time to see yer boyfriend." He reached in and took her arm. His grip was surprisingly strong.

She knew it was important to keep calm. She was sure she could handle the situation once she knew what it was. Watch and see. That was her motto. She was a street kid from the Bronx.

As they entered the ramshackle warehouse, they climbed a flight of stairs and came upon a large empty room. She tried to act casual when it was clear that Dale was not there. "Is this where we're meeting Dr. Harper?"

"Yup, should be here anytime now."

"But I thought you said . . ."

"Never mind what I said." Zimmer pulled a length of rope out of his pocket. "Now I don't want no trouble from ya, Doc. Just go along with what I tell ya and everything'll be fine. Now just set down ag'inst the wall there."

She did as she was told, playing for time. He cut two lengths of rope and dropped them at his feet.

"What are you doing?" she asked, watching him with an almost clinical detachment. He didn't respond.

"Where's Dale?" she insisted.

Ignoring her again, he pulled a handkerchief out of his pocket and said, "Before this goes over yer mouth, I got a present for ya." He got down on his knees and leaned forward, pressing his chafed withered lips to hers. She tried to pull away, but he had her arms and head pinned against the wall. She could smell his sour breath and it made her retch.

He drew back and licked his lips. She spat at him. "You're crazy," she screamed.

"We'll see," he chortled. "Too bad ya cain't keep that kisser of yours quiet." With that, he gagged her.

48

Dale was acutely aware of the faces turned in his direction. But what impressed him most was the table. It looked like the bottom of a huge coffin, hoisted up on legs. The stony-faced jurors positioned around it were the pallbearers, and he the sacrificial lamb. He could almost feel the nick of the blade on the nape of his neck.

As he took his seat his eyes passed down the table, stopping at Carleton. His head was down. He was immersed in his writing. Dale wondered how much it all had to do with his funeral.

Lawrence Orwell, dean of student affairs, sat at one end of the table. Dale tilted his head respectfully. His dealings with Orwell had always been pleasant. The perfect dean. Fatherly and kind with a polished diplomacy and, unfortunately, a certain indecisiveness. Somewhat like Carleton, he thought glumly.

"Thank you for taking the time to meet with us, Dr. Harper," said the dean across the vastness of the table. "I believe you know everyone here." He waved a hand in the air.

Dale looked more closely at the men who were to decide his fate. Moran; Carleton; Dr. Hunnicutt, head of physiology; Dr. Tao, head of anatomy; and three other department heads. No sign of Heffron. But there was Jon Werner, a permanent sneer on his face. A jury of eight men and one asshole. They all knew him. He had clashed with a few, especially Hunnicutt. Hunnicutt had never forgiven him for turning all the laboratory dogs loose to prevent their sudden demise in a Hunnicutt vivisection massacre. There was one sure vote.

He looked back to Carleton, still absorbed in his note-taking. He glanced at Moran. Herman's vacant expression suggested his mind was elsewhere. Probably on his wife.

Orwell cleared his throat. He was a frail-looking man with a sallow complexion, thick rimless glasses, and a few strands of white hair. He gave Dale a kindly look.

"You know why you're here today, Dr. Harper. The board is concerned with your conduct. We like to think ourselves tolerant of human foibles. Understanding is part of being a physician. But we're here to serve our patients. When their care suffers, measures must be taken. Or the system suffers."

Silence. No one looked at Dale. He stared at the ceiling, trying to trace a pattern in random whirls of paint. Yes, the system suffered. And the people, what of them?

He saw that Orwell was having trouble with his throat. He kept bobbing his Adam's apple. Nerves, or maybe he needed a good ENT man.

Orwell had regained his voice. "There have been problems with your patient care in recent weeks. Dr. Harper. Unusual problems. You have been . . . preoccupied, it appears, by matters not under your purview. You have pursued these matters against the advice of your department head." The dean nodded toward the chief of medicine.

Carleton finally lifted his eyes. The room was quiet. As though, thought Dale, an execution was in progress.

The dean poured himself a glass of water. "If anyone has anything to say regarding the matter of Dr. Harper, please do so now." He peered over his glasses, his eyes traveling from face to face. "Dr. Hunnicutt," he said, acknowledging the raised hand.

"Well, I'm sure Dr. Harper has many fine qualities," said Hunnicutt with a smile that came and went like a blinking neon sign. "But a doctor has to be a . . . team player. We all work together, and I must say I've never seen that as a strength of Dr. Harper's. It does not surprise me that matters have reached this, er, proportion." Hunnicutt appeared to have more to say, but Orwell was ready to move on.

"Dr. Werner? You have worked with Dr. Harper recently. Your thoughts?"

Werner stared at Dale with narrowed, calculating eyes, as though he suddenly realized a portion of power had been thrown into his lap and he needed to decide rather quickly how much to use.

"Dr. Harper allows nonmedical matters to distract him," Werner said in his clipped, unemotional tone. "He's bright and he's a good worker. But if you're going to be a doctor, you have to make a full commitment to medicine. Nothing can sway you from the singular purpose of patient care. I'm sorry to say I haven't seen that kind of commitment from Dr. Harper." Werner sat back with a superior look on his face, averting his gaze from Dale, who watched him with obvious contempt.

Orwell smiled and glanced around the table. "Are there any other comments? Dr. Harper?"

Dale shook his head. "No, sir." He knew it was pointless to try to argue with these men. Someone once told him that the more you talked at these funereal meetings, the dumber you sounded. He believed it.

Orwell inclined his head benevolently and once again cleared his throat. "Now, it is ordinarily the duty of the board to decide whether you will be allowed to finish out your residency, Dr. Harper. There has, however, been an unexpected development." He paused. "In a burst of generosity, your chief approached me prior to this meeting and offered to take full responsibility for you if the board would lift your probation."

Dale sat stunned. Carleton had turned his face away. Dale could tell by the looks passing back and forth that the others were as surprised as he. Moran's face had taken on a purplish hue.

Dr. Hunnicutt was the first to respond. He seemed slightly agitated. "We should take Dr. Carleton's offer under consideration, but surely the decision lies with the board as a whole."

The dean managed a benevolent smile. "Since Dr. Carleton has taken it on himself, I see no need to proceed further." Again he paused. "In the last analysis the decision is mine. If there are no objections, this meeting stands adjourned." He smiled at Hunnicutt, who turned and stalked out, his face livid with rage.

The others rose and began drifting out, murmuring among themselves. Dale started after Carleton, but Moran came up behind him and caught his arm.

"This is a complete turnaround! Carleton's up to something." Moran was beside himself. "He's trying to fool you, he's . . ."

Moran smelled of stale alcohol and sweat. Dale pushed him off in disgust and turned to find Carleton. But he was gone.

As he left the meeting, his mind twirling with this gift from the blue, Dale's beeper told him to call the switchboard. He found the nearest phone and dialed zero. The operator excitedly told him about a garbled message she received from a woman with a name like Vronsky. The woman had sounded distressed.

"Where was she calling from?" he asked, all his antennae screaming at him.

"I'm sorry, Doctor. I really wasn't sure. It sounded like she said Franklin Street, but I couldn't hear the number. She sounded very upset and said it was a matter of life and death. That part I did hear."

Dale dropped the phone and was out of the hospital

and into his car in a matter of seconds. His Mustang screeched around the corners on two wheels.

Franklin Street. He knew where it was, thank God. As he put the pedal to the floor, his mind kept racing with the direst possibilities. Was she being tortured, poisoned, threatened? The blood throbbed in his temples, but he was never more controlled, never readier.

He ran two red lights and just missed a pedestrian as he peeled around the turn onto Franklin Street. His heart sank as he saw how barren it was, with old beat-up cars parked all along the curbs. Fortunately, the street was only a few blocks long. He cruised slowly with a steely eye on anything that stood still or moved.

Then he saw it. He couldn't believe his luck. The green City Hospital parking sticker stuck out like a salutation on the windshield of a moribund brown Chevy. He pulled into a nearby alley and parked. Afraid whoever it was might see him, he slouched down and sneaked in and out of shadowed doorways until he was opposite the Chevy. He looked up at the building and listened intently.

Going on the only clue he had, he decided to explore first the building closest to the Chevy. He went up the steps and his heartbeat quickened as he saw the old warped wooden door ajar. He stuck his head in and heard a scraping noise coming from inside. He slipped all the way in and determined it was coming from one floor up. He found the stairs and stealthily climbed them. He promptly came upon a giant storage room and spotted two human silhouettes.

He hid behind a box and strained his eyes against the light from the giant window. And what he saw he had a hard time believing.

There was the old security guard, Zimmer, with his hands and feet tied. Standing talking to him was Nina! He was about to call her name when something told him maybe it was a trap. But just as he stood up, Nina spotted him and waved.

"Dale," she cried. "Over here!"

He rushed to her and they embraced, Dale never taking his eyes off Zimmer who watched them with a dull look of defeat.

"Thank God you found us," she said.

"What happened?" he asked, pointing in amazement to the bound-up Zimmer.

She shrugged with a modest smile. "My street-wise upbringing and a little karate finally came in handy."

He looked at her with approval. "I don't know why I worry about you. Why did he bring you here?"

"I haven't been able to pry it out of him."

"I'll find out," Dale said, squatting down before Zimmer. "Tell me who put you up to this, or you won't be needing your dentist anymore," he said, giving Zimmer a fierce look.

Zimmer shook his head. Dale grabbed him by the hair. "Talk, you bastard."

Nina came up beside him. "Dale, he's an old man. Don't hurt him."

Suddenly, as though Nina had said the magic word, Zimmer opened his mouth and spoke. "Heffron," he said. "Dr. Heffron."

"Why?" Dale still had Zimmer by the hair.

"Dunno. He just paid me good to bring the lady here."

"And then what? Where is he?"

"I was s'posed to call him at his office, but that woulda been a while ago. I thought he'd of come here when I didn't call."

Dale finally let go of him and took a deep breath. He could feel his insides shaking. Nina came up to him and rested a hand on his arm. "You want to find Heffron?"

He looked at her, nodding, regaining some of his composure as he saw her calmness. "Let's take Zimmer with us and head to the micro department first."

She looked at Zimmer, stewing in his bonds.

"Okay. We can leave him in the backseat. Believe me, he's well tied."

They entered the microbiology department by the rear door and headed for Heffron's office. There was no one there, not even his secretary. As they stood in the hall trying to decide where to look next, Mike Bancroft came up to them with a worried expression on his face. "Where the hell have you two been?"

"What is it, Mike?" Nina asked with an intuitive flutter of her stomach.

Mike's voice quavered with excitement. "I have a buddy in pathology. A resident. Maybe you know him—Ray Phillips. He called me a few minutes ago."

"I don't know him," Dale cut in. "What takes you so goddamn long to say anything?"

Mike, beside himself, motioned them into an empty room. "All I'm trying to say," he whispered hoarsely, closing the door, "is you won't find Heffron here, if that's who you're looking for. He's in the morgue. Stone-cold dead."

"Jesus." Dale's jaw dropped. He saw Nina's look of disbelief out of the corner of his eye. "When was he brought in?" It was all he could say.

"Late morning, I think. Ray says it's all very hush-hush. Looks like he died in his sleep last night. 'Apparent heart attack.' You know, standard diagnosis for the tabloids."

Words seemed banal, but the questions were piling up in Dale's head. "Any autopsy results yet?"

"That's what's weird. No autopsy."

"There *has* to be an autopsy. It's an unexplained death. That makes it a coroner's case."

"Not if the patient's doctor vetoes it."

"Who's his doctor?"

"I don't know, Dale. You're the detective. Good luck with this one." He opened the door to leave. "I've got to run. I thought you'd want to know."

"Thanks, Mike," Dale said, easing into a chair next

to Nina. They sat quietly, trying to deal with what they had just heard.

Heffron dead. It hadn't quite hit home yet. Heffron had made a dent in their lives and now he was gone. Whatever else he was, he had been very much alive. Vital, charismatic, impactive, while undeniably ruthless and corrupt. And at the end, a cold slab in the morgue.

Dale brushed his hand across his face. He had seen a hundred people die. Better people, younger people, people who deserved to live. So what made this so great a shock? Was it because Heffron had affected the course of his life like no one else—not even Nina, not Carleton? Heffron. How strange life was. And how strange death. Always on call, when least expected.

The color had drained out of Nina's face. "My God," she cried. He felt her body shake and drew her close. He stroked her back with his hand as he tried to collect his thoughts.

"It's strange there's no autopsy," Nina said. "It's hard to believe a heart attack would get him. I heard he was a fitness nut."

Dale grunted. She looked at him, wondering what he was thinking. "What should we do?"

"I want to go over to the morgue."

"First let's turn Zimmer loose." Certainly Zimmer was no longer a threat. Yet she could feel her heart thumping against her chest.

Dale shook his head. "We can't let him go, Nina. He's a loose cannon. The next woman he victimizes may not have your strength."

She knew he was right. They were doctors. Zimmer needed help. He would have to be reported and examined. Taken out of circulation, maybe placed in an institution. "You're right," she said.

He held her face in his hands, stroking her forehead until she smiled. Thank goodness for her strength. Where would he be without it?

*   *   *

The morgue was all that people imagined and worse. It stank of formaldehyde and Lysol, and underneath the acrid stench of chemicals lurked the sharper stench of death. So many medical students passed out or came close to it when they witnessed their first autopsy, Nina remembered only too well. Some never got used to it. Nothing prepared them for the smell. It usually didn't hit them until the intestines were sliced open, just when they were congratulating themselves on how different they were from the other students.

Ray Phillips was definitely not pleased to see them. His face had a greenish tint from the fluorescent lighting. He was in the middle of an autopsy, and wore a gown and mask. He peered up from the corpse. His eyes were like flint. "So you're Dale Harper."

Dale ignored the belligerent tone. "Yes, and this is Nina Yablonsky."

Nina tried holding her breath. It was worse than the sewers her father used to slosh around in. She spotted the surgical masks on a nearby table and put one to her face while handing one to Dale.

"Mike warned me you might show up," Phillips said. "You want to see the body?"

"We can wait till you're through," Dale said. "What do you have there?"

Phillips unbent somewhat at this nod to his expertise. "Fairly routine. Old gomer found down outside a bar. Coroner's case." He held up the lungs, which he had already dissected out of the cadaver. "Either of you smoke?"

Nina stared at the black organs dangling from the resident's gloved, bloody hand. "No, I'm happy to say. But it looks like he did." She swallowed down a wave of nausea.

"Among other earthly pleasures," Phillips said with a pathologist's indifference. "Get a load of what the booze did to his liver. It looks like a chunk of volcanic rock." He turned to the table behind him and held up the abused organ.

"End stage," Dale said, eyeing the gray-brown cirrhotic liver that was about half normal size. "What's his heart look like?"

"A bag of blood. Dilated cardiomyopathy." Phillips pointed with his scalpel at what looked like a piece of macerated meat on the table.

Dale moved in closer while Nina held back. "You think this was alcohol-induced?"

"Too early to tell. Need microscopics for confirmation. But that's the most likely cause. The coronaries are clean."

Dale nodded. He knew that alcohol had a direct toxic effect on heart muscle, but he had never seen such a dramatic example. Like most residents, one or two autopsies was about all he wanted. He had never understood the appeal of pathology.

Noting Dale's interest, Phillips unbent even more. "Glove up if you want, and take a feel of that heart muscle. You'll never take another drink."

Dale looked at Nina.

"You go ahead," she said. "I'm content to get it all secondhand."

He donned a pair of latex gloves and picked up the heart. It had been cut open and sagged lifelessly in his hands. He felt the thickness of the muscle. It was not quite paper thin.

"Hard to believe that was once a guy's pump, huh?" Phillips said.

"Incompatible with life, as they used to say in medical school." He carefully put it back and felt the liver. It was indeed hard as a rock.

"Well, you won't see any life here." Phillips seemed in his element.

"You think it was his heart that did this one in?"

"Take your choice. Liver, lungs, heart. You name it. The question here is not why this guy died—it's why he was alive. I'm about to cut open his stomach. We'll probably find another cause of death there."

Dale stood over the cadaver. He was getting used to the stench, and the mask helped stifle it some. He decided he liked Phillips. Coldly competent. It was hard to get an image of what the guy looked like, ensconced as he was in all his garb. But he was short and on the chubby side.

Dale craned his neck to get a better look as Phillips removed the stomach and put it on a table next to him. He then sliced it open. "Voilà," he said. "There's your flaming alcoholic gastritis and you can also see he has esophageal varices."

The inner lining of the stomach was bright red with inflammation, as though it had suffered a bad case of sunburn. Higher up, where it joined the esophagus, there was a network of bulging veins, one of which had a small ulceration. Varices—a common cause of bleeding in alcoholics.

"Maybe he bled to death," suggested Dale.

"Possible. His hematocrit was twenty-two percent. But he could've been walking around for years with a 'crit that low. Considering the sorry state of his liver, his coagulation factors probably stunk, so he could've bled because of that. Like I said, take your choice. I usually sign these cases out as total body failure. Not very scientific, but nobody gives a damn anyway. No next of kin. Not even a friend. If you ask me, it's a waste of the taxpayer's money doing posts on these guys."

Phillips took a hose and washed down the organs on the metal table, then rinsed out the inside of the cadaver. He moved to a door connecting to another room. "Ready to close up here, Kim." A short Oriental man suddenly appeared, pulling on a pair of gloves.

Phillips removed his mask and gloves and washed up at the sink. "So, what exactly is your interest in

Heffron?" he asked. He no longer sounded grumpy, Dale was pleased to note.

Dale snapped off his gloves and joined Phillips at the double sink, lathering his hands vigorously as though he didn't trust the protectiveness of the gloves. Nina came closer, now that the cutting was over. Her nausea was beginning to let up.

"I'd just like to take a look at the body," Dale said.

"What do you think you'll find?" Phillips sounded interested. He turned a round, mustached face to Dale. He had a pair of dark, probing eyes.

"I'm not sure. Perhaps signs of foul play."

Phillips arched his eyebrows. "Ah-hah! And why would you expect that?"

Nina came up beside Dale and gave him an admonishing look.

Dale shrugged with exaggerated nonchalance. "The man had a lot of enemies."

"That's not how I heard it. He's a celebrity around here. People worship the ground he walks—walked— on. Though personally, the guy struck me as a phony." He dried his hands and faced Dale, his bright eyes peering intently. "You one of the enemies?"

"Maybe."

Phillips wadded up his paper towel and arced it toward the wastebasket. "Have it your way. Your shenanigans are not exactly a secret, you know." He wiped his brow with his sleeve. "Whew, I'm beat. You two want some coffee?"

Dale saw Nina nod. "Sure," he said.

"So, what do you want to know?" Phillips leaned back in the plastic chair, raising its front legs off the floor.

"Suppose someone smothered Heffron with a pillow. Would there be any obvious telltale signs?" Dale poured three cups of coffee. He hoped the coffee would cover up the scent of formaldehyde so strong he could taste it.

"Depends. If he was a heavy sleeper, maybe not. His color might be a little on the blue side, but that's not real objective. Everybody's blue after they die. If there was a struggle, you might see signs of that—impressions of the pillow on the face, bruising around the mouth, petechiae, abrasions."

Nina leaned forward, suddenly involved. "What about poison?"

Phillips turned to her appraisingly. "That's a woman—you and Agatha Christie. Like what?"

"What poison could you give that would make it look like someone had just peacefully drifted off?"

Phillips looked upward as he thought. "Any narcotic or opiate in strong enough doses. Cocaine, Insulin. Cyanide. Strychnine. Potassium." He smiled acerbically. "Technically, it's easy to kill someone. It's the ethical part that some people have difficulty with."

Phillips stood up. "This coffee is lousy. You came to see Heffron's body? Let's do it."

They entered a chilly, garishly lit room with a lineup of gurneys. Three of the gurneys had bodies on them tastefully covered with sheets. Phillips approached Heffron's gurney and threw back the sheet. "There he is."

They stared in silence at the still, naked form of Robert Heffron. He looked like a statue. Even in death, the great equalizer, he had an insidious quality about him, Dale thought. His lips seemed to be fixed in a permanent smirk. Fascinated, Dale commented on the deep purple discoloration of Heffron's skin. "Is that shade of purple typical?"

Phillips nodded. "Maybe a little purpler than most. But we don't know how long he was dead. His wife had a separate bedroom. She discovered him around . . ." Phillips picked up a folder on the gurney and turned to the first page. "Eight this morning. She last saw him around eleven last night."

Phillips tugged at the chain on the overhead light and produced a magnifying lens. He leaned down and inspected the head and neck area carefully. "I don't see any signs of smothering. No neck marks, either, in case you were entertaining the idea of a strangling." He straightened. "God, my back hurts."

Dale said, "I don't suppose we could get a blood sample?"

"Why not?"

"I was told there would be no autopsy."

"So what? You think I give a damn whether you take blood or not?"

"You won't get in trouble?"

Phillips laughed. It was a jolly sound. "I didn't say that, did I?"

Dale smiled. Phillips, with his screw-you attitude toward the big boys, was his kind of people. "I can put a fictitious name on the sample."

"If you want. But like I said, it's no skin off my nose." He held up a hand. "Before we take any blood, let's check his arms and legs for needle marks." He handed them each a magnifying lens.

49

Dr. John C. Carleton was in the midst of sorting out the papers on his desk. He had an important report to compile, and he was engrossed in thought. His secretary, the evanescent Veronica, had taken an extended lunch and he was mercifully alone. Or so he thought. He looked up with a start at the shadow in the doorway. He smiled, almost in relief.

"It's you, Dale," he said. "An unexpected pleasure." He dotted a few more i's, crossed a few more t's, and motioned Dale to a seat.

"Have you had lunch?" Dale asked in a tone that seemed no more than polite inquiry.

Carleton looked up from his desk and smiled, passing a hand over his bulging waistline. "I'm not much for midday meals. Dinner is my downfall."

"I want to thank you for the other day," Dale said. "You really stuck your neck out for me."

His voice was subdued, too subdued, and Carleton gave him a second and longer look. Whatever he saw made him put his pen down. He stared at the papers on his desk. It was never over, he thought, until it was over. He always knew it would be that way. He knew too that it would be Dale. How could it be anybody else? Life had a way of coming full circle, however you tried to alter the course of events.

He felt an unusual calm as he met Dale's level gaze. He had a fondness for this boy—no, man. The realization startled him. This young, bullheaded resident, the son of his dearest friend, had gone and become a man

on him. He suddenly saw it—the transformation—
clear as day. A shiver ran through his body, which
both surprised and baffled him.

He looked into the pair of probing eyes before him.
"It was no more than you had coming," he said at
last. "As chief of medicine I had to support you in
the end. You've been my best resident. One of the
best this hospital has ever seen. I may not have ap-
proved of your activities, but they could be put down
to youth and a spirit of adventure. Sometimes the
young become so caught up in changing the world and
looking to the future, they lose sight of the present.
Whatever, these activities of yours plainly had nothing
to do with your aptitude for medicine." He smiled.
"You must have your father's genes. There was never
a better doctor, God knows. Unless it is you one day."

Dale shifted in his chair and looked down for a
moment. "I'll always be grateful to you. Whatever
happens."

Carleton gave him a slow smile, arching an eyebrow. "Whatever happens?"

Dale watched Carleton eye the clock, then turn
back to his papers, as though dismissing him. He knew
he must get on with what he had to say but all he
could come up with was one word. And now he uttered it, with an inflection that left no doubt as to its
urgency.

"Why?" he said. "Why?"

Carleton sat back and steepled his hands together.
With his graying temples and his regular features
made wise by the weight of age, he looked just like
what he was—the chief of medicine of a prestigious
and massive medical center.

"Why what?" he said. "I'm afraid you will have to
help me."

Dale's voice had a mechanical ring, as though what
he said was being forced out of him by some inexora-
ble machine. He felt oddly numb. "I started to ask
myself that question when I discovered that you were

Heffron's doctor. Why, with you of all people, was there no autopsy, when the sudden, unexpected death fairly screamed for one?"

Carleton brushed a veined hand across his forehead. He looked tired. "So there was no autopsy. Why should that be so important to you? People like Heffron die of heart attacks every day. He had all the risk factors—high blood pressure, smoking, high cholesterol. Why submit his poor wife to the agony of an autopsy when the findings were certain?"

"Yes," said Dale in that metallic voice. "All quite understandable if it were anyone but you. You, the author of the celebrated precept, so well remembered by your protégés." There was no sarcasm, no mocking tone, only a deep and abiding sadness.

Dale pressed on. " 'Autopsies,' you said, 'cast a light on the dark mystery of death.' That's what you always told us. Prodding us to go against our sense of propriety, and to ask grieving family members, in their greatest moments of sorrow, if we could cut open their loved ones in the name of enlightenment, the advancement of medical science."

Carleton forced a smile. "And so why, you ask, did the author of this famous motto betray his own elementary principle? This is what you want to know?" He was trying to collect his thoughts. It had been a hectic few weeks, and he felt his reserves buckling. There was only so much a man could take, even a leader of men.

"You will have to forgive me," Carleton said, his voice barely a whisper. "I seem to have lost my train of thought." His eyes had a glassy look to them. "You want to know why I did or didn't do something? Is that the gist of it?" He folded his hands on the desk and sat back as though meditating, seemingly oblivious to Dale's presence.

Dale nodded. He understood. He reached into his pocket and drew out a crumpled sheet of paper. He offered it to Carleton. As Carleton leaned forward, wiping his glasses, Dale said, "This is a copy of your office note on Heffron, the morning before he died. He had high blood pressure, poorly controlled. You changed his blood pressure medication to Optivil. 'Start at bedtime,' it says here." Dale looked up. "You gave him a sample capsule to save him a stop at the pharmacy."

Carleton had little room left for indignation. But his cheeks flushed as he said, "How did you obtain a copy of a confidential patient file?"

He reached for his intercom, as though summoning Veronica would resolve the whole matter. He slowly put the receiver back, sighing. It was all so—unreal. For a moment he allowed himself the thought that the young man sitting across from him was no more than an illusion, the product of a bad dream. He did not really expect an answer to his question, and none was forthcoming.

Dale went on in the same deadly monotone. Neither prosecutor nor defender. Only narrator. "Heffron's blood was saturated with cyanomethemoglobin." He paused, looking his mentor in the eye. "He died of cyanide poisoning."

Carleton held the younger man's gaze. Dale thought for a moment there was a sly look of approval in Carleton's eyes.

"And you think I poisoned him? Is that it?" Carleton made an effort to laugh, but it trailed off into a pathetic cough.

"I know you did."

"And how, Mr. Sherlock Holmes, did I manage that?"

"The Optivil. You laced the capsule you gave him with cyanide."

Carleton nodded thoughtfully. "I see. Now why would I kill Dr. Heffron? Such an able man, and of such help to the hospital and the medical school."

Dale smiled. It was a wistful smile, mixed with puzzlement. "I don't know. That's where I need your help."

Carleton seemed amused. "But still, my dear Holmes, you offer no motive. Motive is everything."

"I'm sure you can supply that."

Carleton gave a little sigh at what he saw in Dale's face. It was a different Dale. Mature and determined. Dale Harper, M.D., had come of age. Carleton began to understand why he had felt the shiver down his spine earlier.

His eyes dropped now to the sheet of paper he had been working on. He picked it up, slowly tore it to shreds, and tossed the pieces into the wastebasket. "I won't be needing this," he said. "It's an application for a research grant—a study I was designing on asthma. All I had to do was fill it out and send it in." He paused. "It doesn't matter now."

Carleton stood and moved over to the window, looking out on the vast fortress of granite and marble that had been his life for so many years. He turned and half faced Dale. His voice was soft, quavering slightly.

"Robert Heffron was an evil man. I think you knew that. Not many people did. He defaced everything he touched. Men, women, everything we believe in. Goodness, kindness, charity to our fellow man. He was rotten to the core. He was charming and he was clever. And he was dangerous. Like so many of the drugs and opiates we use to control pain and sustain life—wonderfully effective in the beginning, then manifesting rippling and devastating side effects that extinguish the benefits."

He resumed his seat. "So what will you do now?" It was not so much a challenge, but more a sincere question, as though willfully surrendering his fate to the hands of the man opposite him. Yes, the man.

Dale's face had grown somber. He seemed to have aged as he listened. "You and I," he said in a voice suddenly ringing with the clarity and energy of conviction, "made a sacred vow, the Hippocratic Oath, to sustain and preserve life. Ours is not to judge whether a life is unworthy, or to play God. If that were the case, then anyone who offended us would be in danger. As you well know, a doctor has the ability to take a life much more easily than he can save it."

Carleton seemed wrapped in his own thoughts. There was a faraway look in his eyes that Dale had never seen before. It was as though he was thinking out loud, muttering to himself, going over again in his mind what had brought him to his present state.

Finally, he spoke, his eyes coming back into focus. "In a way, it's because of you that Heffron died," he said, a distinct irony in his voice. "If you hadn't been about to expose him, we could have lived with him a little longer. I did what I could to throw you off. I threatened you, spearheaded Heffron's schemes to discredit you, and was in fact behind the effort to suspend you." A harshness crept into his voice. "Then one night, after a particularly offensive rift with Heffron, I thought, this is all so insane. Here I was trying to destroy you, the good, so the evil might survive. I knew then that Heffron had to go."

A painful lump came to Dale's throat. As with death, no amount of preparation made a soul laid bare easier to take. He had realized it had to be Carleton, but somehow hearing it from Carleton's lips had an impact that stunned and silenced him. He felt unaccountably betrayed. Moran had been right about Carleton. And yet, in the end, Carleton had come through for him. And now he knew why. Carleton had made a vindicating, and perhaps insane, choice—the elimination of Robert Heffron.

As though he understood what Dale was thinking, Carleton went on with his confession—now unstoppable—in the manner of a man hopelessly seeking absolution. "I couldn't have you finding out about Heffron. I knew you didn't give a damn about the system as a whole. You would bring us all down by exposing him."

Carleton saw by Dale's expression that he still didn't understand. "Heffron was stockpiling plutonium in the microbiology department, then marketing it, making huge profits for himself, but siphoning off enough money to the hospital so we could maintain our programs. He sold it to whoever wanted it, with no qualms as to the consequences. He even tried to use the third world students he brought in under his foundation as contacts. Millions of dollars were involved. We only learned of this after you started poking around. None of us had ever questioned where the money came from."

The Heffron Foundation. It was beginning to make sense. Carleton's knowledge of its source was the only surprise. "You mean you were running a black market in plutonium."

"Not I," Carleton said quickly. "Heffron. I, and others in the administration, turned our heads for too long. We suspected something illicit, but it was you who made us see it. It wasn't the money we cared about. It was what it could do—it allowed us to help thousands of people."

There it was again. The system. The goddamn system. Dale felt his numbness lifting and beneath it erupted a swirl of powerful emotions. Among them anger and pain. "You mean like Jesse Munoz, Hector Cantrell, and young Lincoln Lee, who blindly idolizes our profession." Dale emitted a short, bitter laugh. "You all but helped them to the nearest mortuary. And Ron Orloff. How about him? Your own intern?"

"I had nothing to do with them. When I learned about the plutonium poisonings, I told Heffron he needed to end it all. Apparently he had stored the material in improper canisters that led to corrosion and leakage. Very irresponsible. I told him to do what was necessary to keep you from finding out it was his plutonium—leaking and escaping onto the tables and floors, and into the air—that had poisoned those people. And I ordered him to get the plutonium out of the medical center the moment I suspected its devastating effects. He laughed and dared me to stop him. A man without a conscience. I never knew it would come to this."

"You never wanted to know."

"You are wrong there. All that concerned me was what was best for our hospital, our medical school. And for the multitudes of people who gained health and a new life inside our walls."

"What about Christine Anselm? Did you have Heffron 'take care' of her too?"

"If he killed her, it was completely his own idea."

"And Moran?"

Carleton gave a hollow laugh. "Moran never did figure out what was going on. He was no part of this except that his incompetence allowed Heffron the opportunity to do as he pleased."

Dale felt a burning need to understand the man sitting across from him. Was he talking to a rational human being? He had always thought so. Did rational men commit premeditated murder? He thought not. Yet his mind screamed at him to reason with Carleton—to show him how he'd gone wrong. Perhaps such impulses were simply manifestations of the naiveté and fervor of youth, as Carleton had so often reminded him. But it was all he knew.

"How," he demanded, "could you let all this happen?"

"Survival," Carleton answered with a certain self-righteousness. "Sacrifice. It's the sad story of the history of man. Living with a Heffron to enlighten a Harper."

"What about survival of the soul? That means nothing to you? The end justifies the means? The preservation of a hospital, a system, an institution? Is that all there is? Does this justify a broken trust and the betrayal of innocent lives?"

Carleton let Dale's anger wash over him. He understood it. And now, as he saw clearly that all that ever meant anything to him was now behind him, he would bestow upon this boy who had become a man his last legacy of truth, his last outpouring, and then he would find peace. He stood up and resumed his post by the window, looking out on a world he had tried to preserve.

"What I am about to tell you I've told no one. Listen closely. It is only fitting you should be the one to hear it." His voice was rough with suppressed emotion. "Twenty years ago," he said, staring out the window, "I killed your father."

Dale felt every muscle in his body go taut. As he swallowed it felt as though a hot poker had been jammed down his throat. His breath stopped. His hands went cold. He said nothing.

Carleton turned and gave him a pitying look. "No, it was nothing like Heffron. Your father was a wonderful man. It was an accident, but I killed him, as surely as you and I are here today." Carleton looked back out the window. "We were idealistic starry-eyed radiologists, excited about a new machine that was going to revolutionize radiation therapy, cure cancer.

"Shortly after it was installed, we were playing around with the various buttons and calibrations. While your father was in the room with the machine, as a lark I hit a button that I thought would simply take an X-ray picture of him. He got zapped with a lethal dose of radiation. His insides were incurably seared. He lived a creeping death, tortured beyond human endurance. He never blamed me. We never told anyone. He made me promise not to, for my sake. That's the kind of man he was."

Carleton's voice cracked. "I jammed the machine so it would never harm anyone else. Later it was taken off the market due to insufficient safety backups. But your father was long gone, and I alone held the secret to his death. Now I turn it over to you. I have carried the burden long enough. I can see now only too well what that burden has done to me."

Dale sat motionless in his chair. Carleton's words, like the eyes of the Medusa, had turned him to stone.

Carleton turned to Dale, his chin trembling, his eyes moist. "Your father and I were like brothers. He was so vibrant, full of life, with a limitless, inquiring mind." His voice dropped, nearly inaudible. "And I killed him."

Dale closed his eyes. He saw his father, lying in his deathbed, pleading with his son. *Promise me you will be a doctor and heal the sick. Let them know you care. There is too little caring in this world.*

He saw his father, his body wasted from chemotherapy and disease, the skin excoriated, oozing blood and pus, his hair sticking out in ragged patches from his scalp, his eyes sunken with dehydration and the specter of death.

He could feel his father's withered hand resting on his own as the dying man murmured, "I love you, my son. Let them know you care." They were his last words.

Dale felt a swell of grief wash over him as his head sank in his hands, and huge dry sobs racked his body.

Carleton reached out a hand to comfort him, but Dale shrank back. Maybe one day it would be all right, but not now. He was too hurt, too confused. Looking at Carleton's sorrowful face, thinking of the years lost with his father, he could not bring himself to say the three words he knew this terribly disturbed man wanted to hear: "I forgive you."

Epilogue

Dale and Nina sat down in the narrow pew. The bench had the pungent odor of aged wood, and Dale could imagine the years of rituals that had taken place in this church.

He held her hand, and he could feel the sweat on his palm. She looked so beautiful in her white linen suit. While every hair was in place, her face like a marble mask, he knew how hard she was struggling not to cry.

He was dressed in a three-piece black suit with a black tie. He felt uncomfortable. It seemed confining, unreal, in a circumstance that was all too real. He was aware of the somber organ music. He glanced upward at the pillars of stone as they joined the grandly vaulted ceiling, then shifted his gaze to the radiant colors of the stained-glass windows.

He could understand why people would come to a place like this to worship. Its very structure seemed to exalt the human spirit. The inspirational surroundings notwithstanding, he felt himself swimming in a sea of chaotic emotions, none of which seemed to have any connection with the other.

He looked up at the podium and saw the minister mouthing words. But he heard nothing. The feelings kept everything else out. Or was it the other way around?

Finally the sermon was over. He was aware of the sniffling and coughing of people fighting back their sorrow. Nina patted her moist eyes with a tissue. It was time now to rise and view the casket. How archaic, he thought. The living, marching in procession, to view the dead. What was it they sought?

Reluctantly he stood, taking Nina by the elbow as they moved out of the pew into the procession. Finally they came upon the casket, surrounded by the most brilliantly colored flowers Dale had ever seen. Nina walked ahead of him, incongruously making the sign of the cross and genuflecting before the casket, vestiges of an upbringing she had long ago renounced. He moved along behind her, then stopped to gaze inside.

There was John C. Carleton, former chief of medicine, lying in repose. He was supposed to look peaceful, as with all the honored dead. But there was no peace in that stony face. Dale was dismayed at his own reaction as he peered into the casket. He hadn't fully realized what the older man had meant to him. He began to feel faint and his eyes stung as he fought for control. He was vaguely aware of the people behind him, restlessly awaiting their turn.

But he lingered, searching the glazed, still eyes of his former mentor, of the man not just a teacher but a father to him. He remembered their last conversation, the day before Carleton took his life. He remembered how he had drawn back from a man desperately asking him for help. He remembered Carleton touching his arm. He could feel the gentle tentativeness of that touch, and the memory was wrenching.

He leaned now over the casket, his arms supporting him when his spirit could not. Tears streamed down his cheeks. His body was convulsed with emotion.

When he could summon enough control, he whispered into the ear of the departed, "I forgive you, John Carleton. May you find the peace elsewhere that you could not find here. I forgive you."

He rose and drew himself to his full height, and walked on down the steps with Nina at his side, realizing now the full meaning of the words "Rest in

Peace." Nina stopped and embraced him, kissing his wet cheek. Never before had he known such a powerful blending of joy and pain.

Love. The best medicine of all. This Dale thought with a smile as he saw Nina's dark hair streaming in the breeze. She spurred her horse on with a cry of triumph.

In a final burst, horse and rider streaked across the makeshift finish line and drew up to a sharp stop. Nina turned in the saddle with a gleeful laugh as Dale trailed behind her.

"You sandbagged me!" he cried as he pulled up his horse. "You told me you couldn't ride."

"I couldn't," she agreed happily. "You're a great teacher."

He eyed her suspiciously. "Okay, you win," he said with mock grumpiness. They were both breathing hard, the blood flowing through their veins, their eyes sparkling. It was good to feel the vigor of their youth and the thrill of the future that beckoned. Youth was not always wasted on the young, Dale thought, contrary to what Carleton had so often gravely observed.

They dismounted and tied their horses to a tree. They were in the field behind Juan's restaurant. The finish line had been a tree branch overhead. It was a sunny spring morning, the birds were chirping their hello, and a light breeze chased the perspiration from their faces. They sat under the tree and chomped on the apples Nina had taken from her fanny pack.

She tapped Dale on the shoulder with a flourish. "My valiant knight. The man who saved the medical center from a fate worse than death."

"And what would that be?" He laughed.

"Oblivion. Sprawling, insidious mediocrity—the kind that provides a nourishing environment for a perfidious soul like Robert Heffron." She shuddered.

Dale lay back and stared at the blue sky. It was hard to think about mediocrity or perfidy when looking at something so pure and limitless. Maybe there was a place for rules in this world after all, he thought. Had the medical center enforced the radiation safety standards, Heffron would never have been able to enjoy his lucrative little sideline. He felt a twinge of melancholy as he thought how pleased Carleton would have been with him for this observation. Carleton, who had chewed him out time and again for his impatience with rules.

As though affected by his thoughts, Nina said, "What do you think passed through Carleton's mind before he took his life?"

He sat up, tossing the core of his apple in the air so that his horse could reach out with its long neck and take it. He remained silent for a long moment, eyeing the horse pensively as it gulped down the remains of the apple.

"Would you rather not discuss it?" she said, giving his hand a squeeze.

"Oh, no. It's just that I'm trying to sort things out in my mind. I've thought about it a lot. The way he died told me more about the man than anything I knew about him in life."

"You mean with the Optivil, and the cyanide."

"Yes, that and something else. It told me it wasn't easy for him to kill Heffron. There was a form of retribution in the way Carleton died. But there was more."

She gave him a curious look. She loved to watch the change in moods as they reflected themselves on his open face. His blue eyes became tinted with gray when he was solemn, and azure-blue, like the sky overhead, when he was cheerful and ebullient. Now they were gray, so completely gray that she wondered why she had ever thought them blue.

"It was time for him," he said in a heavy voice. "He made good on what he thought he owed me, and redeemed himself for what he thought to be the murder of a man like a brother to him—my father. I realize now how much he must have suffered." His eyes were a little misty. "I never said the words he wanted so much to hear. Not while he was alive."

"I am sure he knew what was in your heart." She sat up and faced him. "Don't be ashamed of what you feel, Dale."

She lay down by his side, snuggling close, sharing her warmth. He drew her to him, looking up as Miguel lowered his head and nudged him in the back. The horse's ears were pointed like arrows toward the restaurant. Dale and Nina turned to see what had captured Miguel's interest.

They sat up abruptly, like a couple of exclamation points. In the distance, emerging from the back door of the restaurant, they saw a lone figure walking toward them. As the figure drew closer, Dale shook his head and said, "I'll be damned."

Nina squinted into the sun. "Who is it?"

"It's our long-lost Ron Orloff."

They waved, and Ron waved back, breaking into a jog. He was smiling, wrinkling his face in a broad grin that Dale hadn't seen for a long time.

"You're back, all back!" Dale stood up and embraced him.

Ron gave him a hug, then leaned down and kissed Nina. It was a different Ron Orloff. He was calm and relaxed, his voice had a bounce to it, and his handclasp was firm and dry.

He noted their appraising glances. "My wise old Jewish grandmother used to always tell me that some good comes out of bad. Heffron was trying to get me out of the way. He even had me thinking you two were trying to do me in. I was one of his dangerous exhibits. So he shuttled me off to New York, like he was doing me a favor. Turns out, they really did help me. I'm in remission, and I feel good. Somehow, getting away helped me deal with the fear, accept my illness, and get on with living. It isn't all medicine, radiation, and chemicals. It's the passion for life. That's the secret ingredient."

Dale and Nina applauded with a smile and cried out in unison, "Bravo, Ron!"

"I guess the old place will never be the same. Heffron and Carleton gone, the micro department closed down until the state safety board sweeps up all the dark corners."

Dale nodded. "A fresh start. New chiefs, new thinking, new respect for old rules."

"Yeah," echoed Ron. "I heard old Terminal got dumped."

"And Audrey Moran's going on trial for what she did to Jesse Munoz and Hector Cantrell. Heffron left her that legacy."

As they looked at each other, reliving in a kaleidoscopic moment the past weeks of confusion, Miguel nickered impatiently.

"Let's ride back," Dale said.

They came to their feet enthusiastically, as though ready to meet a future that beckoned with its endless promise.

"But there are only two horses," Ron pointed out.

"Nina and I will ride double, right, Nina?"

They mounted and let the horses open up into a run. Nina's arms were firmly around Dale's waist.

The wind carried his words back to her as they raced through the spring air, leaving Ron far behind in a cloud of dust.

"Will you marry me?"

"Yes," she cried. "If we're still alive at the end of this ride!"

"Don't worry, I can see it now," he shouted. "Harper and Harper."

"Yablonsky and Harper," she said, with a joyful laugh.

"Women!" he teased. And then he laughed with her.

There's an epidemic with 27 million victims. And no visible symptoms.

It's an epidemic of people who can't read.

Believe it or not, 27 million Americans are functionally illiterate, about one adult in five.

The solution to this problem is you... when you join the fight against illiteracy. So call the Coalition for Literacy at toll-free **1-800-228-8813** and volunteer.

Volunteer Against Illiteracy. The only degree you need is a degree of caring.